# THE RIDDLE

## A James Acton Thriller

# By
# J. Robert Kennedy

## James Acton Thrillers

*The Protocol*
*Brass Monkey*
*Broken Dove*
*The Templar's Relic*
*Flags of Sin*
*The Arab Fall*
*The Circle of Eight*
*The Venice Code*
*Pompeii's Ghosts*
*Amazon Burning*
*The Riddle*

## Detective Shakespeare Mysteries

*Depraved Difference*
*Tick Tock*
*The Redeemer*

## Special Agent Dylan Kane Thrillers

*Rogue Operator*
*Containment Failure*
*Cold Warriors*
*Death to America*

## Zander Varga, Vampire Detective

*The Turned*

# THE RIDDLE

A James Acton Thriller

J. ROBERT KENNEDY

CreateSpace



ISBN-10: 1503118967

ISBN-13: 978-1503118966

First Edition

10 9 8 7 6 5 4 3 2 1

For Warrant Officer Patrice Vincent and Corporal Nathan Cirillo.

#OttawaStrong

# THE RIDDLE

A James Acton Thriller

"The world is on the brink of a new Cold War. Some are even saying that it's already begun."

*Mikhail S. Gorbachev, November 8, 2014*

*On the 25th anniversary of the fall of the Berlin Wall*

"If you prick us do we not bleed? If you tickle us do we not laugh? If you poison us do we not die? And if you wrong us shall we not revenge?"

*William Shakespeare*

*The Merchant of Venice*

## PREFACE

On June 28, 1914 the Archduke of Austria, Franz Ferdinand, and his wife, Sophie, the Duchess of Hohenberg, were assassinated in Sarajevo, Bosnia. A man named Gavrilo Princip, a Bosnian Serb, was the assassin of the future heirs to the Austro-Hungarian throne, the Empire a significant power in Europe.

Bosnia was insignificant in comparison.

The empire had existed at this point for 47 years.

It would be gone in four, one man and his gun triggering a war the likes of which the world had never seen.

And hoped would never see again.

Enter World War II, and almost fifty years of new conflicts, many of them proxy wars between Communism and Capitalism as part of the Cold War.

Capitalism won.

With the end of the Cold War the world thought peace might finally be at hand, but with a belligerent Russia inexplicably attempting to return to the old ways of the failed Soviet Union, many think the Cold War we thought long gone is already back.

And if it is, could a single event trigger another crisis that might lead to a third, and possibly final, world war?

## AUTHOR'S NOTE

A portion of this book recreates the night the Buddha died. It is inspired by the actual accounts of that evening, with fictional intrigue added, the death a backdrop to the historical portion of the novel.

No disrespect is intended.

*Vietnam National Museum of History, Hanoi, Vietnam*

*Present Day*

Archeology Professor James Acton leaned forward, examining the ancient drum crafted by the Dong Son civilization of the Red River Delta in Northern Vietnam over two thousand years ago. Made of bronze and intricately carved, it was nearly three feet tall and according to their guide, weighed in at over two hundred pounds.

"It's beautiful," gushed his wife, Archeology Professor Laura Palmer as she circled the roped off artifact. "I've seen pictures of these but I've never seen one in person."

Acton dropped to a knee. "Me neither." His finger twitched, the overwhelming urge to reach out and touch the artifact killing him.

"Would you like to get closer?" asked their guide, Mai Lien Trinh, grinning.

Acton's head bobbed rapidly, Laura slightly more dignified in her response. "Could we?"

"Only honored guests are allowed—" began Mai.

"I guess that means 'no'," winked Acton at Laura.

She gave him the eye.

Mai looked at him curiously, then apparently decided he must be joking. She lifted the belt from the retractable stanchion and waved them inside. It was almost symbolic, the barrier only a couple of feet from the drum, but Acton felt like he did the day Guns 'N Roses had released their Use Your Illusion double-album and the clerk at Tower Records off Broadway had unlocked the doors letting the gathered throng inside.

He had bought his two CDs and it had only cost him three hours in line and a Classical Literature class. He had torn the plastic wrapping off before he had even paid, clicking the first CD in his Sony Discman before handing over the cash to pay for his purchase, falling in love with Right Next Door to Hell before he had even left the store. By the time he had reached his apartment, Coma's bass drum had him hypnotized.

It had been a great day.

His best friend and mentor, Gregory "Corky" Milton had chastised him, not understanding the appeal. "They're pussy metal. Give me Megadeth or Metallica any day."

"Don't forget Anthrax!"

"Don't act like you listen to it. You only like Bring the Noise, poser."

Acton smiled at the memory as his fingers danced tantalizingly close to the ancient drum, tracing the repetitive carvings ringing the instrument.

"Fantastic!" he hissed as he bumped into Laura who was rounding it in the opposite direction.

"It is one of our greatest treasures. It is called the Ngoc Lu drum. It was discovered by accident south of Hanoi in 1893 by a crew building a dike. It is thought to be well over two thousand years old."

Acton's head bobbed in appreciation. "The carvings are remarkably well preserved. It almost looks like you could play it right now. He rose slightly, positioning his hands to play.

"No!" cried Mai.

Acton laughed, grinning at her. "Just joking."

Mai's hand darted to her heart as she ushered them outside the barrier, quickly blocking off the artifact once more.

"I'm sorry, Mai, I shouldn't have scared you like that."

Laura punched him in the shoulder. "No, you shouldn't have."

Mai smiled shyly. "I'm sorry, I'm just not used to dealing with Americans."

"I'm British. We're even stranger," said Laura with a laugh. "At least to Americans."

Mai shook her head then suddenly paled slightly as her eyes darted toward the entrance to the room they were in. "Oh no, we shouldn't be here."

Acton turned and saw a group of about ten or fifteen people enter, immediately recognizing the United States Secretary of State, Jill Atwater. She had several others with her, clearly American, several Vietnamese and a four man security team.

Acton smiled, recognizing two of them immediately, despite the dark sunglasses hiding where they were looking. The two who had entered the room first he knew quite well, Command Sergeant Major Burt "Big Dog" Dawson and Sergeant Will "Spock" Lightman, two members of the Delta Force's Bravo Team. Acton took a step toward them to say hi when he noticed Dawson shake his head almost imperceptibly. He caught Laura by the arm as she made toward them.

"We don't know them," he whispered, turning to Mai. "Perhaps we should move on?"

Mai emphatically agreed, leading them to an archway that opened into another room, but before they could make it through, another delegation entered, blocking their path. Mai stepped aside, as did Acton and Laura, this delegation similar in nature to the American one, the center of attention vaguely familiar looking but the man's name escaping him for the moment.

Until he heard them speaking Russian.

*Anatoly Petrov, Prime Minister of Russia!*

He whispered the name to Laura who nodded, taking another step backward. Neither of them were fans of the Russians, especially since they had reverted to their old Soviet ways. There was some debate among the group of friends on who had coined the term Soviet Union 2.0 first, Acton thinking he had, but Milton had begged to disagree. It didn't matter who had come up with it first, it simply mattered that the nickname had stuck, and that it was far too apropos to be laughed at.

The Soviet Union was back, with oil money behind it, and Europe on its knees, too dependent upon Russian natural gas to heat their homes, leaving them powerless to counter Russian aggression in the Ukraine and elsewhere.

"Ahh, Secretary Atwater," bellowed Petrov, holding his arms out as he stepped past his security. Acton saw Dawson imperceptibly nod at Spock as they both moved aside, allowing the two dignitaries to greet one another.

"Prime Minister Petrov, an unexpected pleasure."

The smiles were genuinely forced, the long practiced art of diplomacy on display as Acton, Laura and their guide stood off to the side, both exits from the room now blocked with the two delegations.

"If I had known you were coming here today, I would have joined you," said Petrov, shaking Atwater's hand. "But our hosts neglected to mention it." The look he gave the Vietnamese delegate who was accompanying him was withering in its polite disparagement.

"An oversight, I am sure," mumbled the man, bowing deeply and taking a step back. "The appropriate people will be disciplined, I assure you."

Petrov laughed, waving off the assurance. "No need. This is merely a pleasant coincidence, nothing more. Why should I care where the Secretary of State will be on any given day?"

Acton found it impossible to believe that Petrov hadn't known exactly where Atwater would be, this being the highest level visit since the normalization of relations by President Clinton in 1995. It was all over the news with large crowds welcoming Secretary Atwater upon her arrival.

Acton had been shocked to learn that almost 75% of the Vietnamese people had a favorable view of Americans—he had done a little research before accepting the invitation to visit the museum. It had been proffered by Professor Duc Tran while on exchange to St. Paul's University where Acton taught archeology, and eagerly accepted. When they had arrived two days before Acton had been devastated to learn that Professor Tran had been killed in a car accident while they were in the air.

Mai had met them instead with the tragic news.

It was too late to simply turn around and Mai had convinced them that Professor Tran would have wanted them to complete their visit as a matter of honor. Tran was proud of his collection and Acton was anxious to see artifacts that few Americans had seen in nearly forty years.

They had agreed to stay.

If he had known the Russians were going to be here today, however, he might have suggested another venue to visit.

"I understand we are staying at the same hotel," said Petrov.

"Yes, my team informed me that you had requested to stay there."

Petrov's eyes narrowed. "Odd, I thought we had booked first, and it was *your* people who wanted to stay at the same hotel as *me*."

Atwater laughed—slightly. "I'm sure the truth must lie somewhere in the middle, Prime Minister. But not to worry, my security chief"—she nodded toward Dawson—"assures me the hotel is quite secure, so we are both safe."

"As does mine," said Petrov, nodding toward one of his own sunglass sporting men. "Perhaps you will do me the honor of joining me for dinner? I understand the restaurant in our *secure* hotel is quite excellent."

Atwater smiled, her hands out, palm upward. "Unfortunately, Prime Minister, I have a full schedule. Perhaps another time?"

"I look forward to it," bowed Petrov.

A Vietnamese man walked out from behind a tapestry, marching straight toward Prime Minister Petrov, gun extended in front of him, lead already belching from the barrel. Acton spun, extending his arms as they enveloped Laura and Mai, pulling them all to the ground. Out of the corner of his eye he saw Dawson and Spock grab Secretary Atwood and put themselves bodily between her and the shooter, the entire delegation exiting the room within seconds, apparently deciding ensuring the safety of their charge more important than taking out the shooter.

Looking over his shoulder he saw Petrov's four security men down, the rest of his delegation gone, Petrov now. alone with the man's gun pressed against his chest.

"I swore the next time I saw you I would kill you," said the man, his eyes narrowed, glaring up at the taller Petrov, his gun hand steady, there no fear here.

"How dare—"

"Silence!" barked the man. "You do not recognize me, Anatoly Petrov?"

Petrov shook his head slowly. "Have we met?"

"Nineteen-seventy-four. You led the Viet Cong who massacred my village."

Shouts could be heard, heavy boots drumming the marble floor as security from elsewhere in the building sped toward the shooting. Acton rose to his feet, still crouching, ushering Laura and Mai toward the opposite door, all the while keeping a wary eye on the shooter.

"I cleansed a lot of villages in those days, all sanctioned by the legitimate government." He glared down at the man, one corner of his mouth curling into a smile. "You'll have to be more specific."

The gun was pressed harder against Petrov's chest. The man reached into a bag hanging at his side, producing a clay bowl, painstakingly glued together from previously shattered shards. "Now do you remember?"

Petrov's eyes popped wide, a smile spreading across his face. "Young Phong, is that you?"

The man nodded. "You remember me."

"Of course I remember you," said Petrov, the smile still in place, his arms open wide as if trying to set the man at ease. "I let you live!"

"After killing my mother and father and my entire village. After burning everything I had ever known to the ground."

Petrov shrugged. "That was war. It has been over a long time."

"Not for me."

The man squeezed the trigger, the look of shock on Petrov's face something Acton knew he'd never forget. Mai screamed, Laura slapping a hand over her mouth to prevent her own. The man stepped over Petrov's gasping body, aiming the weapon at his head. "Today my village can finally rest."

He squeezed the trigger one more time, blood and brain matter squirting across the floor.

Shouts from the security team were close now. The man looked at Acton then dove through a nearby window, shattering the glass with his body, disappearing from sight as the soldiers charged into the room, guns pointing at the only three people alive.

Acton and the others raised their hands as guns were pressed against their backs. Mai spoke rapidly to no avail, the weapons still held painfully in place as the room was secured. Another man entered whom Acton recognized from earlier introductions as the curator of the museum. His words succeeded in lowering the soldiers' guns, and once removed, the three of them rose cautiously to their feet.

"I'm so sorry, Professor Acton, Professor Palmer. Of course you are not involved in this most unfortunate incident."

"Did you catch him?" asked Laura.

"No, but we know who he is!" said the man, shaking a piece of paper. "The fool showed his ID when he entered!" He held the page up so they could see the enlarged face, a scan of the man's identification card having been taken when he entered.

And it was everything Acton could do to not gasp.

For he recognized the face despite the poor copy.

It was Delta Team-Bravo member Sergeant Carl "Niner" Sung.

*Kusinara, Malla Kingdom*

*Near modern day Indian/Nepalese border*

*401 BC*

Cunda wept.

For the Buddha was dying, deathly ill, and it was his fault. It was he who had provided him with his last meal, a dish made of his favorite local mushrooms, herbs and other delicacies from the lands surrounding their small village. It was a meal he had been proud to gather the ingredients for, a meal his hands had trembled in nervousness while preparing, and a meal he and his only son had delivered with pride, though pride wasn't a virtue becoming of a follower of the Buddha.

He was disappointed in himself for feeling it, and he would meditate on it later tonight.

At least that was what he had planned.

Before he had killed the Buddha.

"He is an old man," reassured Ananda, the Buddha's personal attendant. "He was ready for Parinirvana which is why he travelled here. He knew before he even sat down to eat your delicious dish that this would be his final meal. He asked me to convey to you his thanks and assurances that your meal has nothing to do with his illness. He said your meal was a source of the greatest merit as it provided him his last sustenance before leaving his physical form and entering the next stage of existence."

Cunda, still on his knees, his head nearly touching the floor as he humbled himself beside his son, turned his head to look up at Ananda. "H-he said that?"

Ananda nodded, reaching out a hand which Cunda accepted. Ananda pulled the bereaved man to his feet. "You are to be honored for your service in feeding the Buddha in his final hours." Ananda turned and took a clay bowl, intricately hand painted, rings of colorful flowers and plants adorning it from top to bottom, and handed it to him. "He wanted you to have this."

Cunda extended his hands, shaking more than earlier. His son's hands covered his own, steadying him.

"I do not deserve such a gift."

Ananda smiled. "The fact you say such a thing is proof you do."

Cunda didn't bother continuing to argue. "Why?" was all he could manage to ask.

"You came with a question for the Buddha and instead he asked you to prepare him a meal."

Cunda nodded. It had been a challenge, this not his home, but he had managed to find the ingredients he needed and his wife had sent him with the traditional seasonings from their tiny village as part of their pilgrimage to see the Buddha and seek his advice.

It had been his duty and his honor to undertake this task, though it had left him bewildered and he had to admit, a bit angry. He had travelled for weeks, their journey grueling, but necessary. Their village had been beset by years of misfortune. Flash floods triggered by heavy rains had washed much of their village away only to be followed by two summers of drought leaving parched earth and a nearly dry riverbed. And once they thought their prayers had been answered and their crops had once again blossomed, raids by nearby villages to plunder their limited resources began under the guise of punishment for following the teachings of the Buddha.

He had come to the Buddha to seek an answer to the question that burned in his heart.

*Should we leave our home to find peace elsewhere?*

He had asked the question when granted an audience, but instead had been given the 'honor' of providing the Buddha with a meal.

No answer had been forthcoming.

And now he was given a clay bowl instead.

With the luck his village had been having, if word got out that he had provided the last meal before the Buddha had become violently ill they would be destroyed for certain.

"But what of my question? What is the Buddha's advice?"

Ananda motioned toward the bowl. "The Buddha says, 'Trust in what you see.' Now go, we must prepare for the passing."

Cunda and his son, Asita, were ushered out by guards and found themselves on the street, the sun having set only minutes before. Word of the Buddha's illness had obviously spread, a large crowd already gathering around the home where the Buddha was staying as a guest.

"Is he okay?" asked one.

"What have you heard?" demanded another, grabbing Cunda's arm. The clay bowl fell from his hands as his arm was torn away by the man demanding information.

Asita caught it, tucking it under his arm and grabbing his father, leading them away from the crowd.

"I-I've heard nothing," he said, shame in the lie already gripping his chest.

"I heard he became sick after eating!" shouted a woman, her voice laced with anger. "Somebody must have poisoned him!"

Asita tugged on Cunda's arm harder as he navigated them through the growing crowd as quickly as he could. Cunda continued to shake, his mind shutting down as the shouts grew, his heart fluttering in his chest as fear gripped him, his stride slowing.

"Come on!" hissed his son, squeezing his arm sharply, the pinch snapping him back to reality. "We have to get out of here before it's too late!"

Cunda nodded, his surroundings coming back into focus as he picked up his pace, following his son through to the edge of the crowd toward a group of houses that led to their camp outside the village.

"That's him there!" shouted someone. Cunda looked over his shoulder and nearly soiled himself as the entire throng turned toward him, someone pointing. "He's the one who brought the meal!"

"He poisoned him!"

"He killed the Buddha!"

Asita and Cunda both broke into a sprint, the younger Asita quicker off the mark, darting between two houses, a narrow alleyway extending almost a dozen houses from the main village square they had just come from. They ran as fast as Cunda's older legs could carry them, Asita continually slowing down to urge him forward, but Cunda was gripped in fear. He glanced over his shoulder once more as the crowd tried to shove its way through the narrow opening at the beginning of the alley.

And he tripped.

His left shoulder hit the ground hard, pain shooting through his body. Powerful hands had him in their grasp quickly, pulling him back to his feet as the crowd surged like ants over an obstacle, a flash flood of humanity on a previously dry riverbed.

Cunda drew his sword.

"Go!" he yelled to his son. "I will hold them off."

"No, we will fight them together!" His son drew his own sword.

"No, there is only room for one to fight, and you must survive. Take the bowl and tell our village what the Buddha said. Seek the wisdom in his words."

"But, Father, I can't leave you!"

The first of the bloodthirsty crowd was almost upon them. "You must! If we both die, the Buddha's words will be for nothing. Our village must be saved, and after today, you are its leader!"

He swung his sword hard, sweeping across the breadth of the alleyway, removing the head of one man, cleaving halfway through another.

"Go, my son! Now!" he shouted as he swung again at the leading edge of the crowd, suddenly slowed, pushed forward by the surge of flesh behind them. He raised the sword over his head and swung down, a startled man's head splitting like a log, his blood spurting over the man beside him who screamed in fear, pushing back against the crowd-surge that would have him challenge the now recovered Cunda.

Cunda stole a glance behind him to see his son, halfway down the alley, backing away, keeping a pleading eye on his father, tears rolling down his cheeks as Cunda took another step back, swinging his sword, slicing through a fleeing man's back, removing the outstretched arm of the man next to him.

He looked over his shoulder. "Pray for me!" he shouted, knowing the sins he was committing would condemn him to eternal damnation, the killing of so many unforgiveable no matter the reason. He wasn't a soldier with the luxury of war as an excuse, he was merely the leader of a simple village, leadership thrust upon him purely because of family lineage rather than popular choice.

A reluctant leader, a desperate leader.

He swung again but now saw swords held high nearing him as those who were unarmed tried to squeeze back through the alley, those with swords shoving forward to engage the murderer of the Buddha.

"You will be avenged, Father!"

He spun toward his son. "No! Do not avenge me! They know not what they do! They are blinded by lies and fear and hatred! Just go! Save yourself! Save our village!"

Metal scraped the ground behind him as a roar erupted from what sounded like an impossibly loud man.

Cunda swung around, his sword rising from near his ankles to waist height as he faced the enemy, the blade continuing upward, knocking the man's blade aside and removing his hand.

But there were more blades now, rushing toward him, their owners desperate to get into the battle, blocked only by those in front of them. He swung furiously now, left and right, battling two blades at once, neither able to get a full swing at him, each blocking the other.

Yet he was tiring.

If energy weren't his enemy, he could potentially hold them for hours, but it wasn't, and with each one he took out of the battle, a fresh body faced him moments later.

He retreated another step and looked behind him.

Asita was gone.

*Be safe, my son.*

His heavy heart threatened to overwhelm him as he thrust forward, burying his blade into a man's stomach. As he withdrew the man collapsed on Cunda's sword, causing the blade to drop to the ground. He fell back several steps quickly, dragging his sword free but it was too late. A blade descended upon his left shoulder, burying itself deep. He screamed out in pain, grabbing the sharp metal with his left hand, pushing it up and out of his flesh, slicing through his palm as he did so.

He had no time to even look at the bloody stump that now lay dead on his shoulder, instead swinging weakly at the next thrust, his parry almost useless now.

His sword clattered to the ground.

His leg was sliced open and he dropped to his still good knee, his now free hand pushing against the dirt as he looked up at the attacker who had finally bested him.

Rage filled eyes, so much hate it was inconceivable in the heart of this simple villager, glared down at him, freezing his soul with fear, the descending death blow going almost unnoticed as time seemed to slow down. The crowd roared their anger, screams of pain echoed through the alleyway, swords clanged as they tried to get into the fight. His nostrils flared with the smell of his own blood and those of his victims, the smell enough to make his mouth fill with bile. The air, thick with a mist of carnage, had a metallic taste that mixed with the sickness in his mouth, threatening to make him gag.

And the agony in his neck, as the unnoticed sword sliced clean through, was mercifully short lived, his thoughts of the Buddha's last words.

*Trust in what you see.*

And as his head tumbled to the ground, rolling several times, he died knowing he'd never decipher the riddle meant to save his people.

*Outside the Vietnam National Museum of History, Hanoi, Vietnam*

*Present Day*

Command Sergeant Major Burt "Big Dog" Dawson nearly shoved the Secretary of State into the back of the armored limousine, jumping in after her as the driver floored it, the door closing of its own accord. Four escort vehicles, two in the front and two in the rear were manned by his team and Bureau of Diplomatic Security personnel, the entire procession accompanied by half a dozen Vietnamese military vehicles with police motorcycles leading, blocking off intersections as they made the rush back to the hotel.

"Are you okay, Madam Secretary?"

Atwater nodded, visibly shaken. "Do we know what happened?"

Dawson shook his head, activating his comm. "Bravo One-One, Bravo One. Sit rep, over?"

Sergeant Carl "Niner" Sung's voice came in clear. "Bravo One, we're secure at Echo Two but there might be a problem, over."

"Explain."

"My security pass was stolen from my room. I've reported it and a new one is being issued. We're double-checking all IDs here, over."

"Roger that, ETA seven minutes, out." Dawson chewed on his cheek. A stolen ID. He knew Niner and there was no way he had lost it or screwed up. Protocol would be to secure the ID in the room safe, but hotel room safes were notoriously unsecure.

The question now was whether or not it was a targeted theft, or simply unintentional, the thief grabbing everything he found. He had to assume targeted. He turned to Atwater. "Once you're secure I'll find out what happened, but I'm reasonably certain you weren't the target."

"I'm not waiting seven minutes, I want to know what happened now." She snapped her fingers at her aide. "Call the Embassy, tell them what happened and tell them I want to know the status of the Russian Prime Minister ASAP!"

Ronald Greer pulled out his cellphone and quickly began dialing. Dawson frowned. "Madam Secretary, that phone isn't secure, the conversation could be monitored. I highly recommend we wait until we have access to our secure comms."

Atwater dismissed his concerns with a bat of the hand. "Nonsense. We have nothing to hide."

Dawson turned his head toward the window so as not to betray how moronic he felt the Secretary's statement was. He had lost count of the number of times they had found themselves in hot water because some politician who thought they knew better ignored the advice of him or one of his team.

And this day, he had a feeling, wasn't going to end well.

He had heard four shots before they had exited the building, all from the same type of weapon, his quick glimpse and the sound of the shots suggesting a Makarov PM, probably a leftover from the war. The man appeared Vietnamese and it was pretty clear he was specifically after the Russian Prime Minister.

*This is probably going to be the biggest international incident since the assassination of Franz Ferdinand triggered World War I.*

Another intersection was cleared, their speed at best thirty, Hanoi's streets not accustomed to unexpected emergency motorcades. His mental counter ticked down another intersection, six to go. When they arrived and the Secretary was secure in her room, he would be recommending an immediate return to Washington, the Russian response to the assassination of their Prime Minister unpredictable.

But he already knew the answer would be 'no'.

Greer was speaking in hushed tones and Dawson was half-listening, updates coming through his comm from the security detail, he more concerned with securing his package.

*Five to go.*

"The Prime Minister is dead," said Greer, fear and shock in his voice. "Along with his entire security detail."

Dawson resisted the urge to raise his eyebrows. *The entire detail?* They were clearly caught off guard, the four shots he had heard rapid, the four shots fired within less than three seconds, and with there being no return fire, they were obviously all accurate.

"Has there been a response from the Russians yet?" asked Atwater.

"Not yet. We're not even sure if they know."

"Christ, there's going to be hell to pay, and we were there when it happened!" She jabbed a finger at Dawson. "Why didn't you do anything?"

The muscle memory in Dawson's right hand mimicked tearing her throat out, the accusation idiotic. "I did, ma'am. I immediately evacuated my charge and am in the process of securing them."

A puff of air escaped Atwater's lips as if she thought it a pathetic answer.

"The Russians are going to blame us for this. We have an enhanced security detail—what are you, Delta? SEAL?—and you let him get killed!"

*Thanks for blowing my cover, asshole.*

He kept quiet.

*Three more.*

"What?" Greer's exclamation was one of pure shock as he turned to Atwater. "They're saying he was killed by an American!"

Atwater's jaw dropped and Dawson felt his chest tighten.

*This is going to turn into a Charlie-Foxtrot in a hurry.*

*Outside Kusinara, Malla Kingdom*

*Near modern day Indian/Nepalese border*

*401 BC*

Asita skidded to a halt as he heard his father scream. He turned, gripping his sword but heard the dull thud of the deathblow echo through the alleyway he had left only moments before, then the cheers of the crowd.

He bent over and vomited.

Spitting the harsh liquid from his mouth he said a quick prayer and turned, rushing into the forest to the east of the village, weaving left and right through the dense foliage, the roar of the crowd still behind him as they discovered only one of the two they were after had fallen.

Heading directly for the camp they had made several days earlier upon arrival, tucked on the other side of this small thick of trees, he began to shout to the servants who had accompanied them, hoping they heard him.

“Pack immediately!” he cried. “We must leave now!”

He burst through the trees and into their small camp, a large tent shared by he and his father, several smaller ones for their entourage of four and supplies. The servants stood dumbstruck at his shouts, their faces questioning what there was no time to question.

“They’re coming. They mean to kill us all!”

Action.

He dove into his tent, surveying the room and quickly decided nothing was worth saving. He grabbed a small satchel and slung it over his shoulder, placing the now precious clay bowl into it then reemerged to see the supplies inside the tents quickly being tossed from within.

"Never mind that!" he yelled. "Arm yourselves and leave the rest. We'll find food and water on the way."

The snapping of branches and shouts from within the trees grew as the crowd surged forward in an effort to find the one who had escaped. A branch snapped nearby and a man burst from the forest, his sword wielding arm held high.

"I found them!" he shouted at Asita rushed forward, drawing his sword, swinging at the surprised man emboldened from the crowd, but now alone and apparently inexperienced in the art of war.

His innards spilled on the ground, a river of crimson flowing on the slight downslope leading to a meandering stream their camp was straddling.

More shouts and Asita knew it wouldn't be long before they were overwhelmed.

"Run!" he shouted, turning from the forest and sprinting along the streambed, his feet splashing through the shallow water, the footfalls of his servants, including his trusted companion Channa close behind.

The forest belched forth dozens of pursuers at once.

Asita slowed to defend himself allowing the others to catch up and position themselves between him and the approaching throng.

"Run, Master! We will protect you!"

He hesitated for a moment as the four men, all highly adept warriors advanced on the crowd, leaving him shivering in the cool mountain runoff.

"Run!" cried Channa with a final look over his shoulder as swords clashed.

He ran.

The battle soon began to fade, the clashing of swords crushing his spirit with each splash in the water, his thoughts of Channa, a servant he had grown up with and he had chosen to be his official companion upon becoming a man and heir to the leadership of their tribe.

Channa had been elated.

And Asita had been careful to never abuse his friend, instead rarely needing to ask for anything, Channa knowing him so well his needs were usually anticipated.

And now his friend would die defending his master.

A stabbing pain in his right shoulder overwhelmed him, sending him tumbling to the ground. His grip on his sword loosened and it clattered onto the bed of small rocks as he reached for the source of the pain, his head turning to look at what was causing so much agony.

An arrow, embedded deep, blood flowing freely, stood menacingly upright. He tried to reach it, but couldn't, his fingertips irritatingly close but not enough to grip the shaft and pull it free. He pushed himself to his knees and another arrow skidded past him. He looked back and saw the archer marching toward him as he readied another arrow.

He ran.

Or rather stumbled forward.

The pain was nearly unbearable and he thought of the agony his poor father must have gone through. The satchel containing the clay bowl swung out from his body then back, hitting his hip. His heart leapt. He stole a glance inside the bag and breathed a painful sigh of relief as he confirmed the bowl hadn't broken when he fell.

Another arrow, this one too close, his stumbling and zigzagging thankfully enough to keep the man's aim from being true, his first shot apparently lucky, the man's skill thankfully limited.

But his pace was slowed, less than half his healthy self.

And he could hear fewer swords now.

*I'm sorry, Channa!*

He said a silent prayer as he continued away from the battle but could feel himself getting weaker and weaker.

He dropped to a knee, reaching again for the shoulder, the throb now overwhelming.

He couldn't go on.

The clatter of horses' hooves on stone had his head turning painfully to the side and he caught a glimpse of a man on horseback charging toward him, the blood thirsty mob behind him, stained blades held high as they surged forward, his companions finished, the numbers against them overwhelming.

His head sagged as he collapsed on all fours, gasping for breath, exhausted and weak. The bowl was heavy in his bag, pulling down on his neck, but he refused to think ill of it, to resent its weight, for it was the last thing his father had held, and one of the last things the Buddha had held. It contained the key to saving his village, should he solve the riddle that accompanied it.

Unfortunately he would never know the answer to that riddle.

And his village would continue to founder, and eventually fall.

"Master!"

The voice was instantly recognizable. *Channa!* He looked up as the mighty beast neared, slowing down, and felt a surge of hope as he saw his friend leaning over, reaching out for him. He held up his left arm, his right nearly useless, but knew he had no hope of gripping his friend and companion's arm.

But he needn't have worried.

Channa grabbed his forearm with an iron grip and pulled him from the ground, swinging him onto the horse behind him, urging the beast forward once Asita wrapped his one good arm around his friend's waist. He looked over his shoulder and saw the crowd come to a halt in frustration, and he prayed that his ordeal was over.

The adrenaline that had been fueling him began to wane and within moments his head fell on Channa's back, the horror of the day fading to black as he passed out from the pain and blood loss, the Buddha's riddle in his head.

*Trust in what you see.*

He felt a moment of frustration and anger at the source of the cryptic message. His father had died for a riddle when what he needed was sage advice, not clever words. His eyes burned with tears in his final moments of consciousness as he thought of his dead father and his final words, his chest filling with the shame of hating the Buddha.

*Seek the wisdom in his words.*

It was his father's final commandment to him.

*But what in the name of the ancestors does the riddle mean?*

*Vietnam National Museum of History, Hanoi, Vietnam*

*Present Day*

The curator sped away before Professor James Acton could say anything, leaving nothing but Vietnamese guards behind. And they still looked edgy.

"Was that who I—"

Acton cut Laura's whispered question off. "Yes."

"But—"

"I know." He turned to Mai. "Do you know what hotel Secretary Atwater is staying at?"

Mai nodded, still clearly terrified. "The same hotel you are staying at. It is the best Hanoi has to offer."

"Excellent. I think it's best we return to our hotel immediately."

Mai asked something of one of the soldiers who appeared in charge and he replied with something sounding like an uncertain affirmative then adding a burst of dialogue just before they exited the room. They froze. The man approached, his walk cocky as he clasped his hands behind his back, his body almost at an obtuse angle as he approached, kicking his feet out in a slightly exaggerated manner.

*Ministry of Silly Walks, anyone?*

"You are American?" asked the man, his accent thick.

"I am. My wife is a British subject."

"You witnessed what happened here today?"

Acton nodded. "Yes."

"You saw the man who did this?"

"Yes," said Acton.

"Yes, we all did," added Laura.

"No, I saw nothing!" yelped Mai, clearly terrified. "I closed my eyes as soon as the shooting started."

Acton knew full-well that Mai had seen the shooter, but decided she must have her reasons for lying.

*Probably pure terror. She knows if she doesn't say what they want to hear, she's liable to end up in some labor camp.*

It made him yearn for a quick return home.

"I can attest to that," said Acton, deciding to cover for Mai. "As soon as I saw the man appear from behind that tapestry"—he pointed to the far wall, their interrogator turning to look for a moment—"I grabbed them and pushed them to the floor. I'm surprised either of them saw anything."

"I only did because I turned to look," added Laura, playing along. "Miss Trinh was closest to this wall"—she motioned toward the near wall—"so she had both myself and my husband in her way."

The man pursed his lips, not looking convinced. He shouted something and one of his men disappeared after a heel-clicking snap to attention. The man looked back at Acton then Laura, his eyes finally resting on a trembling Mai. "Why do I think you are lying?"

Acton shrugged. "Why would we lie? There was a shooting. We were simply trying to survive without getting shot."

"Why didn't you run like the others?"

"We were in the direct line of fire. If he had missed one of the guards he might have hit us. I felt it was more important for everyone to get on the ground."

"Or perhaps the assassin knew you, and let you live."

Mai failed to stifle a yelp.

Acton sensed his wife getting pissed off.

"What a ridiculous notion!" she cried, jabbing her finger at the five corpses. "A tragedy has occurred here today, a tragedy that *we* had nothing to do with. Clearly *your* security failed, which is unbelievable considering who your guests were today!"

Acton shifted slightly in front of Laura under the guise of getting a better look at the bodies on the other side of the room. He wagged a finger at her behind his back.

"Sir, we would be happy to cooperate in any way we can, but we didn't really see much."

"You saw the shooter."

"Yes, *I* did," said Acton. "Miss Trinh had no opportunity, and my wife had minimal."

"And you would recognize the man should you see him again?"

"I'm not sure."

"Why, because all us Charlie's look alike?"

Acton hated to admit it, however it had been proven scientifically that people were programmed to be able to recognize people of their own ethnicity far easier than those of another, and his exposure to Vietnamese had been limited, Maryland not exactly bursting at the seams with the descendants of former refugees. "No," he said deliberately, "it's not that at all. It's just that we were worried about getting shot the entire time. I was more focused on the barrel of his gun."

The soldier dispatched earlier returned at a run, handing a folder over to his commander. The man opened the file, revealing the same photo they had seen earlier of Niner, a member of Delta Force's Bravo Team. A man Acton knew and trusted with his life.

And definitely not the shooter.

"Do you recognize him?"

Acton was about to answer truthfully when he remembered Dawson's subtle headshake.

*They're undercover.*

"No."

He almost sensed Laura's heart race.

"But you must."

Acton felt a lump form in his throat.

*They know!*

"Why *must* I?"

"Because he is the shooter."

Acton shook his head. "No, he isn't."

"How can you be sure? You said you were looking at the barrel of the gun? How can you be so sure it wasn't him?"

Acton tried to steady his pounding heart. "I just know," he said, digging his finger nails into his palms clasped behind his back. "This man looks completely different." He decided to play a card, leaning forward and squinting. "He looks Korean to me."

"So?"

"So? So the man who shot the Prime Minister said he was Vietnamese."

"You heard them speak? Why didn't you say so before?" The man's tone was becoming more pressing, more belligerent by the moment, and Acton wasn't sure how to diffuse him.

"Because you simply didn't ask, officer," said Laura for the save, her voice sultry and sweet. "My husband said we'd cooperate fully. We simply haven't had an opportunity to tell you what happened yet, since you've been focusing on *who* did the shooting, not how it happened. We would be happy to give you a statement."

The man visibly relaxed, if only for a moment.

"What was said?" he snapped, his tone back.

Acton thought back, trying to recall exactly what was said. "He asked the Prime Minister if he recognized him, and when he said he didn't, he said they had met in nineteen-seventy-four when the Prime Minister had led a group of"—he paused, searching for a word other than 'Viet Cong'—"*soldiers* that massacred his village. The Prime Minister said his name as if he recognized him, said the war was over, then was shot by the man."

"There were no Russian soldiers here during the civil war."

Acton shrugged, knowing that if he called bullshit on the statement it might just get him killed. "All I can tell you is what I heard."

"I think you're lying."

Acton's chest tightened. "Why?"

The man held up the photo again. "Because this man is the shooter, and he's an American spy!"

*Oh shit!*

Again he shrugged, trying to remain calm. "*That* man"—he nodded toward the picture—"might very well be. But he isn't the shooter."

The man turned his head, shouting something, and immediately the entire security detail descended upon the three innocent bystanders.

*Outside Pataliputra, Vrijji Kingdom*

*Near modern day Indian/Bangladeshi border*

*401 BC, three months after the Buddha's death*

Asita rotated his arm gingerly and Channa smiled.

"See, I told you, good as new!"

Asita frowned, not certain he would describe his healed shoulder that way, but he had to admit, other than some general weakness which he hoped would go away in time, it felt remarkably well. Thanks to Channa's tender ministrations, the bleeding had been stopped once they had escaped the bloodthirsty mob, and he had kept it clean and free of infection, treating it with various plants and herbs as he had been taught by the village elders. Part of his job as companion was to treat his master's wounds during and after battle, which meant an extensive knowledge of medicine.

It had saved Asita's life.

He had feared that should he survive, his arm surely wouldn't, but Channa had refused to give up and his confidence infused Asita with his own, allowing him to fight back from the brink.

But it had been hard. Once the bleeding had been stopped they had been back on the horse almost immediately, trying to put as much distance between themselves and their pursuers. It had been a long, arduous season, the chill in the air blowing down from the mighty mountains now noticeable, and with all their supplies left behind at their camp, they had been forced to scavenge.

All they had had were the clothes on their backs and the clay bowl his father had died for.

Asita shrugged his robe back over his shoulder and eyed the bowl sitting on a nearby tree stump. Whenever they were camped he placed it in plain view—if they were alone—and contemplated the meaning. Both he and Channa were at a loss.

*Trust in what you see.*

"I see a bowl! A cursed bowl! A bowl that my father died for!"

Channa nodded knowingly, sitting beside his master and staring at the riddle. "How do you figure your father died for it?"

Asita's head spun toward his friend, his jaw dropping. "Isn't it obvious?"

"Apparently not."

A flash of anger raged through him. "If we hadn't have waited for the bowl, we would have left the village long before the Buddha died. My father would be alive and we would be free of those pursuing us."

Channa's head bobbed as he poked the small fire with a stick, the flames jumping, burning embers floating in the air in front of them. "You assume too much, Master."

Asita sucked in a deep breath, holding back his desire to cuff his friend as he had every right to do, but had never done. "Explain."

"You assume they wouldn't have been able to find out who your father was, and then followed us all back to the village. We—" He stopped, his jaw dropping just as Asita's did.

"The village," whispered Asita, his heart climbing into his throat. "We've been gone so long—"

"If they knew, they surely would have reached it by now!" finished Channa.

"We have to go. Now." Asita began to push himself to his feet when Channa grabbed his arm.

"No, Master, we must wait until morning. It is too dangerous to travel at night. We will rest and leave at the crack of dawn, making all haste home."

Asita sat back down, reluctantly agreeing with his friend. And as they both lay down to sleep, Asita found himself tossing and turning most of the night, his thoughts consumed with images of his friends and family being massacred because he hadn't been man enough to survive the initial battle, then had spent three months trying to save his own life rather than those of the villagers who would now call him their leader.

*Father, forgive me!*

*Daewoo Hanoi Hotel, Hanoi, Vietnam*

*Present Day*

The car came to an abrupt halt and the door was pulled open. Command Sergeant Major Burt Dawson stepped out first, nodding to Niner who held the door. They were at the Echo Two location, the rear entrance to the hotel where they could avoid the press and public during emergencies. Vietnamese security had kept it clear and seconds later they were within the walls of the hotel, the hallways already emptied to the service elevator.

The elevator ride to the ninth floor was a flurry of Atwater on the phone along with her aides who had been there to greet them upon their arrival. All had cellphones to their ears or in their hands, updates being shouted out, none of which raised any concerns until the last one.

"They've got a photo of the assassin," said one, holding up his phone to Atwater.

Her jaw dropped as she looked at the photo then at Niner.

"It's you!" she exclaimed, taking a step backward.

Niner said nothing, his eyes covered by his sunglasses, ignoring her. His job was to get her safely to her room then worry about false allegations later. Atwater grabbed the phone, shoving it in Dawson's face. "He's *your* man! You're supposed to have vetted him! You let an assassin on your team! On *my* security detail!"

A chime sounded and the doors opened. Dawson and Niner stepped out, Spock and Jimmy there to greet them, the hall cleared, Diplomatic Security Special Agents lining the walls. They marched quickly toward the Secretary's suite then stepped inside. Dawson and Niner cleared the large room then Dawson motioned for Niner to leave as he turned to face Atwater who hadn't stopped her tirade since stepping off the elevator.

"I want him under arrest, now!" screamed Atwater, pointing at the departing Niner. "Now!" The screech was shrill, something he had heard rumors about but hadn't experienced yet in person.

The phone rang and Greer jumped at it. "Yes? One moment." He cupped his hand over the receiver and looked at Atwater. "The police are here to arrest Agent Green."

"We can't let that happen. You know he had nothing to do with it," said Dawson.

"I know nothing of the sort! For all we know he killed the Prime Minister then returned to the hotel."

"Madam Secretary, with all due respect, that's ridiculous and you know it."

"I know nothing!"

*Clearly.*

"Madam Secretary, he's an American citizen. We can't hand him over to the Vietnamese police. We'll never see him again."

"It's precisely *because* he's an American citizen that we *will* see him again." She inhaled deeply, holding up her hand, telling the world to pause while she regained control.

Dawson said nothing, hoping a modicum of sanity would return to the room if Atwater could check her emotions.

"He's your man. Do you trust him?" she asked, her voice remarkably calm compared to moments before.

"With my life, ma'am. I am one hundred percent positive he had nothing to do with it. I saw the shooter. It definitely wasn't him."

Her head bobbed as she dropped into a wingback chair. "Of course you're right, I apologize. It's just—" She stopped as if searching for words.

"We're all in shock, ma'am. We witnessed the assassination of the number two man in one of the most powerful nations in the world. This day is only going to get worse, and it will get out of control if we give in to their allegations that an American security agent on *your* detail murdered him in cold blood. We have to get this situation under control, now."

"How?"

"*Everyone* gets on a plane, now. Once in Washington we can deal with it—not here."

She shook her head. "No, if we run away it looks like we've got something to hide."

"That may be," agreed Dawson, "but my responsibility is to ensure your safety, and I can no longer guarantee that here. The situation has become untenable. Within hours dozens of Russian security will be arriving, and before tomorrow morning there will be hundreds, including their own FSB people. Their delegation is in the same hotel as us, only six floors down. They could assassinate you in retaliation far too easily."

Atwater blanched a little, motioning toward a carafe of water. Greer poured her a glass and handed it to her. She drank then dipped her fingers in what remained, wiping some on her forehead and cheeks. "This job will be the death of me," she muttered. "Vietnam! Of all the damned places he could have sent me, he had to send me to Vietnam!"

Greer put the phone back to his ear. "One moment, please." He looked at Atwater. "What do I tell them?"

Atwater looked at Dawson. "What *can* I tell them? We have to be seen as cooperating otherwise they'll think we *were* involved." She paused, splashing some more water on her face. "But why do they think he's involved?"

"I'm guessing his ID was used to gain access to the museum," replied Dawson.

"What?"

"Agent Green reported that his ID had been stolen. I just found out as we were evacuating you. I haven't had time to investigate."

Atwater shook her head. "This just keeps getting worse and worse." She sat up straight. "Tell them that Agent Green will be available for interrogation in one hour, under *our* supervision on *this* floor."

Greer nodded, repeating the message then hanging up before there could be an argument.

"Thank you, Madam Secretary."

Atwater rose and took Dawson aside. "Listen. I know you're not DSS, and I know your man isn't. I have a pretty good idea who you are. You're right, I don't believe for a second your man is involved, but I have to play the diplomat here. If we can't prove that he isn't involved, the Russians will demand he be handed over, and we'll have no choice but to do it."

"I understand, ma'am."

"I'm not sure you do, Agent." She placed a hand on his chest, lowering her voice further. "Do whatever it takes to prove his innocence. You might just be preventing a war."

*Gandhara Kingdom*

*Modern day Myanmar*

*401 BC, four months after the Buddha's death*

Asita dropped to his knees, burying his head in his hands as sobs racked his body. His shoulders heaved with each cry, his chest tightening, his stomach a knot as bile began to fill his mouth.

His village was gone.

His home, his family, his friends.

Gone.

His wife and three children.

Gone.

He felt the comforting hand of Channa on his shoulder as he too collapsed. For Channa had a family as well. A wife and two daughters.

The two of them were all that was left.

"We are alone," whispered Asita.

Channa for once said nothing, there no words of comfort that could be said. Instead he pushed himself to his feet, stumbling toward what had been his home, it now a burnt out hulk, the thatch roof gone, the mud and stone walls collapsed to half their former height.

Asita couldn't bring himself to look at his own home, the happy memories like daggers to his surviving heart. The horrors his poor wife and children must have endured at the hands of those who would have their revenge had his fists pounding the earth over and over as grief and anger overwhelmed him.

In a fit of anger he reached into his satchel, grabbed the bowl and flung it into the stream that had once been a small river, just one of the curses their village had suffered over the years. The bowl landed on its side and quickly filled with water, sinking enough to be caught up on the streambed, it too shallow.

The satisfaction he felt ridding himself of the albatross that had been around his neck all these months was brief, he returning to pounding the ground in grief.

"They're gone!"

It was Channa's excited voice that had him stop, his fists shoved hard against the dirt as he looked up through tear-burned eyes at the excited utterance.

He said nothing.

Channa was running to the next home, then the next, repeating his cry. "They're gone! They're all gone!"

Asita's pulse was pounding in his ears, drowning out the words of his friend.

And they were excited words.

Happily excited.

It took him a few moments to comprehend that his friend's mood had changed and he began to look around, to look past the horrors he had initially focused on, and to see what wasn't there.

Bodies.

There were no bodies anywhere. Surely if his village had been massacred then there should be bodies.

But there were none.

*Scavengers?*

There would be evidence. Bones, blood, something.

He rose, joining in the search, and after examining the final burnt-out hulk of a former family's home, he came to a stop. Channa was standing in a clearing used only for solemn occasions.

Cremation.

The funeral pyres had clearly been used, a large amount of ash and dust accumulated, more than he remembered seeing. And there were still remains visible, as if there had been no one left behind to tend to the fires to make certain all had been properly dealt with.

He looked at Channa whose renewed spirit had taken a hit, he again on his knees.

But Asita smiled, a smile that began in the corners of his mouth, then spread across his cheeks as he realized the implications of what he saw.

*Someone* had survived.

For the dead don't cremate themselves.

*Vietnam National Museum of History, Hanoi, Vietnam*

*Present Day*

James Acton was shoved into a simple wood chair, handcuffs, clasped too tightly, tore into his flesh. He looked over at his wife, Laura Palmer, who had been forced into her own chair just as roughly, and wondered where poor Mai must be.

*I hope they don't hurt her too much.*

He had no illusions that their passports would protect them. They were in Vietnam, not France. Nothing beyond shouts in Vietnamese had been said to them since their arrest, but everything said had Mai sobbing harder and harder and Acton was pretty sure he had seen her wet her pants.

*That poor woman!*

His own bladder had wanted to let go a few times but he had managed to remember his training, keeping calm through tactical breathing and focusing on Laura instead of the chaos surrounding them. He had done a stint in the National Guard years ago, serving in Gulf War One, and more recently had received intensive training from Laura's security team, mostly made up of former British SAS.

The training was paying off.

The man who had been interrogating them entered and dropped into a chair opposite them, tossing several file folders on the table. The room was a reasonable size, some sort of meeting room at the museum, and the fact they had been taken here instead of some police station or worse had Acton still hopeful they might get out of this relatively unscathed.

"I am Captain Nguyen, Hanoi Police Department." He opened the first folder and put a pair of glasses on, peeking over them at Acton then back at the page as he read, his accent thick but his command of the English language clear. "You are Professor James Acton, American citizen residing in St. Paul, Maryland. You teach archeology at St. Paul's University and were once a member of your National Guard. You have also been involved in a rather large number of international incidents over the past few years." Nguyen removed his glasses. "Care to explain why you always seem to be at the wrong place at the wrong time, as you Americans might put it?"

Acton decided glib wasn't the way to play it. "As an archeologist I often find myself in parts of the world that are inherently dangerous. Unfortunately these are troubled times and I've found myself caught in the middle on occasion."

"Yet you manage to survive. As if someone is protecting you, almost as if you were meant to be in these situations, not an innocent bystander as you claim."

Acton thought of his guardian angels, the Bravo Team and CIA Special Agent Dylan Kane, a former student of his.

And said nothing, instead merely flashing a 'what can I say?' face.

Nguyen grunted then replaced his glasses. "And you are Professor Laura Palmer, Professor of Archeology at University College London, and now at the Smithsonian. Recently married to Professor Acton, you now live at his residence—"

"Our," interrupted Acton, mentally kicking himself for opening his mouth.

Nguyen smiled slightly. "Forgive me. You now *share* a residence in St. Paul's, Maryland. And you are apparently quite wealthy, inheriting a rather large sum of money from your late brother upon his death at one of your own dig sites."

Laura said nothing, merely nodding.

Acton was impressed at how up to date their files were, however since American's visiting Vietnam were few in number, they had most likely been vetted well in advance.

"Where is Miss Trinh" he finally asked.

"She is being questioned by my colleagues."

"I deman—" Acton stopped himself, smiling conciliatorily. "Sorry, I *request* to see her. She, like us, is innocent. We were merely bystanders."

"So you say. *I* say you were advance scouts for the assassin." He opened the third file folder. "Mr. Jeffrey Green, United States Bureau of Diplomatic Security, attached to the Secretary of State's security detail." He flipped the page and turned the folder around, the photo shown clearly Niner.

*Thank God they don't know who he really is.*

"Professor Acton, I ask you, how are you involved?"

"I'm not." Acton could feel his chest tighten and he forced himself to take deep, steady breaths without it being too obvious. He leaned forward. "Listen, can we get these handcuffs taken off? It's really quite uncomfortable, and I'm sure you're quite safe with your men on the other side of the door.

A smile climbed one side of Nguyen's cheek. He barked an order over his shoulder and the door immediately opened, a police officer stepping inside, the cuffs quickly removed. Acton rubbed his wrists as the door closed behind the officer.

"Thank you," said Laura, flexing her own. "Can I ask you something?"

Nguyen leaned back in his chair, crossing his arms over his chest, an amused expression on his face. "Of course, Professor Palmer."

"What possible motivation would we have to assist in killing the Russian Prime Minister?"

Nguyen shrugged. "Revenge for what has happened in the Ukraine? Revenge for threatening European natural gas supplies? Revenge for the liberation of the Crimea? Revenge for not cooperating with respect to Syria?" He paused then leaned forward slightly. "Or perhaps you just wanted to embarrass Vietnam for you losing the war."

Laura smiled pleasantly. "But Captain, I'm British. We weren't in the war."

Nguyen jerked back in his chair. "You live in America and are married to an American. You might as well be American."

Laura shrugged. "We are two archeology professors, invited here by *your* Professor Duc Tran to visit this very museum on this very day. The plans for this trip were begun months ago and finalized weeks ago. The Secretary of State of my *husband's* country announced her visit a week ago, and I never heard that the Russian Prime Minister was going to be here. When was his trip announced?"

Nguyen said nothing, merely tapping on the tabletop for several seconds as he bit his lip repeatedly, the skin turning an uncomfortable white.

*Nothing to say when presented with a logical argument?*

Acton decided to leave the talking to his wife, she apparently better at it than him.

"Captain," continued Laura, her voice gentle as she leaned forward, looking up slightly to try and catch his eye. "You strike me as a very intelligent, very capable man"—*Way to butter him up!*—"and I have no doubt that deep down you *know* we aren't involved. I think an officer with your intelligence and experience knows we were simply bystanders. We're simply teachers who were in the wrong place at the wrong time. If we were involved, we certainly had plenty of time to flee like everyone else did. We were too busy trying to avoid getting shot because we had no idea what was going on. If we knew, we would have fled." She leaned forward even more. "Surely a man of your intelligence must see this?"

Nguyen looked away almost as if he were uncomfortable with Laura's proximity. He clearly seemed flustered, unused to dealing with Western women.

Acton kept his mouth shut and his expression as earnest yet non-judgmental as he could while he swelled with pride for the woman he loved.

Nguyen finally spoke, closing the folders and stacking them. "Professor, you have seen through me. Clearly I knew you were not involved, I was merely trying to shock your minds into perhaps revealing something you had seen, but weren't aware you had."

Laura leaned back in her chair, throwing her hands out in appreciation. "See?" she said, looking at Acton. "I knew he was a clever man." She smiled at Nguyen. "*Very* clever. You had me completely fooled."

Nguyen smiled, looking away awkwardly as he rose. "You are of course free to go. Most likely we will need to talk to you further. Your files indicate you are staying at the Daewoo Hanoi. This is correct?"

"Yes," replied Laura.

"Then you may go, but please do not leave without permission."

"Of course, and we'll need Miss Trinh to accompany us as I'm sure you'll understand," said Laura as she rose from her chair. "She's our guide and also our ride. You wouldn't want us to get lost in your lovely city, would you?" She laughed, Acton joining in, Nguyen doing a chuckle-grunt.

"Of course."

He opened the door and bellowed an order, clearly not having a problem looking strong in front of his men. As they walked out of the room, Acton still biting his tongue, Nguyen held out his arm, directing them down a hallway. They began to walk, two of Nguyen's men in the lead, the Captain bringing up the rear.

A door opened farther down the hall and Mai appeared, makeup smeared, cheeks flush from crying, her hair a mess.

And her nose bloodied.

Acton looked at Laura out of the corner of his eye and could tell she was about to erupt. He took her hand and squeezed it tightly.

*Let's just get out of here!*

Laura squeezed back indicating the message had been received then took Mai by the hand when they reached her, saying nothing. They were led out of the building and to the parking lot where Mai's car and driver, supplied by the museum, were waiting.

Laura helped Mai into the backseat then climbed in after her, Acton squeezing in beside her. Nguyen looked inside. "Don't leave the hotel."

He slammed the door shut before Laura could say anything.

"Take us to our hotel, please," said Acton. The man nodded, apparently understanding English, and they were soon off the museum grounds. Acton fished a clean handkerchief from his pocket and handed it to Laura who began to clean up a still terrified Mai.

"Crack a window, would you, dear? It's stifling in here."

Acton rolled his window down about halfway, the din from outside remarkable. The noise seemed distracting to Mai and her face was soon cleaned up, but it was obvious she was going to have two black eyes tomorrow. Acton found one of the bottles of water they had been offered earlier rolling on the floor. He stopped it with his foot and reached down, cracking it open. He handed it to Mai who smiled gratefully then winced. She drank then took a breath.

"I can't believe they let us go. Not that quickly, at least."

Acton squeezed Laura's leg. "You can thank my wife for that. Her smooth talking convinced Captain Nguyen we weren't involved."

Mai frowned, fear returning to her eyes. "You mean it was *his* decision, not headquarters?"

Laura nodded. "Why? What difference does it make?"

"Nguyen is nothing. He's like the first officer on the scene. It's his supervisor that we need to worry about."

"What do you mean?" asked Acton, suddenly becoming even more concerned than he already was. "He said not to leave the hotel, which I guess is sort of like saying 'don't leave town' back home, but he seemed to realize we couldn't have had anything to do with it."

Mai shook her head furiously. "No, he's nobody. This isn't over. I highly recommend you ignore what he said and get out of the country as soon as you can."

"If we flee won't we look guilty?"

Mai grabbed her face with both hands. "What am I going to do?"

Laura put a hand on her shoulder. "You stay with us until this has blown over. Once they realize the man in the photo had nothing to do with it they'll know *we* had nothing to do with it." She patted Mai. "Who knows, maybe by the time we get to the hotel they'll have caught the guy who did it!"

Acton frowned as he looked out the window.

Vietnamese troops were surrounding their hotel.

*Gandhara Kingdom*

*Modern day Myanmar*

*401 BC, four months after the Buddha's death*

Asita hugged Channa as they both realized someone had survived whatever massacre had happened here. Someone had gathered the bodies, someone had cremated them, and with the effort involved, Asita had already jumped to the conclusion that more than one had survived.

"How do we find them?" asked Channa, tears of joy and hope staining both their cheeks. "Where could they have gone?"

Asita rose and looked about for some indication of where the survivors might have fled to, but saw nothing. "We must assume they went east, away from their attackers."

"Half the world is 'east'," said Channa, sounding discouraged. "I can't believe they would leave without knowing what happened to you and your father."

Asita strode around the funeral pyre. "Perhaps they were certain we were dead, or told we were by their attackers."

Channa now rose, looking at the sky. "It is getting late. We should set up camp."

Asita stopped. "Here?" He looked around, a shiver climbing his spine. "It doesn't seem right."

"No, but I don't think there is any danger in remaining, and there are supplies here, though few."

"Few." Asita barely whispered the word, it sending another surge of hope through him. He raised his voice slightly. "You said there were only a *few* supplies remaining."

Channa seemed to pick up on his train of thought, but shook his head. "Parasites from other villages probably took what was left."

Asita wagged his finger. "No, parasites would have taken *everything*. Word would have spread and nothing would have remained." He walked toward the shell of what was once his home and found little inside of use, mere trinkets and broken pottery along with some rudimentary furniture that had escaped the fire. "Parasites would have taken this table," he said, pointing. "It is in near perfect condition."

Channa stood by his side. "Are you thinking that they all survived?"

Asita shook his head rapidly. "Never would I dare hope for such a thing, but it does appear that those who survived must have been great in number to have stripped the village of only what could be carried. The large items have been left behind, but the clothing and supplies are all gone."

"I fear wishful thinking, Master."

Asita sighed. "As do I, my friend, as do I. But perhaps wishes are all we have. We must trust in what we see before our eyes, and my eyes tell me that some of our village survived, that they took what they could, and left this place. And that their numbers were not insignificant."

*Trust in what we see before our eyes.*

His own words repeated themselves, and he thought of the message from the Buddha before he died.

*Trust in what you see.*

He cursed, running for the stream, his eyes scanning the water for the clay bowl he had tossed in earlier.

It was not where he had last seen it.

His chest got tight as he held his breath, scanning downstream. He sprinted as he saw the bowl farther down, the current having managed to move it past the edge of their village. He slipped on the slick stones, falling, painfully banging his knee. As he winced, he grabbed the bowl before it rolled farther, and as he leaned forward on his knees and one hand, he looked into the bowl, and gasped.

*Trust in what you see.*

For what looked back at him from the half-filled bowl was his own reflection, and he suddenly realized what the Buddha had meant. *Trust in yourself.* He fell back on his haunches, holding the bowl in both hands now, the pain in his knee forgotten as he smiled to the heavens, the riddle deciphered. He closed his eyes, picturing his father in happier times, and how excited he would have been to understand what the great man had been telling him.

*Trust in yourself.*

His father hadn't needed advice from the Buddha on how to save the village; the Buddha was telling him that he had all the wisdom necessary to save the village himself. He and his father had discussed many times moving the village farther to the east. They had been ravaged by neighbors, floods, drought and famine. The location for their village seemed cursed in recent years, and his father had thought moving was the best option.

But moving meant change, and people feared change. They feared the unknown, preferring the familiarity of their own misery rather than the uncertainty a new beginning would bring.

So the wisdom of the Buddha had been sought.

And all along, his father had been right.

*Trust in yourself.*

He smiled, every muscle in his body relaxing as everything became clear. His father had been right all along, his greatness and wisdom as a leader reaffirmed by the Buddha. He looked down at his reflection again and wondered if the Buddha's message extended to him.

*It must.*

He rose, his body chilled to the bone, his shivers unnoticed as he rushed back to share the revelation with his friend as the sun began its rapid descent in the west, the trees casting long shadows across the stream and the ruins of his home.

Something snapped in the forest to his right.

And he gasped.

*Daewoo Hanoi Hotel, Hanoi, Vietnam*

*Present Day*

James Acton stepped out of the car, the museum emblem on the side granting them access to the main entrance valet parking area. He helped Laura then Mai out as they were immediately approached by several deceptively uniformed police officers, the police in Vietnam merely an extension of the military.

Something was said in Vietnamese.

"They want to see our identification," translated Mai, producing her ID with a shaking hand. Acton reached into his shirt pocket, producing his passport as did Laura.

"American?" asked the officer in a thick accent.

Acton nodded. "I am. My wife is British."

Words were shouted and a more senior man appeared who could apparently speak more English. "I am Major Yin. You are an American?" he asked.

"Yes."

"What is your business in our country?"

"We were invited by your National Museum of History to view some of their artifacts. We're both archeologists—university professors."

"Archeologists?" The man's eyes narrowed then understanding dawned. "Ahh, like Indiana Jones!"

Acton smiled, nodding. "Nothing so exciting, I assure you."

*If only that were true! At lease we haven't encountered Nazis yet.*

"You are staying at this hotel?"

"Yes."

Yin nodded at Mai and said something in Vietnamese.

"She's our guide from the museum," said Laura. "We've invited her to join us for dinner."

"You were at the museum?"

Acton felt his heart rate ratchet up. "Yes."

"Did you see the shooting?"

A moment long debate of whether or not to lie ended with a decision to tell the truth. "Yes. We were questioned by Captain Nguyen and released. He said we might be questioned further later."

Yin nodded, waving over one of his men. He handed them their passports, snapped an order and the man disappeared. "We're just going to confirm you are a guest of the hotel and verify your visas."

"Of course," smiled Acton, already resolving to get on a plane as soon as possible and get the hell out of the country. "May we wait inside?"

Yin snapped his fingers and took a piece of paper from one of the others. He held up the now familiar picture of Niner. "Have you seen this man?"

Acton shook his head. "No."

"But you saw the shooting?"

"Yes, but he wasn't the shooter."

Yin's lips pursed and Acton immediately flicked through half a dozen better responses than the truth, none of which would have been lies. Yin flipped the photo around, looking at it, then turned it back toward Laura. "And do you agree with your husband?"

"I didn't get much of a look," replied Laura. "I was trying not to get shot."

*Smart woman!*

Acton assumed the same question was barked at poor Mai who the police seemed to have no compunction against intimidating. She shook her head, spitting out a response that didn't please the man.

"None of us had much of an opportunity to see anything," said Laura. "We were too busy ducking."

"Yet your husband said this man, who we *know* is the shooter, wasn't the shooter." Yin's eyes narrowed as he looked up at Acton, the man a full head shorter. "I wonder why that is? You sound so certain that the man we are positive is the shooter, isn't the shooter. Since we know this man is American, and *you* are American, perhaps you were involved?"

The officer dispatched earlier to verify their identities returned, handing the passports back to their interrogator as he delivered a verbal report. Yin nodded. "It appears you are indeed guests of this hotel and your visas check out. You may enter, but go straight to your room for your own protection."

Acton held his hand out for his passport but Yin shook his head, waving them at him. "I'll hang on to these. You'll get them back once this investigation has been completed."

Acton bit his tongue. "Can we at least get a receipt or something?"

Yin's eyes narrowed inquisitively. "Receipt?"

"Something that shows you have them."

"Ahh, I understand. No." He turned on his heel and walked away, suddenly stopping and turning back toward them. "And do *not* leave the hotel. You *will* be questioned further."

Acton felt Laura's hand squeeze his, cutting off any verbal retort. He merely nodded. Laura grabbed Mai's hand and practically pulled her after them into the hotel. Acton led them directly to the elevators, immediately boarding a newly arriving car.

He nearly bumped into Spock, one of the Delta Force Bravo Team members he had come to know over the years.

No looks were exchanged as the Delta operator disembarked.

"Honey, we'll need to call Mr. White as soon as possible with our room number."

"You mean he doesn't know we're in room eighteen-oh-two?"

"I think I forgot to tell him," replied Acton as the doors closed. Mai looked at Acton with a puzzled expression but said nothing as they rode up to the penthouse level in silence. The doors opened and they found the hallway deserted.

Laura swiped the keycard and they were finally inside the privacy of their own room leaving them all to breathe a sigh of relief as the door clicked closed behind them. Acton quickly looked in the bathroom and separate bedroom, confirming they were alone.

"What are we going to do?" asked Laura. "We can't leave the country without our passports."

Acton sat down in one of the chairs, catching an ice cold water bottle tossed by Laura who was bent over at the fridge. He pushed aside a curtain to look out across the city. "We'll need to get new ones."

"How? We're not allowed to leave the hotel."

Acton made a face, letting go of the curtain as he cracked open the lid. "We need to get the British Embassy to issue a new passport for you, and the American for me. I wonder if we can do this by phone."

Laura nodded. "Possible. But even so they'll have our names at the airport and stop us from leaving."

Acton bit his lip as he crossed his legs. "Maybe we're looking at this in the wrong way."

"How so?"

"We're assuming we have to flee the country. We've done nothing wrong. Perhaps we should just let justice take its course and eventually we'll be allowed to go."

"Ha!"

All eyes turned to Mai. "Sorry, I apologize for my outburst, but Professors, this is Vietnam. Every crime *will* be solved and *a* perpetrator *will* be brought to justice. Never does that guarantee the *right* person is brought to justice. Do not put blind faith in the police. If they think you're involved, you could find yourselves very quickly in prison, and me along with you."

"So what would you suggest?" asked Laura, motioning for her to sit down on the couch, the poor woman flitting about, a bundle of nerves.

Mai perched on the edge of the floral patterned couch, Laura sitting in another of the chairs. "I think you need to use whatever means you have at your disposal to get out of the country. For whatever reason the police are either convinced this American committed the assassination, or they are intentionally trying to frame him for the murder. Either way they are dead set on convicting an American."

"I wonder how they got his photo," said Acton. "It looked like a photocopy of an ID."

"All ID's were being copied today because of the diplomatic visits," said Mai. "Just as yours were."

Laura instinctively reached for where her passport would be. "It said Bureau of Diplomatic Security. Who are they?"

"They provide security for embassy staff and government officials while traveling in foreign countries," explained Acton. "He's obviously part of Secretary Atwater's security detail."

"But I didn't see him in her group."

"Neither did I."

Mai leapt to her feet, pacing nervously. "I understand you are rich, Professor Palmer."

"Well, I…"

Laura's brother had sold his hi-tech company before the bubble burst netting him hundreds of millions, the exact amount Acton wasn't even sure about. Laura had given him full access to everything when they married, but he didn't care enough to actually look. All he knew was that she had inherited it all when her brother had been killed, and from all appearances most of it still remained, if not more, the interest on that kind of money obscene.

"If you have money, then I suggest you use it to get out."

"How?" asked Laura. "We still need passports to get on an airplane."

"I might be able to get you fake passports."

"How?"

Mai flushed slightly. "My brother isn't exactly an honest man."

"We can't choose our family," said Acton. "But if we were caught with fake passports we would be going to prison for a very long time."

Someone knocked on the door gently.

It still startled them all, Mai jumping to her feet and running around the couch twice, trying to find a place to hide if Acton weren't mistaken. He rose and walked quietly to the door, looking through the peephole. "It's okay," he said, opening the door.

Burt Dawson stepped inside and quickly closed the door behind me. "I've only got a minute. I understand you wanted to speak to me?"

Acton smiled. "Glad you got our message. Are you aware that they're claiming Niner was the shooter today?"

Dawson nodded, his lips a thin line. "Yes."

"I told them he didn't do it, but they don't care. They've got a photocopy of his ID. Apparently it was used to enter the museum."

Dawson stepped deeper into the room, his eyes coming to rest on Mai. "And you are?"

Laura answered. "Mai Lien Trinh, a grad student from to the National Museum of History."

"She's our guide," added Acton. "I trust her."

"With your life?"

Acton wasn't sure what to say without embarrassing everyone, since he had to admit he couldn't answer truthfully. Right now he trusted very few people within a few thousand miles.

Dawson was one of them.

As was Niner.

"We have no choice," he said instead. "Where's Niner?"

"On the Secretary's floor for now. They've demanded we hand him over but we've instead agreed to an interrogation supervised by us on our turf."

"What do you plan to do?" asked Laura, now standing beside the two men.

Dawson lowered his voice, glancing at Mai. "I've been ordered to do whatever it takes to prove his innocence." He lowered it even further. "There's fear that war could break out if we can't prove an American didn't do this."

Air burst from Acton's lips. "How can we prove it wasn't him?"

"You saw the shooter?"

Acton nodded. "Clearly. And it wasn't Niner, of course."

"I had little doubt," said Dawson with a wry smile. "Could you describe him?"

Acton shrugged. "Honestly I doubt it. I don't even know if I'd recognize him if I saw him again. He was about five-four, hundred-twenty pounds maybe? Vietnamese in appearance. He had hair." Acton shrugged again. "I really don't think I can be of much help."

Mai stepped forward. "There are cameras in the museum."

"Can you get the footage?" asked Laura, turning toward her.

"Possibly. But they would already have seized it I would think." She paused. "Wouldn't they?"

"Most likely," agreed Dawson. "Are they digital or tape?"

"Digital." Mai's mouth opened a little wider. "Ahh, yes, maybe they just copied them!"

"Let's hope," said Dawson. "I'll call in some favors to see if we can get our hands on that footage." He paused for a moment as he saw the evidence of Mai's interrogation. "Did they do that?"

She nodded.

"What about you two? Did they hurt you?"

Laura shook her head. "No, but they tried to intimidate us into agreeing Niner was the shooter."

"Who is this Niner?" asked Mai. "You know the shooter?"

Acton looked at Dawson who nodded slightly. "No, we don't know the shooter, but we do know who they *think* is the shooter. He's a friend of ours and definitely not involved." Acton's eyes narrowed. "You *did* see the shooter, didn't you?"

She nodded.

"And you agree it wasn't our friend?"

She nodded again. "Yes, sorry, I'm just upset." Her eyebrows popped. "*I* could describe him! Maybe someone could draw him." She smiled slightly at Acton. "After all, all Vietnamese don't look alike to me."

Acton felt his cheeks burn red. "I—" He stopped himself, not sure what to say, Laura delighting in his discomfort.

"I think that's a great idea, Mai." Laura frowned. "But where are we going to find a sketch artist?"

Dawson shook his head. "No need. We've got software. I'll have a tablet brought down to you. In the meantime I'll try to get a hold of the footage.

This is going to turn into a he said-she said incident and we need to get it before they erase it."

"I don't think your people will be able to access the tapes," said Mai. "I remember somebody saying that the security computers weren't networked."

Acton cursed. "We need that footage if we're going to prove Niner's innocent."

"I can get it."

All eyes turned to Mai.

"How?" asked Laura.

"I work there. I could go back and get it. The office computers are networked, but only a few isolated computers are connected to the Internet for research purposes." She dropped her head shyly, looking up as if ashamed of her country. "They don't want us communicating with the outside world too much."

Acton shook his head. "Ridiculous. You're educators. How are you expected to do your job?"

Mai shook her head quickly, as if wanting to defend her native land. "No no, don't misunderstand me. Things are getting much better. Just slowly." She sighed. "I went to Australia once and couldn't believe how they lived. Such…" Her voice drifted off as she was lost in a memory.

Dawson brought them back to business. "We'll need to get you out of the hotel."

"How?" asked Acton.

"We've got a secure egress route manned with our personnel through the basement and into the parking garage. We can get her into a diplomatic vehicle and off the premises then into the American Embassy. From there she can just leave as one of the visitors."

Laura shook her head. "No, they took her ID as well."

"I need to get to my brother. He can get me ID."

"Fake ID. If you're caught…" Laura was clearly not happy with the idea.

"Out of the question," said Acton. "We can't have you risking your life for something you have nothing to do with."

Mai shook her head. "I'm involved. I was there. If we don't get proof that your friend is innocent then they will eliminate anyone who might deny the official story. You two are probably safe because you're foreigners. Me? I and my family will be thrown in prison or worse." A tear rolled down her cheek. "If I don't help you, I'm dead," she whispered, her voice cracking.

Laura took the diminutive woman in her arms, comforting her as a few sobs escaped. Acton looked at Dawson whose face was grim. Dawson motioned toward the door with his head and they both moved away from the two women.

"She's right," Dawson said quietly. "Right now they seem hell bent on pinning this on Niner. Unless we get irrefutable proof that he's innocent, they'll eliminate anyone who doesn't support the party line. And we are talking the *Party* line. This is a communist country and we're being accused of assassinating the Russian Prime Minister. Ten years ago that wouldn't have worried me too much, but now that they're essentially the second-coming of the Soviet Union, it *does* worry me. They'll use this as an excuse to get away with an awful lot."

"Such as?"

Dawson shrugged. "Who knows? He could take the Ukraine within a few weeks with relative ease and NATO will do nothing about it because they're not a member. They could become even more uncooperative at the UN using their Security Council veto to block efforts to fight Ebola, ISIS, Assad, Iran's nuclear program, Chinese belligerence in the South China Sea. Hell, they might even try to sink a few of our ships then quickly call a truce after they've done some damage. Remember, these people aren't Western European in their thinking no matter how much they like to think they are. Their thinking is much different. I fully expect retaliation at any time unless we can get ahead of this. And video footage showing someone other than Niner entering the museum would be gold."

Acton had to admit he agreed with every word Dawson had said. The Russian mindset was still buried in its Communist past, distrust of all with an ingrained superiority complex had them thinking they could do no wrong, that they were always right. And with their President controlling the press with an iron fist, their main source of information was spoon fed to them from their essentially renamed Politburo. Americans liked to think the Cold War had been won and Russia was now democratic because they had elections.

Saddam Hussein had elections too.

He was the only name on the ballot.

In today's Russia, in order to run, your party had to be approved, and their President has simply changed the rules as needed if a significant challenger appeared. The icing on the cake was the rule that if someone wanted to run for President, their party had to have at least 7% of the seats in the Duma, their equivalent to Congress. But in order to have a new party register their leader, they had to have 7%, but how could they have 7% if their party hadn't existed in the previous election to earn that 7%? It was now impossible for a new party to have a candidate for President.

An iron fist.

The Russian President was KGB, loved the Soviet Union, had repeatedly implied its demise was a great catastrophe, and his ultimate desire was to undo that mistake in history.

And an assassination blamed on the United States could be his ticket to do just that.

Somebody hammered on the door.

*Gandhara Kingdom*

*Modern day Myanmar*

*401 BC, four months after the Buddha's death*

Asita spun toward the sound, peering into the darkness, the canopy of the forest thick beyond the clearing of the village, little light penetrating it.

"Master, is that you?"

The voice was old, weak, rough as if having gone unused for a long while.

And it was instantly recognizable.

"Mutri! Is that you?"

"Yes, my Master!" cried the old voice as an emaciated man emerged from the darkness, a cane fashioned from a branch helping him along.

"Grandfather!" Channa rushed toward the old man, embracing him before Asita could. "You're alive!"

The old man's head bobbed up and down as the rest of his body shook with fatigue. "Yes, yes, obviously. Though for how much longer, I can't be sure." He motioned toward the village. "Gather your things, it isn't safe to remain here."

"Why not?" asked Asita as he embraced the old man. "What danger is there?"

"Those who attacked us continue to return. I think they have a camp nearby, downriver. They return each evening to try and surprise us. After we managed to tend to the dead and salvage what we could, we left, only I remained behind."

"Why, Grandfather, why did you stay?"

The old man jabbed at the air. "Why do you not listen to an old man? Gather your things, we must leave now!"

Channa smiled, patting his grandfather on his shoulder. "I'll be right back." Channa hurried into the village and grabbed the bags they had been carrying for so long, the horse long dead from a fall, returning moments later, tossing the satchel to Asita. Asita returned the bag to its too familiar spot on his shoulder, then emptied the clay bowl of the water that had revealed the secret to the Buddha's riddle, and placed it gently inside, thankful his momentary lapse hadn't shattered the now precious vessel. He looked at Mutri's back as the man led them into the forest.

"You haven't answered our question, Grandfather. Why did you stay?"

"Because I am too old to make the journey."

Channa stopped. "I don't believe that for a second. There are others as old as you. Surely—" He gasped as he came to the same realization as Asita had just.

"They're all dead, aren't they?" asked Asita, his heart heavy.

"I was the only one of the elders to survive, the others were cut down as they tried to flee." The old man paused for a moment. "My wife"—he nodded toward Channa—"your grandmother, was among the first. She was washing clothes in the stream when they arrived. It was her cries of warning that saved most of the others."

"Most?" asked Asita, hope surging within.

The old man nodded, resuming his slow shuffle into the trees. "It was midday, everyone was gathered to eat so few were in their shelters. At the first sight the men sent the women and children into the trees, fighting off the attackers who were thankfully few in number at first and exhausted, they had apparently been running for some time." The old man stopped and looked over his shoulder toward the now out of sight funeral pyre. "They fought bravely, repelling the first attack, but their numbers were too few when the second wave arrived. Most fled into the forest knowing it was hopeless, a few, cut off, fought like tigers, delaying the murderers so the others could escape."

"When was this?" asked Asita.

"Almost two moons ago."

A lump in his throat silenced him as he realized they would have had been able to warn the village if they hadn't spent so much time trying to evade their pursuers and allowing him to heal.

"We should have come here directly," he whispered.

"Then we would both be dead," admonished Channa. "There was no way the two of us on one horse could have made it this far without being caught. And besides, you were in no condition to travel."

Asita's head sank into his chest as he realized his friend was right, the words bringing little comfort.

"He's right," agreed Mutri. "You are here now. That is what matters. Your people need you. They need a leader." He paused. "Your father?"

"Dead."

"Did he receive the counsel of the Buddha?"

"Yes." Asita tapped the bowl. "Just before he died."

"The Buddha is dead?" the old man paused, shocked. His step faltered for a moment, Channa grabbing him to steady the frail bones. "How?"

"They blamed us," said Asita. He sucked in a breath, steeling himself as he relayed the story of the last meal, the bowl, the riddle, the pursuit, then his father's valiant last battle.

"He was a brave man," smiled the old man, patting Asita on the arm. "A very brave man." He held up a thin finger as he resumed walking through the near pitch black. "And a wise leader. *He* would have figured out the riddle of the Buddha's riddle." He nodded toward the satchel containing the bowl. "Have *you*, the *new* leader of our people, deciphered it?"

Asita said nothing, suddenly uncertain, stopping. The old man turned to face him, reaching up a trembling hand and gripping Asita by the cheek. "You are a leader now! Never show hesitation!" Asita nodded, sucking in a breath and squaring his shoulders. "Now, I ask you again, as one of your people. Have you deciphered the Buddha's riddle?"

Asita nodded, his confidence still buried deep, but realizing the old man was right. He *was* the new leader. It was his by birthright and there was no refusing it without death. And he being the only son, it could destroy what remained of his people should conflict arise over a successor.

"I have."

The old man squeezed Asita's shoulder. "Good!" He continued forward in silence for some time, curiously not asking for Asita's explanation. Asita glanced at Channa and could see during the occasional shaft of moonlight that broke through the trees overhead that he was dying to know.

And Asita was dying to tell him.

As they continued in silence, Asita's confidence grew. He was certain now more than ever that he was right. He could see no other way to interpret the Buddha's last riddle, last counsel, possibly last blessing. *Trust in what you see.* And he had seen his reflection in the bowl. It made perfect sense.

And perhaps that's why the old man had not asked him for the answer. He knew his leader needed time to be certain what he had puzzled out was correct, and to gain confidence in the interpretation.

For soon he would have an entire village to convince.

*Daewoo Hanoi Hotel, Hanoi, Vietnam*

*Present Day*

The loud knocking at the door caused them all to jump except Dawson who merely retreated deeper into the room. Acton looked through the peephole then stepped back quickly and quietly. "It's the police," he whispered.

Dawson cursed. "I can't be seen with you." He looked around. "Is there another way out of here?"

Acton shook his head. "No." He thought for a moment then pointed at Laura. "Both of you get in the shower, quickly."

Both Laura and Dawson said, "Huh?"

"They'll come in, I'll say you're in the shower, then get you. You'll come out and they won't think to look in there for him."

Dawson nodded, clearly thinking it was a good idea.

Laura shrugged. "If you want me to get naked with another man, then so be it." She headed toward the bathroom with a wink. Dawson grinned at him as the hammering on the door resumed, this time accompanied by shouting.

"Just a second!" called Acton as the bathroom door closed and the shower turned on. He opened the door and was surprised to see a white man in a business suit, the uniformed police standing to the sides, including Major Yin.

"I am Igor Sarkov, Russian Ministry of Foreign Affairs. May I come in, Professor Acton?"

Acton decided cooperation was the name of the game since they had a Special Forces operator in their shower with his wife. He held out his arm, inviting him in. Yin began to follow when Acton decided he should at least pretend to be American.

"Are the police really necessary, Mr. Sarkov. We're all friends here."

Sarkov bowed slightly. "Of course." He looked at the officer that had taken their passports earlier. "Wait outside." Yin's eyes flared in momentary anger, but he was immediately subservient, barking an order that had the uniforms scurrying down into the hallway, the door closed behind them.

Sarkov slowly circled the room, glancing into the bedroom, his eyes narrowing. "And where is your lovely wife?"

"In the shower. She needed to relax after what happened. A long shower helps."

"I'll need to speak to her, preferably now."

"Of course." Acton went to the bathroom and opened the door slightly, poking his head in. "Hon, the police are here. Can you come out?"

"Give me a minute."

He closed the door and motioned toward the seating area. "Please, have a seat. Can I get you anything?"

"Do you have any bottled water? Preferably cold?" asked Sarkov as he squeezed his large, rotund but imposing frame into a too small chair.

"I'll check," said Acton, entering the small kitchenette and opening the fridge. Fully stocked with ten dollar bottles of water. He grabbed three.

He handed one to Sarkov and another to Mai, giving her the opportunity to occupy her hands that were nervously fidgeting about. Acton sat in a chair as far from Mai as he could, hoping to force Sarkov to at least split his attentions, giving Mai a break from constant scrutiny.

The shower turned off.

Sarkov rubbed the ice cold bottle over his forehead and cheeks, finally dragging the perspiring vessel over his neck. He twisted the top off and took a long drag, sighing in satisfaction. "The one thing I hate about being stationed in Hanoi is the heat." He patted his large stomach. "Men my size were never meant to live in tropical climates," he said, laughing, his smile quite genuine in appearance.

*Remember, this man is most likely a spy.*

Sarkov took another drink and Acton decided to open the conversation. "First, Mr. Sarkov, I'd like to pass on my condolences on behalf of my wife and I. This entire situation is horrible. Have you been able to catch the man who did this?"

Sarkov nodded his appreciation. "Unfortunately we have not taken him into custody, however we have him contained."

"Oh, so you found him!" Acton decided to play dumb. "I'm happy to hear that. The police were after the wrong man for a while there so I'm glad that's been cleared up. Do you know why he did it?"

Sarkov's eyes narrowed. "Wrong man?"

Acton continued his charade deciding it was best he continue with the truth with the stakes so high. "Yeah, they showed us a photo of a man, some Asian American I guess, saying he was the shooter. But I had a clear look at him and it wasn't the same man. I'm glad they got that sorted out." He took a sip of his water, sweat trickling down his back.

"I'm afraid you're mistaken, Professor. We know who the shooter is, and we know where he is. At the moment however your government is shielding him. I wonder why that is?"

The bathroom door opened and Laura stepped out in a bathrobe, her hair tied up in a towel atop her head, her face flushed. Acton noticed she left the door open only slightly. "Forgive my appearance," she said, smiling. "You caught me in the shower." She paused, her smile still in place. "I'm sorry, I was expecting Vietnamese police."

Sarkov struggled out of his chair. "Igor Sarkov, Professor Palmer, Russian Ministry of Foreign Affairs," said the man, walking over and shaking Laura's hand with a bow. "A pleasure to meet such an accomplished woman."

Laura returned the handshake. "Thank you, Mr. Sarkov. Do I have time to dress? It will only take a moment."

"Of course, madam, please."

Laura disappeared into the bedroom, the door closing behind her. Sarkov returned to his seat. "You are a very fortunate man, Professor. Not only is your wife a wealthy woman and accomplished in her field, she is remarkably beautiful."

"Thank you, I shake my head every day that she agreed to marry me," Acton said with a smile. "You said I was mistaken. How?"

"In your insistence that the man we know entered the museum and assassinated our Prime Minister is not the man you saw."

Acton shrugged, slightly. "All I can tell you is what I saw. The man I saw was at least fifty years old and the man in the photo looks twenty years younger. Besides, the ID you had photocopied said his name was Jeffrey Green. The man who was the shooter was named Phong."

"Phong?"

"Yes, Phong."

"How do you know this?"

"Because they spoke. And your Prime Minister knew him from the Vietnam War."

"Tell me more." Sarkov seemed genuinely interested, which gave Acton some hope that perhaps this man *was* actually after the truth.

"This man, Phong, claimed the Prime Minister had massacred his village in nineteen-seventy-four."

Sarkov leaned back in his chair, frowning. "Did the Prime Minister deny this?"

Acton shook his head. "No, in fact he claimed he had wiped out many villages then he seemed to remember the man when he was shown a bowl, saying Phong's name first."

Sarkov's head slowly shook back and forth, as if in disbelief. "*If* what you say is true, then the man would easily be in his fifties."

"Agreed."

A sudden burst of air from between his lips was accompanied by a one-handed scalp massage. "Again, *if* this is true, and I'm not saying I necessarily believe you, but *if* it is true, we will need proof of this. And quickly."

Laura appeared and both men rose, Sarkov again with effort. "Lovely lady!" he exclaimed, admiring her simple outfit. "Isis herself couldn't be more beautiful!"

Laura smiled as she took a seat near Mai. "You flatter me, sir."

Sarkov bowed slightly. "I hope it is not unwelcome." He looked at Acton. "And it is all in good taste, I assure you."

It was Acton's turn to bow. "Your flattery honors me, sir." He motioned for Sarkov to sit down and the man plopped once again in his seat.

"Madam, you I suppose support this story of your husbands?"

"I do," replied Laura. "I saw the shooter and he was definitely not the man in the photograph. And they definitely knew each other."

Sarkov shoved his lips in and out several times. "And how old would you say he was?"

Acton assumed Laura hadn't heard the conversation and just prayed her estimate was in at least the same ballpark as his. "I'd guess fifty or sixty. I only caught a few quick glimpses of him, but definitely an older man."

"Yet he jumped through a window and made his escape. Fairly spry, would you not say?"

"Hey, Stallone is late sixties, Chuck Norris is in his seventies," replied Acton, hoping the references weren't lost on their Russian "guest".

Sarkov nodded. "This is true." He leaned forward slightly. "I must confess I love the Expendables movies. Sylvester Stallone is one of my favorites, though I must also confess that in my country Rambo Three is considered a comedy." Sarkov roared in laughter and the others joined in, albeit with a little discomfort, this man quite possibly holding their lives in his hands.

"What now, sir?" asked Acton. "When will we get our passports back?"

Sarkov's face was red from laughing. As he sucked in several deep breaths and a few more gulps of water, he returned to a more normal pasty white with red blotches. "I am confident that you are innocent bystanders," he said. "Your stories however don't match what my Vietnamese counterparts are insisting is accurate. If it were up to me, I would let you go about your business now, however, unfortunately for us all, Moscow has sent a senior investigator, Mr. Dimitri Yashkin, who will be arriving this afternoon." Sarkov sighed. "I'm afraid he won't be so easily convinced." Sarkov spread his hands out in a conciliatory fashion. "I am but a bureaucrat, exiled to this horrible posting because I have not kissed the proper asses as you Americans might say. Where I see innocence, my counterpart might see conspiracy." He pushed himself out of his chair, the others rising with him. "I will have your passports returned, but I believe you may have a limited window in which to take advantage of them, if you know what I mean." He tapped the side of his nose then headed for the door. Opening it he turned back toward Acton and Laura, Mai remaining behind in the living area. "It was a pleasure meeting you both," he said. "You've been very helpful." He snapped his fingers. "The papers for these good people!"

Major Yin stepped forward, producing two passports.

"And Miss Trinh's papers?" asked Acton as he took the passports.

"Of course," said Sarkov, giving a wink only they could see. He snapped his fingers, holding out his hand without looking. Mai's ID was quickly placed in his palm and Sarkov handed them over. "Have a good day." He closed the door behind him, leaving everyone sighing in relief.

Acton carefully looked out the peephole and saw the procession just disappearing out of sight. He returned to the sitting area as Laura opened the bathroom door. "It's safe to come out now."

Dawson stepped into the room.

"Did you hear that?" asked Acton.

Dawson nodded. "We might just have an ally."

"For a few hours at least," said Laura, plopping onto the couch. "Once this new guy arrives none of us are safe."

"Here's what we're going to do. Miss Trinh, you'll leave as planned with your legitimate identification papers. Go to the museum and see if you can get the camera footage. I'm going to return to the Secretary's floor; they're due to interrogate Niner any minute now and I want to be there."

"What about us?" asked Laura.

"I'm afraid you two are stuck. There's no way you're getting on an airplane without being stopped. I'd suggest you try to leave the hotel with the excuse you're going for a walk. Then try to get to the embassy."

"But she's British."

"They'll let her in. I'll phone ahead so they know."

"Then?"

"Hole up until the dust settles."

*Gandhara Kingdom*

*Modern day Myanmar*

*401 BC, four months after the Buddha's death*

Asita hadn't been hugged this much since his mating ceremony. The tears of joy and relief, mixed with fear and sorrow, were overwhelming, but he kept a smile on his face and a steady timbre to his voice, realizing that his people, for they were now *his* people, needed strength. They needed a leader and his father was gone.

All the pressures of these dangerous and uncertain times now fell on his shoulders.

Already he didn't like the burden of leadership.

He raised his hands to quiet the crowd that surrounded him, Channa and his grandfather keeping a respectful distance, his wife and children at his side, clinging to him as if they feared he might not be real.

"Thank you for your warm welcome. It has been a long, hard journey, but it would appear my hardships were trivial compared to yours."

"What of your father?" asked someone.

A deep sadness spread across Asita's face. "He is dead." He drew in a breath, looking from person to person. "Killed by the same people who destroyed our village."

"They said he killed the Buddha!"

"That's a lie!" barked Asita, immediately lowering his voice as the crowd jumped. "That is a lie told by these murderous fiends. My father was given the honor of preparing a meal for the Buddha. We did, and sampled it ourselves. It was not poisoned. The Buddha fell sick after eating, but his companion assured us that the Buddha had been ill before and had come to the village where we met him in order to prepare for Parinirvana as he knew he was dying.

"The Buddha gave us all his blessing"—this elicited murmurs of excitement—"and this blessed vessel"—he retrieved the clay bowl from his satchel and held it up to oohs and aahs—"along with the answer to the question my father asked of him." He paused as he slowly turned, the bowl held high in the air so everyone could see it. "We have suffered, my friends, for many years. The question had been whether or not to move. As you know, both my father and I have been of the opinion that we should move to more fertile ground, no matter how long this has been our home. But others disagreed."

He lowered the bowl, stopping his spin as his eyes rested on the most vocal opponent to moving. Their eyes dropped and Asita turned, looking at those who had supported his father. "To assuage any doubt, it was agreed that my father would seek the wisdom of the Buddha, and he did, quite possibly the last person to do so before the Buddha's death, which I think to be a great honor and omen, it important we heed the Buddha's words since they were among his last."

"What did he say?" asked someone, desperate for Asita to come to his point. But Asita wouldn't be rushed. There were many here who had forced this journey upon his father, and if it weren't for them, his father would be alive right now.

"When the Buddha gave my father his wisdom, he gave him this bowl. His message was, 'Trust in what you see', and it was left to us to figure out what he meant. Before my father could contemplate the wise one's words, we were set upon by a mob who falsely accused my father of poisoning the Buddha. My father fought a hundred men if it were one, and valiantly held the mob off until we could make our escape, ensuring the Buddha's words and gift would find his people." He held the bowl up again. "And I have succeeded in doing so, in fulfilling my father's dying wish that this gift and the wisdom offered with it reach his people."

"But what does it mean?"

Asita smiled. "I have puzzled over that for many a night, I assure you, but in a moment of grief upon discovering the destruction of our village, the wisdom of the great Buddha became clear to me as I looked into the bowl, filled with water from our own stream."

"What did you see?"

"Myself."

He let the word sink in for a moment, then continued before anyone else spoke. "I saw the reflection of myself, and realized what the Buddha meant. He said, 'Trust in what you see', and I saw myself. In other words, I should trust myself. If it had been my father who had looked in the bowl, he would have seen himself, and known the Buddha meant to trust in himself."

Asita squared his shoulders, inflating his chest to make himself appear even larger than he already was, an imposing figure on any battlefield.

"Therefore I shall trust in myself, as the Buddha has instructed, and trust in my father's wishes. We will move the village. In the morning, we head east, toward the rising sun, until we receive a sign from the Buddha that our new home has been found."

There were murmurs of nervousness and excitement, most happy a decision had been made, others not so certain. The village broke off into small groups, debates beginning to rage, but Asita ignored them, instead waving to Channa who directed him to a temporary shelter that had been waiting for them just in case they arrived.

Settling in for the night, out of sight of the others, Asita broke into a cold sweat, shivering from head to toe as fear and doubt set in.

*How can I trust in what I see when I don't even trust in myself?*

*Daewoo Hanoi Hotel, Hanoi, Vietnam*

*Present Day*

Igor Sarkov rode the elevator down to the ninth floor for his scheduled meeting with the American assassin. In silence. He had read the dossiers on the two professors before meeting them. They were well respected, well connected and well financed. With a knack of being in the wrong place at the wrong time.

He tapped his chin. If he was a more cynical man, he might think that they were always exactly *where* they were supposed to be, exactly *when* they were supposed to be. FSB files on them suggested they had been involved in more than one American Special Forces operation over the past several years beginning with the assassination of the American President a few years ago. And the assassination of the Pope. And the kidnapping of the next Pope. And the assault on the Vatican. There was even an unsubstantiated rumor that they were involved during the Qing coup attempt in China.

They either weren't who they said they were, or they were the unluckiest two people he had ever met.

*How they found each other…*

The door chimed and he stepped out into the hallway, immediately greeted by several men who were clearly security, and one woman he had no doubt was sent to disarm him with her smile.

"Mr. Sarkov?"

He nodded with a slight bow.

"I'm Secretary Atwater's aide, Cynthia Boyle. Please follow me. I've been instructed to tell you that you have fifteen minutes with our agent, and one of our people will be in the room at all times. You may ask him anything you want."

Sarkov said nothing, there being no point. He was actually a little shocked the Americans were giving him any time with the suspect, which suggested to him either they thought he wasn't involved, or he was and they wanted it to appear they were cooperating.

He wasn't sure what to think. The Vietnamese were convinced this Mr. Green—obviously an alias—was the shooter, but for some reason he believed the two professors. Their dossiers would suggest he shouldn't, but he never put much stock in FSB files any more than he had in KGB files when he was a younger man.

He had always wanted to be a police officer, or more accurately a detective, but the Communist government, through his father, had other plans for him. He had become KGB, then after the fall, FSB, then finally part of Foreign Affairs, dealing with embassy and diplomatic security. It had been glamorous work at times and his dear, dear wife had loved it so.

His chest tightened slightly at the thought of her. She had died only two years ago in a car accident in St. Petersburg, their son who was driving dying days later from his injuries.

T-boned by a drunk connected to what many in Russia now called the Party. The Communist party still existed, but it was United Russia that now called the shots, the Communists relegated to the sidelines, and the Russia he had such high hopes for after the collapse was quickly regressing into the old ways.

And it shamed him.

He didn't like Hanoi, it was too hot for his large frame, but it was about as far from Moscow politics as you could get because Moscow really didn't care what happened here. As far as they were concerned Hanoi would remain within the Russian sphere of influence no matter what happened. Their efforts were focused elsewhere.

But now with the Prime Minister assassinated, everything could change. He was now in the limelight, and he didn't like it. He had two more years then he'd get his meagre pension and retire to some place cold.

*Perhaps Canada.*

But if this investigation didn't turn out the way the leadership wanted, he just might find himself in Siberia.

Six feet under the permafrost.

"Right in here, Mr. Sarkov."

He was shown into a small conference room flanked by two DSS agents. Inside sat the man he recognized from the photocopied identification card, and another he recognized by the look on his face as a very dangerous man. His dossier supplied by the Vietnamese said he was Mr. White—what is with the colors?—but FSB pegged him as American Special Forces.

Sarkov sat in the uncomfortable chair, noticing with a slight smile that his suspect was seated quite comfortably. A pitcher of ice water sat on the table and he poured himself a tall glass, downing half of it before refilling. He pulled his chair in and crossed his arms on top of the table. "I am Igor Sarkov, Ministry of Foreign Affairs. Russian, if you don't recognize my accent." He smiled at the suspect as the door closed, leaving him alone with the Asian American and the Special Forces operator in the corner of the room, standing by the window.

*If he's here, then this is one of his men.*

Which had his mind racing. If the suspect was American Special Forces, then perhaps this *was* an assassination by the Americans after all. His ID had definitely been used to gain access to the Museum, the witnesses who said it wasn't him had a long history of being involved in international events, therefore could be spies themselves, which meant none of their answers could be trusted. And if they were lying, then there was a conspiracy here, which meant this man hadn't acted alone.

He hadn't gone rogue.

"Your name is Mr. Jeffrey Green. You're a Special Agent with the Bureau of Diplomatic Security."

"Yes."

"In fact, you're actually a member of the United States Special Operations Command."

Remarkably the man showed no sign of surprise.

"I beg your pardon?"

"What is your motto? Sine Pari? Without equal? I believe some of our Spetsnaz soldiers would disagree."

The man shrugged his shoulders. "I don't know what you want me to say. I'm a DSS agent on temporary assignment to the Secretary of State's detail while in Hanoi."

"Temporary. And where is your permanent posting? Fort Bragg? Coronado?"

"Washington, DC."

"Interesting." He leaned back. "Now, how do you explain that your ID card was used at the National Museum of History today?"

"I reported my card stolen this morning from my hotel room safe."

"How convenient."

"It's the truth."

"Of course it is. A DSS agent would never lie."

"I don't know about that, but I'm not."

"So where were you when the shooting took place?"

"In my room."

"Can anyone verify that?"

"No, I won the bet and got the odd man out room. I'd been on the nightshift and went to bed a few hours before I got the call about the emergency recovery."

"Which took how long?"

"Under ten minutes."

"So you mean to tell me that in under ten minutes you were found, woken, got dressed and into position? Where was your position?"

"At the rear entrance of the hotel where the Secretary would be arriving."

"And you did all that in ten minutes."

"Yes. But I had already showered and dressed beforehand."

"But we only have your word for that. For all we know you weren't in your room at that time and instead were busy assassinating the Prime Minister then returning here."

"How would I have gotten here, sir?"

"A motorbike would get you here *very* quickly. In fact, I wouldn't be surprised if you were in disguise as part of the motorcade. Or perhaps in the Secretary's limousine?"

"That's ridiculous, sir. I'm sure there's security footage at the museum that will show it wasn't me that used the ID."

"Vietnam is a rather primitive country, I'm afraid. I wouldn't count on any video footage being found."

"This is a fairly high-end hotel. I'm sure there are cameras here that could prove I was where I say I was."

Sarkov threw up his hands, shrugging his shoulders. "Sorry, but at the insistence of your own DSS agents, all cameras on this floor were disabled."

"That's unfortunate."

"You may find your attitude won't play well with my colleague who will be arriving shortly. He will no doubt want to interview you, and I am certain will insist it be done, elsewhere, shall we say?"

"I've got nothing to hide."

Sarkov rose, as did his suspect. "Unfortunately, Mr. *Green*, I know you are lying to me about at least one thing."

"And what is that?"

"Your name. And when you lie to me about your name, that means you are lying to me about who you really are. I know you are Special Forces, which means you are quite capable of killing the Prime Minister and his security detail. You are among the best in the world, of that I have no doubt. Your identification was used, that fact is not in dispute. And you are a liar, I think we can all agree on that fact as well." Sarkov shrugged, raising his hands palm upward. "I tried to get the truth from you, and you chose to stick to your story. If you were to confess, then this could be handled through diplomatic channels where your government would most likely have you disappear, or fake your death, or something, sabre rattling would ensue, then life would go on. But since you are going to try and hide your involvement, this will turn into a battle of wills that may erupt out of control." Sarkov walked to the door, putting his hand on the knob. "Remember where you are, gentlemen. You have no friends here, no power here, no influence. Like the last, this is a war you cannot win."

Sarkov excited the room, nodded to Miss Boyle, then walked toward the elevator, boarding the one held for him. He returned to the ground floor, joined by his Vietnamese counterpart, Major Yin.

"Did you find out anything?" asked Yin.

"Only that they are lying."

"Which ones?"

"All of them."

"Should I have the professors arrested?"

Sarkov shook his head. "No. Let's see what they do."

*Valley of the Red River*

*Modern day Vietnam*

*388 BC, Thirteen years later*

The constant shivers continued to rack Asita's bones. His trusted companion, Channa, fixed the blanket draping his shoulders as four of the younger men carried the chair that had been fashioned for him after the sickness had taken over long ago. His fever had come and gone over the years, but it had been bad now for many moons, his body weak though his years numbered less than forty.

The journey made it tougher.

They had been travelling for so long another generation had been born, the eldest lost. Grandfather had been right—he was too weak for the journey. He died only weeks after starting, despite being carried. Asita himself had fallen ill that very night but used it as proof from the divine that this place was cursed and they should leave in all haste.

But nothing he could construe as a sign had made itself known to him. They had tried settling on numerous occasions only to find something to drive them away either days or weeks, sometimes months later.

So they continued.

He knew his people were frustrated and some wanted his son, barely sixteen, to take over. Which would mean Asita would have to die.

Fortunately, or unfortunately, depending on the point of view, Asita's son would never do such a thing and seemed content to let his father take the bulk of the criticism while defending him fiercely.

Asita leaned back and looked up at the canopy of tree leaves overhead, the sun occasionally making its presence known. The warmth, though brief, was welcome on his face, and he closed his eyes to enjoy himself, making a game of whether or not he could sense when the sun was bearing down on him.

His face felt warm.

Consistently warm.

He opened his eyes and found the canopy overhead gone, instead a brilliant blue sky shining down on him with the occasional wisps of clouds in a long, slightly curved line overhead.

His heart leapt.

He pushed himself up onto his elbows, the procession still marching forward, and he looked to his side, instantly recognizing flowers in full bloom along the edge of the clearing as those he had seen a thousand times before from the imagination of an artist unknown to him, painting a ring of flowers never before seen by anyone in his village.

"Stop!" he shouted, his strength suddenly returning. His chair was lowered to the ground and he stepped forward, Channa immediately at his side along with his son, Alara. "Get me the bowl!"

The bowl was quickly produced and Asita pointed to one of the bands that ringed it, second from the top. It was blue, with white circles. He pointed at the sky. "Look!" The others gathered as they looked from the bowl to the sky and back. Then he pointed to the strange flowers nearby, then at the final ring at the top of the bowl.

And they all gasped.

For they were a match.

He shook off the helping hands and plodded forward, toward the sound of running water, looking about him. It was a wide clearing, easily large enough for a village. The river was of a good size, but not so large it would pose a danger, and the embankments suggested a steady height, not one prone to surges during spring.

He dropped to his knees, dipping the bowl into the water, then looked inside.

And he saw his reflection.

And smiled.

He drank from the bowl and raised it to the heavens.

"Father! We have found our home!"

*Daewoo Hanoi Hotel, Hanoi, Vietnam*

*Present Day*

James Acton looked at his wife, not sure what to do. Dawson had just left and Mai was about to. But it didn't feel right. Dawson wanted them to stay put but that wasn't his style. Unfortunately his style quite often got them into trouble, but he couldn't in good conscience let Mai leave alone.

Laura grabbed her handbag.

"What are you doing?" he asked.

"Going with Mai. What are you doing?"

Acton grinned. "I knew there was a reason I married you other than your money."

Mai stood by the door. "You shouldn't come with me, it's too dangerous."

"Which is exactly why we're coming with you," replied Acton. "If you're with us you're less likely to get hassled on your way there."

Laura put her hand on the doorknob. "What about when we get there? Surely they'll get suspicious if we try to go in."

Mai shook her head. "No no no, you mustn't come in with me." She pulled a piece of paper from her purse and quickly wrote down a phone number. She handed it to Laura. "This is the number for my brother Cadeo. If anything happens to me, let him know so he can tell my family."

Laura took the paper and placed it in her purse. "Nothing will go wrong. Just get in, get the footage, get out. We'll come straight back here."

Mai forced a smile, looking unconvinced as Laura pulled the door open. They headed for the elevator, there now several uniformed police on their floor. They showed their ID and were allowed on the elevator with little hassle. The ride down was in silence, Acton's mind going a mile a minute as he weighed the pros and cons of getting themselves in even deeper. But he could see little choice. Sure, going with Mai was near idiotic, but it was the right thing to do. Sticking up for Niner was also the right thing to do. It would have been easier to just say he saw nothing and couldn't confirm or deny that Niner was the shooter. It would probably have allowed them to get on a plane today but it would have been wrong. Niner had saved their lives on numerous occasions and leaving him hanging, to possibly literally hang, wasn't an option Acton could even contemplate.

It just wasn't him.

A friend was in trouble and he was honor-bound to help.

And there would be no keeping Laura away for the same reasons.

Which was one of the many reasons he loved her so much.

Their relationship had been tumultuous, dangerous, terrifying, as well as exciting, passionate and stimulating. He wouldn't change a thing despite the fact they had both been through hell on too many occasions.

It had forged a relationship that had been tested under fire, creating a bond as strong as those shared by soldiers in combat, a bond so strong he was certain it could survive any challenge.

And they had been challenged.

And now, once again, they were leaping into the thick of things, boldly going where no sane married couple would dare.

The doors opened and as they crossed the opulent lobby for the main entrance, the dozens of police officers ignored them completely.

Which Acton found extremely odd.

The doors were held open and Acton spotted the museum's car with the same driver from earlier. They made a beeline for it, this time Acton climbing in the front seat, the two women in the back. Mai said something in Vietnamese and the driver pulled away. Acton lowered himself slightly in the seat and looked out the side view mirror, frowning as he spotted what he assumed was an unmarked police car pulling out after them.

He turned back to look at Laura and Mai. "How are you two doing back there? Comfy?" He motioned with his eyes toward the car following them.

Laura immediately caught on, resisting the urge to turn around, but Mai wasn't as quick on the uptake, her life not one normally filled with intrigue. Laura held a finger up and pressed it against Mai's cheek as she turned to look, pushing it back forward.

"We're okay. Just looking forward to getting this errand out of the way then having a nice dinner tonight at the hotel."

"Sounds like a good idea." He looked at a confused Mai. "You should join us, I insist."

She nodded, fear in her eyes as she eventually realized that their actions must have meant they were being followed. "I w-would be honored."

"Fantastic!" grinned Acton. "We'll take the opportunity to go over those files you're getting us. We barely saw half the museum so we'll have to settle for the paper version!"

Mai seemed to catch on, she now having a reason for returning with them, something the driver could no doubt report to the police that might actually sound legitimate.

"It's unfortunate your visit was cut off. Unavoidable, obviously, but my government would want you to at least read the catalog. I'll try to get an electronic version for you so that you can browse it a little easier."

"That would be even better. Paper is so passé!" Acton said with a wink, turning back in his seat and facing the front again as they pulled up to the museum, hundreds of security personnel everywhere including a fairly impressive foreign press brigade. He turned to the driver. "My wife and I are fairly well known. Perhaps it's best if we stayed in the car so the press doesn't see us."

"No problem," said the man as they pulled through the throng, the police making a hole. Their ID's were checked and Acton noticed the senior officer look behind them then nod as if he had just received instructions.

He waved them through.

And the pit that formed in Acton's stomach almost made him nauseous. He looked back and saw the car that had been following them parked on the side of the road, outside the ring of security, no doubt waiting for their exit.

But were they just watching them out of curiosity, or did they know what they were up to?

*This is too dangerous.*

He turned to tell Mai but before he could say anything she had opened her door and jumped out. Instead he was forced to make eye contact with Laura and try to convey his concerns.

She seemed to already be sharing them.

They watched as Mai disappeared through the front entrance, her ID inspected, but not very closely.

As if she was simply being led deeper into the flytrap.

Leaving Acton to wonder if he would ever see her again.

*Valley of the Red River, Vietnam*

*June 17th, 1974*

Phong shook like the leaves around him, the stiff breeze blowing through the village causing them to flutter, the gentle white noise generated not enough to drown out the horror he was witnessing.

The war had arrived.

His village had tried to stay out of the conflict, its location in a small valley with only a few trails leading to other communities allowing them to enjoy relative peace over the years of conflict, though the sound of planes screaming overhead and helicopters thundering on the other side of the surrounding hills was a constant reminder that the war was close.

Too close.

And today it was here.

He had been in the forest looking for herbs, his future duties as companion to the eldest son of their leader demanding he be able to heal him should he become sick.

But there would be no healing from this.

Screams had sent him running toward the village, his duties forgotten. Orders were barked in unfamiliar voices and as he neared he skidded to a halt, dropping quietly to his belly at the edge of the village.

Men with guns were herding the villagers around the shrine where the holy vessel sat on a covered pedestal, protected from the elements. Oral history taught that it had been drunk from by the great Buddha himself before his death and had been a gift to the village leader on the night of the Buddha's death. The leader Cunda had died, but his son, Asita, had saved the bowl and the wisdom imparted with it, and moved their entire community from what was now near India to Vietnam.

The great Asita had died within days of the establishment of their new community, but they had flourished exactly as he had said, with their numbers growing so much over the years that they had spread throughout these hills, there now dozens of villages that could trace their lineage back to this one, spreading the word of the great Buddha to those already living here. Some said that the great Asita had brought Buddhism to this part of the world so long ago.

And the vessel, a simple clay bowl with faded artwork encircling it, had been preserved, lovingly, the ashes of the village's founder, Asita, contained within, gathered from his funeral pyre.

A man in a uniform stepped into view, a uniform that Phong didn't recognize, though he would admit to anyone he wouldn't recognize any uniform, he having seen so few. All he knew was it was quite different from those he had seen while trading in the bigger towns.

But this man was white, whiter than any he had seen before. He had seen pale faces fly overhead in helicopters, quite often accompanied by faces darker than any he had ever witnessed. He had found it remarkable. And now one of these "white people" as he had heard them referred to was in his village, directing the activities in a language he didn't recognize, his translator crying out his orders with gusto.

"Any man who joins us to fight will live!"

Phong held his breath as the men of the village exchanged glances, the terror in their eyes clear. They were farmers, not fighters. The days of fighting between villages was long gone, generations of peaceful coexistence shattered in one day as these strangers forced an impossible decision on his friends and family.

But to their credit, none moved, none stood to join what was clearly an evil cause, for it must be evil. If it were just, then why threaten those you would ask to join you with death?

The white man stepped forward, aiming a handgun at his cousin Duc's head and fired. Duc's body crumpled to the ground eliciting wails from his wife and children, his mother passing out.

"Who's next?" shouted the translator.

Duc's brother jumped to his feet and charged the white man only to be cut down by one of the Viet Cong soldiers' rifles. He writhed on the ground in agony, his wife crawling toward him, pleading with their captors to let them live. The white man straddled her, waving his gun at the others.

"Who will join us to save her life?"

Nobody stood, but several hesitant attempts were halted by others with the grab of a shoulder. Phong wept silently as his heart filled with pride at the brave display he was witnessing, those who had at first hesitated now stoic in their resolve. They had heard the stories and knew that anyone who didn't join would be shot, including women and children. And should they join these men they'd be forced to commit unspeakable atrocities that went against all the teachings of Buddhism.

Another orange robe was stained with red as the white man fired his weapon.

Phong closed his eyes.

"Kill them all."

Immediately the loudest sound Phong had ever heard erupted as multiple guns opened up on his family. He buried his head in the grass, covering his ears, but nothing could drown out the sound of the guns or the screams of his people.

And then there was silence.

He looked up and his chest heaved with anguish as he saw everyone he had ever known and loved lying in a pile of bloodied flesh, some still alive, though too near death for it to matter. The white man walked around the mound of flesh and put bullets in each of those who still struggled to survive and within minutes there was absolute silence save one baby, still held in his dead mother's arms.

Phong buried his head once again as the final shot rang out, silence reigning, the horrors of moments before lost to the white noise of fluttering leaves.

The sound of the white man speaking Vietnamese had his head lifting from the ground. He wiped his eyes clear as the words set it.

"Destroy everything."

"Yes, sir!"

Torches were lit and the homes he had grown up in, played in, ate in and slept in were quickly set ablaze, memories of a childhood wiped from history as the crackling of fire replaced the gentle rustling of the leaves and the harsh, acrid smoke overwhelmed the sweet smell of the grass he lay on. He cried as he finally spotted the body of his father, draped protectively over his mother, and felt a rage build inside him as he rose to his knees, still unseen by the murderous Viet Cong and their white overlord.

The man turned toward the shrine, stepping under its small roof.

"What's this?" he asked, picking up the bowl and looking inside.

"Some religious icon," replied his translator.

The man threw the bowl against the stone surrounding the shrine, the clay shattering into dozens of pieces, the precious ashes it contained spilled on the ground.

"There is no room for religion in Communism."

Phong roared in anger as he jumped to his feet, charging toward the man who had massacred his village, destroyed Buddha's bowl, disrespecting the founder of their village and their entire culture. Phong didn't care as the weapons were turned toward him, didn't notice that the white man waved off the soldiers, instead walking toward Phong, an amused smile on his face.

He grabbed Phong by the top of the head, halting his advance. Phong's arms swung at the murderer as he pushed forward with all his might but it was useless, and as the Viet Cong soldiers around him began to laugh at his futile efforts to exact revenge, he felt humiliation begin to overwhelm him as he realized there was nothing he could do, his small fifteen year old body no match for the fully grown man in front of him.

And it probably saved his life.

"What is your name, boy?" asked the man in near perfect Vietnamese.

Phong collapsed to his knees, his shoulders heaving in sobs as he fell back on his haunches, crying, self-pity overwhelming him.

"Kill me," he whispered.

"What is your name?"

"Phong."

The man motioned toward the pile of bodies now burning, the sickly sweet smell filling Phong's mouth with bile. "Is your family in there?"

Phong nodded, closing his eyes as he saw the flesh of his father's jaw melt off in drips, his once proud visage now a smoldering mass of sticky goo on the bloodstained ground.

"It's too bad you didn't die with them."

"Kill me, please!"

"Why would you die so readily?"

Phong looked up at the man, dumbstruck at the question. "You killed everyone I have ever known! You have destroyed the Founder's Bowl, gifted to his father by the great Buddha himself on the day of his death. You have scattered the Founder's ashes! And you ask why I want to die?

My heart is filled with such rage and sorrow I am no longer worthy to be with the living. I must leave this existence, endure the bardos and be reincarnated to once again live a life worthy of perhaps one day reaching Nirvana."

The white man shook his head slowly, frowning. "So much of your life has been clouded with the nonsense of religion. Buddha? Karma? Reincarnation? These are the ideas of a weak mind, an existence so frail and worthless that one looks forward to death so they can escape their own pathetic selves in the hopes they will be reborn into some form that might actually be worthy of existence, or to join some imaginary deity in an afterlife of eternal bliss." The man spat on the ashes of the Founder Asita causing the rage to return. Phong's fists clenched.

"So you just might be a man after all," observed the murderer, nodding toward Phong's fists. He kicked him in the chest, knocking him onto his back, a heavy boot suddenly crushing the air from his chest. Phong gasped, grasping uselessly at the black boot as the pressure increased. The man leaned forward, looking down at him. "You will find no quarter with me, little man. Which is why I will let you live. Tell the other villages what you have witnessed here today, and should we not get volunteers the next time we come back, they too will suffer the fate of your village."

The pressure was suddenly removed from his chest as the man stepped back leaving Phong to gasp for breath, his chest heaving painfully as he lay on the ground, his back soaking in the blood of his people, tears rolling into his ears as his beaten self wallowed in misery, silently praying for death.

"Let's go!" ordered the man, walking away, his back turned on Phong, a final insult to the boy, he so pathetic he wasn't even deemed a threat worthy of attention.

Phong pushed himself up on his elbows, looking at the departing Viet Cong, then rolled himself over and onto his knees. The translator wasn't as willing to dismiss Phong as harmless, keeping his eye on him, raising his weapon as Phong rose to his feet.

The white man noticed and turned.

"Until we meet again, young Phong." He nodded and was about to turn when Phong finally found his voice.

"I'm going to kill you if I ever see you again!"

The man tossed his head back, laughter roaring from within as the others stopped, joining in. The man pointed at Phong, smiling. "You've finally found your balls!" The levity wiped from his face as he took a single step toward Phong, Phong taking a reflexive one back. "I look forward to that day."

Phong, trembling with fear and adrenaline, part of him hoping to provoke a quick death, another enraged by the injustice he had witnessed, retook the lost ground, advancing another step closer. "You know my name. What is yours?"

The man's chest inflated as his hands moved to his hips.

"I am Captain Anatoly Petrov. And should we meet again, little one, you will die."

Petrov turned on his heel and disappeared into the forest, the Viet Cong following, and within moments Phong was left alone with the dead, his village a mere memory of what it once was.

And as the embers of hate began to ignite in his heart, he made a promise to himself that he doubted he would ever be able to keep.

*If I ever see Anatoly Petrov again, he will die, or I will die.*

*Old Quarter, Hanoi, Vietnam*

*Present Day*

Phong Son Quan still couldn't believe his luck. Yesterday had started as any other day. A member of the maintenance staff at the Daewoo Hanoi Hotel, a job he had proudly held for almost twenty years since the opening day in 1996, he did his job and he did it well, keeping his head down as expected, ignoring the guests unless spoken to directly.

He was a model employee.

And yesterday had changed all that.

For he had seen a new guest arrive in the lobby, a guest he only caught a glimpse of by accident.

Then couldn't take his eyes off.

It was a face he'd never forget, and other than some wrinkles and gray hair, there was no doubt who he was.

His nemesis.

The murderer of his entire village.

The man who had let him live so that he could suffer the memories of that day for the rest of his life.

The Prime Minister of Russia.

Anatoly Petrov.

Phong didn't care who he was now, all he cared about was who he was *then.*

*Captain* Anatoly Petrov.

And his vow of almost forty years ago, never forgotten, was suddenly no longer an empty threat.

Petrov had looked directly at him as he walked by, apparently not recognizing him. He had resisted throwing himself at the bastard and was now thankful he had, for he would simply have been arrested or worse, his family, friends and home unavenged.

Instead he had remained quiet, dropping his head down, his chin back on his chest as the procession walked by. They were the second VIP delegation of the day, the American Secretary of State having arrived earlier. He knew nothing of politics, nothing of world events. He lived in a communist country that controlled the news, instead only letting the people know about things the Party wanted them to know about.

And since the Party had been responsible for massacring everyone in his home, he hated them with a passion that continued to burn to this day.

Which was why he had moved into the city, taking simple manual labor jobs, eventually getting his prized job at the finest hotel in Hanoi. He shunned the news, didn't have a phone, nor did he have a television. He did his job well, prayed for those who had passed, and kept himself as healthy as he could for as long as he could, in the event this day should arrive.

Which was why he had never known his lifelong enemy had become so powerful a man.

He had finished his shift then went for his end of day briefing on what was expected the next day. Today. That was when he found out the Russian Prime Minister would be going to the National Museum of History, leaving the hotel at exactly 9:45 in the morning, only fifteen minutes after the United States Secretary of State would be leaving for the same destination.

The significance hadn't occurred to him at first until he was sitting in his tiny apartment eating his evening meal of pho noodles and banh chung sticky rice cakes. He knew there was no hope in reaching Petrov at the hotel, security was too tight. But he now knew where the man would be and when.

He had eyed the drawer of the rickety nightstand where he kept his gun, an old Makarov he had found after the war years ago. Over time he had learned how to use it during his mandatory military service and kept it clean and well oiled.

Always ready for the day he would kill Captain Anatoly Petrov.

But what was significant about what he had been briefed on was not just when and where his target would be, but who would also be there.

The American delegation.

And he already knew from his duties that there was an Asian looking man on the security delegation and that his room had a Do Not Disturb request until noon, he apparently serving on the nightshift. Phong knew that in order to get into the museum he would need to pretend to be part of one of the two delegations, since it would surely be closed to the public. He couldn't risk accessing the Russian floors since he might be recognized, and he couldn't speak their language should the need arise.

But he spoke English with little trouble, his hotel offering free training to improve the guest experience.

He had excelled.

His plan came together over the hours lying on his bed and the next morning he arrived early for work, seeking out his friend Duy in the Eco Office, Duy a one-man team that monitored utilities usage in the individual guest rooms, an effort the hotel was undertaking to try and lower their carbon footprint.

"I need a favor."

"What?"

"I need you to tell me when room 804 has a shower."

"Huh? Why?"

"I forgot my key pass in there yesterday. If management finds out, I'll lose my job!"

Duy smiled and slapped him on the shoulder. "I've got your back." He handed him his card. "Use mine for now. I don't need it stuck in here." He hit a few keys on the computer. "Just a second, I have to activate the system for that floor to get at the data. He pointed. "He entered his room about six hours ago and didn't take a shower. He turned out his lights about fifteen minutes later then the TV shortly after. I'm assuming his roommate is in there with him."

Phong shook his head. "He doesn't have one. I heard someone say he 'won the bet', whatever that means, so he got the solo room. He's alone."

Duy examined the keycard log and nodded. "There's only one keycard assigned to that room, and only one has been used since they arrived yesterday. Looks like you're right." He looked at Phong. "His room is flagged as being for security personnel for the American delegation. Are you sure you want to sneak in there? He's liable to shoot you."

"Not if he's in the shower."

"You're taking one hell of a chance."

"I can't lose my job."

Duy tapped a few keys and cursed. "He just turned on his lamp and the television. He's getting up. Go now, I'll call you when the shower starts."

Phong rushed from the room, taking the service elevator to the eighth floor then waiting for Duy's call on his hotel issued cellphone, picked up at the beginning of each shift, handed in at the end. It vibrated on his hip. He answered the call, his heart now pounding as he heard the words he had been waiting for.

"He's in the shower. Hurry!"

Phong stepped out into the hallway and walked straight for the room, pushing his maintenance cart in front of him. He tapped lightly on the door and there was no answer. Swiping Duy's master keycard, he pushed the door open slightly and listened.

The shower along with karaoke quality singing could be heard.

*Louie Louie, oh baby, say we gotta go?*

He quickly stepped inside, closing the door gently behind him, his eyes scanning the room the entire time. The man's clothes were laid out on the bed, but his pass was nowhere in sight.

Something Phong had anticipated.

From two decades of experience he knew that most security personnel locked their passes in the room safe while off duty just to prevent what he was about to do.

What most didn't know was that each safe had a master code, and thanks to those same two decades of experience, he knew what it was.

He opened the cabinet doors hiding the safe and dropped to his knees, pressing ## rapidly then entering the master PIN code of 144639. The safe clicked open, revealing the photo ID he saw all the security personnel wearing. He took the pass then closed the safe and the doors, exiting quickly just as the shower shut off.

It had been the most terrifying two minutes of his adult life.

And things were only going to get worse.

He returned Duy's keycard with a promise of beers later, then booked off sick, feigning a wicked stomach ache. It being his first sick day in years he wasn't questioned for a moment, instead receiving well wishes and advice from the ladies in Personnel on various soups and potions to try, one even offering to come by later with some.

He had bowed his way out, made his way home and changed into his best clothes—a dated suit bought at a secondhand store years ago—donned a pair of dark sunglasses like he had seen the security team all wear, then took his moped to the museum. He no doubt made an odd sight as he rode the fifteen minutes to his destination. Parking just down the street, he waited for the American delegation to arrive. Once he saw they were all in the building, he walked in, aping the movements of the security detail.

The pass was barely looked at, merely photocopied and handed back.

He had visited the museum once before and knew the most popular room would be where they kept the drums. There was no way Petrov would miss it. Entering the room, his badge secured to his chest allowing him to pass unfettered, he found a floor to ceiling tapestry and placed himself behind it. From his position he could lean to the left to see the door he had just come through, and to the right to see the opposing door.

The rest was now history, his adversary dead.

A life's promise fulfilled.

A life no longer with purpose.

He curled up into a ball on his bed and wept for those who had been lost all those years ago.

*Vietnam National Museum of History, Hanoi, Vietnam*

Mai Lien Trinh turned down the hallway containing the museum staff offices, hers at the far end, her position, or lack thereof, warranting a tiny cubbyhole next to the utilities closet. But she didn't mind at all. She found her work fascinating, rewarding, and until today, completely non-political.

She hated politics. Her brother was obsessed with them. He hated the Party, he hated the system, he hated their father for being a staunch supporter of the military, a proud retired member of the Vietnam People's Army and a firm supporter of communism.

Her mother simply never spoke of it right up to her death.

And Mai hated it all. She just wanted to live her life outside of the system as best she could, which was why she had gone the academic route rather than the service route. And she was damned lucky as far as she was concerned.

*Now if only I could find a boyfriend!*

She had been on a lot of dates but rarely received the promised call back. Her brother assured her she was 'hot' but in a bookish way, so it must be something else and she was pretty sure what it was.

She hated her country.

Her work exposed her to the world and she knew it was much better almost everywhere else she had been. Communism was at fault, the Party that imposed this failed system was at fault, and the people who blindly supported the Party were at fault.

Like her father.

Many of the men she went out with were men she wouldn't want to have return her calls, and she made it quite clear they shouldn't call through her lack of interest, and most of the rest simply were shown disdain at their love of their "connected" job.

Yet there were a few that she was disappointed never called her, breaking her heart every time.

And if today didn't end well, she might not need to worry about her dismal record on the dating scene.

She'd be dead or worse.

She closed the door to her office, sitting behind her desk and logging into the computer connected to the internal network. It was an old "clunker" as she had heard them called by other visiting professors, the better yet still outdated computers reserved for the full professors, not the grad students.

But it worked.

One advantage of working at a museum where nobody thought anything beyond physical security was important was that she pretty much had access to everything. Professor Tran had put her in charge of trying to modernize, which meant she had full Admin privileges on the server.

And was quickly into the files for the video cameras, installed just last year.

She pulled open a desk drawer and found a memory stick given to her as a gift at a conference she had once attended in Australia and inserted it into the USB port of her computer. She quickly copied the files over and set the 'Hidden' property on them to True. She then copied the electronic catalog of all their artifacts, pocketing the memory stick. Next she printed the catalog so she'd have something physical in her hand instead of having to use the memory stick to explain her presence.

She was about to log out when she paused for a moment, mentally debating if she had time.

And whether it was worth the risk.

She reached in her desk and grabbed a second memory stick, repeating the process, then slipped the tiny USB key into her bra. If she made it out unscathed, she'd have both copies. If she was stopped, she could hand over the first one and hopefully walk out with the second. And if she were arrested, she'd be in so deep it wouldn't matter how many copies she had.

She trembled at the thought.

Straightening herself in a small mirror stuck to the back of the door, she sucked in a breath and was about to leave when she stopped.

She went to her desk and picked up the phone, dialing her brother.

She got his voicemail.

"Cadeo, it's me." She thought for a moment then realizing they barely spoke, added, "Your sister. I'm in some trouble. I got mixed up by accident with the assassination this morning. I'm at the museum now but I'm leaving. I'll hopefully be with two American professors, Acton and Palmer, at the Daewoo. But if something goes wrong, just let everyone know I was doing the right thing and wasn't involved in this at all, no matter what they say, I was just an innocent bystander." She took a deep breath. "I love you."

Her chest tightened and her eyes filled with tears as she suddenly realized she actually did love her brother, despite his decision to become a criminal, a dealer on the black market. She thought of calling her father but before she could return the phone to its cradle the door burst open behind her.

Causing her to nearly pee her pants as she inhaled suddenly.

The Russian from earlier was standing at the door flanked by two police officers including Captain Nguyen, the first officer on the scene after the shooting.

"Miss Trinh, may I ask what you are doing here?" asked the Russian.

She felt herself begin to get dizzy and grabbed the desk, placing the phone receiver on the top, still connected. The breath she had been holding finally burst free and she began to breathe again. And she realized he was waiting for an answer. She held up the sheaf of papers. "I was printing off our antiquities catalog for the visiting professors."

"May I see?"

She nodded, handing the papers over. Sarkov quickly leafed through them, nodding as he did so. "An impressive collection, I am sure." He handed the papers back. "Certainly this information is available on the Internet?"

Mai shook her head. "No, little of it anyway."

"Are your American guests leaving so soon that this couldn't wait?"

Mai's mind raced for a reasonable explanation but could come up with nothing. "Not that I know of."

He took a step forward causing Mai to take one back. "Did they ask you for the list, or did you offer?"

"I-I offered."

"You don't sound certain."

"No, I-I'm just scared."

"Why?"

"Wouldn't you be?"

Sarkov smiled, his head bobbing as he took another step forward. "I suppose I would be. Which is why I definitely wouldn't come back here today." He held his hand out. "Please give it to me."

She knew she was busted. "Give you what?"

"Whatever storage device you are using for the files you copied from the secure network."

She gulped, her stomach doing butterflies as her mind raced. Glancing past the massive man, Nguyen's glare had her staring at Sarkov's shoes. Wingtips. Polished. She looked for her face in them.

She reached into her pocket and produced the memory stick, regaining her composure for a moment. “I copied the electronic version of the printout in case they preferred that.”

The words came out fast and almost a jumble, her nerves winning out.

“Of course you did,” he said, taking the memory stick. “You won’t mind if I take a look at this a little closer, would you?”

She shook her head, motioning toward her computer. “Please.”

Sarkov smiled. “I think we’ll use my computer in the car.” He held out his hand, inviting her out the door. “If you would be so kind?”

She began to tremble. “Where are you taking me?”

“Somewhere safe, I assure you.”

“B-but I’m a Vietnamese citizen.” She looked at Nguyen. “I demand—I mean I request that my government protect me. I’ve done nothing wrong.”

Nguyen stepped inside, his rage barely contained. “You have stolen files from a secure network belonging to the Vietnamese people! When he is done with you, *then* your government will *protect* you!”

Sarkov looked down at her with a sympathetic smile, waving the memory stick at her. “I’m sorry, Miss Trinh, but should we find anything on this that shouldn’t be there, it is out of my hands. Perhaps it would be best to admit to any wrong doing now?”

Mai’s shoulders slumped in defeat. She had hidden the files from casual observation. Anyone with even a basic knowledge of computers would be able to find them.

“I copied the camera footage,” she mumbled, her chin on her chest.

Nguyen began a tirade cut off with a single raised finger by Sarkov.

“Did the Americans ask you to?”

She looked up at him, eyes wide as she shook her head vigorously. “No! I said I would get it to prove their friend wasn’t the shooter!”

“Their friend?”

Mai gasped, realizing she had made a terrible gaffe. "No, I didn't say that, I mean, I misspoke."

"We both know you didn't. So the Americans lied to me. I wonder why they would do that."

The room felt like it was starting to spin as Mai's heart raced and a vicelike grip took hold of her chest. She steadied herself with a hand on the corner of her desk, closing her eyes which proved to be a mistake, she nearly losing her balance. She opened them quickly and focused on the wastepaper basket in the corner. Sarkov was saying something, the words distant and incoherent.

"Miss Trinh!"

Sarkov's sharp shout brought her back to reality with a roar and she sucked in a sudden breath, everything coming back into focus. She looked up at Sarkov. "They know him from somewhere, and they know he wasn't the shooter, as *I* know he wasn't the shooter. If you're going to kill me because I told you the truth, then so be it."

Sarkov pursed his lips, nodding, giving Mai the impression that he actually respected her response. He motioned to Nguyen. "Take her away. I'll want to interview her later as will my colleague from Moscow." He turned toward the door then looked down at the much smaller Nguyen. "And I expect to find her in the exact same condition she is in now."

Nguyen snapped to attention briefly in acknowledgement, his eyes, burrowing into Mai's, revealing his outrage at the limitation imposed upon him. Orders were barked and she found herself between two policemen being hauled bodily down the hallway, past all of her shocked colleagues.

It would be humiliating if it weren't so terrifying.

As she stepped out in the light of day hundreds of cameras began to snap while she was pushed into the back of a police car, flanked on either side in the backseat by the two officers, another two in the front. The siren was turned on and the vehicle pulled away from the museum and made its way through the police cordon and onto the street.

Where she caught a glimpse of the two professors in the museum car, horror on their faces.

She just hoped they would tell her family how she died.

With honor, doing the right thing.

At the hands of her father's beloved government.

*Outside the Vietnam National Museum of History, Hanoi, Vietnam*

"Get out!"

Acton spun toward the driver. "Excuse me?"

"Get out! Get out! Get out!" screamed the man, motioning toward the door.

Acton decided it was best to follow the order, it clear they were no longer welcome now that Mai had been arrested. Acton looked back at Laura as she frowned, opening the rear door. They both stepped onto the street and looked about.

"What now?" asked Laura, eyeing the guards.

"We walk straight toward that throng of press people and hopefully get recognized."

He took Laura by the hand and walked with purpose toward the street fronting the entrance to the museum where the police had a cordon set up and international press—he was sure there'd be few if any local press—were gathered, cameras rolling.

He spotted an ABC News reporter that he had met after an incident at the Vatican. He raised his hand, hailing him as he pushed a broad smile out over his face.

"Charles!"

The man looked at him, confused for a moment, then an expression of shock mixed with recognition took over. "Professor Acton? What the bloody hell are you doing here?"

"We were visiting the museum when all hell broke loose," he replied, flashing his ID to the guards as he continued to walk toward the reporter.

And just as he had hoped, every camera and microphone was now turned toward them, someone finally engaging them.

"Did you see the incident?" yelled one.

"Do you have a ride?" Acton asked Charles Stewart. Stewart nodded.

"Was it an American?" shouted another.

Security seemed confused, an officer looking about for instructions on whether or not to let these two foreigners off the premises. Acton casually looked for their tail car but it was lost in the crowd.

Suddenly the cordon parted after somebody shouted something in Vietnamese behind them.

They were free, Stewart hustling them toward his van. Safely inside the driver pulled away, the vehicle being chased by the press for a good twenty yards. Stewart turned back toward them from the passenger seat. He jerked a thumb at the driver. "Meet Pat Murphy, my cameraman and chauffeur."

"Bloody slave would be a more accurate description," muttered Murphy, flashing a smile at the new arrivals, his accent thick and Irish.

"He's a scholar and a gentleman and a constant pain in my ass. Why they keep putting us together on assignment I'll never know." Stewart suddenly became all business. "Okay, what gives? How are you two mixed up in this?"

"Wrong place, wrong time, that's all," replied Acton. "We were on a tour provided by the museum when the assassination took place."

"You saw it?"

"From the context of ducking, yes."

"Did you get a good look at the shooter?"

Acton exchanged a quick glance with Laura that the trained Stewart caught.

He pounced. "You did, didn't you? Was it an American like they claimed?"

Acton decided coming clean on that part at least should be not only safe, but his duty. "No, he was definitely Vietnamese."

"How can you be sure?"

"I guess I can't be sure he was Vietnamese, but he looked like he was from this *region*, shall we say."

"They're claiming an Asian American attached to the Secretary of State's security detail."

Acton frowned. "They've already released that?"

"Unofficially of course, but they're not denying it, and they've got his ID on circulation none too discretely."

"We've seen that photocopy and he definitely wasn't the shooter."

"How do you know? You said he was Asian."

"Yes, but they knew each other."

Stewart's eyes narrowed. "Huh? Who? You mean the shooter and this Asian American?"

Acton shook his head. "No, the shooter and the Russian Prime Minister."

"How do you know?"

"They spoke," said Laura. "He claimed the Prime Minister had massacred his village during the war."

"The Vietnam War?"

Acton cocked an eyebrow indicating how stupid he felt the question was.

"Sorry, obviously. And the Prime Minister didn't deny it?"

Laura shook her head. "No, in fact he seemed quite proud of the fact he had, even told the man he'd have to be more specific since he'd cleansed lots of villages during the war."

"Then the guy showed him a clay bowl and that's when Petrov said the man's name."

Stewart's jaw dropped. "Are you kidding me?"

Acton shook his head. "Nope. He said, 'Young Phong, is that you?' and the man nodded and spoke of how Petrov killed everyone in his village."

"There was no doubt they knew each other," said Laura. "This was *not* an American. We saw the photo they're handing around. It *definitely* wasn't him. The guy's at least twenty years younger!"

Stewart was scribbling madly on his pad, shaking his head the entire time in awe. "This is huge," he muttered. "Are you willing to go on camera?"

Acton looked at Laura who shook her head slightly. "Not until we're safely stateside unless it becomes absolutely necessary."

"If they're trying to pin this on the Americans, you might have a hard time leaving the country what with you being there and all."

Laura patted the pocket her passport was in. "They already seized our passports but gave them back. We'd try to leave but we're afraid that might just make us look guilty."

"There was some suggestion by the Russian investigator that a much more hardline guy is arriving from Moscow later today. I expect things to get much more difficult by then."

Stewart lowered his voice as if concerned someone might actually be listening within their vehicle. "Look, this American connection is being pushed, hard. Every press organization worldwide is running his name and photo. The only saving grace is that it's a terrible photocopy, so his identity in the future might actually be protected still. The Russians are already at a heightened state of alert but our government hasn't responded yet, they're denying any involvement, promising to cooperate fully, and are scrambling to deescalate. The Russian President though is already whipping up a frenzy and it hasn't even been four hours."

"Do you really think this could lead to war?" asked Laura, her own voice subdued, a tinge of fear lacing it.

Stewart shrugged. "I doubt it, but that guy's a nutbar. I'm guessing he'll use it as an excuse to take some territory where he feels Russian minorities are 'oppressed'"—Stewart added air quotes—"and perhaps a few limited skirmishes to make his point. I just can't see anyone wanting all-out war, not even that man, no matter how far he's got his head shoved up his ass looking for the Soviet Union's former glory."

Action stifled a grin, Stewart always peppering his conversation with colorful alliterations.

"We've got a tail." It was Murphy that startled them all with the revelation.

Stewart already looking at them in the backseat shifted his eyes. "Yeah. Dark blue sedan, four people inside. None look happy."

"We were followed on the way to the museum," replied Acton. "Probably the same people."

"Which reminds me," said Laura. "I need to call Mai's brother." She reached into her handbag and pulled out the piece of paper Mai had written on earlier then dialed the number. She shook her head, covering the mouthpiece. "Voicemail," she whispered then raised her voice. "Hi, this is Professor Laura Palmer. I'm a colleague of your sister Mai. I have important information about her. Please contact me as quickly as possible as it is urgent." She left her number then hung up. She looked at the others. "Let's hope he understands English."

Half a dozen motorcycles suddenly whipped by them on either side, racing up between the lanes of the wide boulevard.

Chaos erupted moments later.

*Trang Tien Street, Hanoi, Vietnam*

Cadeo An Trinh raced between the rows of traffic on his Yamaha, everyone stopped for the traffic lights ahead. As soon as he had heard this morning that there had been an assassination at his sister's museum he had gathered his gang and headed for the general vicinity. He had one of his men set up surveillance near the front gate while the rest hung back a couple of blocks away. His little sister he knew didn't approve of him, didn't approve of the choices he had made over the years, but he didn't care.

She was still his little sister.

And it was his duty to protect her.

It had only been a precaution to go to the museum, he figured there was no way she could be involved, but by the time they got there the place was swarming with police and she wasn't answering her phone. When one of his friends texted that she had just arrived in a museum car with two white people he had immediately become concerned since the story had broken it was an American that had killed some Russian big-wig.

And now she had come back.

It wasn't even ten minutes later that she was led out by police. His decision had been quick and decisive. There was no doubt they thought she was involved otherwise they wouldn't have arrested her. And since she had arrived with these two Americans—or who he presumed were Americans—they were involved too.

*Could they have framed her?*

The thought had made his blood boil, but he didn't have time for that. He knew in his country, a country he hated, or more accurately, a country whose government he hated, his sister would most likely never be seen again unless it was at a trial where her guilt would be predetermined, the sentence death, carried out with the swift efficiency of the communist state.

He had dedicated his adult life to undermining that very state, not through joining some obscure rebel faction, but by joining the underground community that lived away from the grid of authority and supplied the masses with what they wanted—black market goods. Whether it was American cigarettes or Russian Vodka, he had it in supply or knew someone who did. Guns, DVDs, computers, illegal satellite dishes? He had it all. And every time he made a sale, it gave him a rush in knowing that not only had he defied the government one more time, he had subverted a citizen yet again.

It especially gave him a thrill knowing when it was a Party member that had come to him to fulfil some special need.

Drugs and prostitution weren't his bag, and they never would be despite some members of his gang wanting to branch out into those extremely lucrative markets. He refused to. He had a moral code that he strictly followed. Goods the government banned were fair game if they were freely available in other countries. If Sylvester Stallone and Chuck Norris movies could be freely watched in the United States, why not here? If Smirnoff and Camels could be enjoyed, why not here?

But drugs and prostitution only destroyed lives. A good Rambo movie enjoyed with a few shots of vodka and a cigarette never did.

He whipped past the left side of the news vehicle his spotter had seen the two Americans enter. He'd worry about them later—if anything happened to his little sister, they were dead.

His spotter, Tran, pointed at a car stopped in traffic ahead and he gunned his engine, the front wheel popping slightly off the ground. He grabbed his Beretta M9, his pride and joy, and hit the brakes, skidding to a halt at the driver side window.

He stuck his gun against the driver's temple, the window conveniently down.

The others surrounded the vehicle, screwdrivers used to flatten all four tires within seconds, Tran holding a gun to the officer in the passenger seat. Shouts ensued, the driver silent and trembling as Cadeo's men yanked open the back doors and hauled the two officers out and onto the ground. Mai was screaming as Tran grabbed her, hauling her out. She looked at Cadeo and he could tell she immediately recognized him despite his helmet's visor being closed.

She shut up.

She climbed on the back of Tran's bike and he gunned his engine sending them racing forward. Cadeo kept his gun trained on the driver until he saw Tran turn right and disappear out of sight. Out of the corner of his eye he saw several people running toward them. He turned to see two men, one carrying a television camera, along with what he assumed were the two Americans, a man and a woman.

Rage consumed him as he looked at the two people who had got his sister involved, effectively ending her life as she knew it. He flipped up his visor and glared at them.

Then raised his weapon and shot at the woman.

*Trang Tien Street, Hanoi, Vietnam*

Acton saw the man on the motorcycle raise his weapon at them. He dove at Laura, knocking her to the ground as the shot rang out. They hit hard, Laura yelping in pain and shock as the bullet ricocheted off a nearby vehicle. Stewart and his cameraman, Murphy, ducked, Acton swearing Murphy didn't lose the shot the entire time. The shooter turned and raced away with the rest of the bikers, disappearing around a corner within seconds.

The entire kidnapping had taken less than a minute.

The four policemen suddenly were all business, screaming and waving their arms, trying to get the traffic out of their way, and Acton was sure trying to look like they hadn't just been totally owned by the well-executed kidnapping.

Then they noticed the camera.

"Let's get out of here," said Stewart, putting a hand on Murphy's shoulder as he led him back to the van, the experienced reporters documenting everything as they beat a hasty retreat. Acton pulled Laura to her feet then rushed after the reporters, the police shouting behind them, making sure they were walking very quickly as opposed to running, he hoping the excuse of "I don't speak Vietnamese" might just work if they were caught.

But he knew they had to get out of there. They had just witnessed Mai being kidnapped—or probably more accurately rescued—by what he assumed was her brother.

And they had been with the camera crew that caught most of it on tape, a tape that would embarrass the Vietnamese government.

Something he assumed they wouldn't tolerate with today's events.

He pushed Laura into the back of the van, jumping in after her as he slid the door closed, Stewart grabbing the camera as he climbed in, Murphy starting the engine and looking for a hole in the traffic. Stewart kept shooting as the police began to run toward them. Murphy looked in his side view mirror then suddenly gunned the engine, cranking the wheel to the left. He surged into a gap in the oncoming traffic with a flurry of honked horns and burnt rubber, then quickly forcing his way into the right hand lanes, he was able to make a sharp right turn and leave the police in the distance as he eased off the gas and tried to blend.

"What the hell was that?" asked Stewart as he turned off the camera and handed it back to Acton.

"I'm guessing that was Mai's brother," said Laura as Acton placed the camera beside him. "Apparently he's not quite a law abiding citizen."

"Ya think?" Stewart shook his head looking at Laura. "You okay?"

She nodded, examining her wrists, both with a little road rash. "I've had worse, believe me."

Murphy made another turn. "You're just lucky he missed."

Stewart's phone buzzed on his hip and he grabbed it, swiping his finger to take the call. "Stewart." He listened for a moment, cursed, then hung up. "That was Steve Frost from NBC. He said he just overheard a police broadcast down at the museum." He nodded toward Acton and Laura. "You two are apparently wanted for involvement in what just happened, and so are we."

"Shit," muttered Acton. "What the hell do we do now?"

Stewart shrugged. "We've got video proof we weren't involved. That should get us off."

Acton shook his head. "No, they're trying to pin this assassination on the United States. I'm guessing because their security failed so miserably, they don't want to be held accountable by their closest ally. That video"—he tipped his head toward the camera—"will just be conveniently lost or erased and we'll all be tied into this."

Stewart's lips pressed into a thin line. "You're right." He reached back and flicked open a panel on the camera then pressed several buttons on a touch display. "I'm uploading the video to New York now, just in case."

Acton watched a green bar crawl across the screen at an excruciatingly slow pace, the satellite uplink not the quickest method of transmission but the most reliable when in a moving vehicle in the Third World.

"Aww Christ!" cried Murphy as a siren sounded behind them. The rest of them turned to see a police car several vehicles back in pursuit, its lights flashing, the occupants with their arms out the windows trying to wave cars out of the way. "What now?"

"Let's get to the American Embassy," said Acton. "If we can hole up there until this blows over we just might be okay."

Murphy jerked the wheel to the right and lay on his horn, scattering the pedestrians from the sidewalk he was now driving down. He turned right and managed to just cut ahead of the traffic surging forward from a newly green light. This bought a momentary reprieve but by the time they had caught up to the next light the police car, along with a second, was visible again.

"How far to the embassy?" asked Laura.

"Not far," said Stewart. "Just a few blocks."

"Yeah, but this traffic is ridiculous. I've never seen it this bad."

Acton was about to ask if Murphy was local when he jerked the wheel to the right again, shooting down an alleyway.

*He must be stationed here.*

He seemed to know the roads like the back of his hand, gunning the van into a sharp, hair raising left skid, propelling them up a relatively quiet side street, still heading in the same direction as before but bypassing the busy main roads. Acton looked back through the opaque windows and could see flashing police lights in the distance.

"Almost there!"

He made a quick left and Acton could see the main road ahead, but rather than cars, it seemed to be filled with people.

People protesting.

"Shit!" cried Murphy as he slammed his brakes on, hundreds of bodies blocking the way.

"Where's the Embassy?" asked Laura as Acton threw open the side door.

Stewart pointed in the flow of the protesters. "Half a mile that way, you can't miss it."

"Let's go!" Acton jumped out, helping Laura down to the scorching pavement, the midday sun baking everything. Stewart reached back and grabbed the camera, heaving it toward Murphy as he climbed out. Stewart led the way, pushing through the crowd chanting something Acton couldn't quite make out.

*Yankee go home!*

He cursed to himself realizing that there could only be one reason this crowd was at this particular location.

The American Embassy.

And this was clearly an orchestrated demonstration. Camera crews were in among the throng, beaming the Communist Party's designer message to the world. This was a full court press to convince the world that the Vietnamese people were united in their belief that an American, and not a Vietnamese, was responsible for today's assassination.

"Murph, start rolling!" called Stewart as he apparently realized the crowds were letting the news teams move freely. The four of them bunched together, Acton with a hand on Stewart's shoulder, his other hand gripping Laura's as Murphy raised his camera to his shoulder and began shooting.

As if by magic the crowd parted, their "anger", which to Acton looked half-hearted until on camera, shouted at the lens, fists pumped even harder than a moment before, anger creasing faces that seconds ago looked almost bored.

True propaganda.

Acton was willing to bet barely half the people knew why they were there, too many of them in white dress shirts with dark pants, clearly government workers sent into the streets.

But political manipulation of the proletariat wasn't his problem today, his problem lay directly ahead.

An Embassy ringed by a cordon of police officers.

"There's no way we're getting through that!" shouted Acton, Stewart nodding his agreement. "You try to get into the embassy, they might let you in as a camera crew. We're going to try and get to the British Embassy."

Stewart pulled a business card from his shirt pocket and handed it to Acton. "Call me if you can't get in. I'll see what I can do to help."

Acton nodded, stuffing the card in his pocket as he and Laura pushed through the crowd toward the opposite side of the street. He glanced back and could see the heads of police officers jumping up in the crowd like whack-a-moles trying to spot them.

He ducked down, his six foot plus frame too obvious in a sea of five-foot-five. Even Laura ducked, she too taller than the average male in this country.

Acton spotted an alleyway and pointed, trying to stay low and not draw attention by shoving against the steady forward flow.

Laura's hand suddenly broke free.

"James!" she cried as he spun around, catching a glimpse of her as she was carried with the flow, several men pushing her along, one grabbing her from behind, almost bear hugging her.

Acton rose to his full height, shoving against the crowd, tossing them aside without warning as he fought toward his wife. Suddenly he saw her left elbow lash out, catching one of the men on the chin. He dropped. The man almost carrying Laura slowed to look down at his friend as she threw her entire bodyweight forward, picking the man up off the ground, his body draped over her back. The third man swung his fist, punching Laura in the stomach just as Acton arrived. He thrust the web of his hand hard against the man's throat, partially collapsing his windpipe. As the man dropped to a knee, gasping for breath, Laura flipped her assailant over her back and onto the pavement, dropping a well planted heel on his groin causing him to cry out in agony.

Acton grabbed her wrist again and pushed to the side of the crowd and into another alleyway, the Embassy tantalizingly close, the Marine guards visible behind the wall of Vietnamese police.

Suddenly it was another world, dark and closed in, the crowd almost muffled as they moved deeper into the alleyway, the protest becoming more distant.

Acton stopped, turning toward Laura. "Are you okay?"

She nodded, rubbing her stomach. "He hits like a girl, I'll be fine." She looked back at the crowd at the other end of the alley then continued moving forward as she pulled out her cellphone. Her thumb flew over the touch screen and she held up her phone, surprised. "The British Embassy is only about half a kilometer from here."

Acton felt a surge of hope as they cleared the alleyway and hurried along another a side street heading south. And as they neared a pit began to form in his stomach as chanting in the distance, rather than continuing to fade, became louder.

"It's just up here on this next street," said Laura, pointing ahead. They turned the corner and froze in their tracks.

The British Embassy was surrounded as well.

Acton pulled Laura back and out of sight of the smaller but still significant crowd.

"They obviously don't want us going to either of our embassies," said Acton, frowning as he tried to figure out what to do next. They couldn't get the help of their governments since both sources of assistance were behind police cordons, they couldn't go back to their hotel since they were now wanted criminals, and they had no way of reaching Dawson.

"Could we call Dylan?"

Acton shrugged. "It's worth a try, but his kind of help is probably at least hours away. We need to get off the streets now. You and I stick out like sore thumbs."

Acton was painfully aware of the stares they were both getting and decided that walking with a purpose looked less suspicious. He reached into his pocket and pulled out Stewart's business card. "Let's call Charles and see if he has any ideas." He dialed the number and it rang several times before the reporter finally answered.

"Stewart."

"It's Jim. Are you guys safe?"

"Yeah, we managed to get inside the embassy. What about you two?"

"The British Embassy is surrounded as well. And I doubt we can go back to our hotel."

"Definitely not! I just spoke to one of the guys here and they said you two have been named co-conspirators in the assassination. Every cop in the country is looking for you."

"Shit!" exclaimed Acton, lowering the mouthpiece, turning to Laura, her inquisitive look demanding an explanation. "We've been named co-conspirators."

"Bloody hell!"

"You two need to get off the streets and hole up somewhere," said Stewart. "I'm going to see if we can work out something here and I'll get back to you."

"Okay, thanks Charles."

Acton ended the call as Laura snapped her fingers.

"I know who we can call."

*Over the Arctic Ocean*

*184 nautical miles from Alaskan coast*

Major Terry "Sandman" Johnson pushed the engines of his F-22 Raptor hard, his entire body pressed into his seat, the feeling of the g-forces pressing against him familiar and comforting. He had always wanted to be a pilot from the time he got his first toy airplane, and with his father in the Air Force having flown dozens of missions in Gulf War One and his grandfather over Vietnam, he was now carrying on the family tradition. After meeting his wife and the birth of his two daughters, earning his wings was probably the greatest thing that ever happened to him. He loved his job, loved his life and wouldn't change a thing.

Except perhaps the mindset of these asshole Russians.

He and his wingman Captain Larry "Hagman" Ewing were racing to intercept eight Russian long range bombers, Tu-95 Bears, approaching American airspace. These challenges to American and Canadian Arctic sovereignty had been frequent during the Cold War, stopping almost completely after the collapse of the Soviet Union. But a newly resurgent Russia had begun sending bombers toward the borders again, turning back at the last minute after being intercepted by American or Canadian fighters coordinated by NORAD.

And the dance long thought over with had resumed.

It made no sense.

He simply couldn't understand the arrogance of the Russians and why they had to bring back a state of the world that had almost led to nuclear war on at least one occasion the public knew about, and several others they didn't. It frustrated him and his fellow pilots why anyone would want to try and trigger an incident like this. They were flying at high speeds at high altitude in the middle of nowhere. If something went wrong, which it easily could, people would die and who knew what kind of international incident that might trigger.

He never worried about what his fellow pilots were doing. They trained together, flew together and knew each other's moves like they were their own.

It was the Russians that worried him.

He had no idea what they would do. The last time they had intercepted two bombers he had pulled up beside the cockpit on the starboard side and looked at the pilot who promptly banked directly into him. If he had been checking his own starboard side he might have missed the maneuver and been taken out by the massive airframe.

And it wasn't the first time the Russians had tried to hit one of them.

But this was the first time he had ever seen eight bombers and he had to admit he had some butterflies. He had heard about the assassination earlier in the day in Vietnam and their briefing had told them to expect trouble over the coming days and possibly weeks until things simmered down, but as soon as the reports broke that an American was suspected of committing the murder, NORAD had reported the launch of bombers from across Russia. Challenges were already happening in Europe and Guam and several carrier groups had been buzzed.

*If everyone isn't careful, this could turn into a shooting war very quickly.*

He buzzed the lead bomber with full afterburners, giving their fuselage a shake as he banked around to take up position on their wing, showing the proverbial flag. He and Hagman were on the starboard side of the bombers, two others from his command on the port. As he examined the nearest Bear, his cameras taking plenty of photos, he couldn't help but wonder if their payload truly was nuclear, or if they were carrying dummies just for training.

*Knowing these assholes, it's probably the real thing.*

The squadron leader made no attempt to make radio contact with the Russians as was protocol. International airspace was quickly running out and the bombers would soon be turning back at the last second.

Assuming they stayed true to form.

Sandman kept a cautious eye on the nearest bomber, his shoulder and instrument checks brief glances, not willing to risk a near-miss like last time.

He looked at his coordinates and his HUD display showing the rapidly approaching border.

*They're not turning!*

The lumbering beasts the Russians were flying couldn't turn on a dime. They weren't meant to. They needed a lot of distance to do a 180, and if they didn't turn now, they'd actually stray into American airspace.

His HUD indicated four more aircraft arriving, friendlies from Canadian airspace. Now they were about to be eight, a show of force that hadn't been needed in a long time, but with tensions so high, the message being sent by NORAD was any incursion wouldn't be tolerated, no matter how justified Russia might feel with their moment of sympathy on the international stage.

He listened as the squadron leader broke radio silence, another new experience for him.

*Today's just full of firsts.*

"—turn now or you will be violating United States airspace, acknowledge, over!"

The Russians ignored the hails and continued forward, the border now only seconds away at these speeds.

*Shit! What the hell are we going to do?*

They trained for this, but never expected it to actually happen, the Russians *always* turning back just short of violating the sovereignty of whoever they were challenging. He had to assume they were merely "pushing the boundaries", hoping to provoke some reaction that they could then play to the folks back home, claiming they had been in international airspace.

"Antler, this is Sable Leader. Russian bombers have violated the twelve-mile limit and show no sign of turning back. Request permission for weapons lock, over?"

"Sable Leader, this is Antler. Permission granted, over."

"Acknowledged, Antler. Maple Leader, Sable Leader. Proceed with weapons lock, over."

The Canadian squadron leader acknowledged the order, both squadrons coordinated through NORAD and listening in on the same frequency, their tactical computers able to recognize each other. Sandman watched on his display as the Canadians repositioned slightly then his HUD indicated that weapons locks had been attained. He watched the Russian cockpit of the nearest bomber and saw some excited pointing, but they continued forward, now well into US territory, the first time he could recall this ever actually happening.

His adrenaline was flowing freely and he steadied his breathing, remembering his training. What happened in the next few minutes could be the end of a long, hard, cold peace.

"Antler, Sable Leader, weapons locks attained, no effect. Request permission to fire warning shots, over."

"Sable Leader, Antler. Permission granted, over."

*Shit! This is really happening!*

Sandman leaned forward and watched as his squadron leader broke off and out of sight. His instruments showed the experienced pilot put some distance between himself and the bombers then suddenly bank back toward the large group of planes. Tracer fire was clearly visible as the M61A2 Vulcan 20 mm cannon opened up, the bullets whipping harmlessly past the lead aircraft with plenty of room to spare, the intention not to scare the Russians but to show the determination of their escorts to turn them back.

Again nothing.

Sable Squadron Leader opened up with another volley, this one closer, and again nothing.

*These guys are determined to get shot down.*

As the harsh Alaskan terrain rushed past almost forty thousand feet below them, he felt sweat trickle down his spine as another volley, not thirty yards ahead of the lead Russian bomber flashed past.

And still nothing.

His squadron leader reported back to NORAD, requesting permission to engage.

And permission was granted.

*Jesus Christ!*

He looked over at the cockpit of the plane he was shadowing and the Russians still seemed oblivious to the fate about to befall them. Orders had been granted to splash the lead bomber. As he began to pull up to reposition himself to open fire from the rear his threat alarm suddenly sounded as chaff erupted from all eight bombers, flooding his display and canopy. Momentarily blinded, he held up his hand to block the intense light when he saw a massive shadow coming toward him.

Collision alarms sounded and he pushed hard left and down as the bomber banked into him. He felt his plane jerk as if a mighty force had grabbed his portside wing and yanked it up like he was the log in a caber toss. He struggled to regain control as his entire cockpit began to protest, alarms and lights demanding attention.

Suddenly a sound he had only heard described before and never dreamed he'd hear himself filled the cockpit, the entire aircraft shaking and groaning. He looked over his shoulder and felt his heart drop into his stomach as his wing separated from the fuselage. His ejection alarm sounded and he heard shouting in his comm to bail. He reached for the ejection control between his legs and gripped the handle as his aircraft began to spin out of control. He could feel himself about to blackout, and in a final moment of lucidity yanked on the handle. His canopy tore away, the whipping of the ice cold wind bringing him back to reality just as the seat was catapulted out of the plane.

The spinning stopped almost immediately and he felt the rockets fire to push him away to avoid any potential shrapnel from his plane in case it exploded. When the rockets finished he felt his freefall begin, his altitude too high for the chute to open yet. He found himself falling backward with a perfect view of the chaos overhead. His own plane was long gone, the bomber that had hit him had smoke trailing from its wing as it rapidly lost altitude. The other bombers were all banking in unison now, still spitting chaff, his squadron and the Canadians now simply shadowing as there was no need to engage, his own wingman, Hagman, breaking off to keep an eye on his descent.

And as he continued his fall, waiting for his chute to open, he wondered just what the hell the Russians had hoped to accomplish.

And prayed he hadn't just started a war.

*Daewoo Hanoi Hotel, Hanoi, Vietnam*

"You've gotta see this!"

All heads turned as Secretary Atwater's right-hand man Ronald Greer burst into the room, making for the televisions they had set up with satellite feeds to all the major networks. Half a dozen displays in one corner were all on but muted, Atwater speaking to the President only moments before.

To say he was concerned would be an understatement. Apparently an F-22 Raptor had bumped a Russian Tu-95 Bear less than half an hour ago. The Raptor was lost but the Bear was able to make an emergency landing at Joint Base Elmendorf–Richardson, it unable to make it home. The Russians were screaming bloody murder, as was the White House, blaming the Russians for violating the twelve-mile limit to the tune of over one hundred miles. It was the greatest incursion in history and according to the Pentagon they were seconds away from splashing one of the bombers.

It was an incident designed to provoke.

Again demonstrating the different mindset of the Russian.

Americans wouldn't sacrifice an aircrew to gain points in the foreign press, but the Russians wouldn't hesitate to do it. They'd sacrifice their men for the greater good of the country. Dawson would die for his country in a heartbeat, but he also knew his country wouldn't tell him to go provoke a war with the biggest bully on the block by getting himself killed. He had met quite a few Russians over the years, some he even liked. But he had to admit the supreme arrogance was overwhelming at times. He was confident. His men were confident. But arrogance could get you killed, arrogance could start wars.

Which seemed to be just what the Russians were trying to provoke.

He knew it wasn't actually the case. Russia wouldn't go to war even if they had lost all eight bombers. But they would take advantage of the situation. A lightning strike into the Ukraine was something Dawson was fully expecting to hear of within the next few hours if things didn't simmer down. Latest intel had Russia activating armored divisions already deployed to the borders of Ukraine, Belarus, Latvia, Lithuania and Estonia. And with NATO's policy of not stationing troops in former Warsaw Pact countries, the Baltic States were vulnerable, and Poland, just west of Belarus, was as well.

And would NATO actually stick to its mandate of going to war should a member state be attacked?

He had his doubts.

The only solution to this entire situation was to prove that Niner wasn't involved. He hadn't heard from the professors since they had left, and he couldn't risk calling their phones, just in case it was traced back to Atwater's security detail. The last thing they needed was the Russians or Vietnamese thinking they were interfering with the investigation.

But it had him worried.

And he became even more so when the audio was cranked on CNN International, split screen file photos of James Acton and Laura Palmer displayed with a talking head in the corner. He stepped closer, as did everyone.

"*—now wanted in connection to today's assassination of the Russian Prime Minister. Vietnamese authorities are saying the two professors, husband and wife, are co-conspirators, along with a Vietnamese national named Mai Lien Trinh. They are accused of assisting the assassin, whom Vietnamese and Russian authorities have identified as a member of Secretary of State Atwater's security detail, a member of the Bureau of Diplomatic Security named Jeffrey Green. A photocopy of his ID card, taken just before the shooting when he entered the National Museum of History, has been* *released by Vietnamese authorities. Authorities are also claiming that Professor James Acton and Professor Laura Palmer, along with an American camera crew from ABC assisted in the assault on a police car transporting the Vietnamese suspect Mai Lien Trinh. Several police officers were injured in the incident and the suspects escaped.*

*"The White House denies any involvement in the assassination, instead insisting their Agent's ID card was stolen from his locked hotel room safe and he was at Secretary Atwater's hotel when the incident occurred.*

*"In further developments, a joint American and Canadian operation sent to intercept eight Russian bombers that eventually violated United States airspace resulted in an F-22 Raptor being lost today in a mid-air collision with one of the bombers. The Kremlin is claiming it occurred outside the twelve mile limit and are demanding the United States immediately provide access to their bomber that was forced to make an emergency landing in Alaska. The American pilot was recovered with only minor injuries. This was only one of over a dozen incidents today with Russian bombers around the world violating American, British and European airspace, an unprecedented move that resulted in several shooting incidents before the bombers turned back.*

*"At the UN—"*

"I've heard enough," said Atwater as she dropped back into her chair. "The Vietnamese and Russians are certainly working overtime to get their version of the story out to the press."

"And the press are eating it up," observed Greer. "This situation is rapidly getting out of control."

"Agreed," said Dawson. "They now have named a second American as involved, along with his wife who now lives in the United States."

"I've heard that name before. Acton was it? Where do I know it from?"

"They've been involved in a few incidents over the years, Madam Secretary." Dawson hesitated. Should he reveal his relationship with them? Could it send Atwater back into her initial conspiratorial bend when she thought Niner might actually be involved? He decided he better tread lightly. "The two professors made the papers a few years back when President Jackson targeted them for some reason. They testified before congress."

"Oh yeah, the London incident, I remember now. Didn't they also show up at the Vatican, involved somehow with the death of the Pope?"

Dawson nodded. "Professor Palmer had been kidnapped."

"Please tell me these two aren't in any way connected with the United States government, military or intelligence community."

Dawson shook his head. "Professor Acton was in the National Guard about twenty years ago but other than that, not that I'm aware of."

"Not that you're aware of." Atwater sighed. "Where have I heard that before." She paused and Dawson decided it was best to say nothing. Finally Atwater spoke. "I think it's time we leave Vietnam."

*Finally!*

"I'll arrange it immediately." He turned then paused, looking back at Atwater. "What about the two professors?"

"What about them?"

"We know they weren't involved. Shouldn't we try to help them somehow?"

"How do we know for sure?" She quickly held up her hand. "Just playing devil's advocate."

"They were in the room when the shooting happened, just like we were. They were standing in the corner between the two delegations."

"They were there?" Atwater was clearly surprised.

Dawson nodded. "Yes. When the shooting began they hit the floor and we evacuated you."

"But they were there." It was a statement which made Dawson uneasy. The tapping of her finger on her chin made him even more so. "I can see now why the Vietnamese are so sure we're involved." She sighed. "They're on their own. We need to get our personnel to safety. I'll instruct the Embassy to provide whatever assistance they can, but *we* and your friend need to get out of the country."

Dawson didn't like the answer but she was right. His responsibility was her safety and that of the delegation, not to a private citizen and a foreign national who were here under their own accord. "I'll begin the arrangements immediately. Fifteen minutes?"

Atwater nodded.

A flurry of activity instantly began as the staff executed their orders, each having a list of duties they were responsible for. As Dawson left the room equipment was already being broken down and packed. He walked down the hall to the room set up as their security center and entered. He pointed to Spock. "We're evacuating in fifteen. Tell the jet to be ready and have the cars brought around to Echo Two." He looked at Niner. "What the hell are we going to do with you?"

"Have me go in whiteface? All you honkey's look alike to us Asians."

"I always knew it," grinned Dawson. "But perhaps a disguise isn't actually that bad an idea."

Niner dropped his chin and raised his eyebrows. "Huh?"

"Not whiteface, jackass. But you're going to stick out like a sore thumb in our security detail because they're going to be watching us. Wander out like a tourist or a local and you might just blend."

Niner's head bobbed as he contemplated the idea. "I did bring some casual clothes for when I was off-duty. But what if things go haywire?"

"Make for the Embassy."

"Which is surrounded."

"Hole up until it isn't. As soon as we're off the ground we'll release that you are onboard with us and that will lighten up the security pretty quickly."

"Unless it's in place for the docs. Those two are still out there somewhere."

"True." Dawson squeezed his chin. "Atwater wants us to basically abandon the professors."

"I don't like that."

"Neither do I. They've helped us too many times for us to turn their backs on us."

"So, perhaps you're suggesting I try to meet up with them?" asked Niner with a suggestive inflection.

"Me? I'd never violate orders like that."

"Sure you wouldn't. Neither would I. But *if* I were to, hypothetically of course, run into them, where exactly might I be running into them?"

Dawson dropped into one of the seats as a team entered, beginning the dismantling of the equipment. "I have no idea." Dawson pulled out his secure phone and wrote down several phone numbers. "These are their cellphone numbers."

"Which you just happen to have."

"As soon as we got back from the museum I pulled together all their info just in case."

"Good thinking," said Spock as he stepped aside to let the crew finish their work. "But we're only doing this *if* Niner can't make it out with us."

"Yes." "No."

Dawson looked at Niner. "No?"

"No. Like you said, these two don't deserve this."

"If you get caught you'll be put on a show trial and it could lead to war." Dawson shook his head. "You'll be coming with us, understood?"

Niner peered at Dawson through narrowed eyes. "Understood? Or understood, wink-wink-nudge-nudge?"

Dawson stifled a chuckle. "The first one." He pointed at him. "I mean it." He rose as the last of the equipment was removed. He looked at Jimmy. "Make sure he gets his ass out of here."

Jimmy gave a two figured salute. "I'll beat his ass like there's no tomorrow if he tries anything."

"You know the egress route, meet us outside the security cordon, we'll stop for you. Jimmy, you drive the lead escort vehicle like planned, keep a constant connection with him and pick him up. All of our vehicles are diplomatically plated so they can't touch him once he's inside. They won't dare interfere with the motorcade. Once the vehicle is within the security perimeter of the plane he's on US soil." Dawson jerked a thumb over his shoulder. "Now go."

Niner and Jimmy left the room, Dawson and Spock following. "Let's walk the route." The hallway was still a buzz of activity. By now the eighth floor where the security staff were lodged would have been cleared, protocol dictating that they were constantly packed in the event of a quick egress. Their luggage would already have been collected and placed in front of one of the two service elevators. Since this wasn't an emergency egress, but still an unscheduled one, the majority of the equipment and luggage would be left behind for embassy staff to collect and return to Washington.

The priority here was to get the personnel and classified equipment out of the hotel and onto their airplane as quickly and efficiently as possible without a panic.

He looked at his watch.

*Five minutes.*

They would leave in two waves, the first with his team and other DSS agents, would evacuate Atwater and the senior staff—essentially anyone who could fit on the first elevator. The second wave would be larger and would be purely DSS agents providing security. They would wait until all staff had been evacuated then follow the first motorcade. The delay should be no longer than ten minutes between the two, and should it become absolutely necessary, the Secretary's plane would leave without them.

He hoped it wouldn't come to that.

The elevator chimed and he and Spock stepped on, two Vietnamese police with assault rifles standing in the rear corners. They both held up their passes and turned their backs on them, Dawson watching their reflections in the polished elevator doors just in case.

They rode in silence as the floors ticked down without any additional passengers boarding.

*Everyone is probably too terrified to leave their rooms.*

The doors opened to shouting. Dawson immediately spotted several police chasing a man in shorts and a t-shirt with ball cap and sunglasses.

*Niner!*

His comrade whipped around a column and made eye contact just as Dawson heard the distinct rattle of a weapon being moved behind him. He swung his left hand, chopping at the side of the man's neck as Spock whipped around, collapsing his man's windpipe. Dawson finished the soldier off with several rapid punches to the face, Spock's still gasping for air, his hands nowhere near his weapon. The doors began to close and Dawson turned, grabbing it just as Niner dove inside.

He hit the rear of the elevator just as gunfire erupted from the lobby. Dawson jumped back, hugging the wall as Spock did the same, Niner grabbing the gasping guard and using him as a human shield as he dropped prone on the floor. Dawson hit the button for the eighth floor then kept jamming his finger on the *Close* button as the glass in the rear shattered, shards raining down on Niner and the two police officers.

Dawson had his Glock in his hand but refrained from shooting, hoping to not make the situation worse, they hopelessly outnumbered regardless.

The doors finally began to close, the bullets now impacting the metal on the other side but none penetrating completely. He activated his comm.

"Code Red, Code Red, Code Red. We have taken fire, I repeat, we have taken fire. Secure the package and prepare for hostile assault, over." He looked at Niner as the acknowledgement came in over his earpiece, Niner pushing the now dead cop off him. "You okay?"

He nodded. "I'm having a better day than him."

The second cop groaned and Niner punched him in the face, knocking him out cold again. He leaned over and pushed the button for the fifth floor. The doors opened and he peeked out. "Not a soul." He dragged the now unconscious cop out of the elevator. "See you soon."

Dawson simply shook his head. "I assume you've got a plan?"

"Yup. I intend to blend." He motioned toward the guard's weapon that still lay on the floor of the elevator. Dawson bent over and tossed it to him. Niner snatched it and winked. "See you on the other side."

The doors closed leaving Spock and Dawson looking at each other.

The police officer moaned.

Spock looked down at the man. "Whadaya know? He's alive."

Dawson kicked the man in the head, silencing him.

*Noi Bai International Airport, Hanoi, Vietnam*

Igor Sarkov stood at the foot of the stairs, looking up as Dimitri Yashkin surveyed his surroundings from the door of the Aeroflot Airbus A320. He was younger than Sarkov by twenty years, but his squared jaw and determined, arrogant eyes suggested a throwback to the Soviet era.

*He would have fit right in.*

It was the new Russia. *Or was it the* new *new Russia?* More like the old than ever before, and those who would go far would be those who agreed with ironfisted rule from a single, central authority led by a single, charismatic leader who yearned for the glory days.

The problem was Sarkov remembered those glory days. He had spent the first almost forty years of his life living in the Soviet Union during those glory days.

And they weren't very glorious.

Their President was drinking his own Kool-Aid, as the Americans might say, believing his own propaganda about how great things once were, and how great they would be once again. The only thing that had been good before was that the Soviet Union was indeed a superpower with an arsenal that could destroy the world a dozen times over. The world respected it, and for good reason.

Because they feared it.

But for the Soviet people themselves life was anything but glorious. Food shortages, sketchy utilities, no freedoms of any kind. Why anyone would want to return to such times was beyond him. Yes things weren't perfect now, far from it. But the new Russia was less than 25 years old. It still needed to grow and develop, to learn what it truly meant to be a democracy, to have freedom of religion, speech and a free press.

Unfortunately almost none of those existed anymore thanks to their glorious President.

The new Russia was dead.

And who might resurrect it he had no clue. Unfortunately it would probably take an old Soviet style coup to actually deliver democracy back to the people, and with their new dictator shoveling money into the armed forces, he doubted deliverance would come from them.

It made him sad.

It made him look forward to retiring elsewhere soon.

He forced a smile on his face as Yashkin descended the steps. Hugs and the traditional cheek kisses were exchanged, another thing he didn't miss about Mother Russia, then they quickly climbed into the back of a waiting SUV supplied by the Embassy.

Pleasantries were pushed aside as soon as the doors closed.

"Have you arrested the American assassin yet?"

Sarkov shook his head. "No, the Americans have refused to hand him over."

"Is he still on the Secretary of State's floor at the Daewoo?"

"Yes. But some doubt has been raised as to his involvement."

"Explain."

"They're claiming his pass was stolen, and witnesses to the shooting have said the assassin was an older Vietnamese man who knew the Prime Minister, not this younger American."

"And these witnesses are these two professors you reported on earlier?"

Sarkov nodded. "Yes, Professor James Acton—"

"An American."

"—and Professor Laura Palmer."

"A British subject, married to an American, now living in the United States."

"Yes. And one Vietnamese national who says she saw nothing but I'm pretty sure she did. She even went so far as to try and steal a copy of the camera footage from the museum to prove their story."

"And you arrested her?"

"Yes, but she escaped."

Yashkin's head dropped slightly as he expressed his surprised outrage. "Explain." The single word was delivered as hard as any Sarkov had ever heard. He almost shivered with the memories it brought back.

"According to the Vietnamese Police a dozen men on motorcycles assaulted the officers escorting the suspect to the police station. Several were hurt in the attack. They fought valiantly but there were only four of them and a dozen attackers with automatic weapons."

Yashkin grunted. "More likely there were half a dozen men, few weapons, and these police officers are telling a tall tale to cover their collective behinds."

Sarkov had to admit it appeared Yashkin had a firm grip on how any story from the Vietnamese authorities should be interpreted.

"These professors. I've read their dossiers. They're clearly involved."

Sarkov indicated his disagreement with a tilt of the head and a bounce of the eyebrows. "Perhaps, but I don't think so."

"You *have* read their files, haven't you?"

"Of course. I admit they are colorful, but having met them, I get the distinct impression they are simply what they are—unlucky."

"You are naïve, Comrade."

Sarkov bristled at the word. *Comrade!* This man was definitely yearning for yesteryear. He hadn't heard the word used in years, the mere thought of it bringing back the sickening feelings of decades ago. The traditional greeting of Party members to each other, or those who wanted to look good when they thought they were under surveillance.

*Tovarishch. Comrade.*

It hadn't been nearly as common as Hollywood would have you believe, though it was all too common, there being millions in the Communist Party and the military who used it habitually.

And here this young Kremlin stooge would dare use it on him.

His displeasure clearly had registered with Yashkin.

"You are offended?"

Sarkov caught himself, knowing full well how he handled himself over the next few days, perhaps hours, would determine if he retired in peace like he had planned, or met his maker far sooner than intended. "Not at all. But we need to examine the footage before we jump to conclusions like the Vietnamese did."

"Have you seen it?"

Sarkov nodded. "Yes, but there's only a camera at the front entrance. We can see the man enter who used the pass but it is of poor quality."

"Does he at least meet the description?"

Sarkov shrugged. "He was Asian, male, that's about it. I've asked the embassy to send it to Moscow for enhancement. But like I said, I think these professors are telling the truth."

"I will want to speak to them."

"We don't know where they are. The Vietnamese have ordered their arrest for involvement in the escape of their citizen from police custody, but they managed to escape."

"So they are definitely involved then."

Sarkov pursed his lips. "I wouldn't want to be arrested by the Vietnamese any more than I'm sure they would. If I were them I'd be trying to get to either the American or British embassies."

"Have they tried?"

"They might have, but the Vietnamese authorities organized protests around both embassies so they've been cordoned off. I doubt they'd be able to get anywhere near either building."

"I want people put on all Western embassies plus other traditional allies. Australia, Japan. All of them. The Americans are liable to swing some sort of deal to hide their accomplices."

"I already sent the order immediately after their escape."

Yashkin smiled broadly. "Good work, Comrade! Perhaps we think alike after all."

*That I sincerely doubt.*

"Now that the professors have nowhere to go, they will get desperate. They will stick out among a sea of Vietnamese and soon be arrested." He lowered his voice. "You should know, I am under direct orders from Moscow to make certain that the story of the American assassin sticks. Any evidence that shows otherwise is to be destroyed or eliminated."

"Including people?"

"Especially people. We must recover the escaped Vietnamese witness, destroy the video evidence from the museum if it doesn't show what we need, and eliminate the professors before they can talk to their own officials." He jabbed the air with his forefinger. "There can be no dissenting voices."

"But what of the truth?"

Yashkin tossed his head back. "So you *are* naïve." He shook his head as if pitying Sarkov. "My dear old man, there is no such thing as the truth, only the story. The story here is that an American on the Secretary of State's security detail, with the assistance of at least one American, one British and one Vietnamese national, assassinated the Prime Minister and his security detail in cold blood, then was given the protection of his government from immediate prosecution." Yashkin almost looked like he wanted to rub his hands together in glee. "The public relations coup this will bring is immense. The sympathy at the UN is already unprecedented. Almost every country has expressed their condolences and over one hundred have condemned the United States for their involvement or lack of cooperation."

"Mostly Arab and African countries, I would assume."

"Yes, but it's the optics. So many in the West believe the UN is an institution that is of value because they think it is made up of countries like theirs. They can't fathom the fact that only eighty-seven of the hundred-ninety-three countries are actually democracies. When the news reports that the majority on the Security Council or in the Assembly passed resolutions condemning the United States, they have no idea it's simply a bunch of dictators and theocracies pushing their own agenda. The United Nations is like the useful idiot that serves its purpose on days like today."

They pulled up to the Daewoo Hanoi hotel, a complete cordon of security now in place.

"I assume you're going to want to interview the suspect?"

"You should get in the habit of calling him the 'assassin'. And yes." He smiled as he looked toward the entrance. "Good. I see they received their orders."

Sarkov looked and his jaw dropped as he watched at least a platoon's worth of Vietnamese soldiers decked out in assault gear disappear into the main lobby.

*Daewoo Hanoi Hotel, Hanoi, Vietnam*
*Fifth floor*

Niner grabbed the guard and tossed him over his shoulders in a fireman's carry. He rushed toward the end of the hall and where he knew the service elevator was on each floor. And privacy. Kicking open the door, having no time to bother with security passes, he dumped the man on the floor and quickly undressed him. Pulling his own sneakers, shirt and shorts off, he hiked on the man's pants and zipped them up.

He cursed.

They were about four inches too short.

He cringed for a moment at the thought of putting the man's socks on but he had no choice otherwise he'd be sporting bare ankles and too much calf. Slipping on the socks, he shoved his feet into the man's shoes.

It wasn't happening.

He removed the laces and pushed his toes in as far as he could, shoving the rear of the shoe down with his heel. Using the shoelaces, he tied the shoe around the middle, strapping them to his feet. The man's shirt fit just as poorly but it was short sleeved making it a little less obvious, and one thing he had noticed since being in Vietnam, the uniforms were always very baggy.

He placed the man's hat on his head, rolled up his own clothes into as tight a roll around his sneakers as he could and tucked it under his arm, parallel to his forearm. Shouldering the local variant of an AKM assault rifle he hogtied the still unconscious man with some sheets from a laundry basket, dumped him inside, then stepped into the hallway, making for the stairwell.

Boots were pounding on the steps below. He looked over the railing and could see black-clad troops, possibly SWAT or Vietnamese Special Forces, rounding the second floor. He looked up and saw a familiar face looking down from the eighth.

He didn't acknowledge it.

Stepping back through the stairwell door he took up a position to the side of the door, out of view of the elevators.

And listened.

He glanced down at his highwaters, the too short pants looking ridiculous.

*I look like Spaz doing the Poindexter dance.*

He smiled at the memory of his late buddy, killed the first time he had encountered Professor Acton. Killed by Professor Acton. He didn't blame the professor, not anymore—he was simply defending himself against the Bravo Team who were sent to kill him under orders they now knew were illegal. Acton and his students weren't domestic terrorists like they were told.

They were innocent.

The team had been torn up for some time after they found out the truth. Dawson had taken it the hardest. He had known from the beginning something just didn't feel right so had taken it upon himself to do most of the dirty work so the others wouldn't have to live with the consequences.

It was something they never spoke about.

Not to their wives, girlfriends, shrinks or brothers-in-arms.

They just tried to make up for it every day.

Which was why he had such strong feelings about helping the professors now. He and Jimmy had decided it was best that he leave alone, being spotted with a pasty white American would be too easy. Jimmy was to act as his spotter from the eighth floor window if he should make it out, but he had lost his comm in the excitement down in the lobby where he had been spotted and challenged almost instantly.

He was on his own.

Just like the professors.

Boots pounded past the stairwell door and he waited a few seconds before peeking through the small glass window. He could see shadows moving above and nothing below but it was hard to tell. He opened the door and cocked an ear. Shouting erupted above, some in English, ordering the approaching force to stand down as additional boots began their ascent.

Niner glanced down and saw they were still on the first level. He rushed down the stairs, two at a time, his pace hindered by the makeshift shoes he was wearing. He cleared the fourth level containing the Russian delegation and decided to chance the third. Leaping over the railing to the next flight, he pushed through the third level door just as the next wave of troops rounded the bend.

And found himself face-to-face with two Vietnamese police officers.

He flicked the butt of the AKM upward, catching the first on the chin, knocking him to the floor, then spun around, swinging his cocked elbow at the other, catching him on the side of the head. He finished him off with a quick blow to the temple with the rifle, then pressed his shoe into the other man's neck, slowly cutting off the oxygen to his brain.

He let up as soon as the man was out.

*No need to kill anybody unnecessarily.*

He pulled the two unconscious men away from the door and noticed one of them was taller than the other. He pulled a shoe off and stepped beside it.

*Shazam! I got me some kicks!*

He yanked off his makeshift shoes and pushed his feet in the much better fitting new ones, his toes still scrunched, but at least inside completely.

There was no time for pants.

He approached the stairwell door again just as gunfire erupted, the distinct sound of AKM's and AK-47's echoing through the confined space.

Glocks and MP5's responded.

A scurry of green uniforms, regular police, rushed back down the stairs. He stepped out into the stairwell after the last passed and quickly descended the stairs behind the cowards, soon reaching the main floor. The lemmings burst through the door leading to the main lobby but Niner turned and headed out another door that led to the rear of the building, a tense standoff developing as the gunfire from above could just be heard outside. The DSS agents guarding the motorcade vehicles had their weapons drawn, pointing them at the confused police who had their own guns aimed at the American security detail.

*If someone doesn't get a handle on this, a lot of people are going to die.*

And he knew they'd mostly be his own people.

He skirted the edge, behind the uncertain police officers, knowing there was nothing he could do here to help the outnumbered DSS agents. The best thing he could do would be to escape the premises and somehow get back home. He had a funny feeling that there was no way he'd be meeting the motorcade in the next five minutes.

He just hoped the situation would end in a stalemate soon.

And his buddies survived.

*Near the British Embassy, Hanoi, Vietnam*

Laura and Acton waited, trying to be as inconspicuous as possible, but with little success. They kept getting looked at, the chanting just around the corner still loud, attracting more and more onlookers as the minutes ticked by.

The conversation had been short. She had dialed Mai's brother's number, still in her purse, and was relieved to hear the young woman's voice on the other end.

"Are you okay?"

"Yes," Mai had replied. "It was my idiot brother who rescued me."

"We just may need his help too."

"Why, what has happened?"

"We're wanted fugitives. They're claiming we helped you escape."

"But that's not true!"

"No, but they don't care about the truth. Both embassies are surrounded by police and protesters. We can't go back to the hotel for the same reason."

"I'll send my brother to get you. Where are you?"

James had been leaning in, listening to the conversation and held up his phone with the Google Map of the area. She gave Mai the street address.

"Someone will be there to pick you up as soon as possible."

The call had ended leaving the two of them waiting with plenty of time to wonder in silence, English probably not the best language to be speaking out loud right now. Even James though couldn't hold his tongue at the sight that came slowly down the street. Two men were pushing a Jaguar

XK-8 Cabriolet, its engine still steaming with what looked like a high-priced call girl steering. James pulled out his phone and began taping it.

"It's a wonder he can afford her what with all the repair bills."

"You're sending that to Hugh, aren't you?"

He grinned at her. "Am I that predictable?"

Laura shook her head, smiling as they watched the broken down vehicle slowly make the next left turn, eventually pushed out of sight.

The sound of a motorcycle engine caught Laura's attention. It was distinctly different from the others, this one clearly driven by someone in a hurry. Then the sound changed, her ear discerning a second engine as they neared.

"I think our rides are arriving," observed James, nodding down the street.

"Lovely."

"You were expecting a limo?"

"I don't know what I was expecting. Can we trust these people?"

Laura shrugged. "We can trust Mai, I think, but her brother? I don't know."

"He could turn us in for a reward."

"He could," agreed Laura. "But at least that might be a controlled situation. Right now we're liable to get shot by some trigger happy street cop."

Two men pulled up to the curb, their heads covered by helmets, their visors down. The first one flipped his up. "You professors?"

James nodded. "Did Mai send you?"

"Yes." He jerked his thumb toward a car that pulled up behind them. "Back seat, now!"

Laura looked down the street and saw two police officers looking their way. "James, look."

James followed her stare and cursed. "No time like the present." They climbed into the rear of the car as the motorcycles pulled away, the car following, Laura stunned it could actually still drive, it having more square inches of dents than smooth metal. Smoke churned out the tailpipe as oil was burnt at an alarming rate while the engine roared from a faulty muffler.

"Definitely not a limo," she muttered, James squeezing her leg. She looked at the police officers, one of whom was now pointing, the other on his radio, shouting. A siren behind them had her driver looking back and shouting something in Vietnamese that she assumed was a curse.

He jerked the car to the right, around the corner just as they both yelled, 'No! Not that way!"

The driver cursed again as the two motorcycles suddenly turned around, the massive crowd, protesting in front of the embassy, blocking both directions just ahead. Shouts could be heard from the two police officers now chasing them on foot as the driver eased off the gas, his head desperately looking left and right, wondering where to go.

"You've got to turn around!" shouted James, the crowd now taking notice, the police shouting something and pointing.

"What are they saying?" asked Laura.

"American! American!" translated the driver as he came to a halt, indecision ruling him. Suddenly the crowd swarmed them, pounding on the car. James leapt over and slammed down the door locks as they all rolled up their windows. The car jerked forward as their driver lay on the horn, but the crowd refused to give. The pounding became rhythmic, like a drum beat, as the 'Yankee go home!' chant, not present only moments before, became deafening, each word punctuated with a slam on the car.

Laura's window shattered and she screamed, pushing back from it toward James, whose fist darted out, bloodying the nose of the man who was unfortunate enough to push his head inside, reaching for her. Several more jabs to the face and the man was trying to get out but James held him in place, obviously figuring a bloodied, under control man blocking the window was better than some unknown.

Gunfire rang out and the crowd screamed, scattering away from their car. The whine of motorcycle engines was suddenly heard over the mob and the lead motorcycle pulled up beside them.

"Get out!" yelled the man. James opened his door, pulling Laura out after him then helped her onto the back of the first motorcycle. He jumped on the back of the second as the car pulled away, making a U-turn and blasting past the police officers causing them to dive out of the way.

Laura's motorcyclist gunned the engine, peeling away before she even had a chance to grab on. She looked over her shoulder and breathed a sigh of relief as she saw her husband's ride shoot after them.

They rushed up between the lanes of traffic, easily doing three or four times the speed of the slow traffic, leaving the chanting mob behind. Her heart was slamming into her chest and she wondered for a moment what had happened to their driver, there no way he could follow them in this traffic.

*Hopefully he gets away.*

After wincing in anticipation of a collision for the umpteenth time she decided she was better off closing her eyes and holding on.

Only to find it was more terrifying that way.

She opened her eyes and looked back to see James' bike close behind and a motorcycle cop gaining. Her driver must have noticed as well, gunning the engine even harder toward a red light, the opposing traffic still crisscrossing the intersection.

She screamed.

The light changed, the stragglers clearing just as they entered the intersection leaving them on almost open road for about a quarter mile where they really opened up. A quick glance back resulted in a sigh of relief as she saw James on their tail, the motorcycle cop cut off by the flow of traffic.

"Hang on!" yelled her driver and she gripped him around his waist, tight. They banked sharply to the right, into an alleyway, the high pitched whine of the engines echoing through the confined space as they blasted through the tight quarters, both motorcyclists hitting their horns to try and clear any pedestrians out of the way. Suddenly the rear brakes were locked up in a puff of smoke, a hard turn to the left almost toppling Laura from the bike. Several more repeats of this maneuver had Laura swearing off motorcycles for life.

She looked back at James then ahead.

And gasped.

They were racing full speed to what appeared to be a garage door in an old industrial building. Three honks of the horn and with less than a hundred yards to go the door rolled up, two men revealed yanking chains on either side of the rollup door. They burst through, both ducking, the brakes locking up again, her journey ending with a skid just before a pile of empty crates, the other bike sliding up beside them as the rattle of the garage door closing cut off the outside sunlight.

They were in the dark.

Lights flickered on and Laura remained on the bike, shaking.

"Are you okay?"

She looked toward the voice and saw Mai rushing up to them, a concerned look on her face.

Laura nodded and climbed off the bike, embracing Mai then James. Mai motioned toward the man who had driven her. "This is my brother, Cadeo."

The man nodded at her as he removed his helmet.

She looked into his eyes for the first time, and a chill raced up her spine as she suddenly realized he was the man that had shot at her. James realized it at well, jabbing a finger at him. "What the hell was the idea, shooting at my wife?"

Cadeo looked at James with disdain. "I'm sorry I missed."

She placed a hand gently on her husband's chest as he advanced on Cadeo, the sound of weapons being needlessly cocked all around them. "I'm sure he doesn't mean it, otherwise he wouldn't have helped rescue us." She turned to Mai, hoping she might defuse the situation. "Thank you for helping."

"No problem." Mai looked at Cadeo. "Thank you, Cadeo, for getting my friends."

Cadeo grunted and walked away, dropping on a threadbare couch parked in front of a large plasma television, two of his "gang" playing a split screen game of Grand Theft Auto. He grabbed the remote control and surprisingly put on CNN.

"What's the latest?" asked James, turning to Mai.

Mai pointed toward the television with her chin. "Look for yourself."

Laura turned and gasped at the headline.

*Vietnamese Forces Assaulting Secretary of State's Hotel.*

*Daewoo Hanoi Hotel, Hanoi, Vietnam*
*Eighth floor*

Scattered unaimed bullets tore at the underside of the stairs Dawson was standing on, a single round making it through the gap and tearing a hole in the concrete leading to the ninth floor. He fired three more rounds into the floor of the flight below, shards of concrete spraying in all directions, powdered rock clouding the steps.

It continued to keep their attackers at bay.

Atwater and her team were working the phones trying to get the assault stopped, the 7th Fleet already steaming toward Hanoi, jets already in the air from the USS George Washington in a show of force. It had been fifteen minutes since the Vietnamese had begun shooting. One of the DSS agents had been wounded in the leg in the initial unexpected volley, but since then, nothing but close calls. He had immediately issued orders for suppression fire only unless they reached the landing below the eighth floor. So far the assault had been halted at both ends of the floor.

They had lost contact with Niner but the DSS agent who had been shot said he thought he had caught a glimpse of him several floors below wearing a Vietnamese police uniform.

It made sense.

Niner had obviously put the officer he had dragged out of the elevator to good use. He just wished he knew that he was safely off the grounds. He was assuming he was, otherwise the assault would have most likely been stopped, their target captured.

Another burst from an AKM had he and the others hugging the wall, Spock leaning out as soon as the shooter stopped to reload, firing three rapid rounds, the thunder of the shots almost overwhelming in the tight space.

Heavy gunfire from the other end of the hallway caught his attention. He activated his comm.

"West stairwell, status."

"Taking heavy fire!" came Jimmy's reply. "Request permission to repel!"

"Permission granted."

Bursts of MP5 and Glock rounds, distinctly different from the AK's they were facing, overwhelmed all other sounds as Dawson shot a glance down the hallway, the doors at both ends held open in case the men in the stairwells had to retreat quickly. So far the assault was only from below, but he had deployed men to the tenth floor as well just in case, and they were hijacking the elevators as they passed, the Vietnamese not thinking to shut them down. Right now all but two had been stopped on the eighth or ninth floors, their doors jammed open to prevent the elevator cars from moving.

A disturbingly familiar sound, metal bouncing on concrete had him whipping back around, his eyes immediately spotting the grenade that had just been tossed, hitting the landing they were standing on. He grabbed one DSS agent by the suit jacket, throwing him back into the hallway as the others all turned away from the impending blast.

But not Spock. As Dawson lunged toward the grenade Spock was way ahead of him, and with the swiftness and accuracy of David Beckham, he kicked the grenade, still bouncing in midair, back down the stairs, the tiny orb of fury sent toward the landing between their floor and the one below.

Dawson reached out and grabbed the slightly off balance Spock as the follow-through prevented him from retreating quickly enough, the grenade still able to spit its deadly shrapnel directly at him. Dawson yanked with all his might, pulling Spock toward him then launching himself backward with a bend then shove of his knees. As the two sailed through the air toward the door, the grenade detonated. Shrapnel raced in every direction, shredding the walls and steps, the concrete shards resulting in even more deadly material desperately seeking flesh to mutilate.

Dawson landed on his back, hard, the shockwave blasting over them as he closed his eyes tight, there nothing he could do about his exposed ears, the comm in one protecting him slightly. Powerful hands grabbed him by the vest, pulling him through the door and into the hallway as four DSS agents rushed forward to replace the now disoriented men.

Spock rolled off him and hit the floor groaning as Dawson lay stunned for a moment.

"Are you okay?"

It was a DSS agent leaning over him, shouting the words, words that sounded a thousand miles away. Words that weren't registering.

Reality kicked back in though his ears were still ringing. He nodded to the DSS agent then rolled toward Spock to find him lying on his back, facing him. "Are you okay?"

Spock pushed himself up on his elbows and paused for a moment as he did a self-assessment.

"I'll live."

The DSS agent pulled Dawson to his feet then Spock. "You sure you two are okay."

"We're good," replied Dawson, brushing himself off, both of them sporting a good covering of pulverized concrete. Dawson activated his comm. "West stairwell, report."

"Attack repelled, one casualty, she'll live," replied Jimmy. "We're pressing our advantage, pushing them back two levels, over."

"Roger that. Hold at the seventh floor, we don't want them getting in behind you, over."

"Holding on seven, out."

"We've got troop transports arriving at the front!" yelled a DSS agent over the comm. "Looks like a company of heavily armed troops!"

Dawson looked at Spock as they returned to the stairwell, the DSS agents now a floor below them. Spock frowned. "We're two dozen. There's no way we're holding off a company."

"You can put a thousand men in a stairwell. They're no more effective than the two guys in the lead. Our problem is ammo. Their problem is willingness to die."

They began to descend the stairs. "Enough grenades and we're done for. We got lucky."

"Thanks to your soccer skills."

"Nothing like the one you batted with the stock of your MP5 last year."

"That's different, that was baseball, my sport. I've never seen you kick a soccer ball before." Dawson eyed the large amount of blood splattered on the walls and floor at the landing for the seventh floor. Clearly those who had thrown the grenade hadn't been as lucky as he and Spock. "Besides, I got damned lucky on that one. If the guy had done a proper count I'd have been ground beef."

They reached the landing with four DSS agents, guns aimed down at the next flight, sporadic gunfire being sprayed blindly up, the miscue on the grenade seeming to have taken some of the fight out of their opponents, a bloody trail where a body had been dragged down the stairs a stark crimson reminder of just how lucky they had all been that Spock was on the ball.

A DSS agent squeezed the trigger of his MP5 sending a short burst of lead down to the next landing. Dozens of sets of boots could be heard rushing up the stairs from below as the new arrivals flooded the stairwell. Dawson activated his comm. "Prepare for assault. Reinforcements have arrived. If we have to fall back retreat to the ninth floor. Send a two man team to check out the upper levels then the roof. Control, contact the

George Washington and see if there's any chance of getting a chopper here to evac the Secretary, out."

Dawson holstered his Glock and motioned for one of the agents to hand him their MP5. He checked the weapon as Spock switched as well. "I'll take point, you stay back. You take over while I'm reloading. We'll pile the bodies if we have to. We're not losing the Secretary on my watch." He pointed at the four DSS agents with them. "As we advance past the bodies, relieve them of weapons and ammo. Let us know if they've got grenades. Those could be the great equalizer."

"Yes, sir," they echoed, clearly nervous. Dawson didn't blame them. This wasn't like anything they had ever experienced. They were security guards. Best damned trained security guards in the world, but they were never meant for all-out war like this.

"Here they come," announced Spock as a roar of false bravado erupted from below, boots pounding on the concrete as they rounded the landing. They were firing blindly and Dawson smiled as he saw they were only two abreast as he had predicted. He raised his MP5 and squeezed off two rounds, taking the lead two men out by shooting them in the legs. Cries rang out as they collapsed back on the men behind.

*One wounded man takes two to carry, taking three out of the fight.*

Those behind tried to climb over them, the weapons fire halted. Dawson heard gunfire from the other side of the building and Jimmy's voice came in over the comm. "Holding on seventh, they've begun their assault."

"Take them out," ordered Dawson.

"Roger that."

Dawson shot the next two, one of them dead.

The men behind were now trying to pull their fallen comrades to safety while more stumbled over the bodies attempting to execute their orders to advance. Cries of pain with shouts of anger and confusion and the occasional gunshot echoed through the stairwell. Dawson fired several more rounds, the thirty-round magazine quickly getting used up.

*Too bad we didn't have 100 round C-MAGs.*

He rushed down to the next flight, pressing their momentary advantage, sending off bursts of two and three rounds at a time, their adversary starting to retreat. One of the soldiers, almost a full flight behind, a Captain if Dawson wasn't mistaken by his insignia, glared up at Dawson then pulled the pin on a grenade.

Dawson put a hole in his chest.

The man dropped, the grenade falling from his dying hand.

"Fire in the hole!" yelled Dawson, jumping back against the wall and covering his ears, closing his eyes. The shouts and screams as the men below realized what had happened became muffled then were quickly replaced by the deafening roar of the explosion. Dawson checked his men then looked back down at the carnage below.

It was a mess.

Blood and body parts were everywhere, the confined space shredding those around the lethal weapon. Moans and cries filled his ears as Dawson advanced, Spock and the other DSS agents following. He pointed at two of them then the seventh level doors. They held back to cover them just in case Jimmy's team failed in their efforts.

As they pushed forward panic set in below. Those they could see were all turned now, pushing back against the crowd farther down still trying to advance. As more realized what was happening, encouraged by Dawson sending a burst of gunfire every five to ten seconds into the walls behind them, the tide quickly turned, the group no longer a threat.

Dawson stopped on the fifth floor, the attacking force now well below them, at least a dozen bodies left behind. He pointed. "Strip them of any weapons and ammo. This might not be over." He listened for a moment and could hear nothing from the other end of the floor. Activating his comm, he opened the fifth floor door, looking down the hallway. "West stairwell, report."

"All calm on the western front," replied Jimmy. "They've retreated beyond the fourth floor, still retreating. I get the impression though it wasn't as much us as it was them being ordered back."

"Roger that, return to the eighth floor, police any weapons and ammo that might have been left behind."

"Roger that."

The DSS agents and Spock finished stripping the bodies of weapons and ammo, a decent haul including a few grenades. Enough to add at least a few more minutes of resistance should it become necessary.

But judging from what he could see below, that resistance might not be necessary for some while, the sounds of the last boots going silent as the door at the main level clicked shut, returning them to an eerie quiet.

Somebody moaned.

Dawson looked over at one of the bodies, not quite dead yet. He motioned to Spock. "Check him out."

Spock knelt beside the now conscious man and checked him over. "Sucking chest wound," he said. "He's lost a lot of blood. He won't make it unless he gets immediate help."

Dawson frowned, pulling out his phone. "Time for an olive branch." He hit the speed dial for the hotel security booth.

The phone was answered on the first ring, the initial words Vietnamese, followed by English. "Hotel Security, Bao speaking."

"This is Special Agent White of Secretary Atwater's security detail. Put me through to whoever is in charge down there."

"Y-yes, sir."

There was some clicking then a man's voice, deep and thickly accented, answered. "This is Dimitri Yashkin of the Russian Foreign Ministry. To whom am I speaking?"

"Special Agent White, DSS."

"Are you prepared to surrender?"

Dawson smiled. "I was about to ask you the same thing, sir. I have a wounded man—"

"We will be happy to provide medical attention to all of your wounded—"

"One of *your* men, not ours. By my count we also have about a dozen dead here, all your men. We have returned to our positions and will not fire upon medical personnel who retrieve the dead and wounded, as long as they are unarmed."

"You will be held responsible for any deaths that occurred here today."

"Considering it was your men that attacked us with guns and grenades, I think not. We were merely defending ourselves." Dawson paused, deciding to give the man a diplomatic out that he could take whether or not he was guilty. "Sir, I'm willing to bet that you did not order this attack and that it was someone on the Vietnamese side of things. We are prepared to evacuate our personnel and equipment and return to the United States immediately, as is our right under international law. Are you going to let us exercise this right, or continue to deny it to us as your Vietnamese counterpart has done?"

"I cannot let you go until the assassin has been handed over."

"Sir, Agent Green is innocent of the crime you have accused him of, however I am under orders to cooperate fully, so I will tell you this. Agent Green is no longer on the premises, and hasn't been for some time."

"What?!"

The man was clearly surprised by the revelation and immediately the line went silent as he was placed on hold. Dawson heard an update through the comm that the upper floors and roof were clear and that a helicopter rescue wasn't in the cards. He had doubted it, but it was worth the call. It also conveyed a message to Washington about how desperate the situation actually was.

The phone line clicked.

"We will be sending in medical teams now."

"Unarmed."

"Unarmed. I also request a meeting with your Secretary Atwater."

"I will try to arrange it. I will call you back shortly."

The line went dead and Dawson took the stairs two at a time to the ninth floor, jogging down the hallway to Atwater's suite. He entered the large multi-roomed suite to find all the windows blacked out as per protocol, the senior staff, including Atwater herself, located outside the direct line of sight of any window or door.

"Are you okay, Madame Secretary?"

The woman clearly wasn't, her face red, her eyes wide with fear. But to her credit she hadn't lost it yet, though her white knuckles as she gripped the arms of the chair she was sitting on suggested she was close.

"What-the-hell-is-going-on?" she managed, each word punctuated with a gasp for air.

"Vietnamese troops assaulted both stairwells simultaneously. We repelled both attacks successfully and they have since withdrawn. I have established a dialogue with a Russian Foreign Ministry representative—"

"The one from before? Sarkov was it?"

Dawson shook his head. "No, I'm suspecting this is the senior man Mr. Sarkov referred to. He demanded we handover Agent Green but—"

"I don't see how we have much choice."

"We don't, ma'am. He's no longer on the premises."

Atwater's eyebrows shot up, her eyes opening even wider. "Excuse me?"

"He managed to escape just before the attack began. I haven't established contact with him yet, however the fact the attack continued for as long as it did suggests he made a clean escape."

"Why the hell would he run? It just makes him look even more guilty!"

"Keeping in mind he isn't guilty."

Atwater caught herself. "Of course, of course. But still, the optics!"

"I ordered him to effect an escape and meet us if possible on our evac route. If not, to make his way to the embassy when things cooled down." He could see Atwater was about to blow a gasket. "By getting him off the premises and separating him from you, there should no longer be any reason for them to try and hold us here." He lowered his voice. "Ma'am, based upon what just happened, there was no way they were going to let us leave with him. We can now let them confirm he's gone then leave. There's no way they'll risk furthering this incident when their prime suspect isn't even here anymore."

"And what are we going to tell them? Are we just going to say he ran away?"

"Not at all. As you said, that would just make him look guilty. We'll tell them that I ordered him to leave the hotel so we could evacuate you, and to get to the embassy immediately. He left under orders given to him by your head of security, unknown to you. You were shocked to hear this—"

"I am!"

"—and you didn't authorize his departure, but now that he has left, you and your team will be leaving, promising full cooperation in the investigation and access to Agent Green when he arrives at the American Embassy."

"You've really thought this out, haven't you, Agent?"

Dawson smiled slightly. "Experience, ma'am. This is what we're trained for. Now, Mr. Dimitri Yashkin would like to meet with you. I suggest we do so in about ten minutes. That will give us a few minutes to regroup and finalize our prep for evac, and give Mr. Green some additional time to escape, though I have no doubt that every cop in the city is now looking for him."

"He better get to the embassy quickly."

Dawson shook his head. "If I know him, he'll be nowhere near it."

*Kentucky Fried Chicken, Nguyen Thai Hoc Street, Hanoi, Vietnam*

Niner marched into the ground floor of a three story building, the large red KFC logo shocking the hell out of him until he remembered his briefing. Fast food joints were popping up everywhere in Vietnam, including the biggies like McDonalds. KFC had actually been one of the first in 1997.

He eyed the menu as his stomach grumbled from the smell. It reminded him of home. Growing up he used to bike past the local KFC, swearing they intentionally pumped the delicious smell of deep fried chicken to the outside just to lure people in. It drove his mother nuts every time they rode past the place, his young nostrils catching a waft, immediately triggering the required, "Can we, Mom, can we get some?"

Too often she had spoiled him.

Fortunately he was blessed with the skinny gene so was able to indulge in the finer points of American cuisine when he was younger, and now as an adult, training constantly, he had no clue if he was still blessed, or just burned off every damned calorie he got near. His eating habits were shit, fast food and pizza the order of the day, but when you lived a job that might kill you tomorrow, the saturated fat content of a meal enjoyed today meant little.

Besides, his cholesterol was fine and his doctor had let him in on a little secret—they really had no clue whether dietary cholesterol was important or not, since the body produced the vast majority of it.

He chose to ignore it all. As part of the job they were monitored constantly, bloodwork being taken all the time just in case they had been exposed to something while on assignment. He didn't do drugs, drank like a fish when it was appropriate to do so, and ate what he wanted.

And today his stomach was telling him it wanted KFC.

Too bad he'd only be seeing the inside of their bathroom.

*Which is where?*

He spotted the universal blue sign pointing up a set of stairs and stood almost bewildered as he watched the customers who had just placed and paid for their orders climb the same stairs. He followed, most giving him a wide berth and avoiding eye contact, the AKM still slung over his shoulder. Reaching the top he saw a dining area where there appeared to be a large number of disgruntled customers waiting for the food that they were apparently supposed to pick up here.

And a group of teenage staff playing what appeared to be tag.

*Corporate should hear about this.*

The arrows pointed him to the third level and he climbed some more steps, soon finding the bathroom on the top floor. He prepared himself for disgusting but was pleasantly surprised at how clean they were, especially by Third World standards. He had been on assignment in the Middle East and South Asia enough to know that the dirty water bucket beside the hole in the ground was for rinsing off your left fingers.

Here there was modern plumbing.

He locked himself in the far stall, stripping out of the police uniform and donning his Hawaiian shirt, Bermuda shorts and sneakers. He rolled up the uniform, removed the bullets and firing pin from the AKM, then making sure he was alone, stuffed them all above the tiles in the drop ceiling. He tucked his Glock behind his back, the shirt covering it, then took care of some overdue business while flicking through his phone contacts.

He decided his best bet would be to reach out via text rather than voice. Selecting Professor Acton's number, he sent a quick text.

*this is niner. contact me asap.*

He waited.

And waited.

Then he grew concerned.

*Old Quarter, Hanoi, Vietnam*

Phong woke, still curled in a ball, the sounds of ceremonial drums beating rhythmically on the street below waking him. He looked at the ancient alarm clock sitting on the floor by his bed. It was barely evening, the sun still casting a gentle glow through the dirty window. He sat up, wiping his eyes with his knuckles, moistening his teeth with his tongue.

*They're starting early.*

The drums and the festive sounds of happy revelers wafted through the half open window, and as he realized he had finally avenged his loved ones, he decided it was time to celebrate. He stepped behind the only wall outside of the four framing his one room flat and used the toilet he considered himself lucky to have. Showers in his building was shared, but he was fortunate to be allowed to do so at the beginning and end of his shift at the hotel, management wanting their staff to be clean and well groomed.

They even supplied the soap and antiperspirant, a concoction he had never heard of until getting his job.

Now he couldn't live without it.

He now found the pungent smell of body odor almost unbearable, and almost felt ashamed that he had gone through more than half his life smelling the same way. But with too many of his neighbors poorer than he, it just wasn't something brought up in polite company.

He washed his hands and face, straightened his hair and checked his clothes.

His heart almost stopped.

There was blood on the front of his shirt, as if he had been sprayed by it. He quickly pulled it off and his mind raced along with his heart as he wondered if anyone could have seen it before he got home. He began to rinse it out in the sink, the dried blood quickly coloring the water, thankfully most of it washing out, but he knew he'd have to get rid of it.

He frowned.

It was his best shirt. His only dress shirt. And it had been more expensive than any other shirt he had ever bought. He could count on one hand how many times he had worn it. During the day he wore the clothes supplied by the hotel, far nicer than anything he could justify, then in the evenings and his days off he wore simple, cheap but respectable clothes. He took pride in his appearance, never wearing dirty or overly worn clothing, but he didn't believe in dressing to impress when outside of the work place.

He was a lonely man who led a lonely existence. What had happened to him as a boy had stained his entire life, avoiding any type of relationship that might lead to an attachment that would break his heart should it end.

He couldn't, he wouldn't, go through that pain again.

*There's nothing worse than loss.*

The pain of loneliness, of seeing everyone around him eventually meet people, get married, have children, have someone to talk to at night, was nothing compared to the loss of that day, of knowing you would never see the ones you loved again.

His heartache was still fresh, as if it had happened just yesterday.

It did feel raw, more than usual, and he attributed that to all of the memories flooding back the moment he had spotted Petrov. His head dropped, his shoulders sagged and he gripped either side of the sink, a flurry of sobs racking his body for several seconds before he held his breath, stopping himself. He lifted his head and looked in the cracked mirror.

He looked old.

As if he had aged another ten years since yesterday.

And he felt old.

He was exhausted.

It was a mental exhaustion, not a physical one, and he realized that almost forty years of obsession had consumed his life. The first few years, when he had left the village to live with cousins in the next valley, he had been commanded by hatred, but he had eventually let most of that go, realizing there was nothing he could do about it, though he allowed it to continue simmering, preventing almost any joy from permeating the thick crust he had allowed to incase his heart.

It had been a lonely life.

But now his promise was fulfilled.

He had his revenge.

And he could die now in peace, knowing that his family, friends and lineage had been avenged, no matter how contrary to the teachings of the Buddha his act had been.

He was willing to be punished after his passing, to endure the demons and the suffering, to come out the other end a lesser form, but with a chance at redemption in a later life.

For he had no illusions that nirvana was his fate, not in this life. He knew the rest of his life would be tortured with the memories of today, just as it had been tortured by the memories of a teenage boy, helpless against grown men.

He looked into his red eyes, tired eyes.

*It's time to move on.*

It had been said to him a thousand times by his cousins, so much so that when he had the first opportunity he had left them behind, leaving his adopted village and moving to the newly renamed Ho Chi Minh City. A few years later, in his early twenties, he had moved to Hanoi with several friends, a brief folly as street vendors wiping out what little savings he had managed to scrape together when the two brothers stole everything.

It had hardened his heart even further.

A life of manual labor had been his lot until he had been lucky enough to get his job at the Daewoo Hanoi. It had changed his life. Though his existence was meager, it was better than most. He had a decent roof over his head, no need for any more than he had, he was well fed, and his hobby of reading was well taken care of by the unbelievable amount of books left behind by hotel guests.

He had used them and the hotel training to learn English, and felt a shameful amount of pride in his ability.

"Tonight we celebrate."

His voice was rough, it the first words spoken since his retribution had been delivered.

And it lacked confidence. Even he didn't believe it.

"*Tonight,* we celebrate!"

He forced a smile on his face, his fairly decent teeth one of the reasons he had scored his good job. It almost made him believe that he could have a good time.

But he knew he'd need some lubrication.

He went into the bathroom and stood on the toilet, reaching into the tank high on the wall. He pulled out the plastic resealable bag and stepped down, wiping it dry with the towel hanging off a rack salvaged from a recent renovation at the hotel.

Inside was his life savings.

A pittance compared to the excess he saw day in and day out at the hotel, but it was his. He had earned it, no one could deny he had. What he was saving it for, he wasn't sure. There was really nothing he wanted. He had no need for a car, his moped, bought cheap and secondhand, suited him well. He had a small radio that he listened to music on and had no desire for television, it filled with too much news and lies.

Part of him had already decided what the right thing to do was. Leave it to the monks. He pulled out several bills, enough to have a great time tonight, then returned his secret cache to its hiding place. As he stepped down he wondered though who would give the money to the monks if he were to die.

He had friends, but he had learned long ago you couldn't trust them, not with money, not in a poor country. People were too desperate. He might be able to tell Duy, but Duy also had a gambling problem, losing most of his money each week to the cock fights.

No, there was no one he could trust.

He did have family. Cousins. His adoptive parents might still be alive since they were only about fifteen years older than him when he came to live with them. They'd be old now, but he had no idea if they were still in the village. He hadn't seen them in over thirty years.

And going back would be too painful.

Death had never really been a topic he dwelled on. He was going to die. Everyone did. It was inevitable and nothing to fear. And it was always so far away. But with what happened today, perhaps that inevitable ending was much closer than it had been just this morning. He must have been caught on camera entering the museum. He had tried to avoid looking at the one camera he had spotted, but really had no clue if there were others. He had no doubt that if they had footage of him it would be all over television by now and someone would recognize him.

He sucked in a deep breath.

*You'll be arrested tomorrow morning at work.*

The drums outside his window beckoned. It might be his last night as a free man. His last night in this body, the long process of reincarnation perhaps about to begin before soon.

*Or they might torture you for years.*

That didn't frighten him. In fact, he didn't care at all. There was nothing they could do to him that could match what had happened decades before.

A decision was suddenly made.

He sat down and wrote a letter to his cousins, telling them where to look for the money, but not that it was money, and of the sacred bowl. It deserved to be preserved. It *had* to be preserved. His entire community, the entire foundation of Buddhism in this region of the world, had been as a result of that bowl, and though it was a patchwork of its previous self, its significance remained.

Especially its contents, kept in a sealed bag so they wouldn't leak out the too numerous holes.

He eyed the floorboards where he kept it hidden, counting them out from the wall and writing exactly where to find it. Folding up the letter, he stuck it in an envelope with the hotel logo in the corner then left it on his bed, happy this final duty was almost complete. He'd mail the letter tomorrow morning at work, then not worry about his legacy again.

He left the apartment, locking the door behind him and descended the flights of stairs to the streets below. They were filled now with revelers, the Vong Thi Festival in full swing. Colorful garb ruled the evening and he felt a little out of place in his drab shorts and t-shirt, but he didn't care. He watched the young people laughing and dancing, his generation joining in at times, the elders lining the streets, clapping in unison with the drums.

A smile slowly creased his face.

A hint of joy, just a hint, began to invade that darkened heart. His people could rest in peace now, and so could he. He found his hands clapping to the beat, a bounce in his step as he headed for Duy's apartment, hoping his friend was still home. He wanted to celebrate. He wanted to celebrate the end of a long dark chapter of his life.

And forget that tomorrow might be the short, final chapter.

*Daewoo Hanoi Hotel, Hanoi, Vietnam*

Dawson stood at the doors of the elevator on the eighth floor, the only one they hadn't blocked, the rest all held on one of the two floors they controlled. They had swept the upper floors and he had a spotter on the roof just in case the Vietnamese tried to insert troops by helicopter. Medical personnel had arrived to tend to the Vietnamese wounded, and unarmed soldiers, as agreed to, had retrieved the bodies, all stripped of their weapons.

Dimitri Yashkin had upped the stakes, however.

Electricity and water had been cut off about twenty minutes ago, power just now restored for the meeting.

Apparently no one wanted to climb nine stories.

With their egress halted, comm gear had been set back up again, batteries powering it. It was almost nighttime outside now, leaving the floor and rooms eerily dark with all the drapes closed to prevent snipers from spotting their targets easily. The Secretary's room had custom drapes that blocked thermal sensors from picking up the bodies moving around, but the security meant even the light of the city couldn't provide comfort.

Fortunately these were luxury suites and one of Atwater's staff had found bags of tea lights in the maid's supply closet. These had been broken out and lit to surprising effect once the eyes were adjusted.

Spock joined him, looking at the tiny candles lining the hallway, no longer necessary now that the power was back on. "It was almost romantic."

"Don't get any ideas. I'm a taken man."

"So how *are* things going with Maggie?"

Dawson shrugged. "Good, I guess. We're still seeing each other, if that's what you mean."

Spock chuckled. "Nooo, that's not what I mean. She's at all the events with you, so obviously you're still together. I mean, *how's* it going?"

Dawson glanced over at his friend. "How are things with your girlfriend?"

"Stacey?" Air burst from Spock's lips. "That's going nowhere. We're just having a good time."

"So am I."

Spock cocked an eyebrow causing Dawson to immediately regret his dismissive response. "Really? I thought you two were more serious."

"We are. I just mean we're having a good time."

"Uh huh." Spock didn't sound convinced. "Wedding bells in the future?"

The elevator chimed, saving Dawson from answering. The doors opened revealing Sarkov and another man whom Dawson assumed was Yashkin, the man he had spoken to earlier and Sarkov's boss.

"I'm Special Agent White," said Dawson.

"Dimitri Yashkin."

"Follow me, please." Dawson was about to start walking when Yashkin stopped him.

"First I want to speak to you." Dawson paused, turning back toward their "guests". "You are in charge here?"

"No, Secretary Atwater is."

Yashkin smiled, shaking his head. "I mean in charge of security."

"Yes."

"I have confirmed your man escaped, disguised as a Vietnamese police officer. He also had an assault rifle with him, and perhaps other weapons. We also found the body of the man he killed to get the uniform.

*That doesn't sound like Niner.*

"*If* Agent Green killed one of your men, then I have no doubt it was in self-defense."

"They are not *my* men, but those of the Vietnamese government, your hosts while you are *guests* in this country."

Dawson said nothing, semantics a waste of time.

Yashkin waited a moment before realizing Dawson wasn't taking the bait. "You say your man is innocent. Why would he run?"

"I ordered him to."

Yashkin's eyebrows popped. "Interesting that you would do such a thing."

"My responsibility is Secretary Atwater's safety. By separating the two of them, she is safer. Now that he is gone, I fully expect that our Vietnamese *hosts* will respect international law and allow us to leave."

Yashkin shrugged. "I have no control over the Vietnamese."

*Bullshit!*

"We expect your people to hand over Agent Green immediately."

"I have no idea where he is."

"You no doubt have some way of contacting him."

It was Dawson's turn to shrug. "I'm afraid he's gone silent until he makes it to safety." Dawson glanced at Sarkov. "Have you retrieved the footage from the museum?"

Sarkov was about to open his mouth when Yashkin replied for him. "No. Unfortunately none of the cameras were functioning this morning."

Dawson didn't believe that for a second. "Unfortunate."

"Indeed. This *is* Vietnam after all. The government isn't known for its state of the art security, especially at facilities like a museum with little strategic value."

"Of course. Fortunately this hotel is private and does have state of the art security."

Yashkin's eyebrows narrowed. "What are you saying?"

"No doubt there will be footage of Agent Green leaving the hotel in order to assassinate your Prime Minister."

"I wouldn't rely on that, Agent White. After all this is—"

"Vietnam, I know. However I'd have to ask, if the hotel cameras are not functioning, then how did you confirm Agent Green escaped earlier disguised as a police officer?"

Dawson caught a slight smile almost break out on Sarkov's face and had to admit he took a little delight in catching the slight flare in Yashkin's eyes.

"I think I'll speak to Secretary Atwater now."

"Of course."

Sarkov grunted. "If you'll excuse me, sir, I'm going to see to the security situation downstairs."

"Yes, yes, of course, go," replied Yashkin, dismissing Sarkov with a bat of the hand without looking at him. It was clear he had little respect for Sarkov, the older man bowing slightly to Dawson before disappearing into the elevator. Dawson's impression of the older Russian continued to be that he was interested in the truth, rather than the message, whereas Yashkin had no interest in what had really happened, rather he was only concerned with how to exploit the situation.

And from the intel reports continuing to arrive, it appeared things were only going to get worse if this farce of an investigation continued.

*Pushechnaya Street, Moscow, Russia*

"What do you think's going on?"

Jake looked at his girlfriend, Sarah, then back at the television. "I'm not sure." It was still only mid-afternoon and they had a big day planned. They had already been to Red Square after an early start and were planning to finish it off with a tour of Saint Basil's Cathedral after a light lunch. His stomach rumbled, their breakfast a little too light for his liking, but Sarah was a health nut and had him watching his calories.

*A man's gotta eat!*

Sure he could stand to lose twenty or thirty pounds, but she had met him this way and if she didn't like it, why had she started dating him? He was trying, but it was hard. She made it easier, the sexual incentives huge having a girlfriend far hotter than he was handsome. But sometimes he just wanted to have the double-quarter pounder with large fries and large diet coke.

And a snack sized Smarties McFlurry.

But now it had become something he hid.

He hated lying to her and he knew it was wrong. But he had his addictions and didn't want to change, didn't feel he had to change. The doctor said his cholesterol was fine, he wasn't diabetic, his blood pressure was normal.

And he was twenty-eight damned years old.

*I'm going to eat what I want while I can!*

Yet he still hated lying to her.

And on this trip, with them spending 24/7 together, there was no opportunity to cheat. He was eating every meal with her, spending every waking moment with her, which meant his caloric intake was what she had believed it had been for months.

A pittance.

He was starving the entire time.

And it was ruining his dream vacation.

He had always wanted to visit Russia, ever since hearing the stories of the Cold War from his now retired father, a former Colonel in the Air Force. He had never been able to visit the country due to his job but Jack had always wanted to see Moscow. His father had no problem with it, but told him last Christmas at the dinner table when they were all discussing it something that echoed in his head now, as if his father's words foreshadowed this very day.

"Do it while you can. That country is heading back to Soviet times and pretty soon you won't be able to go there. It's already not very safe, but at least they don't kill you for being American. I give it tops five years before Cold War Two starts."

His mother had pshawed him, turning the conversation instead to Jack's love life, or lack thereof, his extra pounds seeming to always be a hindrance to his success with the ladies.

He had been proud to announce he was dating Sarah at the time. And now here they were, spending one full week in Moscow almost a year later.

It was the longest relationship he had ever been in.

To say he loved Sarah would be an understatement. He adored her. In fact, he had to catch himself on occasion elevating her to a pedestal no one could live up to. She wasn't perfect. No one was. And he was far from perfect, though he'd admit to being his own biggest critic. But she was the type of girl who made him want to be a better man, so he put up with her healthy ways, knowing her heart was in the right place.

But when he had seen what looked like a good Western style burger on the menu posted in the window, he had been determined to order it, whether she wanted him to or not.

His stomach rumbled again. "Do you see a waitress?" he asked.

Sarah motioned toward the television. "Everyone seems glued to the TV."

They finally seemed to be noticed and a waitress hurried over. Short and large, she was the type of server he loved—you never felt guilty ordering whatever you wanted. She said something in Russian and Jake replied with the standard Berlitz greeting he had practiced, then asked if she spoke English.

"Da."

And she said it with a frown.

"Can I get the house salad please, dressing on the side?"

"To drink?"

"A bottle of water, please."

The waitress turned to Jake. "And you?"

"Cheeseburger with fries and a diet coke."

"Jake!"

"Hey, I'm on vacation." He sighed. "Hold the cheese." He winked at Sarah as the waitress walked away. "That'll save a few calories."

"But you were doing so well!"

Jake wasn't sure if this was the time to dump a truckload of truth on his girlfriend, but he figured there probably never would be a good time. It wasn't like she could break up with him here in Russia. They were staying in the same hotel room and flying back together in three days.

*Perhaps it's the* perfect *time to tell her the truth.*

"Honey, I hate dieting." Her eyebrows jumped, her eyes opening slightly wider. "I love my fast food, my greasy hamburgers, my pizzas with extra cheese. It's just the way I am, the way I always have been. I don't mind eating the foods you like, but I also have to indulge every once in a while." He slapped his belly. "I've always had this and I don't think it's going away any time soon."

Sarah looked aghast.

*Uh oh.*

"I feel horrible," he started, but was quickly cut off by her hand darting out and grabbing his wrist.

"No, *I* do."

"Huh?"

"For making you do all those things." She squeezed his wrist tighter then let go, grabbing his hand. "I love *you.* I don't care if you've got washboard abs."

"Hey, I've got those, they're just washboard abs for delicates."

Sarah laughed. "See? *That's* why I love you. You make me laugh. If I had a problem with your weight I never would have started dating you." She lifted his hand off the table and raised it to her mouth, kissing a knuckle, her eyes glistening. "I'm so sorry I made you uncomfortable," she whispered, her voice cracking.

Now it was his turn, and he was delayed by the return of the waitress.

Empty handed.

"The cook wants to know if you're American."

"Why?" asked Jake, alarms suddenly going off as he felt Sarah's grip tighten.

"Are you American?" the woman demanded.

"So what if we are?" asked Sarah.

The woman pointed at the television, the gathered crowd of locals beginning to take interest in the conversation. "The Prime Minister has been assassinated! By an American!"

"Of England?" asked Sarah.

The waitress glared at her. "Of Russia, you ignorant American pig!"

"Hey, there's no call for that kind of language," said Jake, standing. "I think we'll be leaving." He grabbed his jacket off the back of the chair, folding it over his arm as several of the men at the far end of the café left their seats. Sarah rose, grabbing her jacket as well, still holding Jake's hand across the table.

The woman shouted something at the crowd, the only word he understood being "Amerikanskiy!" More rose from their chairs as Jake led Sarah out the front door, pulling his jacket on as they stepped out onto the chilly street.

"We need to get out of here, quickly," he said, hustling Sarah along as she fumbled with her jacket. He paused to help her as several men stepped out of the café, angry expressions on their faces and shouts of vodka infused bravado spilling across the cobblestone street. He grabbed Sarah by the arm, hauling her along. "We need to get to the car, fast."

Their rental was within sight, just near the end of the block. He reached into his pocket, fumbling for the key, a momentary panic setting in when he couldn't find it. His fingertips touched something and he grabbed, relief flowing through him as he felt the key fob in his hand. He glanced behind him and the crowd was larger now, several marching toward them, shouting, one with a fist pumping the air, a drink in the other.

He kept them moving fast, resisting the urge to run, knowing that like an animal, a mob was more likely to pursue if they thought their prey just might get away.

And their pursuers had no idea they had a car only yards away.

"You get in and lock your door right away," he said as they approached the car. "Are you ready?"

"Y-yes."

He could feel her trembling, his hand still gripping her arm. He pulled the fob out and pressed the unlock button twice. The car chirped and the lights flashed.

Somebody yelled.

"Now!" he yelled, letting her go as he dodged behind the car and grabbed for his door. He stole a quick glance back and saw several of the men racing toward them, far too close. Sarah's door slammed shut as he jumped in. He jammed the fob at the dash, missing the slot as his elbow pushed down on the lock. His foot shoved on the brake as his second attempt was successful.

He pressed the ignition switch and the engine roared to life, someone slamming their fist on the roof at the same moment. Sarah screamed as a hand slammed against her window. He put the car in drive and lifted his foot off the brake just as someone slid across the hood, blocking his path.

He slammed the brake back down, bringing them to a jerking halt.

Another slam on Sarah's window, the car quickly surrounded.

"Jake! Do something!"

Her voice was desperate, terrified.

It sounded like he felt.

Something swung at the windshield, splintering the safety glass on the passenger side.

"Screw it!" He eased his foot off the brake and the car began to move forward. "Get the hell out of the way!" he shouted as those in front began to push back on the car, hatred in their eyes, mob mentality having taken over.

These people meant to kill them.

He removed his foot from the brake completely and gently pressed on the gas, cranking the wheel to pull out from the curb, his view of the road blocked.

A horn blasted but he committed himself, pushing down a little more on the gas, the bumper shoving those in front, some moving to the side, one jumping on the hood.

It didn't matter anymore.

They had to get out of here, they had to get to safety.

Something slammed into his side of the car, shoving the front end back toward the car that had been parked in front of them. They hit with a jolt, a car alarm suddenly blaring as they were brought to a halt, he instinctively hitting the brakes.

Somebody pulled full force on Sarah's door handle.

He hammered his foot down on the gas, squeezing between the car that had hit them and the parked car, shoving the car and its angry driver aside as they began to gain speed. He looked in his rearview mirror and saw the crowd chasing after them, the only pursuer now on their hood.

He pulled the stock to wash the windshield, the wipers flicking past, hitting the man's hand, a finger stuck through a hole in the passenger side of the windshield where it had been hit.

The man lifted his hand.

And Jake slammed on the brakes.

The man's eyes popped wide open as he slid down the hood and onto the cobblestone. Jake hit the gas, cranking the wheel around the man, trying not to hit him but not really caring when he heard a thump and a cry.

"Get your phone out and look up where the embassy is!"

"What?"

"Just get your phone out!"

Sarah fumbled in her purse, finally pulling out the phone as Jake looked in the rearview mirror, cursing. The car he had hit was racing up behind them. He pressed on the gas a little harder, but had no idea where they were going.

Sarah held up her phone.

"Get the address for the embassy then program it into the GPS."

She nodded, no longer bothering to try and speak, instead trying to get trembling fingers to work on a touch screen phone.

*What I'd give for an old Blackberry right now.*

He spun the wheel, cranking the car around a corner and onto a busier street, trying to watch ahead for any chance of being stuck in traffic while pressing the buttons on the built in navigation system, it thankfully already set up for English instructions.

"I've got it!" exclaimed Sarah, holding it up.

"Type it in! Type it in!"

Sarah typed in Moscow, a list of streets appearing, it narrowing as she continued typing. A second car seemed to have joined the chase, probably filled with drunken patrons from the café. Several waving arms were shoved out its windows as well as a few from the car he had hit. Either it had passengers before the collision or others had joined the driver in his pursuit.

Either way it didn't matter.

From what he could tell they had at least eight people after them.

"There!"

*"Turn left at the next intersection in one hundred meters."*

He cut across two lanes of traffic, taking the turn just as the light changed. He glanced at the display and saw they were less than five minutes away from the embassy.

"Call them!"

"What?"

"Call the embassy. Tell them what's happening!"

Sarah worked the phone and suddenly he could hear ringing over the speakers, forgetting they had paired the phone with the car when they first rented it.

*Thank God!*

"American Embassy—"

"Thank God, we need help!" he cried, only to hear the automated voice hell system begin. Sarah began selecting options and finally the phone rang. Jake slammed on the brakes as a car cut in front of them, his arm darting out to protect Sarah from jerking forward, neither of them with their seatbelts on. "Put your seatbelt on!" he shouted, glancing in his rearview mirror. "Hold on!"

The car was suddenly slammed from behind as their pursuers caught up. He jammed down on the gas, the car leaping forward as he glanced back, a nervous laugh erupting as he saw the airbags had been deployed, most likely killing the car's engine as a safety measure.

The laugh was soon stifled as the second car pulled around.

"American Embassy, how may I help you?"

"We're being pursued by a car full of Russians!" he shouted as the GPS signaled another turn silently, the phone in control of the audio. He cranked the wheel.

*Three minutes.*

"I'm sorry, sir, you'll have to calm down, I can't hear you properly."

Jake wanted to shout even louder, but bit his tongue. "We are two American citizens. We were attacked by a mob of Russians when they found out we were American. They are pursuing us now in our car. We are about three minutes away from the Embassy. You have to let us in or they're going to kill us!"

"One moment please."

Music played.

"Is she kidding me?!"

Strains of a Muzaked version of More Than Words by Extreme filled the car.

Sarah's seatbelt finally clicked into place, reminding him to grab his own, yanking it across his chest. Sarah grabbed it and shoved it into the buckle when the music stopped. It was a man's voice. "This is the Regional Security Officer. Give me your situation."

"We're American citizens. Right now one car is pursuing us, probably four individuals inside. They assaulted us and we escaped in our rental. We're"—he glanced at the display—"two minutes out from the embassy."

"Do you have your passports?"

"What the hell kind of question is that?"

"Do you—"

"Yes!"

"Good. Just show those at the gate and you'll be let inside."

"These people mean to kill us!"

"Once you are inside the gates we will protect you. There's nothing we can do outside those gates. Are you coming from the east or west?"

Jake glanced at the map.

"East!"

"Okay, good, it's a one way street. The gate is on your right. Just stop right there and get out of the car. Just leave it, forget the keys. Make sure you have your passports raised in the air and announce clearly that you are American."

"Okay, okay. We're almost there!"

A siren sounded behind them.

"What's that?" asked the man.

"We've got a cop following us now."

"Okay, don't stop. Just keep going."

Jake made a hard right, seeing the gate ahead. And two police cars, sirens and lights blaring, raced toward them in the wrong direction.

"There's more cops coming right at us!"

He heard the Officer shout something unintelligible. The gate was only a couple of hundred yards away. The light traffic ahead was veering to the left and right as the police cars tore toward them.

"Go! Go! Go!" urged Sarah as she gripped the dash, her passport rolled up in her palm. It was going to be down to feet. He could see Marine Guards running toward the gate now, the red and white boom barrier still down, manned by what looked like Russians, the large gray iron gates behind that still closed.

He hammered on the brakes, shoving the car into park with a jolt. "GO!" he screamed as he unlocked his seatbelt. Sarah threw open her door and tried to jump out, forgetting her belt. She cried out, struggling for a moment as Jake leapt from the car. He reached back in and pressed the button, releasing Sarah and she flew forward, shrugging off the shoulder belt.

The boom barrier was still down, the two Russian uniformed guards stepping toward them with their hands out as the three police cars and their pursuers screeched to a halt, shouts erupting as ear splitting sirens drowned out most everything.

Jake reached into his pocket and pulled out his passport, rushing toward the gate. "We're Americans! We're Americans! Let us in!"

Somebody was running toward the front gates, a phone pressed to his ear suggesting he might be the Regional Security Officer. "Open the gates! Open the gates!"

A Russian guard tried to block him but Jake knew it was all or nothing now. He dropped his shoulder and hit him square in the chest, bowling him over, hard. The jolt was jarring, but he kept forward, leaping over the boom gate, Sarah right beside him, a steady scream still sounding from the moment she left the car, her face one of pure terror like he had never seen in his life.

The iron gates started to slide open when he heard gunshots erupt behind him. He didn't stop. If they were willing to shoot them now, then there was no way they'd survive an arrest. He opened his arms wide, trying to shield Sarah as he slowed slightly to let her through the narrow opening first.

Something hit him from behind, hard.

He flew forward, his arms out front breaking his fall as he smacked hard into the ground, excruciating pain radiating throughout his back. It didn't feel like a gunshot, at least not how he'd have guessed one would feel, but he had definitely been hit by something, and it had been preceded by a shot.

*Rubber bullet?*

He pushed himself to his elbows, looking up at the gate not five feet away. Sarah was inside, trying to leave to help him but she was being held back by two Marine guards, her pleas thankfully being ignored, Jake knowing the moment she crossed the threshold of those gates she'd be back in Russian territory.

"Shots fired! Shots fired!" yelled someone, the hammering of boots on pavement nearing, a platoon of Marines rushing toward the scene.

But nobody crossed the line, nobody moved to help him

He pushed himself to his hands and knees, crawling forward, his passport still gripped in his hand, his back breaking in pain, when someone kicked him, hard. He felt his entire torso lift up as ribs cracked, the pain in his back a sudden distant memory. Instinctively he tried to curl into a ball as a flurry of kicks ravaged him. He heard shouts of protest in English, Sarah's begging for them to stop, and the Russians continuing to deliver street justice.

He opened his eyes and saw that the Russian police were holding back, four men from the café the ones actually doing the kicking. He looked up and saw a boot raised, about to stomp on his head. Sarah screamed, someone shouted something, and suddenly all hell broke loose. The pounding of boots approaching, a chorus of "Move back!" ordered repeatedly and the sight of military issued black boots rushing toward him almost made him forget the boot about to drop on his head. He looked up at the man, rage and hatred etched over his face, Russian expletives spitting from his twisted mouth. Jake raised his hands to try and block the blow when a rifle butt suddenly hit his attacker square on the chin, knocking him to the side. The sounds of hand-to-hand combat surrounded him then he felt someone grab him under the armpits, hauling him to his feet.

He looked behind as he was dragged through the gates and saw a cordon of Marines, their weapons aimed at the Russian attackers and police, covering his rescue as the entire procession quickly retreated behind the safety of the Embassy perimeter. As he felt his feet drag over the speed bump he cried a gasp of relief, knowing that at least for the moment he was safe, that he wasn't going to die. He was placed gently on his knees and he collapsed in pain, rolling over onto his back, the cold pavement slowly biting into his skin through his jacket. The gates rumbled closed as Sarah dropped to his side and began to hug him, crying uncontrollably, her sob filled words incoherent.

He just reached up and hugged her, his ribs aching in protest.

But he didn't care.

They were alive.

They were together.

And they'd never be coming back to Russia again.

*Daewoo Hanoi Hotel, Hanoi, Vietnam*

"It is my understanding that you have allowed the assassin to escape."

Dimitri Yashkin seemed nothing if not direct. Dawson could sense Secretary Atwater was already bristling at his presence, his figure imposing and the Russian arrogance almost unbearable under the circumstances.

To Atwater's credit, however, she stood her ground and refused to be intimidated by the man, at least from all outward appearances. Inside she might be quaking, but Dawson doubted it. He had no doubt she felt safe at this very moment, there half a dozen security with guns within twenty feet, including himself.

He could drop Yashkin in two seconds if it became necessary.

But it wouldn't.

This was a "diplomatic" visit.

"I wasn't aware of that until a few minutes ago," replied Atwater.

"You should have better control of your security detail. If one of my men did what your man did"—he nodded toward Dawson—"he would be in prison before the day was out."

Atwater smiled. "In America we have due process. I thought Russia had the same?"

Yashkin's turn to bristle.

"We do, of course. It was merely a figure of speech."

"Of course. And since Russia has due process, where someone is innocent until proven guilty, I would have to assume that Agent Green would be given the same consideration."

*Good one, Madame Secretary!*

Yashkin's fake smile eased slightly. "We are interested in the truth, of course. But—"

"Excellent!" interrupted Atwater, motioning toward a nearby chair as she sat down. "Since we are both interested in the truth, I suggest you rein in your Vietnamese allies. Clearly they do not have due process like our two democracies have, and they don't seem interested in the truth."

Yashkin was about to say something when Atwater held up a finger, cutting him off again.

"Our Agent is innocent. We intend to prove that. In order to diffuse the situation, my head of security ordered him to leave the premises and make his way to our embassy. I'm sure he will be there shortly if he is not already. In the meantime, as our Vietnamese hosts clearly have terminated the approved schedule for our visit, we will be departing immediately. You are welcome to visually ID each of our personnel as we leave to confirm that Agent Green is not among them." Atwater leaned forward. "Now, since we're both agreed we all want the truth and that both our countries believe in due process and the concept of innocent until proven guilty, and since no demands have been made for access to any of our other personnel, I assume you will be encouraging your Vietnamese allies to obey international law and let us leave freely, immediately."

Yashkin smiled, opening his clasped fingers in a dismissive manner. "Unfortunately the Vietnamese are beyond my control in these matters. While I agree with you on every point you mentioned, my government seems to have little influence with the Vietnamese anymore, at least where today's events are concerned." He leaned forward, lowering his voice slightly. "I'm afraid they are very embarrassed at the lapse in security, and perhaps fear retaliation on my country's part." He sat back upright, smiling. "Of course retaliation is something from our past. A democracy never attacks its neighbors."

Dawson had to hold back his laugh.

*Umm, Georgia? Ukraine?*

But he was right. A democracy never attacks its neighbors. And a democracy never attacks another democracy, no matter where it is. Which was just further evidence Russia wasn't a democracy.

Atwater held her tongue, something Dawson might not have been able to do if he were in her position.

*Further evidence I'm no diplomat.*

"I'm certain your neighbors would be happy to hear that." Atwater rose, signaling the end of the conversation. "Embarrassment or not, the Vietnamese government must respect international law. We are a diplomatic mission and are entitled to leave freely. I expect you to deliver that message to our hosts."

"Of course," said Yashkin as he rose, extending a hand. "I am pleased we had this discussion."

Atwater shook the man's hand, looking up at him. "As am I." She nodded to Dawson. "Please show our guest to the elevator."

"Yes, ma'am."

Dawson held his hand out as Spock opened the door to the hallway. Yashkin walked toward the elevator, it already opened by one of the DSS agents. Yashkin stepped aboard and turned back toward Dawson.

"Until we meet again," he said, his smile suddenly disappearing. "Sergeant Major."

The doors closed, Dawson saying nothing, careful not to reveal any emotions. He felt no surprise, he had no doubt the Russians had a pretty good file on him. And he was also quite sure they now knew exactly who Niner was.

And he was also positive this had nothing to do with justice, and everything to do with the Vietnamese saving face, and the Russians taking advantage of the situation.

He walked toward Atwater's suite as the lights went out.

"Détente didn't last very long," observed Spock.

"Nope. I don't think they have any intention of letting us leave."

They entered the suite and found Atwater sitting again, sipping from a bottle of water. "Recommendations?" she asked the room.

Nobody wanted to say the obvious.

They were screwed.

Especially if they did nothing.

Her eyes rested on Dawson. "You look like you want to say something."

"Ma'am, there's no way we're fighting our way out of here, and we can only hold off so many assaults. If they really want to take us, there's no stopping them, just delaying them. Diplomacy just failed, but may eventually succeed. It all depends on whose will wins out—the Russians or the Vietnamese." He nodded toward a battery powered television showing CNN. "Right now they're controlling the message. Beyond our denials, we are the guilty party. They have a copy of Agent Green's photo ID, bullshit eyewitnesses and a dead Russian Prime Minister who was speaking to you at the moment of the assassination. *We* look bad. We need to make *them* look bad."

"What are you saying?"

"Take back control of the message. Set up a direct feed with CNN and talk live to them. The Vietnamese wouldn't dare risk killing you on live television for the world to see. As long as you are on the air, we are all safe."

An explosion rocked the room, the windows rattling.

"They just breached the eighth floor!" came Jimmy's voice over the comm. "Probably cord explosives on the seventh floor ceiling!"

"This is White. Reinforcements to the eighth floor. Shoot anything that shows itself, conserve your ammo. Use the grenades we confiscated if necessary, over."

"What's going on?" asked Atwater, fear showing itself as she jumped to her feet.

"They just blasted through the ceiling on the seventh. They now have access to the eighth. We don't have enough personnel to hold them back, ma'am. If they take the eighth floor, they can put explosives directly below us and take this entire room out."

Atwater snapped her fingers. "Set up the camera, get me CNN now!"

Dawson left the room, her entourage, desperate for something to do other than worry, bursting into a flurry of activity.

*Now let's just hope CNN takes her call.*

*Dong Mac Ward, Hanoi, Vietnam*

James Acton sat on a none-too-comfortable chair, Laura beside him at a table on one side of the rather smallish "gang" hangout belonging to Mai's brother, Cadeo. Mai sat across from them, as did a reluctant Cadeo. CNN International was playing on the television nearby, it having been turned so everyone at the table could see it.

He pulled the phone out of his pocket and pressed the button out of habit.

His eyes narrowed.

He held his finger on the sensor and brought up the text message.

*this is niner. contact me asap.*

He showed the message to Laura and her eyebrows jumped. "How old is that?"

Acton looked. "Almost fifteen minutes." He typed a message.

*This is jim. We r safe. R u?*

They waited, Mai rising and rounding the table, curious.

Cadeo simply glared.

The phone vibrated.

*Confirm identity. How did we meet?*

Acton winked at Laura.

*You tried to kill me.*

*LOL. Good thing I failed. Are you secure?*

*For now.*

*Give me location, I will try to make it to you.*

Acton texted him the GPS coordinates, Mai supplying the address.

They waited.

*ETA one hour.*

Acton sighed. "If he can make it here then he should be safe."

"I don't want any more Americans here."

They all turned to Cadeo. "I'm British," said Laura with a smile.

"It all same."

Acton was about to make a quick quip but decided against it, Cadeo's Beretta sitting on the table.

Mai spoke instead. "They are my friends and they need help. If they are not welcome here, then neither am I."

Cadeo growled and jumped from his chair, kicking it to the floor with the back of his knees. He spat something in Vietnamese and walked away, disappearing through a door to the outside.

"I must apologize for my brother."

"No need. He's just scared," replied Laura. "We all are."

"And he's right to be," added Acton. "We're all wanted fugitives and now he is too for rescuing you. He has the advantage for the moment of not being known to the authorities."

"They will figure it out. They know he's my brother."

"But they don't know he's the one who rescued you. At least not yet."

Mai shook her head. "It won't matter. They will just assume because they know he is a criminal." She dropped back into her chair. "At least for now they don't know where he is. But from now on he'll always be connected to the murder."

Laura leaned forward, reaching out to Mai with a hand. "Unless we can get the truth out."

"But what *is* the truth?" asked Acton. And that was the most important question. They had no proof of their side of the story, just their word, which meant little to nothing here in Vietnam. "It's too bad you weren't able to get that footage."

Mai's jaw dropped. "Oh my God, I forgot!" She reached into her shirt, fishing in her bra for a few seconds, then smiled triumphantly as she produced a memory stick. "I made a second copy, just in case!"

Acton wanted to kiss her. "Good thinking!"

Mai grinned. "They did not search me. They took my purse but that was all. I guess they were going to search me at the police station."

"Have you seen it?" asked Laura.

Mai shook her head. "No, there was no time. I just copied the files. They could be blank for all I know."

Acton frowned. "Let's hope not." He looked around. "Do you have a computer we can watch them on?"

Mai asked one of Cadeo's men who pointed to a metal cabinet. She rose and opened a drawer, pulling out an old Lenovo laptop. She turned it on and once booted, inserted the memory stick. A directory listing popped up showing only the catalog.

"There's nothing on it!" cried Acton in dismay. Mai smiled and changed the folder settings, a list of files appearing. Acton chuckled. "Never mind. Premature panic."

"You've never suffered from that before," grinned Laura.

Acton shot a shocked look at his wife then laughed.

Mai looked at them having no clue as to what they were talking about.

*Good thing.*

"Mai!"

They all looked at the shout, one of Cadeo's men pointing at the forgotten television.

*"—true, Wolf, the entire American delegation is under attack by Vietnamese authorities as we speak. I'm not sure if you can hear the gunfire, but I can. A desperate battle is being fought one floor below us right now, our brave men and women of the*

*Bureau of Diplomatic Security, hopelessly outnumbered, are trying to delay our capture, and perhaps death, at the hands of those who would claim to be our hosts."*

*"You are in danger now."*

*"Absolutely, Wolf, we have wounded and at least two dead already. Unless this unwarranted, and may I say unprecedented attack is halted immediately, I'm afraid many more will die."*

*"Why not surrender? Isn't it true that the Vietnamese have accused one of your security team members of the assassination of Russian Prime Minister Anatoly Petrov? Why not hand him over and end this?"*

*"That isn't an option, Wolf. Even if I was willing to ignore all of the principles we believe in such as due process and innocence until proven guilty, the Vietnamese have proven with this brazen, brutal attack that justice is not their goal. Our man is not guilty, he was here at the hotel during the time of the attack, and other than a photocopy of a stolen identification card, the Vietnamese authorities have provided no actual proof our agent was involved.*

*"We have eyewitnesses to the attack that have sworn it was a Vietnamese national, at least twenty years older than our agent, who was the assassin, and that the shooter was known to Prime Minister Petrov. I won't say on the air what the Prime Minister admitted to before he was shot, as I'm sure the Russian government will want to confirm these stories before they are made public, however should it look like we may lose this battle, I will of course provide you with the full details of the accusations, as I would hate to see it lost with our deaths."*

*"Are these eyewitnesses the two archeology professors, Professor James Acton and his wife Professor Laura Palmer?"*

*"Yes, among others from my security detail and a Vietnamese national, all of whom were in the room when the shooting began."*

Acton and Laura stood in front of the television, even Cadeo having returned after one of his men called. The fear in Atwater's voice was plain, though she was doing an admirable job of trying to hide it.

But no one could.

The gunfire was plain to hear, and Acton was certain he had heard at least two explosions, Atwater wincing both times. What they were, he couldn't be sure, but he had to assume grenades.

Which meant this was either an all-out attack, or an all-out defense.

Either way it would mean a lot of deaths.

He felt Laura's hand grip his as his thoughts immediately went to Dawson and the others. He knew Spock was there with him and Niner had escaped, but he had no idea who else was there that they might know. It could be the entire team for all he knew.

*If it's all of them, they'll hold out until the last man.*

Suddenly Atwater turned her head as shouting was heard off camera. Dawson's face appeared momentarily as he came into view, grabbing Atwater from the stool she was sitting on, lifting her as he yelled, "Get to the tenth floor, now!"

He disappeared off camera as screams and shouts could be heard, then a terrific explosion tossed the camera off its tripod, it bouncing off the floor, then seeming to freefall as the CNN announcer was left dumbfounded.

And Acton was left with all hope cleaved from his stomach.

Just then the channel went blank and a message appeared that looked like a Windows error message.

"What happened?" asked Laura.

Rapid fire Vietnamese was shot back and forth as Cadeo hammered at a keyboard sitting on a nearby table. Mai turned to them. "He said they were streaming that over the Internet. It looks like they've shut it down."

"What, the Internet?" asked Acton. "How?"

"It's very easy to do here. All providers are controlled by the government. They simply need to make some phone calls. Anyone who disobeys is thrown in prison."

Acton checked his phone. "Cellular network is down too."

As if on cue the rest of the room checked their phones, grumbling and cursing following.

Laura pulled her satellite phone out of her purse. "This may be our only lifeline."

Acton pointed at the laptop. "We need to get proof that Niner wasn't the shooter."

*Daewoo Hanoi Hotel, Hanoi, Vietnam*

Igor Sarkov knocked on the door to the security office, not waiting for a response, instead opening the door and stepping inside. The room was cramped, as most were, one side filled with banks of monitors and computers, still functioning as the main floor had power. Two men watching the monitors as if tuned to an American movie network ignored him.

Sarkov glanced at what they were looking at and frowned.

The Vietnamese appeared to be positioning themselves for an assault from the seventh floor, if his reading of the security feeds was correct. He could see the American positions on the eighth floor, the ninth dark.

*They must have used the elevator shafts to get to the seventh floor.*

He had to admit the tactic surprised him. He had never been overly impressed with the Vietnamese government or its adjuncts. They were competent but lacked creativity, their thinking trapped in the past, hindered by a communist mindset that hadn't evolved like China's had. Though he had no love for the Chinese government, and they were clearly still a brutal regime, they at least were moving forward with economic reforms, if not political. And if there was something he was certain of it was that a healthy middle-class, which in today's China was growing rapidly—from only 4% of urban dwellers in 2000, to 68% in 2012—was something a communist government was ill-equipped to deal with. People with stable, comfortable incomes had time to think about politics and democracy when they weren't obsessed with how they were going to put food on the table the next day.

China's economic growth would be its political undoing.

But Vietnam was far behind, though he imagined the Chinese would have reacted much the same way. The difference though was again economic. The Chinese would weigh the economic benefits of pissing off the United States versus pissing off Russia. And they would most likely side with the United States in the immediate aftermath. About the only thing Russia could offer was oil, natural gas and military hardware, and those deals took time.

Vietnam's economy was far less dependent on the Americans with less than 20% of their exports going to the United States and less than 5% of their imports coming from them. Russia was even more insignificant, however China wasn't.

But economics didn't enter the mindset of a communist when there was an opportunity for political embarrassment or gain. He had no doubt that the Vietnamese government was not only trying to avoid embarrassment, they were trying to curry favor with his own country to get a cut rate deal on military hardware, about the only thing the American's weren't willing to offer.

But if they killed the Secretary or a significant portion of her entourage, even the Russian government, he would hope, would distance itself.

Part of him, most of him, wanted to warn the Americans of what was coming, but that would certainly earn him a quick trip back to Moscow. He watched helplessly for a moment as the camera showed a security detail monitoring one of the eighth floor stairwells.

When he sucked in a breath of realization.

*Eighth floor!*

"The cameras on the eighth floor are working?"

"Yes," answered one of the men in English.

"But I thought the Americans ordered the cameras on their floors disabled."

The man looked uncomfortable and remained silent.

Sarkov decided intimidation would work on the diminutive man and glared at him, leaning in while jabbing a finger in the air. "Well?"

"It was!" the man sputtered. "I swear! But when I came on shift they were back on!"

"How?"

He shrugged, but not convincingly so. "I-I don't know."

"But you can find out."

The man's head bobbed rapidly as he turned back to the computer, furiously hitting keys. He pointed. "I-I can't be sure, but Duy from the Eco Office must have turned them back on for some reason."

"Eco Office?"

"It's an environmental program that monitors individual utility usage."

"Why would he turn the security cameras on for that?"

"They're connected. Why, I don't know. I just watch the cameras."

"Where is he now, this Duy?"

"At home. His shift ended a few hours ago."

"I want his employee file. Name, photo, address, phone number."

"Y-yes." The man hit a few keys and soon had the employee file printing. He handed it to Sarkov.

"How long have those cameras been on?"

"At least a few hours."

"Check."

Some more keys were hit. "They were turned on at 8:17 this morning."

"And they remained on?"

The man nodded.

"Bring up the footage from this morning."

The screens flipped from the live action upstairs to the calm of the morning, the eighth floor from several views displayed.

"Fast forward."

The footage raced forward several minutes before Sarkov pointed. "There!" A hotel staff member appeared from around the corner, pushing a maintenance cart. "Who is that? Is that him?"

"No, that's Phong," said the other man.

Sarkov nearly froze. "Did you say Phong?"

The man nodded. "He's a maintenance worker. He's been here forever. Since the beginning I think."

Sarkov watched the man knock on a door then swipe his pass, disappearing inside. "Whose room is that?"

The man shrugged. "They're all assigned to the American security detail. We aren't given that information." The man's eyes narrowed as he looked at his terminal. "Wait a minute." He hit a few more keys. "He used Duy's pass!"

Sarkov frowned. "Give me the employee record for this Phong person." Another printout was handed to him just as the door opened, Phong reappearing and pushing his cart back from where he had come. "Follow him."

"No need. He left five minutes later for the day, sick."

*Plenty of time to get to the museum.*

The more he learned, the more he realized the professors were telling the truth. The American Agent Green had nothing to do with this and it was this maintenance man—he glanced at the printout—Phong Son Quan—who was actually the shooter.

He needed to see the museum footage before it was erased. He had handed the memory stick over to security staff at the embassy but had yet to hear anything. If it too showed this man entering the museum, then it should be an open and shut case.

"Keep the camera on that door. Fast forward until someone comes out."

The image sped forward then the door opened, as did several others within the frame, agents rushing out, readying their weapons.

Including one Asian American DSS agent named Jeffrey Green.

At 10:02am.

Exactly when the Prime Minister was being shot.

The entire hotel rumbled.

*Kentucky Fried Chicken, Nguyen Thai Hoc Street, Hanoi, Vietnam*

Niner stretched then flushed to make it sound like he had actually done some business, he having waited for almost twenty minutes before hearing from the professors, or the Actons as he had come to think of them though he wasn't sure if she had taken his name.

He hoped that if he ever got married his wife would take his. He knew it would make his parents happy, especially his mother. He was a traditionalist when it came to that though he had to admit he wasn't overly religious. He prayed before each mission, just a quick, informal affair to remind the Almighty that he was on his side and doing his duty to his country. He didn't enjoy killing with the possible exception of terrorists. Enemy soldiers were at least fighting for their country, just like he was. Terrorists were murdering scum who didn't deserve to breathe the same air as the rest of us.

But the people who were his enemy today were soldiers and policemen, not terrorists. They were just doing their jobs and he would hate to have to kill one of them because of this situation.

Killing was a job, not a joy.

Not to say he didn't love his job. He did. He wouldn't trade it in for anything. He loved the adrenaline, he loved the rush, and he loved knowing at the end of the mission, hopefully successful, they had made the world a slightly safer place. Did he take satisfaction in killing the bad guys, especially the terrorists? Yes, it would be a lie to say he didn't. Did he enjoy it? No, he never went into combat saying to himself or one of his buddies, "Can't wait to blow some asshole's head off today because he was born under a different flag!" then live with the memory for the rest of his life.

He killed because it was necessary. He had killed too many to want to count, but he did, his mind simply unable to let go of the carnage. And the number was probably low. Too many times you sent bursts of gunfire around a corner or at a position to know if you actually did or didn't kill someone.

Yes, the count was probably much higher.

And he didn't want it to go any higher today.

But he had a feeling things weren't going to work out the way he wanted.

His secure phone had satellite web access so he had spent his time reading about the latest developments in Hanoi and around the world. The latest showed over ten thousand Russian troops along with armor, artillery and air support were surging into Eastern Ukraine in what appeared to be a well-planned, well-executed invasion. The Russian's were of course denying it, saying it was Western propaganda, despite footage rapidly filling the Internet of Russian vehicles and men pouring across the border.

Russia's "new" KGB mindset simply didn't understand the modern reality of social media and a free press, having such tight controls in place in their so-called democracy. Russia ranked a dismal 148th out of 179 countries for freedom of the press in 2013.

It was sad how much potential had been lost so quickly under a single leader stuck so far in the past.

Niner stepped out, washed his hands in the for the moment empty bathroom, making sure his Hawaiian shirt and Bermuda shorts were hiding his Glock tucked in the waistband.

Shades and his ball cap completed his look as he exited the bathroom, descending the three floors to the ground level and exiting, turning east, walking at a brisk pace, but not too brisk. He couldn't risk standing out, but the coordinates he had been given were almost a ninety minute walk from his current position. Apparently the Actons had somehow holed up near the Red River, a silt-laden source of water that actually appeared red.

How they had gotten there he had no idea, but he had to get to them, not only to protect them, but for his own protection. Those two were good in a fight and there was strength in numbers. The three of them would become a team, self-preservation and the truth their motivation.

How he could contribute toward the truth he had no idea.

All he could testify to would be that he had been at the hotel when the Prime Minister had been shot, and that his pass had been stolen. Nothing more. Which meant that they had to take his word for it. Sarkov had been right. He very well could have taken a motorcycle from the museum and been back at the hotel in no time.

But right now the truth could wait. Dawson needed to get Atwater and her entourage to safety, and he needed to take himself out of play by somehow getting into the American Embassy, ideally with the Actons in tow.

For now the embassy, according to the news reports he had read, was completely surrounded.

Inaccessible.

Which would mean the waiting game.

He spotted a bicycle in an alleyway, no evidence of a lock or owner.

He walked up to it and climbed on as if it was his own, pushing away and immediately blending in with the traffic, turning down the first road heading south that he could and out of sight of the scene of the crime. As he rode however one thing became painfully clear.

His Hawaiian shirt was screaming tourist.

Unfortunately he had simply tossed a couple of casual shirts in his suitcase for wearing off duty, and both had been from his "fun" drawer since there would be zero time available for socializing outside the hotel.

His current outfit was for hanging around with the guys in one of the rooms, shootin' the shit and playing cards.

Not blending in with the public while on the run from authorities.

He spotted a small shop with a few racks of t-shirts and stopped. They were all printed tees with crazy slogans and bright colors. He spotted a black one and grabbed it, handing the clerk twenty bucks, much to their delight. He biked to a nearby alley and pulled off his Hawaiian shirt, taking the opportunity to move his Glock to the front, it a little too exposed when leaning forward on a bike. He pulled the new shirt on, saying a silent prayer of thanks when it actually fit decently, then looked down at the words emblazoned on the front and laughed.

*THINK LESS.*

*STUPID MORE.*

He shoved down on the pedal, pushing himself back into traffic, quickly picking up speed as he continued to chuckle.

*I should take a picture for Engrish.com.*

The sun was setting rapidly, the buildings lining the streets casting long shadows when he heard drums in the distance. He pulled his phone from his pocket and memorized the upcoming few turns, taking the next street east toward the river. Stopping at a light, queuing up with a gaggle of other cyclists, mopeds and cars ignoring the painted lines, he looked straight forward, his head slightly down as he debated whether or not the sunglasses were attention grabbing at this level of brightness or not.

"Nice shirt, mate!"

Niner turned toward the Aussie accent. A young guy was grinning at him, early twenties with a gorgeous Vietnamese seat cover perched enticingly on the back of his motorcycle.

Niner smiled, deciding being rude would just attract more attention.

"Hey wait a minute, you're the guy that's all over the television. The assassin! You're that American they're all looking for!"

Fear suddenly shoved the tourist's smile aside as he realized his gaffe and he gunned his engine, looking for a way to put some distance between them and a killer. Which was fine by Niner, but unfortunately the word 'American' seemed to have caused almost every head to swivel toward him.

*This can't be good.*

The light changed and he pushed forward, weaving between the gawking cyclists just as one finally shouted something in Vietnamese. More shouts from just across the intersection had him cursing as two police officers rushed toward him.

He pulled his Glock, aiming it directly at the first officer's chest as he gained speed through the intersection, the man and his partner throwing up their hands. He kept pumping forward, aiming the gun behind him as he put some distance between them, finally turning back, the gun still in his hand as he raced forward, suddenly jerking the bike to the left, cutting across two lanes of traffic and down an alleyway. He shoved the gun in his belt and rose off the seat, pumping hard, a siren nearby adding to the urgency.

He banked hard to the right, back onto a busy street, the sidewalks filling with people in colorful clothes and costumes, some with drums strapped to their shoulders, a rhythmic beat beginning as what was clearly some sort of festival was just getting underway.

*Which might be just the diversion I need.*

He removed his sunglasses, hooking them over his t-shirt under his chin and slowed, plastering a smile on his face as he exchanged looks with the gathering crowds, trying his best to blend in. The sun was almost set now, streetlamps, light from shop windows and apartments along with lanterns and candles carried by revelers provided a comforting glow, the dim light his friend.

The chances of being recognized now were slim unless he stopped and someone got a good look.

Instead he made sure he never stopped. He set a leisurely pace, weaving slowly among the crowd now spilling onto the streets. There were few cars that weren't parked, those that were on the road had people hanging out the windows, joining in what was turning into a parade. He checked his phone's GPS and he was less than ten minutes from his destination.

Multiple sirens in the distance suddenly became very loud. He looked over his shoulder and saw three police cars, lights flashing, sirens blaring, turn onto the street.

He smiled.

The crowd was large now, the street thick with humanity as he picked up a little speed, much of the crowd having stopped and turned toward the noise. A loudspeaker announced something and the crowd started to part, the police obviously ordering them to make a hole.

He turned leisurely into another alleyway, gaining some speed but nothing that might suggest to the revelers he passed that he was fleeing. Several more quick turns and the sirens were again distant, and according to his GPS, he was nearly at the location.

Making the final turn, he began looking for street numbers and quickly realized that there were none that he could see. He pulled out his phone and prayed it would at least get him close.

He stopped where the phone indicated, finding a shitty building with a garage door, suggesting it was or had been some sort of business, nestled between more shitty buildings.

This wasn't a good neighborhood, though there were lots of colorfully dressed people milling about, some gathering into small groups who looked perfectly friendly, clearly getting ready to head for the festival or perhaps create their own party right here.

He tried calling Acton's phone but got his voicemail, the cellular network still down.

He didn't leave a pointless message.

He thumbed through the contacts and found Laura's phone which he knew from previous experience was a satellite phone.

She answered on the third ring.

"Hello?"

"I'm outside, but I'm not sure which building."

"Just a second."

He heard muffled talking then a garage door, three doors down from where he was sitting on his bike, opened, a Vietnamese man stepping out, looking about. Niner slowly biked toward him, holding the phone to his ear.

"Garage door? One man smoking a cigarette?"

"That's it," said Laura.

He pushed a little harder, the man nodding at him, tossing his cigarette out onto the street as he dropped the door closed behind Niner entered the nearly pitch black entrance. The moment the door hit the ground with a shudder and a clang lights were turned on and he breathed a sigh of relief, the two professors rushing toward him, Laura giving him a hug as he climbed off the bike, Acton shaking his hand.

"Thank God you're safe!" cried Laura. "We were starting to get worried."

"You should know better than that," grinned Niner as he surveyed their surroundings. It appeared to be some sort of hangout, about half a dozen young men milling about looking like they had never been up to any good in their life. A television showing CNN had been turned toward a table with half a dozen chairs surrounding it, a laptop with a Vietnamese girl sitting at it had what looked like security footage playing on it. "So, where are we?"

Acton motioned toward the girl at the computer. "We're at Mai's brother's…place, shall we say. They rescued her from the police then saved our asses a little while later."

Niner noticed what was on the television and his jaw dropped. "What the hell's been going on since I left?" He walked toward the television, footage from the outside of the hotel on a loop showing what looked like a fairly large explosion blasting out several windows, then footage of Atwater being hustled away off camera. A tag line in a red bar across the bottom of the screen read, "Secretary of State Dead?"

"They cut cellphone and Internet access a little while ago. This is from a satellite dish on the roof," explained Acton. "I'm pretty sure that's BD"—he pointed at the screen, Niner nodding in agreement with the identification—"and since that explosion nothing else has been heard, it's just talking heads right now."

"I pulled some updates down while I was waiting for you guys but didn't see this. Apparently the Russians have sent troops into the Ukraine?"

Acton nodded. "Yeah, over ten thousand of them. It looks like they basically sent everything they had in the area across. The NATO Secretary General has already given a press conference suggesting it was a well-planned, well-coordinated attack."

"Timing?"

"They think coincidental. The troops had already been in place for weeks if not longer. The Russians are simply taking advantage of the situation."

"How are the Ukrainians doing?"

Acton shook his head. "Not good. The Russians basically splashed anything in the air within the first hour, bombed the airfields so nothing else could launch, and have told the Ukrainians that any military units that don't lay down their arms in Eastern Ukraine by midnight will be eliminated, and any units moving into the east will be bombed."

"Christ. Can't say that's a surprise though."

"Nope. Everyone knew it was just a matter of time. NATO's scrambling to send as many forces as they can to the Baltic States. Russia's got dozens of bombers in the air right now."

"And us?"

"The President's saying he won't play their game so has kept ours on the ground for now."

"I'd have to say I agree with that. De-escalation is the key right now. The Ukraine was lost long before today. We should have put a few hundred advisors in there months ago. The Russians wouldn't dare risk killing American troops." He looked at the laptop. "But world politics aren't our concern right now. Right now we need to figure out how the hell to get out of here."

"That's going to be a problem. All our photos are on every television station in the world."

"Lovely."

"Don't worry, yours is still a pretty grainy photocopy."

"Thank God for small favors, but I did get recognized a few minutes ago." He nodded to Mai. "What's that footage of?"

Mai didn't turn, instead her eyes remained glued to the footage she was fast forwarding through. "It's from the museum security cameras."

Niner's eyebrows rose. "Really? How the hell did you get that?"

"I stole it."

"That's why she was arrested. She's wanted by the police too as a co conspirator."

"Co-conspirator? You two as well I suppose?"

"Yup."

"What a joke. This whole thing is a joke. It makes no sense. Why are the Vietnamese so hell-bent on arresting me that they'd risk—hell, already cause—an international incident?"

Acton nodded toward the television. "Apparently the Vietnamese are about to sign a massive weapons deal with Russia. The Chinese are causing problems in the South China Sea so the Vietnamese are using their growing oil money to purchase a whack of new hardware. The talking heads think the overreaction is an effort to please the Russians who've been hemming and hawing on whether or not to sell them the weapons."

"The Russian I met with seemed reasonable though he toed the party line."

"Sarkov?"

Niner nodded. "Yeah, same guy. You met him?"

"Yes, at the hotel before he went to meet you apparently. I got the sense he was willing to hear the truth. What good that will do now, I don't know. What with Atwater's appeal being ignored, the Vietnamese seem to have committed."

"Appeal?" Niner turned back to the television. "Is that what they're showing?"

"Yes," said Laura. "She was broadcasting live to CNN, telling the world what was happening when they think the Vietnamese blew out the floor from under her."

Niner cursed. "I hope the guys are okay." He motioned toward the laptop. "Any luck yet proving I'm innocent?"

Mai shook her head, pointing at the screen. "This is the only footage showing the shooter. He comes through the main doors, hands over his pass, then heads toward the room where we all were a few minutes later. You can't really make out his face, at least not with this."

Niner leaned in and replayed the footage. He frowned. "Nope, this won't prove it's not me."

"Sure it will."

Niner and the others turned to Laura. "How?"

"That guy's half a foot shorter than you."

Niner turned back to the screen. "You can tell?"

"Not really, I just remember from the shooting. The guy who shot Petrov was far shorter. You're what, one-hundred-eighty centimeters?"

"Huh?"

Acton laughed. "Europeans!" He looked at Niner. "You're about five-nine?"

"Ten."

"Ten then," said Laura. "He was five-two, five-three at best?"

"So how does that help me?"

Laura leaned forward and backed the footage up to when the man entered, pausing it. She pointed at the metal detector. "That height can be measured. From the video any pro will be able to see exactly how tall he is." She snapped her fingers. "Bring up the footage from when *we* arrived. Leave that one open so we can compare James entering. He's taller than you but close enough that we should be able to make a comparison."

Mai brought up the footage and paused the image showing Acton entering. She split the screen to show both images.

And it was obvious. The man who had used his ID was a head shorter at least than Acton, and clearly far shorter than his own 5'10".

"Okay, so that pretty much proves I'm not the guy. Now what? How the hell do we get that footage into the proper hands while we're stuck here?"

Acton smiled. "I've been thinking about that."

*Daewoo Hanoi Hotel, Hanoi, Vietnam*

Dawson grabbed Secretary Atwater, swinging the small woman into his arms as he charged from the room. The eighth floor had been lost and Jimmy, the last out, had reported seeing a group entering the room directly under Atwater's suite. He cleared the threshold, Atwater at first struggling against the indignity, he ignoring it. Screams from the staff left behind who hadn't reacted as quickly as he had filled his ears but they weren't his concern at the moment. The others would get them out. His job was to get Atwater to the tenth floor before the Vietnamese had a chance to blast through the floor. The fact they would actually blast through the floor of her suite had him convinced this was going to be a fight to the death.

Which meant it was time to get dirty.

He deked to the right, shoving hard, his legs pumping toward the stairwell before it was lost to the enemy.

An explosion ripped at the air behind him, screams of terror turning into screams of pain.

And far too many screams suddenly silenced.

He reached the stairwell and put Atwater down, handing her over to two DSS agents. "Get her upstairs, now!"

They each grabbed an arm and practically lifted the aging woman up the stairs. He pointed at Spock and Jimmy. "It's time to go on the offensive."

"It's about damned time," said Spock, readying his MP5 as they ran back toward the room, gunfire erupting as the DSS agents returned fire while they tried to evacuate the survivors from the room. Dawson took a quick look and saw a ten-by-ten hole in the floor, several bodies and even more wounded scattered about the suite. He motioned for Spock and Niner to follow him, running to the other end of the hall. Six DSS agents were holding the stairwell.

"Status!"

"Holding for now, they don't seem to be making an assault from here yet."

"Okay, hold this stairwell but be prepared to retake the eighth."

The DSS agent's eyes narrowed. "Are you serious?"

"I never kid."

"He doesn't," added Spock with a smile. Dawson retreated back to the hallway and opened the first door on his right, entering the room. Spock and Jimmy followed. "Umm, BD, just how are they going to take the eighth?"

"We're going to drop in for a little visit."

Spock cocked an eyebrow. "Beg pardon?"

Dawson slid open the door to the balcony and Spock grinned. "Now I got you."

Dawson pointed to the two double beds. "Three sheets."

Jimmy and Spock stripped the sheets, returning to the balcony. The hotel and the grounds surrounding it were pitch black except for vehicle headlights and several spotlights that had been set up, randomly swinging across the façade of the building. They quickly tied one end of the sheets to the railing, spaced apart by several feet.

"We drop down, try the door, break the glass if necessary, clear the room. Understood?"

"Yes, Sergeant Major."

"Let's do this."

Dawson wrapped part of the sheet around his hand and swung a leg over the railing. He didn't wait, the risk of a spotlight catching them too great. He pushed out and let himself swing away from the building as he let the sheet slide through his fingers. Timed perfectly, he swung onto the balcony below, immediately reaching for the handle of the sliding door. He lifted the door up and off the track, out of the locking mechanism, an old trick that unfortunately worked with too many patio doors.

*Security eight floors up is always overlooked.*

Spock and Jimmy surged into the room the moment the door was out of the way and within seconds the whispered 'Clear!' was heard from all three operators. Dawson approached the door and looked through the peephole. He couldn't see anyone but it was nearly pitch black and the gunfire from down the hall was loud. He pointed toward the left where the stairwell was. "Spock with me, Jimmy cover our sixes. Stay low, conserve your ammo, and if we're lucky, anyone down the hall won't know what happened with all the noise."

Spock pulled open the door and Dawson poked his head out. An emergency light in the stairwell showed at least half a dozen silhouettes. He could see shadows at the far end, near the room under Atwater's suite, but no one close. He stepped into the hallway, breaking left, Jimmy to the right, taking a knee, Spock beside him to his left. Dawson raised his MP5 and squeezed the trigger, single shots, Spock doing the same.

The Vietnamese, eight of them as it turned out, didn't know what hit them. Dawson stepped into the stairwell. "West landing, eighth floor secure," he said into his comm. Immediately he heard footsteps rushing down the stairs and the six DSS agents joined them. "Hold this stairwell as long as you can."

"Yes, sir."

Dawson pointed at the bodies. "Get their weapons and ammo, one of you deliver it to the tenth." Spock was already searching the bodies. "Grenades?"

"One each."

"We'll take those. This battle will be fought here, now."

Spock tossed three grenades to Dawson. He shoved them in his pockets as they joined Jimmy, still taking a knee at the door to the room they had swung into. "Status?"

"It's so loud down there they didn't hear you guys. I'm counting at least six in the hall, but I could be wrong, it's just shadows." He pointed to a door about midway. "I'm pretty sure that's the room they blasted through from the seventh. The door's open and I've seen several people moving back and forth through there."

"Ok, somebody is going to check this end sooner rather than later." He looked at Jimmy. "How's your arm?"

"Fantastic. Let me guess, east stairwell?"

"Yup."

"No problem," he said as Spock handed over two grenades.

"Good. Put two in the strike zone as soon as we've cleared the soft targets, Spock you put two into the room under Atwater's suite. We'll clear that room so our guys can clear the ninth of anybody who made it up, then join us."

"Roger that."

Dawson activated his comm. "Ninth floor, prepare for grenades under Atwater's suite and the east stairwell. East stairwell, prepare to take the eighth floor landing. Ninth floor prepare to join us on the eighth."

Confirmations were heard through his earpiece just as someone came out of the seventh floor access room, turning right toward them. Dawson dropped him as the three advanced at a crouch, squeezing off single shots at the now alerted men in the hall. As they approached the first target room Dawson pulled the pin on a grenade, tossing it around the doorframe as he pulled the pin on a second, still firing one-handed at the quickly diminishing Vietnamese. He tossed the second grenade inside. "Fire in the hole!" he shouted as they all rushed forward, away from the blast. Spock dropped the last man in the hallway as those at the stairwell took notice. Jimmy's first grenade was already whipped down the hall, speed and accuracy key as the ceiling was too low for a traditional lob. It was a fastball pitch that in the darkness they had no way of knowing if it were successful or just bouncing back at them.

The second was thrown as they continued to advance, Spock already tossing his first grenade into the second target room just as Dawson's grenades erupted behind them. Screams and secondary explosions tore into the hallway through the open door behind them as the stairwell was suddenly shredded in a brief flash, the emergency light taken out bathing the entire area in darkness. Gunfire erupted, the distinctive sounds of Glocks and MP5s, unchallenged as Spock's grenades tore apart the eighth floor suite.

Dawson spun on his heel as the last of the debris burst through the door. He rushed inside, weapon high and on full-auto, squeezing short bursts at anything that moved, Spock joining them, Jimmy covering their asses.

"Clear!" announced Dawson, the others echoing their confirmation. The entire assault had taken less than sixty seconds but it wasn't over. "Ninth floor, you up there?" he shouted.

"Yeah. That you, White?"

"Affirmative. Get as many men down here as you can." He pointed at a tipped over ladder and Spock grabbed it, putting it back in place. Almost immediately someone began to descend the ladder as another update came through the comm.

"Eighth floor east stairwell secure."

Dawson pointed at the first man. "Make sure this room is secure, then begin a room by room search. Try to stick to the hallways, they won't risk blowing those." He motioned for Spock and Jimmy to follow as he stepped back into the hallway. Flashlights at either end showed DSS agents in position, weapons being stripped from the dead. He jogged down the hall toward the room with the hole to the seventh floor and took a quick peek around the door.

Nothing was moving and the windows, curtains opened, were providing enough light from the city for everything to be seen clearly.

Including the large hole in the center of the room and half a dozen dead or dying men around it. Shouts and sounds of movement from below could be heard. He tossed his third and final grenade down the hole, taking cover in the hall.

The blast was still deafening, even if fifteen feet below. The screams and cries seemed louder.

Suddenly the lights came back on, revealing the carnage for them all to see.

And signaling, Dawson hoped, the end.

*Daewoo Hanoi Hotel Lobby, Hanoi, Vietnam*

Sarkov looked up as the lights came back on. The hotel had been rocked by what seemed like a dozen explosions over the last few minutes, the vibrations carrying through the structure and up his legs, though the sounds were muffled and distant. He rounded the corner and found Yashkin standing near the check-in counter with several Vietnamese senior officers and a couple of suits.

"What's going on?" asked Sarkov as he approached. "Why are the lights back on?"

Yashkin nodded to the men then took Sarkov aside, out of earshot. He lowered his voice. "The message has been sent."

"What message?"

"That the Vietnamese should be taken seriously in their desire for justice to be served."

"Justice? How is violating international law justice?"

Yashkin looked at him, almost as if disappointed. "International law? The Russian Federation does not concern itself with international law when one of its leaders has been murdered in cold blood. However, that being said, *publicly* we have implored the Vietnamese to show restraint in dealing with this security emergency and they have agreed, halting the attack that was so inappropriate a response."

"An attack you ordered."

Yashkin shrugged. "Orders from Moscow, though I must admit the Vietnamese were a little overzealous in blasting through the floor directly under the Secretary while she was live on international television."

"A brilliant defensive tactic on her part."

Yashkin pursed his lips, examining Sarkov's face. "I sense admiration."

"Perhaps, though that should not be misinterpreted as doubting where my loyalties lie. One can always express admiration for one's enemy's tactics. The key is to then use the knowledge gained for a successful counteroffensive against them."

Yashkin nodded his head slowly. "I wonder if your time has come."

Sarkov felt a pit begin to form in his stomach. "I beg your pardon?"

"Perhaps it is time for you to retire. I think you are too soft for the job."

Sarkov chose his words carefully. "I have only two years left before that fateful day. However, if I weren't here today, we would not know that the Americans are telling the truth."

Yashkin's eyes narrowed. "What do you mean?"

"I have just seen security camera footage of the eighth floor showing that Agent Green was indeed in the hotel at the exact moment of the Prime Minister's assassination."

"Show me this."

Sarkov led Yashkin to the security office, a bit of hope building within that perhaps Yashkin might just be interested in the truth after all. "Bring up the footage showing the American coming out of his room," said Sarkov as they entered. Within moments they were watching Agent Green exit his room then run to the elevators with several others. "See the timestamp? Only two minutes after the fatal shots were fired."

Yashkin leaned in, watching the footage loop. "Interesting." He stood back up. "How did this footage come to be? I thought the cameras were supposed to be deactivated on that level."

"They were, but an employee reactivated them to help a man named *Phong* enter the room, presumably to steal the security pass of Agent Green."

"And I assume there is footage of this as well?"

"Yes. And Phong is what the Prime Minister called his assassin. The same name as the employee seen entering the DSS agent's room."

"So then this would suggest our theory is wrong."

Sarkov almost let out an audible sigh of relief. "Yes."

"It would appear then that this Phong was acting on behalf of the Americans. He went to Agent Green's room, Agent Green gave his security pass to this Phong, who then assassinated the Prime Minister and his security detail, while the American delegation did nothing to stop it, then two witnesses, both with known ties to several international incidents involving the American government and its military just *happen* to be in the room at the same time, to name this Phong patsy as the killer, claiming that the Prime Minister knew him and he was killed for something he allegedly did during the war and not for political reasons." Yashkin shook his head. "I'm afraid this proves nothing. All it proves is how the professors knew the name of the individual. They were *all* in on the plot to assassinate the Prime Minister. All that has changed here is that the actual shooter is a different person than we thought, and that the two professors are *definitely* involved."

Sarkov's eyes had opened wide, his eyebrows climbing his forehead as he resisted all temptation to let his jaw drop. The story being spun by Yashkin was brilliantly ridiculous, exactly the type of thing the Kremlin would come up with in situations like this. Yashkin definitely had a bright future, unfortunately it was a future Sarkov wanted no part of.

He shook his head. "I can't believe what I'm hearing. There's no proof of anything you say. The entire case has been that Agent Green was the shooter. We now know definitively that he wasn't. This information must be presented to the Vietnamese *and* the Americans."

Yashkin shook his head, a frown on his face. "I'm *very* disappointed. Moscow will be too." He turned to the man at the keyboard. "I want all of the eighth floor footage erased. *All* of it. It should be as if the cameras had never been activated." He pointed a finger at the man, then his partner, glaring down at them. "And *no one,* I repeat *no one* will ever hear about this otherwise there will be *dire* consequences. Understood?"

The terror in the men's eyes made it clear they understood perfectly as they nodded, the first man attacking the keyboard to execute his orders. Yashkin left the room, Sarkov following. When they were alone in the hallway, Sarkov stopped and Yashkin turned toward him.

"Why?"

Yashkin squinted. "Why?"

"Why delete the footage? Why aren't we pursuing the truth?"

"Moscow isn't interested in the truth."

Sarkov shook his head. "Why not? We have an opportunity here to shine on the international stage, to bring out the truth ourselves, to show that no matter how much everyone wanted to believe it was the Americans, we were more interested in finding out what really happened, and when we did, we revealed it to the world, showing we aren't the monsters so many think we are. By destroying this footage we become the very people the West accuses us of being!"

"You are indeed naïve," replied Yashkin, his head shaking slowly from side to side. "You have no idea what is going on here. We've had troops massed on the Ukrainian border for months just waiting for something like this to happen. And it finally has. Ebola and ISIS provided the distraction so the Western public would forget about what had happened in Eastern Ukraine and the Crimea, and now this event, this one, single event, carried out by a madman, gave us the opportunity to pull the trigger. Our troops at this very moment are invading and should have control of the traditionally Russian portions of the Ukraine within days. There is nothing the West can do to stop it, and there's nothing they *will* do because with this murder of our leader by an American, they have no credibility on the world stage.

"The *truth* as you call it is unimportant, and it may very well come out in time. But at *this* time, it is more important to further the ambitions of Mother Russia and its diaspora by bringing them back into the fold. Once we have done this, the world will once again tremble at the might of Russia and will never dismiss us again."

Yashkin's face was beet red, the passion in which he had delivered the last few sentences was terrifying in its zeal, and Sarkov had taken a step backward as the onslaught of the diatribe had hit home.

The man was mad.

The men he followed were mad.

And Cold War Two had begun with the actions of a single Vietnamese man seeking revenge for an affront carried out forty years ago.

Sarkov remained silent as Yashkin's face returned to its normal pale self. The man pulled in a deep breath, pursing his lips as he seemed to examine Sarkov for a reaction.

Sarkov gave him none.

Yashkin finally spoke. "I think we will no longer require your services today. Go home and report to the embassy tomorrow morning for instructions."

Sarkov said nothing, merely nodding as Yashkin continued to stare at him, then spun on his heel and walked briskly away.

*Go home.*

Sarkov shook his head. He knew his dreams of retirement in a foreign land were finished. He'd be ordered back to Moscow in quiet disgrace and probably stored in some hole for years or decades. And some way, somehow, he'd die accidentally or in a staged prison fight.

A wave of self-pity swept over him and his shoulders collapsed, his chin dropping as he reached for a wall, both hands held high, holding his body up as he fought for control.

He thought of his wife.

She had been a good woman, not political in the slightest, but supportive of his career from the start, putting on the public face required and tolerating his sometimes late hours and long absences.

And it had been her dream to retire outside of Russia as well.

She hadn't made it.

And neither would he.

He shoved himself away from the wall, squaring his shoulders.

And if he was going to go down for doing the right thing, he was going to give them a real reason.

*Too soft my ass.*

*Daewoo Hanoi Hotel, Hanoi, Vietnam*

Dawson took the stairs two at a time to the tenth floor as the bulk of the security team redeployed to the eighth and ninth floors. He entered the room Atwater was now located in and found the woman sitting on a chair near the hallway door. He pointed at the open windows.

"Why aren't those covered?"

"Sorry, sir. We just relocated here sixty seconds ago when one of the guys said there was a support beam here. We figured they won't risk taking the entire floor down." Two agents closed the curtains over as the explanation was given.

"Good thinking," said Dawson as he turned to brief Atwater. "The Vietnamese have pulled back. We've retaken the eighth floor and with the lights back on, I'm thinking we've got a reprieve, at least temporarily. We should take the opportunity to relocate our equipment to this floor, recharge our batteries and pool all the resources we can including food and water."

"The water's back on," said one of the staff.

"Good. Refill every water bottle we've got and everyone, I mean everyone, use the bathroom now while we've got toilets that can flush. Search every room on the floor and evacuate any civilians if there's any left. Empty their bar fridges and distribute food. I want everyone fed and hydrated. Police all weapons and ammo from the bodies of the fallen, ours and theirs." He looked about. "Where's the wounded?"

"Next room. We've got two serious that need immediate medical attention, five walking wounded that will need attention and half a dozen with minor scrapes and bruises."

"Dead?"

"Two caught in the initial blast. We got lucky."

"Lucky?"

When Atwater finally spoke she sounded beaten. Dawson took a knee and lowered his voice. "Are you okay, ma'am?"

Atwater shook her head. "They tried to kill me."

"Yes, ma'am. It appears that way. But your team did its job and you're uninjured. If need be, we'll do our job again and protect you."

She raised her head and looked at him, her eyes red. Someone handed him a bottle of water. "You do this every day?"

He chuckled. "No, not *every* day." He leaned in a little closer. "Listen, ma'am, it's okay to be scared. We all are. That's human nature. The immediate danger is over. Your people need you. Now I'm going to teach you a trick. In situations like this control has been taken away from you and given to your security staff. That's procedure. While you don't have to make decisions, use the time to get control of your adrenaline. It's your adrenaline that's got you shaking and it feeds your fear. Think of fear as a chemically induced artificial state rather than some personal failure. If you can get control of the adrenaline flowing into your bloodstream then you'll be able to calm down. You know when you're really angry sometimes you shake?"

She nodded, looking up at him.

"Well that's adrenaline, not fear. So if anger can be fueled by adrenaline, it's time to turn the fear you now have into anger at what's happened to you. You should be indignant, mad. Frankly, it's time to get pissed off. So here's the trick. While you're in a situation where you're not talking and running around, use tactical breathing."

"What's that?"

"It's a trick us soldiers do to keep us calm and it's very easy. Just breathe in through your nose for four seconds, hold it for four, breathe out through your lips for four, then hold for four, and repeat. Just keep doing that and eventually you'll calm down. If you remember to do it enough, it just becomes habit." He smiled as she began doing it. "It also works at the negotiation table. Do it while the other guy is talking, then when it's your turn, you appear calm, no matter how idiotic the other guy's demands are."

She nodded, smiling slightly, as she continued the breathing technique.

Dawson heard a phone ring down the hallway, the doors of the rooms obviously now opened by the staff. It went unanswered then another rang. "I think they're attempting to make contact," he said, looking at Atwater. "Do you want me to deal with it?"

She shook her head. "No, I'll do it." She pushed herself to her feet, taking a breath, the color returning to her cheeks. She smiled slightly at Dawson and placed a hand on his arm. "You're a good man, Mr. *White*."

"Thank you, ma'am."

The phone rang and she nodded toward one of her staff who picked it up. She covered the receiver. "It's Mr. Yashkin for you, Madame Secretary."

"Put it on speaker and someone record this."

Several cellphones quickly appeared.

"This is Secretary Atwater."

"Thank goodness you are okay, Madame Secretary. As soon as I heard what was happening I requested the attack be stopped at once."

Atwater rolled her eyes, seeming back to her normal self. "I'm happy to hear that the Russian government was not responsible."

"Of course we weren't, Madame Secretary. We are a peaceful people"—the entire room rolled their eyes—"and only want justice to be served. Clearly that does not involve further violence."

"I am happy to hear that, Mr. Yashkin. Now there is a matter of the wounded. We have two people who need emergency access to a hospital and several others who will need medical attention. Can I trust that you will see to it?"

"At once, Madame Secretary, at once. In fact we have medical personnel already here just waiting for your approval."

"Sent them up at once. Make sure they are unarmed."

"Of course."

"And we have four dead. We will require body bags for them and transportation of the bodies to the Embassy."

"I am indeed sorry to hear that. It will be arranged."

Atwater took a deep breath, almost glaring at Yashkin through the speaker. "Now there is the matter of our departure. Since you seem to have significant influence with the Vietnamese authorities, I expect you will be able to *convince* them to allow us to leave at once."

"I have already spoken to them and they have agreed that you may leave in one hour, provided all of your personnel lay down their weapons and submit themselves for a visual inspection to confirm Agent Green is not among them."

Dawson shook his head slightly.

"I'm afraid we can't agree to disarming, Mr. Yashkin. I'm sure you'll understand that after what has just happened we simply cannot put our lives at risk."

"So you do not trust our Vietnamese hosts?"

His mock shock was almost comical. "Would you?"

Yashkin laughed heartily, the man clearly a well-trained diplomat. "No, I suppose I would not. I will speak to our hosts on your behalf. Perhaps they will allow your staff to at least keep their sidearms."

Dawson nodded slightly.

"That would be acceptable. And please inform our hosts that I will be resuming my interview with CNN and conveying our expectations and our thanks to the Russian government for their assistance. Good evening, Mr. Yashkin."

She signaled with a hand in front of her throat to end the call then dropped back into her seat, sucking a breath in through her nose, her head bobbing almost imperceptibly as she counted.

Dawson pointed to one of the staffers. "Get the equipment set up immediately, I want the Secretary on with CNN in five minutes." He pointed to one of the DSS agents. "Coordinate the medical evac and let's get the bodies ready to go to the Embassy."

Atwater motioned for him to come closer. He knelt beside her.

"Any word from Agent Green?"

Dawson shook his head. "No, but if they had him I'm sure we'd have heard."

"Can you reach him?"

"Not without possibly compromising his location."

"They'll be controlling the phones into here, but he might reach out to the embassy. Make sure they know the plan. He needs to get himself to the airplane if he can."

"Yes, ma'am."

"And what about those two professors they're accusing of being involved?"

"If I know Agent Green he's probably already made contact with them."

"They know each other?"

"Some things you're better off not knowing."

Atwater chuckled as she shook her head. "It's the secrecy of the job that I hate the most."

"Funny, I thought it was the gunfire." Dawson grinned and Atwater swatted at him, finally laughing genuinely.

"Let's just hope your friends are able to get to the airplane in time. I don't know when there will be another opportunity."

Dawson nodded, his face grim as he pushed himself to his feet. "I'll call the embassy right away."

He stepped away to make the phone call as the first paramedics arrived in an elevator down the hall, Spock and Jimmy checking them and their equipment over.

As he activated the secure phone, part of him wanted to reach out to Niner right then and there, to let him know, but he couldn't risk that their conversation might be monitored and his friend's location traced, especially with the Russians and their eavesdropping equipment most likely in play.

*You're on your own for now, buddy.*

*Tay Ho District, Hanoi, Vietnam*

Phong was in a good mood. The best he could remember in a long time. A weight had been lifted off his shoulders that he had forgotten was there, an albatross that had tied him to an impossible promise made by a grieving, angry teenager forty years ago.

And karma had brought justice and balance back to the world.

A grave injustice had been done, and the man responsible had been punished.

And now Phong could rest in peace along with his ancestors.

A rest he expected to soon find, he having no doubt he would be arrested tomorrow when he went to work. They would surely know by now that the American agent's pass had been used, they would check the hotel footage for the agent's room and see it had been him that had stolen it, and he would be immediately arrested. In fact he was kind of shocked they hadn't arrived at his apartment to arrest him while he slept. It had been over eight hours since he had killed Petrov, plenty of time for them to have discovered the truth.

*Maybe I'll get away with it?*

He had to admit the thought of continuing his job into his old age like he had planned just yesterday morning appealed to him.

*The cameras were turned off!*

The sudden recollection had him pause, the parade he was marching in surging around him like a stone in a river. He resumed walking, gaping in wonder at the thought. If he had managed to avoid the cameras at the museum, and there was no footage of him stealing the pass, then it could be anyone who killed Petrov.

*They might have no clue who I am!*

It made sense. In fact, it was the only reasonable explanation. They hadn't arrested him yet because they had no idea who he was, and if they didn't know yet, there was almost no way they'd ever know.

His step felt a little lighter as the last of the day's pressures began to lift. His nemesis was dead, and as if the divine Buddha himself had wished it, he had been the instrument of karmic retribution, and so as not to further imbalance the life forces surrounding them, he would not be punished for being the deliverer.

He spotted Duy sitting in a lawn chair in front of his apartment building, a bottle of liquor being handed around among him and several others he knew from the hotel, their wives and girlfriends sitting in their own row behind them.

He waved.

Duy leapt to his feet, a smile on his face as he greeted his friend. "Phong! I was beginning to wonder if you were going to make it. I guess you're feeling better?"

Phong had to think for a quick moment when he remembered he had left work faking stomach issues. He nodded, taking an empty seat. "Yeah, just one of those things that a couple of good visits to the toilet cured."

"I hope you lit a candle!" laughed Duy, the others joining in as the bottle was handed to Phong. He took a long swig of the vodka.

*Russian. How appropriate.*

He passed the bottle down the line of chairs and looked at the parade, the colorful garb accentuated by the dancing of the young people.

*To be young again!*

His youth had few pleasant memories, and as he watched the happy couples pass he found himself thinking of a life lost, a life wasted. He took another swig as the bottle passed, nobody saying anything except to point out a particularly beautiful woman.

There had been plenty of women in his life, plenty of women who had wanted to be with him. But he had denied them all. He didn't want to bring a child into this world, a world where such hate and evil could exist. He wouldn't contribute to the misery that was life. His lineage would die with him.

And at this moment that brought him a profound sadness.

The great Asita, who had never given up for decades, had founded their village in this land over two thousand years ago.

And now it would all end thanks to him.

*No! Thanks to Petrov!*

Yes, Petrov was to blame, but not completely. It wasn't Petrov that had thrown away a young life to hatred and despair. It was him. He had done it to himself. He should have tried to move on, to honor his family by continuing their lineage, rather than living a lifetime consumed by hate.

Another swig. Another pass.

"I need a wife."

Duy nearly dropped the bottle. "Were you drinking before you got here?"

The others laughed as Duy's wife came up behind her husband and massaged his shoulders. He leaned his head back against her and smiled. "Phong says he needs a wife."

"He's still a catch!" she said, winking. "I'm sure I can find him one. There're some good widows around here." She motioned toward an old grandmother with no teeth, mushing her rice with her gums. "Old Qui is available."

Qui reached out her hand to Phong, her fingers covered in sticky rice. "Come here, baby, I'll give you a good time!"

Everyone roared in laughter.

"I need to have babies, lots of babies," said Phong, oblivious to the humor at his expense. "Sons!"

"I'll give you a good time but forget about babies!"

More laughter.

Duy seemed to sense Phong's mood was serious. "What's wrong my friend, why all this talk of children?"

"I've wasted my life."

The bottle was about to be handed to him again when Duy shook his head, motioning for them to be skipped. "No you haven't. You've got a great job, good friends. You've made the most of what this country can offer people like us."

"My village was wiped out in the war."

Duy's eyes opened wide, this the first time Phong had ever told him anything about his past. He remained silent, drawing Phong out to share more.

"The Viet Cong came into our village with a Russian, looking for recruits. I was in the forest collecting herbs when they came. I watched them murder everyone."

"I'm so sorry," said Duy, placing a hand on his friend's shoulder, his wife dropping to her knees beside him, taking his hand in hers as tears rolled down her face.

"You must have been a boy," she said.

He nodded. "Fifteen. I tried to kill the Russian but I couldn't." His head dropped to his chest. "I was too weak."

"You were only fifteen!" She squeezed his hand, holding it to her chest. "You can't blame yourself."

"I know that now, but I did. For forty years."

"Is that why you never took a wife?" asked Duy. "Never had kids?"

Phong nodded. "I was ruled by hate and self-pity. I punished myself for surviving by denying myself happiness."

"But you're finally talking about it," said Duy's wife. "You obviously want to move on."

"I finally *can* move on."

"What do you mean?"

"I killed him."

Everyone looked at him in shock, the bottle forgotten, the parade only feet away mere background noise now, the drums a heartbeat they all felt in their chests.

"What do you mean?" asked Duy, sounding almost afraid to ask. "Who did you kill?"

"The Russian who slaughtered my family."

Duy gasped as did the others. "*You* killed the Russian Prime Minister? At the museum?"

Phong nodded, another weight lifted off his shoulders. He realized he was putting his friends at risk, but he had to tell someone. And part of him hoped they would turn him in out of fear, thus protecting themselves and ending a future that he felt was uncertain. "They haven't arrested me yet, though, so I guess they don't know it was me."

"I guess they don't!" exclaimed Duy. "They're blaming the Americans! They're saying one of their agents is the assassin!"

Phong suddenly snapped out of his self-pity. "What? What are you talking about?"

"You stole that agent's ID, didn't you?"

Phong nodded, suddenly ashamed he had involved his friend. "Yes. I'm sorry, but as soon as I realized who he was, I had no choice. I promised him I would kill him the next time I saw him, and when I heard he'd be at the museum at the same time as the Americans, I took the ID of the Asian agent from his safe."

"You used me!"

He turned toward Duy. "I'm so sorry, Duy. I didn't mean to, but if they knew you were involved they'd be here, wouldn't they?"

Duy grabbed the bottle of vodka and took a long swig, his Adam's apple bobbing. He was about to hand the bottle down the line when his wife grabbed it and took her own swig. "You'd think so." He sighed, lowering his voice from its excited state. "Phong, don't you realize what's been happening today?"

Phong shook his head.

"They're talking war! The Russians are accusing the Americans of assassinating their Prime Minister. Two professors who were guests at the hotel and a grad student at the museum have been named as being involved. The Russians have invaded a country already and there was some sort of air battle. An American plane crashed!"

"And don't forget the hotel!" added his wife, jabbing at the air. "Don't forget what's happening there!"

"Yeah, the police went in and attacked the floors the Americans are on."

"What happened?" asked Phong, his chest tight as he realized everything happening was his fault.

"I don't know. They shut down the Internet and cellphones. I saw it down the street on a television with a satellite dish."

Phong wasn't sure what to say. "Has anybody died?"

"Phong, they invaded a country! Of course people have died!"

His chest dropped to his knees as he leaned over, grabbing at his hair. "What have I done?!"

No words of comfort came from his friends. Everyone was in shock. The events a world away never affected their day to day lives. Yesterday if someone had said Russia had invaded a country, he would have paid it no mind as long as it wasn't Vietnam they had invaded. But the events at the hotel were on everyone's mind since it was where most of them worked. It affected them immensely.

And it was all his fault.

In his wildest nightmares he couldn't have imagined things spiraling so far out of control. He had killed a bad man and those protecting him. He had delivered justice, restored balance, then moved on. There were witnesses who should have been able to tell the police that the shooter wasn't the American whose pass he had used. There were cameras at the museum.

*We spoke!*

And the conversation was in front of witnesses.

*Why are they doing this?*

"What am I going to do?"

Duy put the bottle on the ground. "You have to disappear."

Phong sat back up, wiping the tears off his cheeks. "No, I need to turn myself in, to tell everyone that it was me."

"They'll kill you before you get a chance to tell your story," said Duy. "People are dying because of this. The news says they don't care who did it as long as there's confusion." Duy shrugged. "You know me, I don't know anything about politics, all I do know is this situation is dangerous."

A phone rang and Duy's wife jumped in shock. She stepped over to where she and several of the wives were sitting and picked up the cordless phone. "Hello…one moment." She handed the phone to her husband. "It's for you. It's the hotel."

Duy exchanged a scared look with Phong. He took the phone and Phong leaned it to hear the conversation. "This is Duy."

"Duy, it's Bao. I've only got a minute."

"Bao? You've got to speak up, the festival has started."

"They're after you and Phong!"

Phong's heart nearly stopped.

"What do you mean?" asked Duy.

"Some Russian guy was in here looking at the tapes from the eighth floor—"

"The eighth floor cameras are disabled."

"Yes, but you turned them back on. There's footage of Phong going into the American agent's room using *your* pass, the same agent they're saying killed the Russian guy. But the footage showed that he couldn't have done it because he was here when it happened."

"That's good, isn't it? It means they can prove the Americans didn't do it?"

"No, it's not! Another Russian ordered me to delete all the footage. But Duy, the first Russian guy had me print your personnel file and Phong's too. He knows where you guys live. You've got to warn Phong and the two of you have to disappear. I don't know why you did it, but killing the Russian Prime Minister? What were you thinking?"

"I-I didn't! I mean, it wasn't me! I—"

Duy stopped, looking at Phong, uncertain what to say. Phong took the phone. "This is Phong. I killed the Russian Prime Minister. Duy thought he was helping me get my key pass from the American's room. I told him I had forgotten it there. He didn't know anything. I'm the one they want."

"I don't think they care," said Bao. "They deleted all the footage." There was a pause. "Does that mean you got away with it?"

Phong wasn't sure, but with this footage not existing anymore, then it did make him wonder whether or not he was actually safe

"Why did you kill him?" asked Bao. "Did the Americans hire you?"

And that was when Phong knew this would never end. Too many people knew now, and if he didn't tell his side of the story, unmolested, the truth would be twisted into whatever story the authorities wanted.

*This has to end.*

"No, nobody hired me." He took a deep breath. "Thanks for letting us know." He hung up, handing the phone back to Duy's wife. He turned to his friend. "I have to get my story out."

"But how?"

"I need to tell the Americans."

*Old Quarter, Hanoi, Vietnam*

Igor Sarkov pulled his car to the side of the street, yet another festival filling the night with revelers. He couldn't remember which one this was, he didn't care. It was just another party. Almost every month there seemed to be some sort of celebration in the city, but they were things to be enjoyed by the younger people at the embassy, not him.

If there wasn't air conditioning, he wasn't interested.

And these celebrations took place on the streets where the air was thick and hot far too often for his liking.

Colorful clothing, tissue paper lanterns, rattles and drums—it was all an assault on the senses. His late wife would have loved it, she being much more interested in the culture of the places they visited, but he could care less.

Which was probably his loss.

But none of that mattered now.

By disobeying Yashkin's order to go home he was putting his life at risk. But he didn't care. He had to know the truth, and the world had to know the truth. His loyalties were no longer to "Mother" Russia, the very term poisonous now, his country a disappointment that crushed his will more every day.

*Only two more years were left!*

It was devastating. A lifetime wasted. He had lost his wife, his son had died with no family of his own, his parents were long dead, and his only brother was lost to vodka a decade ago.

He was truly alone.

With no one to share his retirement years with.

He looked up at the apartment and felt an affinity for this man, Phong. If what the Americans said was true, if his family and village had been wiped out by Petrov forty years ago, then he too was alone, having lost everything.

*It would almost be a shame to bring him in.*

He turned off the car, killing the exquisite flow of chilled air and opened the door, the rapidly cooling evening still an assault on his overly large frame. It was a four story apartment building with a small grocery on the main floor.

And Phong Son Quan lived on the third floor.

*At least it's not the fourth.*

The stairwell to the apartments was on the left side of the building. He stepped through the doorway, there no door to be found, and began the long climb up the stairs. By the time he reached the third floor he was wheezing far too much for someone involved in security.

*That's new.*

He held his hand on his chest for a moment, feeling his heart as it fluttered slightly before settling down. He pulled in a few steady breaths and felt himself begin to return to his normal self. He was getting old—was already old he had no doubt in the minds of those like Yashkin. Time was catching up, a lifetime of enjoying fine foods, then two years of not having his shutoff valve at his side to stop him from overindulging.

Which had resulted in him packing on thirty pounds in two years, on top of the extra thirty he had already been carrying.

Fortunately his job hadn't been to chase people for a long time. In fact, he couldn't remember ever chasing anyone as part of Foreign Affairs. It just wasn't important enough. He was an investigator, but of diplomatic concerns. In a diplomatic post he had no jurisdiction to arrest people, so why chase them? And today, if he ran into the assassin in the apartment he now stood in front of, he had no intention of chasing him either.

He pulled out his gun as he had no qualms about shooting the man.

He knocked.

No answer.

He knocked again, KGB style.

Still no answer.

He tried the door and wasn't surprised to find it locked. A hard shoulder against the flimsy door soon had him in the apartment, his weapon sweeping from left to right, quickly finding the single room apartment clear. It was a simple affair, spotlessly clean, a habit Sarkov wondered helped get Phong his job, or was learned from his job. One thing he had found over the years of being in various levels of developing countries was the common misperception among Westerners that just because someone was poor their homes were dirty.

This was rarely the case.

Like this apartment.

The paint was peeling, the floor was chipped and scarred, the porcelain of the lone sink had lost most of its white and the toilet behind a makeshift wall was equally showing its age.

But the floor was swept clean, the toilet bowl was free of filth and the bed was made.

Everything was spotless.

Everything had its place.

Except one thing.

Sitting on the bed was an envelope with no stamp, it clearly waiting to be mailed.

He picked up the envelope and examined the handwriting. Meticulous. This was a deliberate man, and deliberate men could be dangerous.

*Clearly.*

If the professors were telling the truth, then this was the assassin, not Agent Green. And if so, this would be exactly the type of apartment he would expect to find such a man in. He wasn't crazy. That much was clear. This was a man who had fulfilled a forty year mission if what the professors overheard was true.

He had enacted revenge on the murderer of his family.

Something Sarkov wished he would have had the courage to do when the opportunity arose, but alas, he hadn't. He had sat in the courtroom like a coward when the drunk driver who killed his wife and son was acquitted due to *his* rights being violated when he was arrested.

Sarkov's heart had turned cold against his country when the man had been congratulated by a senior member of United Russia, a man Sarkov knew reported directly to the President.

Which meant there was nothing he could do.

*Except kill the man.*

Instead he had done nothing.

And it shamed him, especially now, when a man like Phong, poor by anyone's standards outside this struggling country, was able to murder one of the most powerful men in the world.

All by having the courage of his convictions, and a simple plan that required nothing more than a gun and some balls.

Sarkov almost felt sorry that he'd have to arrest the man.

He tore open the letter and scanned it, his limited Vietnamese able to at least decipher that it was a letter to his family, telling them of some hidden items including a religious bowl.

*Must be the one the professors mentioned.*

He finished the letter and smiled, not with any sense of joy, but simply with the satisfaction of the truth finally revealed.

For at the end of the letter Phong Son Quan confessed to his crime.

And Sarkov knew the truth.

He folded up the letter, stuffed it back in the torn envelope and placed it in his inside jacket pocket.

*Now to find his friend, Duy.*

*American Embassy, Hanoi, Vietnam*

Charles Stewart sat in the cafeteria sipping a coffee, exhausted. His cameraman, Pat Murphy, sat across from him, his head on the table, snoring. The chanting and drums outside continued to drone on, Vietnamese television looping footage of the rallies here and at the British Embassy non-stop. Of course the 24 hour news channels were as well, mixed in with talking heads spouting off about the crisis, and blowing it out of proportion for the viewing public.

*It's all about the ratings.*

He was happy he was a hard news man. He reported, he didn't comment. Commentary was for commentators, not reporters. And the blurring of that line over the past few years was a blight on the honored history of his profession. Even he as a newsman would be the first to admit there wasn't enough news of interest to fill 24 hours of television, which was why hour long commentary shows had become the norm, and now even CNN was airing canned shows, finally realizing even they couldn't fill 24 hours with coverage they could call news with a straight face.

Hopefully it would lead all the 24 hour networks to trim down the talking heads and instead return to the time honored tradition of the thirty minute news cast that was actually news.

But he wasn't naïve enough to think it would happen any time soon.

One of the staffers, Leroy Donavan, waved to him, sitting down at the table with a coffee and donut. He looked as haggard as they all did.

"What's up, Leroy?"

"Hopefully my blood sugar in a few minutes." He took a large bite of his Boston cream donut, the filling spilling out the hole in the other side, a dollop dropping onto his napkin. He chewed, moaning with pleasure as he wiped up the escaped custard filling with his thumb, sucking it off with a smile. "So good. I missed lunch and dinner and I've got about five minutes to stuff this into me."

"Should have grabbed a sandwich, you'll just crash in an hour from that."

He shrugged. "Shoulda coulda woulda." He took a sip of his coffee then leaned in, bumping Murphy's arm. Murphy jumped in his seat.

"What's going on?"

"Life, liberty and the pursuit of happiness," replied Stewart, nodding toward their guest. "I'm guessing he's about to make us very happy."

"You didn't hear this from me," said Donavan, "but we were just informed that the American delegation from the Daewoo will be leaving within an hour for the airport."

"The attack has stopped?"

Donavan nodded. "The Russians are taking credit for that, and they're taking credit for negotiating with the Vietnamese to let the delegation proceed to the airport."

"Are they going to let them lift off?"

"No word on that, but don't be surprised if they don't. The statement was *very* carefully worded."

"At least though they'll be on the airplane. That has to be safer than at the hotel," said Murphy, swirling his now cold coffee in his cup.

"I don't know about safer," said Stewart. "How do you defend against an assault on an airplane filled with jet fuel?"

"But isn't the aircraft considered American soil?" asked Murphy. "Attacking it would be like attacking the embassy."

"True," said Donavan, swallowing the last of his donut. "But who would have ever thought they'd attack the damned Secretary of State's hotel!" He shook his head. "This whole thing is nuts. The goddamned Russian bastards have launched a full-blown invasion of the Ukraine and they're rattling their sabers at the Baltic States. NATO is shitting right now. They've got a mutual defense pact with them."

"So what are they doing? The news is pretty thin."

"From what I can gather NATO is on full alert and a rapid reaction force is already on its way to Lithuania. Air patrols have been stepped up and the navies are sending pretty much everything they've got in the area toward the Baltic Sea. I think everyone is just praying this settles down."

"Any word from Professor Acton or his wife?" asked Stewart.

Donavan shook his head. "No. I've got one of my staff trying to track them down but there's not much we can do. The cell network is down and so is the internet. The number you gave us for him is obviously down. We've tried sending some emails, but haven't heard anything. My guess is they're stuck just like we are."

"Did you try his wife's number?"

"We don't have it. Hers wouldn't work either."

"No, she's got a satellite phone."

Donavan paused in mid sip.

"Pardon me."

"Satellite phone. She's got one. We need to get that number. They need to know about the plane leaving so they can get on it."

Donavan pursed his lips as Murphy jacked his own satellite phone into his laptop, creating a painfully slow internet connection. "I'm not sure if that could be swung."

"Even if it can't, just knowing that the plane is leaving could be valuable. At least if they are safe for the moment, they'll know to keep their heads down until the delegation leaves. Then things should start to settle and maybe this security cordon will be lifted."

"I don't think the police are going anywhere until Agent Green is arrested."

Murphy swung the laptop around. "Maybe we should call her university? See if they have the number?"

Stewart picked up the satellite phone and dialed the number for University College London. It turned out she was splitting her time at the Smithsonian and was supposed to be there now, but with most people still asleep in Washington, he persisted with the London call. It took several transfers but he was soon speaking to one of her grad students, it still mid-afternoon in London.

"Terrence Mitchel here."

"Mr. Mitchel, Charles Stewart, ABC News. I'm trying to reach Professor Laura Palmer and her husband, Professor James Acton. Do you have a satellite phone number for them?"

There was a pause, then a reply he was used to hearing. "I'm sorry, but I can't give out the professor's private number. If you give me your number I'll see what I can do."

Stewart gave the number for Murphy's satellite phone, his own just a straight cell. "Now listen, Mr. Mitchel. I'm not sure if you're aware of this, but they have become mixed up in this Hanoi business."

"I know! I know! It's always something with them! If she had never met Professor Acton her life would be so much safer!"

Stewart smiled, the concern in the young man's voice plain to be heard.

*Something tells me someone has a crush on his teacher!*

"Marital situations aside, it is essential I speak to them at once. I have urgent information they need to know. Can you try calling them immediately?"

"Yes, I'll do it at once. Thank you, good bye."

The call ended and Stewart checked the phone battery just to be safe.

Half a charge.

"Hopefully we'll hear something soon."

Donavan rose. "If you hear anything, let me know right away. And get their number. We need to be able to contact them so we can arrange a pickup if it becomes possible."

"Will do."

Donavan walked away leaving both Stewart and Murphy staring at the phone.

*Ring dammit!*

It rang.

Two hands darted for it on instinct, Murphy's winning. He shrugged sheepishly and handed the phone over.

"Hello?"

"Hello, Charles?"

Stewart smiled, breathing a sigh of relief and giving a thumbs up to Murphy as he recognized Acton's voice. "Thank God you're okay!" he said, pulling out his pad and pen. He paused. "You *are* okay, right?"

"For the moment. We managed to hook up with Mai at her brother's place, and we have Agent *Green* with us."

"He's with you?!" Stewart looked around, lowering himself and his voice as he realized the entire cafeteria was now looking at him. "How did you manage that?"

"He reached out to us."

"He knows you?"

"Yes. Don't ask me more."

"I won't, I won't. Here's the skinny. The American delegation is leaving for the airport in about an hour. Any chance you can get there? Maybe sneak onto the airfield?"

"I don't see how. We might be able to get to the airport but there's no way we're getting on that plane with all the security I'm sure they'll have. But listen, we might not have to."

Stewart's eyes narrowed. "What do you mean?"

"We've got proof that Green isn't the shooter."

"Really?" He wrote 'PROOF NOT GREEN' and underlined it three times, Murphy raising his eyebrows. "What kind of proof?"

"We've got the footage from the museum showing the shooter. You can't really see his face, but analysis should be able to show that the man in question is easily six inches shorter than the agent."

"Are you sure?"

"There's no doubt. All anyone would need to do is measure something in that room for a reference point like the metal detector."

Stewart was nodding, furiously scribbling notes, Murphy reading them in stunned silence. "Can you send us the footage?"

"No, the Internet is down and the computer we have access to has no way to connect to our satphone. We're stuck here with probably the only copy of the proof with no way to send it."

"What's your location?" He jotted down the address, Murphy already entering it into Google Maps. "We're coming to you."

"Is that wise?"

"Probably not, but I'm a newsman and the truth must be set free, or some bullshit like that."

Acton laughed. "It's your neck."

"Don't I know it." He looked at the notebook with the directions plotted. "We're not actually that far from you. If we can get out of here, we should hopefully be there in about twenty minutes."

"Okay, good luck."

Stewart ended the call as he rose from the table, Murphy already packing up their equipment. His cameraman looked at him. "Just how do you think we're going to get out of here? Aren't we wanted?"

"I've got an idea on that."

He strode over to a nearby table, a CNN crew sitting around it. "Can I borrow your keys?"

Murphy laughed. "Bloody hell."

*Tay Ho District, Hanoi, Vietnam*

"Are you crazy?" asked Duy. "You want to tell the Americans that you're the cause of all this insanity?"

Phong nodded. "It's the only way to stop it."

"But you'll be killed!"

He shrugged. "So? My life's purpose, a purpose that was never supposed to have been fulfilled, has been. If I die now, today, I die in peace."

"You *will* die, don't doubt that."

"And I can live with that." He held up his hand, smiling. "Sorry, no pun intended."

Duy shook his head. "This is no time for morbid jokes." He paused then picked the bottle back up, taking a long swig. "What are you going to tell them?"

"The truth. The entire truth." He motioned to Duy's wife. "Can you hand me the phone?"

She didn't budge. "You don't even know the number."

"I'll ask the operator."

"They charge for that!" She pointed at her son. "Go to the store, they've got a phone book for tourists. It might have the American Embassy number."

He jumped to his feet and disappeared, running back a few minutes later, the bottle making another couple of rounds, Phong partaking again as he fueled himself with courage, his hands shaking slightly as he realized what he was essentially doing was committing suicide.

Something he had been tempted on many occasions to do in his youth.

But this time at least it would serve a purpose. It would save lives.

And perhaps atone for those lost already due to his actions.

He had no sympathy for Petrov, and only a little for his guards, all men who were protecting a murderer, which in his mind made them little better. He wondered how much they knew of their leader's past, and if they knew, would they have still tried to defend him, or would they have stepped aside, letting justice be served.

Phong took the piece of paper with the number, Duy's wife handing him the phone. He dialed.

"American Embassy, Hanoi, how may I direct your call?"

"I need to talk to someone in charge."

"In regards to?"

"I'm the man who shot the Russian Prime Minister."

"One moment please."

The woman at the other end sounded scared after his revelation, the phone ringing again several times as he was transferred he hoped to the right person. "This is Leroy Donavan. How can I help you?"

"My name is Phong Son Quan. I am the man who shot the Russian Prime Minister this morning."

*American Embassy, Hanoi, Vietnam*

Leroy Donavan's jaw dropped. "Everyone quiet!" he shouted as he hit the button on his phone, placing the call on speaker. The bustling office area was suddenly silent, Charles Stewart and his cameraman, just bringing him up to date on the two professors and their plan to meet them, were sitting in front of his desk, equally as curious as the rest of the room.

"Can you repeat your name for me?"

"Phong Son Quan."

Donavan jotted it down, ripping the paper off the pad and waving it in the air. It was snatched within seconds. "And you said you shot Prime Minister Petrov and his security detail this morning."

"Yes."

Some of the room gravitated toward the desk scribbling notes, the rest hitting their phones and computers, immediately trying to gather as much information as they could based upon what they were hearing.

"What proof do you have?"

"I work at the Daewoo Hanoi." Donavan's hand shot up, pointing down at the phone, indicating someone should pick up on that tidbit. "I tricked my friend into giving me his key pass. I told him that I forgot mine in your agent's room and I was afraid of being fired. I then used his pass to enter the room, used the factory security code for the safe and stole the security pass while your agent was in the shower."

"How did you know he would be in the shower?"

"My friend works in the Eco Office. He let me know when the shower was activated but he had no idea what I planned to do. He was just helping a friend."

"Then what did you do?"

"I told Human Resources that I was sick and went home, changed into a suit, then rode my moped to the museum. I used your agent's pass to enter. They thought I was part of your delegation. I then hid behind a tapestry in the room where they keep the Dong Son drums—"

"How did you know he'd go there?"

"Everyone goes there. It's the most famous display in the museum."

"Okay, continue."

"When he entered the room, I waited for a few minutes while he spoke to your delegation, but I thought I saw one of his security guards notice me so I came out from behind the curtain, shot his guards then shot him."

"Why?"

"He murdered my family and massacred my entire village during the war."

Donavan could hear the man's voice crack, immediately removing any doubt he might have had, it clear this man was struggling with his confession. "Did you speak to him?"

"Yes, I wanted to make sure he knew who was killing him and why."

"Did he remember you?"

"Yes."

"Were there any witnesses who could prove your story?"

"There were three, I think. I think they might be who they're saying helped your agent, I'm not sure. But they just happened to be there, I've never seen them before."

"Are you willing to testify to this?"

"Yes."

"Okay, we're going to need to get you to a safe location as quickly as possible. Is there anywhere you can go that the authorities wouldn't know about?"

Phong shrugged. "Not really. They know where I live and where my friends live since they almost all work at the same hotel."

"Okay, give me your number just in case we're cut off." He jotted down the number. "And where are you?"

"A friend's."

"A friend that the authorities will know about?"

"Yes, actually another friend from the hotel just warned us that the Russians are looking for us."

*Shit!*

"Okay, just a second."

He hit the *Hold* button. "Where can we hide this guy? There's no way we're getting him in the Embassy, not with all those police out there."

"We could pick him up."

Donavan looked at Stewart. "Huh?"

"We're taking a CNN truck out in a few minutes to go meet the professors. We could pick him up and take him with us."

Donavan shook his head. "No, it's more important that you get that evidence transmitted than it is to pick this guy up."

"Then have him meet us," suggested Murphy. "We can kill two birds with one stone."

Donavan nodded, taking the sheet of paper he had been making notes on prior to this bombshell phone call. It contained the address for where Agent Green and the professors were, as well as the satellite phone number. He jabbed the hold button. "Are you still there?"

"Yes."

"I'm going to give you an address, do you have something to write it down with?"

"One moment." Talking in Vietnamese could be heard, muffled, then a moment later Phong spoke again. "Go ahead."

Donavan gave him the address and made him repeat it. "How long would it take you to get there?"

"If I get my moped, not long."

"Where is it?"

"At my apartment."

"No, don't go back there under any circumstances. Can you borrow a friends?"

Again muffled voices. "Yes. I can be there in about ten minutes."

"Good. When you get there, have them call us so we know you're safe."

"Okay, thank you. Wait a minute, somebody is coming…oh no!"

There was a sound as if the phone had been dropped followed by shouts and footfalls fading into the distance. More scratching, as if the phone were being picked up and a deep voice in English with a thick Russian accent spoke. "Who is this?"

Donavan lifted the receiver and dropped it back into its cradle, ending the call.

"Our assassin may have just run out of time."

*Tay Ho District, Hanoi, Vietnam*

Igor Sarkov stepped out of his car, the temperature having dropped even further since his visit to Phong's apartment, it no longer stifling with the humidity now reasonable. It had taken him longer than expected, forced to almost inch along with the revelers, none paying too much heed to the cars travelling with them, most drivers appearing to be taking part along with their passengers.

It made him dislike the country a little less.

He didn't like it here. He didn't hate it, but he didn't like it. It wasn't the people, though he couldn't stand most of the senior bureaucrats, their arrogance rivaling those in similar positions in Moscow. The everyday people he had to admit were wonderful. They were simple by Western standards in that they led simpler lives. Consumerism was growing as the economy expanded and barriers were dropped, but it was nothing like that now seen in Moscow. Meals were simpler and eaten at home with family, evenings were spent with friends and family talking and playing games rather than in front of a television or a phone, and it wasn't a constant competition of who owned what or drove what.

Simpler.

Just too hot for his liking, too communist for his liking.

He believed in democracy, even if his taskmasters didn't.

And to preserve any hope of maintaining a possible democratic future for his homeland, he needed to stop this madness. His GPS informed him in her charming British accent that he had arrived. He found a spot along the parade route, there no police or barriers here to stop him, it an informal affair.

Climbing out, he surveyed his surroundings and immediately spotted Phong sitting with Duy and several other men, Phong on what looked like either a cordless phone or one brick of a cellphone from yesteryear.

He strode toward them, unbuttoning his suit jacket just in case he needed to grab for the weapon in his shoulder holster. Suddenly Phong's eyes met his and he knew he had been made.

*Tall overweight white guy in a suit in Vietnam. Real tough.*

The phone clattered to the ground as Phong shouted something then bolted. More shouts and a scream from one of the women sitting in a row with several others behind the men ended when he pulled his weapon, Duy's designs to run with his friend ended.

He picked up the phone. "Who is this?" There was a click as the other end hung up. He handed the phone over to one of the women then turned to Duy, still sitting in his lawn chair. As much as Sarkov would love to sit right now, he knew there was no way the flimsy chair would support his mass.

"You speak English?" He already knew the answer, his personnel file, printed off in English, already told him.

"Y-yes."

He looked at the printout. "Your name is Duy Giang Tran?"

The terrified man's head shook out an uncertain nod.

"You work at the Daewoo Hanoi Hotel?"

Another shaky affirmative.

"How about you tell me what happened?"

"I-I don't know what you're talking about."

Sarkov scratched his chin then absentmindedly tapped the gun in his shoulder holster. "I think you know exactly what I'm talking about. Your friend Phong—and yes, I know exactly who he is and where he lives—must have told you, otherwise you wouldn't be so scared."

"I-I'm not scared."

"Good! You shouldn't be. I don't believe you did anything wrong, at least not intentionally. Why don't you tell me what you know? Perhaps I can help."

A bottle of vodka was suddenly pressed against the man's lip, liquid courage pouring down his throat as he polished off several ounces, one for each bounce of his Adam's apple. The bottle was removed then hesitantly offered to Sarkov.

He shook his head. "No thanks." The woman who had taken the phone disappeared inside, returning a few seconds later with a hard plastic chair, something he had seen at cheap cafés on many occasions. He smiled gratefully as he took a seat. The festivities continued around them, the brief excitement caused by Phong's flight forgotten in moments. He watched as a particularly beautiful woman passed, even Duy unable to ignore her. "Very pretty," said Sarkov. He motioned toward the women. "Is one of these lovely ladies your wife?"

Duy nodded, pointing to the woman who had brought the chair.

"Thank you."

She nodded and said, "Thank you," her nervous smile accompanied with her entire upper body bowing repeatedly in the chair.

Sarkov turned to Duy, smiling, trying to disarm the man at least a little, though he could tell his attempts were unsuccessful so far. "Lovely lady, you're a lucky man."

"Thank you."

"Does she speak English?"

He shook his head.

"Then nothing you say to me can get you in trouble with her, and we both know there's nothing worse than being in trouble with your wife."

Sarkov laughed at his own joke, trying to put the man at ease as he directed his gaze at the crowd again, providing the man with a little relief.

Nervous laughter from Duy, then the others, quickly tapered off.

"Now, let's start at the beginning. What happened this morning?"

The man sighed, his gaze lowering to his shoes as he leaned forward, the bottle rattling on the concrete as he twirled it nervously with his fingers. "Phong told me he forgot his pass in one of the American's rooms. I just told him when he could get in to get it."

"You activated the security cameras to do it."

Duy hesitated. "Y-yes, I guess I did. I mean, I had to in order to access the utility usage data." His jaw dropped. "I forgot to deactivate it!"

Sarkov smiled, nodding, his eyes still mostly on the crowd. "No need to worry. Your forgetting might actually have helped." He waved to a group of young women who were smiling at him. They giggled and rushed off. "You had no idea what your friend was going to do?"

An emphatic headshake. "No! He gave me my pass back, thanked me, and that was it. I didn't know until later that he had left sick."

"And I guess you didn't know until this evening what he had done?"

Duy sighed. "Yes. He told us just before you arrived."

"Did he say why he did it?"

"Yes!" Duy turned his chair slightly toward Sarkov, as if excited he might have a defense for his friend. "He said this man murdered his entire family and village when he was a kid. During the war. He said that he had let him live. He swore that if he ever saw him again he'd kill him."

"And he did."

Duy frowned. "Yes, but it was justifiable, wasn't it? I mean, wouldn't you kill the man who killed your family if you had a chance?"

Sarkov's chest tightened slightly at the question, it something he had been asking himself too often since he had found out Phong's possible motivation. Unfortunately he already knew the truth.

He wouldn't.

Not because he didn't want to, but because he was too scared to.

Until today, he had never thought himself a coward.

But he must be.

He had let the murderer of his wife and child escape unscathed. He would have been able to find the man with little trouble. He had access to a weapon. He could have killed him in a heartbeat.

But he hadn't.

Instead he had requested the earliest transfer so he could escape any possible memories of his wife and son.

And he hadn't even unpacked a single photo of them when he had moved into his apartment here in Hanoi.

Shame swept over him.

And envy for the brass that this man he had never met had shown.

*Phong is to be admired.*

"Who was he on the phone with when I arrived?"

Duy's eyes darted away, his posture changing as he turned slightly away.

He said nothing.

"Tell *me* now, or the police later. Either way you will be telling."

Duy sighed then took another swig from the bottle. "He called the American Embassy."

Sarkov's eyes narrowed. *The American Embassy?* He turned toward Duy, the festival forgotten. "Why?"

"He's a good person!" cried Duy, his words rapid, almost jumbled with his accent. "He is! I've known him for years and he'd never hurt anyone. That's why when he heard about what was happening because of what he'd done, he wanted to turn himself in. We"—he motioned toward his friends and the women behind them—"all thought he shouldn't because they'd kill him."

Sarkov turned back to look at Duy's wife who smiled. "Thank you!"

He nodded with a smile, noticing the old grandmother nearby rocking in her chair, her hands clapping in synch with the drums, her grin of pure joy a pleasant if out of place sight under the circumstances. "You were probably right to advise him to not go to your local authorities." Sarkov turned back to the parade. "What did he tell them?"

"The truth, exactly what I told you."

"And what did they say?"

"They wanted him to go to some address to meet some people so he could tell his story."

"Not the embassy?"

"It's surrounded, isn't it?"

Sarkov nodded. "What was the address?"

Duy shook his head. "I don't know the address. I think it was on Lang Yen street, but I don't know the number."

"Where's that?"

"Dong Mac Ward. Not far." He nodded toward the car. "Maybe ten minutes in car."

Sarkov pushed himself to his feet. "Thank you for your cooperation."

"What should I do? They say the police are after me!"

Sarkov frowned sympathetically. This man had committed a minor indiscretion. Did he deserve to be fired? Probably. Arrested? Perhaps. Tortured and jailed or executed? Definitely not. "I suggest you and your family leave immediately. Call your hotel tomorrow and tell them you have a family emergency and need to take a few days off, don't give them a chance to tell you anything—just talk then hang up. Then go stay with people that the authorities don't know you have any connection with and stay there until you hear on the news that the crisis is over. Hopefully once the truth comes out, you can go back to your job. If what you say is true, your government will probably want to forget this ever happened very quickly and you might just get your life back."

Duy rose and nodded, his face clouded with fear and uncertainty. "I will do that."

"Good luck."

Sarkov strode toward his car and climbed in, entering the street name into his GPS. *Ten minutes, maybe twenty if I'm stuck in this parade.* He pulled out and inched along, looking for a side street that might not be so busy, but it was to no avail. The crowd was parting, smiles and waves rather than shaked fists the order of the evening, but it was slow going.

Which meant he had time to think.

He was already defying orders by being here rather than at his apartment. And he knew Yashkin's report back to Moscow on his performance would be negative, so much so that he would almost definitely face recall. And if the truth didn't come out, there would be more than sufficient reason for the powers that be to have him disappear in some cold, dark corner of Russia, never to be seen again.

Which was why he continued to push forward.

For he had nothing left to lose except his life.

*Dong Mac Ward, Hanoi, Vietnam*

James Acton looked up from the laptop as Laura's phone rang, startling Mai who was still a bundle of nerves. They all were. Cadeo's men were fussing with an impressive cache of weapons and ammo, Mai's brother's black market business apparently booming. If they had to make a stand, they could, but it would be pointless. There were no helicopters or American troops rushing to the rescue here.

They were on their own.

With nowhere to go.

*If only we could get on that plane!*

But he knew there was no way that was even possible. Their only hope was to not be discovered, get their story out so that the world would be convinced they and Niner weren't involved, and then hopefully get into the Embassy.

And perhaps the first step of that plan was about to take place.

"Hello?" His wife's voice was tentative, she clearly as nervous as he was. She breathed a sigh of relief and smiled. "They're here!"

Mai jumped in delight or nerves, Acton couldn't tell, as Cadeo flicked off the lights and opened a door to the side of the garage. Niner stepped ahead of them, his weapon drawn, fresh ammo supplied by Cadeo filling his pockets.

"Do you see the door that just opened?" She nodded. "Okay, bye." She hung up the phone, placing it back in her pocket as they waited.

A couple of minutes later two men casually strode in, the door closing behind them immediately, the lights flickering back on. Acton smiled at Stewart and his cameraman Murphy. "They're okay," he told Niner who lowered his weapon, Cadeo's men following. Acton stepped toward the new arrivals, shaking their hands. "Thank God you made it. Were you followed?"

Stewart shook his head. "We were but Murph lost them. We should be okay."

"I'm surprised they let you go," said Laura, giving both men a quick hug. "You're wanted like us."

Murphy laughed. "Nope, an ABC news crew are wanted men. We borrowed a CNN van."

"They agreed?"

"Once they heard what was going on. At first they wanted to come with us but we agreed that would look suspicious, four guys in the van instead of the normal two. We agreed to share any footage we take."

"Sounds good," said Acton. "Now let's get this show on the air, now. We need to get the word out and the museum footage transmitted before we're discovered."

Stewart nodded. "What format is the footage in?"

"Files on a USB memory stick," replied Mai, walking toward the laptop. She pulled the device out and handed it to Murphy who immediately sat down, setting up his camera to transmit the data.

Stewart looked at Niner. "So you're the assassin."

"Apparently."

Stewart chuckled. "Well, you'll be happy to know that the *real* assassin is on his way here."

"What?!" cried both Acton and Laura, Mai almost fainting, grabbing the back of a chair to steady herself.

"Yeah, this Phong character called the embassy just as we were about to leave. He confessed to everything, said it was in revenge for what Petrov did during the war, exactly like you guys said, and he wanted to turn himself in, but not to the Vietnamese. We suggested—"

"—I suggested," interjected Murphy.

"Mr. 'Takes All The Credit' suggested—"

"That's rich coming from you."

"—that he meet us here so we could get him on tape along with you guys."

"And to correct my esteemed colleague's previous statement, we *think* the real assassin is on his way here."

"What do you mean?" asked Acton.

"The phone call was interrupted when a Russian arrived on the scene. We think though that the Phong guy ran away in time. We're just not sure," replied Stewart.

"He has the address?"

"It was given to him, and we assume he wrote it down."

Niner clasped his hands behind his neck. "A lot of assumptions."

Stewart nodded. "Agreed. But let's try to look at the bright side. That data is about to be transmitted—"

"Already happening."

"—and you're all about to get on the air with your stories."

"Should we do it live?" asked Acton. "We don't want to risk them finding us and confiscating the tape."

Stewart patted him on the cheek. "You're so cute!"

Laura snickered.

"Yeah, yeah, I know there's no tape," said Acton, placing a quick kiss on Stewart's palm causing the man to jerk his hand away.

"I'm not that kind of girl," Stewart said in a feigned huff. "We're definitely going live. I've already talked to the studio and they're waiting."

"Thank God," sighed Laura. "Hopefully once the truth gets out things will settle down."

Stewart shook his head. "Hopefully, but there's a full-fledged invasion of the Ukraine going on, troop buildups on both sides in the Baltic States, a few shells exchanged between ships in both the Baltic Sea and the Black Sea, and there's that F-22 that was intentionally hit. Apparently a couple of American tourists were attacked and beaten in Moscow and Marines from the embassy had to rescue them. The Russians are expressing outrage and demanding they be handed over and that the UN Security Council condemn the violation of international law."

"That's pretty rich coming from them," said Acton.

Murphy grunted. "That's what I said." He pulled the memory stick from the camera, handing it back to Mai. "Sent."

"Good. Do they know what to do with it?" asked Laura.

"Yeah, we already gave them your theory and they used file photos to determine the make and model of the metal detector they were using so they know the exact height for comparison," said Stewart as Murphy set the camera up for the interviews.

Laura shook her head. "I can't believe they let him in with a gun when there's a metal detector."

"Probably because they thought he was a part of the American security team," replied Stewart. "But this is good. It means that even the Vietnamese were fooled or just didn't care enough to carefully check the ID. I'm assuming our friend here"—he nodded toward Niner—"looks nothing like our shooter."

"I'm much more handsome," said Niner, straight-man style.

"Oh much," winked Laura.

"Oooh, Professor, not while your husband's in the room."

Acton shook his head, smiling as Stewart laughed, Mai still not sure what to make of them.

"Who's first?" asked Stewart.

"As soon as Phong gets here, we'll put him on. But for now I think hearing from the eye witnesses rather than Mr. Green is the way to go. If they hear from him they'll just say he's lying."

"Good thinking," said Niner. He looked at Laura. "Shall we go entertain ourselves while your husband is interviewed?" He grinned ear-to-ear suggestively raising his eyebrows up and down.

Laura pointed to the door leading to a side room. "How about you go get started yourself."

Niner's shoulders slumped. "You're not going to show up, are you?"

"No thanks, I'm a one man girl." Laura goosed her husband. He jumped.

Acton, his ass cheeks still clenched, looked at Laura. "Careful, hon, you're liable to lose a finger up there."

"Eww!" she cried, yanking her hand away as Niner bent over laughing.

"I never knew you two were so kinky!" he said, still chuckling as he walked away to check the front.

"We're ready," said Murphy, Stewart standing straight, microphone in his hand, the light from the camera shining brightly.

"We'll have all three of you on camera," said Stewart, but I'll primarily ask Laura the questions since the public will find a woman more sympathetic and believable. I'm a newsman but we need to sell the truth today not just tell it, so I'm not beyond manipulating people's perceptions if you're not."

"Sounds fine to me."

"Okay, good." He touched an earpiece apparently connected with the studio. "Can you hear me?" He nodded then gave a thumbs up to Murphy who began a countdown from five, the last two with fingers, Laura stepping up beside Stewart, Acton then Mai beside her. "Thank you, Terry. I'm here with Professors Laura Palmer and James Acton, and Vietnam National Museum of History grad student Mai Lien Trinh, all witnesses to today's assassination of Russian Prime Minister Anatoly Petrov. They have a much different story to tell than that being provided by the Vietnamese and Russian authorities. As well, they have managed to retrieve footage from the Museum security cameras that appear to substantiate their version of events, footage I might add that the Vietnamese authorities previously said did not exist." He turned toward Laura. "Professor Palmer, please tell us what happened from your perspective."

"We've got company!" shouted Niner from the door, Cadeo's men all leaping from their assorted perches, grabbing their weapons.

"Sorry, Terry, we've got a situation here. Please keep us live. Apparently the authorities may have found our location."

Niner jogged over, readying his Glock. "A car with diplomatic plates just pulled up and there's a couple of police checking out the news van." He pointed to Stewart. "Get their story on the air, fast. We might not have much time."

"What about Phong?" asked Acton, his chest tightening as he realized their entire plan was quickly unravelling.

"Something tells me it's too late for him," replied Niner. He pointed at Acton. "Could use a good man on the door."

Acton nodded. "Call me if you need me," he said to Stewart, pulling his own Cadeo provided Beretta from his belt. He could hear the interview resume behind him with Laura and Mai as he readied the weapon. He looked out the small, dirty window, a clear area in the center made with someone's fist rubbing the dirt away.

And frowned.

*Time's up.*

*Daewoo Hanoi Hotel, Hanoi, Vietnam*

Dawson held the door to the service elevator, Spock on the opposite side, Jimmy in the main hallway organizing the elevators there. Plans had changed. Since they were still blocking almost all of the elevators, they were going to evacuate everyone in one shot. He motioned to Spock to hold the door as he stepped back into the hallway to confirm everyone was loaded.

A thumbs up from Jimmy gave him the all clear.

Dawson activated his comm. "Proceed to ground floor on my mark. Don't let anyone board should you stop at another floor. Do not engage unless fired upon, you're fish in a barrel. When you arrive in the lobby, immediately proceed to the right, then right again, straight through to the rear entrance and get in your designated vehicles. Each agent will report any stops on any floors, your arrival in the Lobby, and the successful loading in the vehicles as per your briefing." Dawson climbed aboard the elevator, nodding to Spock. "Proceed."

The doors closed, the elevator cramped with Atwater and her senior advisors, half a dozen DSS agents along with several pieces of highly classified communications gear. Laptops had already been wiped, hard drives destroyed just in case, and the classified gear could be made inoperable with a touch of a button on the outside of their cases.

As the floors ticked down, Dawson readied himself for anything. He had been assured by Yashkin that the Vietnamese had agreed to cooperate, but he frankly didn't believe any of them. Right now he wouldn't breathe easy until the landing gear smoked on American soil.

"Okay, get ready people. Our directions are simpler. We walk out in an orderly fashion, calmly, no matter what you see, no matter what you hear.

We turn to the left and just walk straight out the door at the far end of the hallway and we'll see the motorcade waiting for us. There's no reason to die here today, so if you hear gunfire, just hit the floor, raise your hands and surrender." He nodded toward one of the aides with a video camera. "And don't forget, we're on TV." The elevator chimed their arrival. "Okay, calmly to the left then straight until we're outside."

The doors opened and they found an empty service room. He stepped out and checked the hallway. Empty. All of the other elevators were reporting unplanned stops, the Vietnamese having obviously pressed the buttons on other floors either to delay them, or had done it earlier during the crisis. Either way it didn't matter.

It meant delays.

He headed toward the door at the far end, Spock covering the one that led to the lobby while the others followed him in near silence, a few of the civilians audibly trembling in fear.

He didn't blame them.

These people were never meant for situations like this. In fact he was always impressed with how often civilians were able to rise to the occasion, some able to compartmentalize their emotions until the crisis was over.

That was when the breakdowns usually happened.

He reached the door, it solid with no window.

No way to see what was on the other side.

He waited for everyone to catch up, Spock still covering the far door by the elevator. "Okay, people. You're all doing great. We're going to go through this door. The vehicles are already in place, not even thirty yards from here. Remember, just walk calmly toward your assigned vehicle. Don't run, that just causes you and them to panic. No matter what you see, you just walk. If they fire at you, hit the ground, surrender."

Several of the elevators continued to report repeated delays, none yet arriving at the lobby.

He couldn't wait.

He opened the door only to be blinded by large spotlights trained on the exit, and as his eyes adjusted he cursed.

Dozens of soldiers pointing a mix of AKs at them stood between them and the idling vehicles.

Jimmy cursed again as the doors opened on the fourth floor, two men staring at them, guns pointed at them, clearly part of the Russian delegation. He didn't react, instead reaching over and pressing the *Close* button. It had been the story the entire way down, the doors opening on every floor except the seventh. Over the comm he could hear the same was true for the others except for Dawson's group, the service elevator apparently cleared.

It had him wondering if it were an attempt to split the security detail into two batches.

The doors closed and they passed the third floor. It chimed on the second.

"Oh for Christ's sake!" cried someone in the back of the elevator, the tension getting to them all. The doors opened and two Vietnamese Police officers pointed guns at them and Jimmy again ignored them, the key to getting out of this alive to avoid any type of provocation.

He hit the *Close* button again.

"Okay people, get ready. Remember, we exit calmly, turn to the right, walk past all the elevators, take our first right then go straight through the rear exit of the hotel where our motorcade is waiting. Get into your assigned vehicles and then we're home free. Just stay calm no matter what you see, and whatever you do, don't run. That just causes itchy trigger fingers to twitch."

The tension level rose as they descended once again. The doors opened and Jimmy resisted the urge to curse, dozens of soldiers, weapons raised, ringed the elevator doors as they all began to open.

He activated his comm. "Everyone stay calm. Follow the plan."

He stepped out, leaving his weapon holstered, there no point in drawing with odds like this. He saw several other DSS agents step out of their assigned elevators as well. The soldiers inched forward, the sound of boots and magazines rattling disturbing enough to cause several of his group to begin sobbing, their attempts to stifle themselves only making it worse.

"Calmly people, follow me," he said, stepping to the right, checking over his shoulder to make sure they all followed, several carrying pieces of equipment, the final DSS agent nodding the all clear as the group he was responsible for finished exiting the elevator. The barrels of the guns followed them, but no one said anything. He spotted the Russian, Yashkin, nearby, staring at them, particularly him.

*I wonder if he knows who I really am.*

Apparently he had called Dawson 'Sergeant Major' so he was pretty sure the Russians had dossiers on them all. He did a shoulder check and saw the last of the six elevators open, the delegation emptying into the lobby, shocked expressions from some along with others covering their eyes, trying to either hide from those aiming weapons at them, or hide the horror from themselves.

It was a pitiable sight.

One he had seen far too often, just never in a five star hotel lobby.

He activated his comm. "Elevator Zero-Three all clear, proceeding to first turn, out."

He heard the others reporting in as Dawson's voice broke in.

"We've been blocked by troops, hold at the rear entrance doors, over."

*Shit!*

He reached the corner and looked to his right, down the hallway leading to the rear exit.

A hallway lined with soldiers, guns at the ready.

But no one had fired yet.

This was a show of force, designed to intimidate, to make someone on their side make a mistake.

The only problem with these types of standoffs was the side creating them was just as scared usually.

Which meant they might set off their own trap.

If just one of these dozens of soldiers fired a single shot, the rest of them would fire as well. The entire delegation would be mowed down in an instant before the order to cease fire could even be given.

He simply walked forward, calmly, his hands open at his sides, slightly out in front, showing he had no weapon at the ready. He walked at a reasonable but not too quick a pace reaching the rear doors, large glass affairs providing a clear view of the situation outside.

A situation that didn't look good.

He checked behind him and found the entire delegation bunched together, no stragglers left behind. Yashkin and his Vietnamese counterparts were walking toward them.

"We're at the rear entrance, awaiting your orders."

"Proceed through the doors when you see us and merge with our group. I'll lead, on my mark." Jimmy put a hand on the door to the left of the revolving doors, a DSS agent doing the same on the right, two queues forming behind them spontaneously.

"Execute."

Dawson stepped forward, a DSS agent holding open the door as he led the delegation forward, directly toward the center of the line of troops. He glanced to his right and saw Jimmy stepping through the glass doors of the rear entrance, two lines following through the doors, merging back together, walking calmly and deliberately toward his group.

Perhaps calmly wasn't the right term.

The civilians were terrified. Even his nerves were on edge. At least he was used to the prospect of dying at any moment. It was his job. These people had probably thought they were simply going on an exciting field trip to a country few of their generation had seen, and far too of their parents' generation had.

The Vietnamese weren't moving.

He kept closing the distance between them and the vehicles, each guarded by a single DSS agent who would double as driver, the doors all opened and ready.

He came face to face with one of the soldiers, staring down at him.

He said nothing.

Neither did the soldier, his weapon almost shaking as it was pointed up at Dawson's chin. If the kid shook any harder he risked blasting Dawson's face off.

Jimmy stepped up beside Dawson, saying nothing, adding his own set of eyes to the staring match, the poor soldier, clearly out of his depth, nervously glancing between the two.

"Let them through."

Dawson turned to see Yashkin standing just outside the doors. The order was shouted in Vietnamese and the young soldier in front of them sighed audibly, lowering his weapon as the cordon of soldiers quickly parted in the middle, retreating in two directions leaving the delegation with full access to the vehicles.

"Calmly people," said Dawson as he led them toward the vehicles, the DSS agents splitting off with their groups. Dawson headed for the main limo, stepping aside as Atwater and her senior aides climbed in. He closed the door behind them then opened the passenger side door, waiting for the rest of the vehicles to be loaded. The all clears came in over the comms and Dawson looked at Yashkin.

The man smiled. "Until we meet again, Sergeant Major."

Dawson nodded at Yashkin, climbing into the passenger seat and closing the door.

*Now let's see how far they let us go.*

*Dong Mac Ward, Hanoi, Vietnam*

Phong turned the corner and nearly pissed his pants. He had run almost the entire way and was exhausted, still gasping for breath. He had always considered himself in reasonable shape, there barely an ounce of fat on him, but he never actively exercised beyond his morning stretches.

His job kept him in shape.

But his job had never involved running for almost thirty minutes.

He had bolted the moment he saw the white man walking toward them, it obvious he was there to arrest him. He had shouted a warning to the others but none had reacted quickly enough. He was dismayed to find himself running alone but knew the best way to help his friends would be to get the truth out.

Which meant getting to the address the embassy had given him.

And now he was here and there were police.

He stepped back into the shadows, weighing his options. There appeared to only be two of them. They were out of their car, examining a white van with English writing. His heart leapt as he spotted the CNN logo.

*This is the place!*

Another car rolled up and he nearly fainted as the large white man from earlier stepped out. He walked over to the police officers, holding up his identification. Phong could hear them speaking but they were too far for him to make out the words. He spotted a street number in small black letters on a gold foil background above the door he was hiding in and determined he was at least on the right side of the street and only a few doors down from where he needed to be.

The urge to run, to disappear into the night was almost overwhelming, but he knew he had to tell his story, to make right what had gone so terribly wrong. He had had plenty of time to think while on his way here, and he had come to two conclusions.

First, he had no regrets over killing Petrov. The man deserved it.

And second, he should have stayed, waiting to be arrested rather than escaping through the window.

Then all of this could have been avoided. He didn't care if he was punished. He hadn't cared then, either. He wasn't even sure why he had run. At the time his plan had been to kill Petrov, nothing beyond that. It hadn't occurred to him that he'd actually be successful, so he had made no plan for what would follow.

On instinct he had run.

If he had truly thought it out, he would have surrendered.

At least that's what he hoped he would do. He had to admit that if the current crisis weren't happening, and countries weren't going to war over what he had done, he would happily be going on with his life, content he had delivered justice and done nothing truly wrong.

*Maybe I would have still run.*

But he didn't have the benefit of hindsight then, and he did now. He had no doubt he would have stayed if he knew what was going to happen because of his actions.

Which meant he had to go through with this meeting. It was the only way to stop it.

He kept to the shadows, moving forward a doorway at a time, unnoticed by the police and white man whom he presumed was Russian rather than American, since he knew none had been sent to meet him.

The next building sandwiched to the side of the one he was currently hiding at was a couple of stories high with a garage door in addition to a regular door to the left of it. He darted forward just as one of the police officers turned toward him and pointed, shouting for him to stop.

Suddenly the door beside the garage opened and hands reached from the shadows, grabbing him.

He screamed.

He was yanked from the street and into darkness, the door slamming shut behind him before the lights turned back on. He blinked rapidly as his eyes adjusted, the hands that had snatched him from the street letting go of him.

Half a dozen men, Vietnamese, had guns pointed at him. His jaw dropped as he saw the Asian American security agent standing nearby, gun in hand but at least not pointing at him. A camera with a bright light turned toward him.

Nobody said anything for a moment and Phong simply stood there, his hands raised.

"I was told to come here."

"Are you Phong?" asked a white man stepping forward.

He nodded.

"I'm Professor Acton. Call me Jim," said the man, stepping forward, extending his hand. "Did they see you coming in here?"

"Y-yes, I think so," replied Phong, shaking the man's hand.

"Then we better hurry," said a woman as she walked toward him, hand extended. "I'm Professor Palmer. Call me Laura."

He had already forgotten the man's name and knew he had no hope of remembering hers. He was too rattled.

"Terry, we've just had some excitement here," said a man holding a microphone as he urged the group back toward the camera. "This is live television in a crisis, folks, so you never know what's going to happen."

Phong stopped beside the man, the professors and a young Vietnamese girl standing beside him. "Can you please tell us your name?"

"Phong Son Quan."

"And where do you work?"

"At the Daewoo Hanoi Hotel."

"As?"

Phong looked at the man, puzzled. "Pardon?"

"What's your job?"

"Oh, sorry. Maintenance man."

"And this is the same hotel that Secretary Atwater is staying at."

He nodded. "Yes."

"And it is also the same hotel that Russian Prime Minister Anatoly Petrov was staying at."

"Yes."

"Had you ever met him before?"

"Yes."

"When?"

"During the war."

"And what happened then."

"He murdered my entire family and village."

"You saw him do this."

"Yes."

"How did you survive?"

"He let me live. I was hiding in the woods when they came. He told them to kill everyone. I watched and did—" He paused, the words caught in his throat. The female professor came up behind him and put a comforting hand on his shoulder. "Sorry. I did nothing."

"How old were you?"

"Fifteen."

"And how many soldiers were there?"

"I don't know. Twenty or thirty. A lot."

"So there was nothing you could have really done then is there?"

He shrugged. "I guess not."

"And how do you know he was the same man all these years later?"

"I recognized him and I recognized his name."

"He told you his name all those years ago?"

"Yes. We spoke for a few minutes when I tried to kill him."

"You tried to kill him back then?"

"Yes. With my bare hands."

"And he told you his name."

"Yes. First he asked me mine then I asked him his. And I told him if I ever saw him again I'd kill him."

"And when did you see him next."

"Yesterday when he arrived at the hotel."

"And you recognized him."

"Immediately."

"Then what happened?"

Phong closed his eyes and tried to control his breathing, the interview rapid fire, the questions non-stop. *Just a little bit more. You're almost done.* "In our end of day briefing for what was happening the next day we were told he would be leaving for the museum." Phong quickly related the rest of the story, the interviewer prompting him along when needed, and within minutes the entire truth had been told, a weight lifting off his shoulders though the terror still remained.

"Is there anything you'd like to say?"

"Yes, yes there is. My friend Duy had nothing to do with this. I lied to him and tricked him. He didn't want me to get fired for losing my pass otherwise he never would have done what he did. Also, also I'm sorry. Not for killing Petrov—he deserved to die for what he did—but for all the trouble I have caused. This man"—he pointed toward the American agent—"is innocent. I stole his pass while he was in the shower. And these people"—he motioned to the professors and the Vietnamese woman—"are innocent as well. They just happened to be in the room when I shot Petrov. None of what is happening in the world should be happening. I'm so sorry that innocent people have been hurt. Please stop the fighting, please."

"Thank you Mr. Quan," said the man, turning back to the camera. "There you have it, Terry, a confession, live on the air, to the most notorious assassination of the twenty-first century. Russian Prime Minister Anatoly Petrov, murdered for a war crime he allegedly committed almost forty years ago. No conspiracy, no involvement by the American or British governments, nobody helping him. A lone gunman, delivering justice for a wrong committed against him in a war that took away the innocence of so many. I understand you are now showing the analyzed footage that we were able to obtain from the museum, showing that the man entering the museum was approximately five-foot-three." He motioned for the Asian American to join them. The man stood beside Phong. "I'm five-foot-ten. You can see Agent Green is essentially my height and Mr. Quan is clearly about half a foot shorter, matching the height shown in the video."

"Somebody's coming!"

He turned to see one of the Vietnamese men with guns open the door and stick his weapon outside, three shots ringing out.

They all hit the ground as a hail of gunfire responded.

*Dong Mac Ward, Hanoi, Vietnam*

Sarkov stepped out of his car, clearly in the right place. Two police officers were inspecting a CNN news van parked and apparently empty. He was pretty sure the reporters wanted regarding the escape of the Vietnamese girl were from ABC, so he doubted they were the same crew. That being said, why a CNN news van would be here at this location at this time of night made little sense.

Unless they were here to interview Phong.

Which is why he had merely shown them his identification and asked them what they had found rather than tell them why he was there and possibly tip them off. One of the officers actually spoke Russian, his father having been stationed in Moscow when he was a child in a diplomatic position.

It was a pleasant surprise, even if the accent was thick.

Though he spoke English well, he did find it a slight mental strain to converse in a foreign language, especially when those he was speaking it with quite often were speaking a language they sometimes only claimed to speak. And with thick accents.

He knew he would sleep like the proverbial log tonight.

But if Phong were being interviewed by CNN right now, it might be a way for this entire situation to be defused, and allow him to slip back to his apartment unnoticed, perhaps escaping Moscow's wrath.

One of the officers shouted and pointed. Sarkov turned to see a man slinking along the street, hiding in the shadows. He couldn't tell if it was Phong, but a door opened beside the man and he was pulled inside, the door slamming shut then a light turning on, highlighting a small square window in the door.

It had to be him.

Which now meant there was no way to keep what was happening secret.

*You better hurry up, my friend.*

Sarkov returned to his car, his back sore from walking and standing for pretty much the entire day except when driving. He sat down, the door open, the evening now cool with a nice breeze. The Vietnamese were on their radio, calling in reinforcements. He wasn't sure they knew what they had gotten themselves into, but they weren't taking chances, not with everything that had happened in their capital today.

Which meant he had a decision to make.

Stay, and possibly be found out by Yashkin, and by extension, Moscow, or leave, not finishing his duty as an investigator, leaving the Americans to still be blamed for something they had nothing to do with, and his government running roughshod over international law and continuing to display generally indecent behavior.

He sighed, his head falling against the headrest as he closed his eyes, fatigue quickly overwhelming him.

Gunshots rang out, startling him out of his sleep. He reached for his gun as he regained his bearings, finding several police cars now lining the street, officers taking cover behind them as a group of four ran for cover. As soon as they were out of the line of fire at least a dozen guns opened up on the front of the building Phong had entered.

And Sarkov sighed.

*I knew this wasn't going to end well.*

*Daewoo Hanoi Hotel, Hanoi, Vietnam*

Dimitri Yashkin watched the last of the motorcade pull away then spun on his heel, entering the hotel. His vehicle was parked in the front but he wasn't leaving quite yet. He pointed to Major Yin. "They will have left luggage and other equipment. I don't want it touched. A forensics team from Moscow will be arriving shortly. They will go through everything. If the Americans arrive from the embassy to pick it up, tell them they can't because the entire hotel is a crime scene."

"You intend to keep the hotel closed?"

"Yes."

"But what of the guests? This is a five star hotel, the most prestigious hotel in the city, and it holds hundreds of guests." Yin shook his head. "My superiors are already demanding updates on when it will reopen."

Yashkin stopped himself from rolling his eyes. He could care less if a bunch of rich, pampered tourists and businessmen were inconvenienced. The Russian Prime Minister had been assassinated. It took precedence. And his orders from Moscow were clear.

Maximize the disruption.

The more people who were inconvenienced, the more people who were pissed off, the better, as long as the message was controlled, as long as they all thought it was the Americans' fault.

And so far he felt he was doing a stellar job, especially with the Vietnamese so eager to please. The weapons deal they were so desperate to close would be the biggest in their history, and with the Ruble collapsing due to economic sanctions over the Ukraine, Russia needed foreign cash to add to the reserves that were quickly being drained to try and stabilize the currency.

The deal was worth billions. His country wanted the money, the Vietnamese wanted the equipment, desperate to be able to show some real muscle with a belligerent China on their border. When he had read his briefing notes on the flight here he couldn't believe how arrogant China was over their claims in the South China Sea. Their aggression was uncalled for, and their claim tenuous at best. But since they had the military might, their neighbors could do little but protest.

He hoped the weapons deal went through soon.

For both countries' sakes.

But tonight he needed to tie up loose ends. The two hotel employees had to be eliminated, the two professors, the Vietnamese grad student, those who rescued her, and the two reporters who had witnessed the rescue.

He could care less if the American agent escaped now. The museum footage had been destroyed, the hotel footage destroyed, and once the witnesses were eliminated, it didn't matter what the Americans or their DSS 'Agent'—for he knew full well the man was no DSS agent—said to the public. They would never be believed.

He knew that if you controlled the message, then you controlled the minds of the people. In Russia a recent poll showed that only 3% of people believed Malaysian Airlines flight MH17 was shot down by Russian equipped separatists in the Ukraine. The Kremlin's message had been accepted by the public, 82% of the people believing it had been shot down by the Ukrainian Air Force.

It was propaganda worthy of Goebbels himself.

One of Yin's men ran up to them, handing Yin a radio. A flurry of Vietnamese was exchanged, Yashkin uninterested, his disdain for the

Vietnamese knowing no bounds. In fact, he hated most things that weren't Russian. Russian music, movies and television were far more appealing than anything Hollywood could produce. Russian cuisine was the finest in the world, its vodka and caviar second to none. And its women! There were none like them.

He thought of his fiancée, Karina.

*She was a face that would indeed launch a thousand ships.*

"There's a gunfight near the river," said Yin, finishing his radio call.

"And this interests me why?"

"Because there's a CNN vehicle there."

"So, reporters are at a gun fight. This is to be expected."

Yin shook his head. "No, you don't understand. They were there before the gunfight started. They aren't in the vehicle, they think they're inside with the gunmen."

Yashkin's eyes opened slightly wider as his heart picked up a few beats. "It just might be worth checking out."

As they walked through the lobby he noticed a large number of the soldiers and police heading toward the lounge. He followed, curious, knowing full well they wouldn't dare to drink on the job. It immediately became obvious what was attracting their attention. The large television on the far wall was tuned to CNN International with a large headline emblazoned across the screen.

*Russian Prime Minister's Assassin Confesses.*

On the left of the screen the museum footage he had ordered destroyed was playing with computer graphics overlaid showing the height of the individual and on the right, an interview was playing showing the two professors, the American agent, the young woman from the museum and an Asian man he assumed was the maintenance worker that had actually done the killing.

His blood pressure ticked up a few dozen points as he clenched his fists.

Then he smiled as he saw the interview was taped, and it had been interrupted by gunfire.

He now knew where almost all of his loose ends were located.

*Dong Mac Ward, Hanoi, Vietnam*

"Stop shooting, you moron!"

Niner hauled Cadeo's man back from the door, tossing him onto his back. The man looked flustered for a moment then jumped to his feet, raising his weapon at Niner.

"We'll have none of that now," said Acton, his Beretta raised and aimed directly at the man's head. "He just saved your life."

The man looked nervously at Acton, the 'would I rather feel shamed or be dead' debate going on. A little too slowly. Laura joined him at his side, her own weapon pointed at the man. "Why don't you go cover the back?" she suggested.

The man nodded, lowering his weapon as Cadeo returned from the back room. "We're surrounded," he said.

The gunfire stopped, the sturdy metal door having held back almost all the bullets, the small glass window in the door shattered. Acton looked back at Stewart and Murphy, Murphy's camera still rolling. "Are we still live?"

"Yes," replied Stewart.

"Good!" Acton faced the camera. "As you can see, we aren't shooting back. It was one local who got scared and fired, and we stopped him. We have no intention of fighting, we just want our story to get out to the world so they know the truth of what happened here today. We want safe passage to the American Embassy, and eventually home. We are willing to cooperate fully with any investigation, but only with consular access and an assurance we won't be harmed." He paused, his eyes narrowing. "Where's Phong?"

Stewart motioned to the far corner. Phong and Mai were both huddled there behind what looked like some sort of large tool cabinet.

"Are you two okay?"

Nods.

"Good. Just stay back there, stay low." He turned back to Niner who was stealing glances out the shattered window. "Status?"

"About two dozen police and Sarkov. All light weapons for now but I'm sure the heavy artillery will be arriving soon. What's our game plan here?"

"I think we need to delay as long as possible without killing anyone else. Our story needs time to circulate so the powers that be can get some control of the situation."

"Which means we need to start negotiating," said Laura. "That should buy us time if they're willing to talk."

"That's the question," said Niner, "are they willing to talk? This isn't back home where they'll spend three days talking down a madman with a Mountain Dew and a hard on. This is Vietnam. Shoot first, burry the evidence so there's no questions to ask except, 'I wonder what ever happened to that nice subversive who lived down the street?'"

"True, but we're TV stars right now," said Acton, jerking a thumb over his shoulder at Murphy. "They never kill celebrities."

"In America."

"This is true too. We could tell them you're a K-pop star on vacation."

"I do have a lovely singing voice."

"Would you two stop?"

Acton turned to Laura, an expression of chagrin on his face. "Sorry, hon. Nervous tension."

She shook her head at them but Acton could tell she was battling a laugh, her nerves on edge as well. He glanced back at the camera and could tell Stewart was fascinated with what he was seeing, Murphy giving him a thumbs up from behind the camera mounted on his shoulder.

"How do we start negotiations?" asked Acton. "Wait for them?"

"I think that question is now moot," said Niner from his position at the door. "Look."

Acton stepped over to the door and took a quick peek.

"Uh oh, this can't be good."

*Dong Mac Ward, Hanoi, Vietnam*

"Mr. Sarkov!"

Sarkov turned to see the police lieutenant who was in charge of the scene rushing toward him. The gunfire had been brief and had thankfully stopped. He had no desire to see anyone inside killed or injured, though he feared death was their immediate future unless someone in Moscow decreed otherwise.

Hanoi was clearly marching to a Russian beat.

"I've just been informed that the American delegation has left for the airport and that your superior, Mr. Yashkin, is on his way."

Sarkov felt butterflies. "Here?"

"Yes."

"How did he find out?"

"I'm assuming the police radio."

Sarkov kept his expression neutral, his overwhelming desire to curse at the news held at bay. "When will he arrive?"

"About fifteen minutes."

"Okay. I'm going to attempt to talk them down."

The lieutenant frowned. "Are you sure that's wise? They have already fired at us."

"Yes, but that might have been nerves. Let's see what happens."

He unholstered his weapon, placing it on the roof of his car, then turned and strode directly toward the door with the now shattered window, his hands held out at his sides. He spotted movement inside, then a second head appeared for a moment.

"We need to talk!" he called, continuing forward. "I'm unarmed!"

"Lift your jacket, take a spin."

He lifted his jacket up, revealing his portly belt line then turned around so they could see he wasn't concealing another gun.

"Okay, keep coming forward, hands up."

He approached the door and it suddenly was pulled open. He stepped inside and as the door closed behind him he recognized Agent Green as the man he had been speaking to and the two professors. A television crew was filming from the other side of what looked like a repurposed garage. Four Vietnamese men with guns were at the far end and what appeared to be Phong with the young Mai girl hiding in a corner.

*All the loose ends except Duy.*

It would be the mother lode if Yashkin got here.

*These people don't stand a chance.*

And he said so.

"You people don't stand a chance."

"What do you mean?" asked Acton as the American agent patted him down.

"He's clean," announced the man before covering the door again.

"My superior, Mr. Yashkin, will be here within less than fifteen minutes. At that point he will order your elimination."

"But why?" asked Laura. "We have proof we're innocent."

"He doesn't care. He's under orders to push the official story from Moscow. He's already ordered the destruction of the museum video and the hotel footage showing Mr. Quan entering and leaving Agent Green's room, and Agent Green leaving his room just after the shooting occurred, proving he wasn't involved."

Acton turned toward the camera. "You got that?" Murphy gave a thumbs up. "We're live on several networks right now."

Sarkov frowned, this an unexpected development, but his fate had been sealed the moment he went to Phong's apartment instead of home. "I understand. Now *you* need to understand *me*. You all need to surrender your weapons and come with me. I'll take you to the airport where we can get on a plane to Moscow. At least there you'll be in a more civilized country."

"Only a *bit* more civilized," said Acton. "Let's just be clear, it's Moscow that's trying to kill us."

"Yes, but this is a proxy war. The Vietnamese are the ones trying to kill you on camera. Once you're in Moscow, you'll simply become pawns. My prediction is you two will be released almost immediately, the Vietnamese nationals would be returned after a cooling off period, and Agent Green would at most get a show trial."

"But we have proof that he wasn't involved."

"Your word is hardly proof."

Laura shook her head. "No, we have the museum footage that proves he wasn't the shooter."

Sarkov's eyes narrowed, his heart skipping a beat in excitement. "Really?" He looked over at Mai, a sudden realization dawning on him. "You made a second copy?"

She nodded.

"Brilliant, brave woman." His appreciation for this young, diminutive woman grew several fold. He looked at Laura. "And this footage proves that your Agent Green wasn't the shooter."

"Without a doubt. And Phong just gave a full confession to the world."

"And we gave our witness statements," added Acton. "The world knows this was a lone gunman, a local man who was taking revenge for a war crime committed forty years ago."

Sarkov thought for a moment.

*This changes everything.*

There was no way Moscow could kill or disappear these people if he got them to Russia. But they were still in terrible danger if they remained here, with Yashkin only minutes away. "This is good news," he finally said. "And it makes it all the more important that we get you out of Vietnam."

"Why?" asked Acton.

"If the world knows you are definitely innocent, there is no way Moscow will harm you. The worst that will happen is you are put up in a hotel under guard for a few weeks while you are questioned and the Kremlin does their dog and pony show for the press, then you'll all be released. Young Mai will probably be released, perhaps even with a demand that she not be harmed by the Vietnamese upon her return, and Phong will be given a trial, most likely quickly found guilty and sentenced to life in prison."

Phong rose from his corner. "I've already accepted that," he said as he walked toward them. "I don't want anyone else hurt. We should do what he says."

One of the Vietnamese men said something, Mai jumping to her feet and rushing over to the man, grabbing him by the arm. Words were exchanged, rapid fire, Sarkov having no hope of understanding. Acton turned toward them.

"What's going on?"

"He says he's not going to Russia."

"Better there than here," said Laura. "At least temporarily."

"He said he has a way out."

Acton's eyes narrowed. "And he's telling us this now?"

"He didn't think he'd need to use it. He says we can all escape."

Cadeo pulled a panel up from the floor and his men began to descend some steps into what was once a mechanic's pit. "Are you coming?" he asked his sister in English.

She shook her head.

Acton stepped toward Cadeo. "Listen, if you run now, you'll be running your entire life."

Cadeo just glared at him then looked at his sister saying something in Vietnamese, his expression softening. She nodded, biting her forefinger as tears flowed down her cheeks. Cadeo disappeared, closing the panel behind him. Laura walked over and put her arm around Mai's shoulders. "What did he say?" she asked softly.

"He said he loved me and to be careful."

Laura hugged her tighter as she began to sob, leading her away, waving off the camera following them.

Sarkov looked at Acton. "We have little time to debate this. Once Mr. Yashkin is here, you will die, perhaps me as well."

"Why are you doing this?"

"Because it's the right thing to do."

Acton seemed to think about this for a moment then walked over to Agent Green. There were whispers as they spoke, the brief conversation breaking with nods of agreement. Acton then spoke to his wife, again in hushed tones. Finally he spoke to the camera crew. He turned to Sarkov.

"What about the reporters? They're not involved."

"Are they the ones that were there when Miss Trinh was rescued."

Acton quickly shook his head, perhaps a little too quickly. "No."

"Then I think I might be able to convince my Vietnamese counterpart to let them leave. I would highly suggest they leave the country as quickly as possible, even *if* they are not the crew wanted by the authorities."

Acton nodded, as if he understood that Sarkov knew he was lying.

"So we are agreed?"

Nods of assent gave him the green light.

"Then we must leave now, we have only minutes."

*Dong Mac Ward, Hanoi, Vietnam*

Dimitri Yashkin rolled up in his chauffeured vehicle provided by the Russian Embassy. The drive had been uneventful but slow, taking more than the promised twenty minutes, a parade of some sort blocking their way, it seeming to stretch across half the damned city. And what he found when he arrived baffled him. Two police cars and nothing more.

"I thought there was gunfire? What the hell is going on here?"

His chauffeur said nothing, simply bringing the car to a halt and climbing out, opening Yashkin's door. Yashkin stepped out into the cool evening breeze and looked at Major Yin as he exited his own vehicle. "What's going on here?"

Yin shouted something in Vietnamese, another man running over. Words were exchanged, Yin seeming confused, continually asking questions, then getting angrier and angrier, his subordinate beginning to cower.

Yashkin stormed over. "What is happening? Where are the suspects?"

Yin looked at Yashkin, exasperated. "They're gone!"

"What?"

"They're gone! He says *your* man took them."

"What? What man?"

"Mr. Sarkov."

"Sarkov!" Yashkin's mouth gaped wide in shock. You could have told him Petrov's ghost himself had been here and he couldn't have been more surprised. "Are you sure? I sent him home!"

"He's sure."

"Where did he take them?"

"To the airport."

"What?"

Yashkin could feel every muscle in his body tighten as fury ripped through him. Through clenched teeth he asked, "When?"

"Almost fifteen minutes ago."

"Stop the motorcade, stop Sarkov. They can't be allowed to reach the plane."

Yin shook his head. "No, he said he's taking them back to Moscow."

Yashkin paused, not sure what to make of that. "Moscow?"

"Yes."

"And the suspects agreed?"

"Yes. Apparently Mr. Sarkov convinced them they would be safer in Moscow than here. It avoided a possible gun battle and many deaths."

Yashkin bit his lip, thinking. Perhaps Sarkov wasn't a traitor after all. He was still a damned fool, and he'd be enjoying his final years in a cold dark cell for disobeying orders and violating Moscow's wishes, but at least he wouldn't die with the shame of being labelled a traitor.

But his orders were to have these people eliminated by the Vietnamese so that his country could claim they weren't involved.

"I want your men to shoot them on sight."

Yin's jaw dropped, then his head began shaking rapidly. "No no no! There's a camera crew following them, broadcasting live!"

Yashkin caught his shoulders before they slumped in defeat. His deflated tone didn't hide his dejection. "Explain."

"There was a CNN crew here, taping them. That's how my men found them, they followed their van from the American Embassy. They apparently lost them for a few minutes but eventually found them. They were allowed to leave freely since they are press—they didn't want to create an international incident, especially since they were broadcasting live to the world."

"And your men let them follow Sarkov to the airport?"

Yin nodded.

"Idiots."

Yin nodded again. "I agree."

The young man in charge of the scene clearly understood English, withering with each word.

"Delay the Americans as much as you can. I don't want that plane leaving before I get there. And detain Sarkov and the others when they arrive at the airport."

Yin nodded, demanding a radio as they headed for their respective vehicles.

*Moscow is going to string Sarkov up by his balls.*

*Approaching Noi Bai International Airport, Hanoi, Vietnam*

Jimmy watched the nearly empty streets whip by, the airport located north of the capital leaving much of the route a clear high speed shot out of the city. It was normally a forty minute drive but they had done it in half the time, their Vietnamese police escort urged to higher and higher speed by the approaching bumper of the lead vehicle driven by him, the normal thirty mile per hour speeds upped to sixty plus.

But it was too easy.

He wasn't complaining, he was just stunned the Vietnamese, and more accurately the Russians, were sticking to their agreement. The drive was long and uneventful, and it had given him a lot of time to think—or more accurately, worry—about Niner. Dawson hadn't been able to contact him directly about their imminent departure, and though he hated the decision to leave without their fellow operator, he agreed with it. Atwater and the civilians were the priority.

But he was also a firm believer in the no man left behind doctrine.

Which was why he was hoping they would quickly be returning to assist in an extraction if Niner didn't make it. He had been watching the entire route like a hawk for Niner to make an appearance like the original plan had dictated, but he hadn't seen him, though at these speeds and at night he might have missed him.

And if he had, and something bad happened to his friend, he'd never forgive himself.

He looked at the GPS in the dash and activated his comm. "ETA less than four minutes."

He knew it was less than the four shown since it was assuming they were travelling at the speed limit.

They were doing anything but, much to the annoyance of the police in the lead, the motorcycle cops' bumpers about three feet ahead of his own.

There was no way he was going to tolerate any delays.

*Three minutes.*

And it had only been thirty seconds. He could see the airport directly ahead, and had been able to for some time, it standing out against the night sky, the planes taking off and landing steady.

*Two minutes.*

Which meant less than a minute. "ETA less than two minutes." Brake lights lit up in front of him and the motorcycles split off in opposite directions.

Jimmy cursed.

Two police vehicles were blocking the road ahead, at least a dozen officers behind them, weapons drawn. "Road block ahead!"

"Can you go through?" asked Dawson over the comm.

"Affirmative. At least a dozen hostiles with weapons."

"Do it!"

"Everyone hold on!"

Jimmy leaned forward and hit a custom installed button on the dash, disabling the airbags and fuel cutoff features for the impending front end collision. He was driving a large, heavy Ford SUV, facing two relatively small Vietnamese vehicles.

He laid on his horn, at least giving some warning to the officers that he had no intention of slowing down.

They didn't move.

Until he was within about ten yards, then they scattered.

He gripped the steering wheel tightly with both hands, tensing up his muscles and shoving his head back against the headrest, bracing for the impact, the DSS agent beside him and his passengers in the back doing the same.

They hit hard, the back end fishtailing for a few moments, the civilians in the back momentarily panicking, but he was trained for this. He took his foot off the gas as he steered into the skid, steadying his breathing as his body demanded an emotional reaction.

Instead he mastered the adrenaline bitch and when enough speed had been taken out of the equation and traction reestablished itself, he straightened the wheel, back in control.

He hammered on the gas, blasting through a set of gates that were being hastily closed, the Secretary's airplane plainly visible in its cordoned off, secure section of the airport to the left.

He cursed again, a company of troops surrounding the area, but thankfully with few vehicles. He glanced in his side mirror and saw the motorcade was still tight behind him. He braked, turning onto an access road that led to the tarmac, moments later turning hard left, eliciting more screams from the back. He was heading directly for the plane now, the soldiers or police, he couldn't tell which and didn't really care, scattering out of the way. DSS agents were posted around stanchions demarking the diplomatic exclusion zone indicating American soil.

One of the agents opened a gap in the simple barrier, jumping out of the way just as Jimmy blasted through, easing off the speed slightly but not locking up his brakes until he reached the other side, leaving enough room for the rest of the motorcade to get inside the barrier.

"Everybody out and on the plane. Don't forget any equipment assigned to you. Stay calm and don't run. We don't need anyone getting injured in the final nine yards."

Doors were thrown open as he stepped outside. The squeal and shudder of antilock brakes surrounded them as the other vehicles stopped, car doors being thrown open as the civilians raced for the steps that had been pushed up against the front door of the Boeing 757, their instructions to not run ignored. He checked the backseats and found an abandoned piece of satellite gear.

*Naughty! Naughty!*

He removed it and handed it to the DSS agent that had accompanied him.

"Nice driving," said the man with a nod of appreciation.

"Thanks, nothing I like better than a Sunday drive in the country."

The man chuckled as they walked toward the stairs. "Remind me to never accept an invitation from you for ice creams."

Jimmy batted his eyes at him. "Why Agent Conroy, whatever do you mean?"

Dawson jogged up to them, smacking him on the shoulder. "Good job."

"Just good? Why Agent Conroy here just hit on me for doing such a good job."

Conroy shook his head, laughing as he climbed the stairs, the last of the civilians now boarded.

"Hugs and kisses later," said Dawson as the last of the abandoned equipment was carried up by DSS agents. Dawson's phone rang as he pointed to the vehicles. "Get some men and move these out of the way. I don't want anything interfering with us taking off."

Jimmy nodded and climbed into his own vehicle, pulling it in behind the wing. He didn't care if the engines blew the damned thing halfway back to the hotel, he just didn't want them hitting or trying to suck the vehicle into them.

He glanced in his mirror and saw Dawson smile.

*It must be Niner!*

"What's your situation?" asked Dawson as he rushed up the stairs, the idling engines too loud to hear properly. Inside he found confusion and chaos as the panicked civilians couldn't seem to decide where they wanted to sit, too many trying to avoid windows. He pointed at Spock. "Start assigning seats. Explain how bullets and jet fuel work." Spock grinned and began to push people into seats as Dawson stepped toward the cockpit.

"We're on our way," said Niner. "I've got the professors, the Vietnamese grad student, and the assassin with me and an ABC news crew in a CNN van following. But there's a change in plans."

Dawson frowned. He didn't like changes in plans. "Explain."

"We're not coming to you. We've surrendered to the Russian agent we met earlier, Sarkov. We've agreed to return with him to Moscow."

"Unacceptable."

"We had no choice. We were surrounded and had only minutes before his superior, that asshole Yashkin, arrived with orders to kill us all."

Dawson's teeth clenched. "That guy deserves a bullet to the skull."

"True dat! Listen, if you guys get a chance to leave, you take it. Don't wait for us. I don't know if you've seen the news—"

"Been a little busy but did catch the latest Big Bang Theory on the way."

"Sheldon is my favorite, he's so dreamily geeky—he's like a white Asian. But, if you had switched the channel you'd see we're being broadcast live so we should be safe. Also, the assassin, an employee from the hotel, broadcast a full confession and the professors managed to get their hands on footage from the museum proving it wasn't me."

Dawson breathed a sigh of relief. "Thank them for me."

"I'll be sure to give Jim a big kiss and Laura a hearty handshake from you."

"Good. Make sure you don't mix them up. Contact me as soon as you arrive at the airport. ETA?"

"I can see it from here, so I'm guessing we'll be there in less than ten minutes, maybe even five at the speed we're going."

"Good luck, my friend."

"Ditto."

The call ended and Dawson felt a little relief though not happy at the prospect of his friends being taken to Moscow.

*But at least they'll be alive.*

He entered the cockpit and looked at the pilot. "Can we leave?"

He shook his head. "They're refusing clearance."

"Then just go."

Another headshake, accompanied by a finger pointing ahead.

"No can do."

Dawson looked and cursed as he saw a police vehicle parked in the way.

*Approaching Noi Bai International Airport, Hanoi, Vietnam*

Acton was sitting in the rear seat of Sarkov's car with Laura, Mai and Phong, Niner up front in the passenger seat. It wasn't that tight a fit, Mai and Phong both slight, but it meant there weren't enough seatbelts and Oh Jesus! handles to go around. Sarkov was clearly an expert driver, taking corners at breakneck speeds, urging their Vietnamese escort on with his bumper, at times leaving their news crew safety net behind as the van's acceleration couldn't match the car's.

But Sarkov appeared to always make sure they were never out of sight.

"How much farther?" asked Laura, leaning forward.

"We're almost there," said Sarkov, motioning with his chin instead of taking his hands off the wheel. "This is a straight road all the way to the airport. We should be okay."

Niner pointed. "Road block?"

Acton's chest tightened as he leaned over to see past Niner's head. Several police cars were on either side of the road, about a dozen officers standing nearby, all turning toward the mini-motorcade.

They blasted through, unmolested.

"It looks like somebody took out two of those cars," observed Niner from the front seat. "Probably our motorcade."

"But they made it aboard," said Acton. "That's the important thing."

"Let's just hope that we're doing the right thing," said Laura, squeezing Acton's hand. "This whole idea of putting our trust in the Russian government has me nervous."

"Me too," said Acton.

"Me three," said Niner. "But we have no choice. We're dead here."

Sarkov said nothing, instead following the police vehicle in front of them as it turned onto the airport property. They could see the Secretary of State's jet less than half a mile away, tantalizingly close, but the police turned in the opposite direction, heading toward the terminal.

Sarkov locked up his brakes then turned hard to the left, toward the airplane, then hit the gas, gunning his car toward the cordoned off area. The troops surrounding it, filled now with over half a dozen vehicles from the motorcade and the large Boeing, raised their weapons and opened fire. Mai screamed as they all ducked, but Sarkov kept accelerating forward, the windshield splintering, the bullet resistant glass of the embassy issued vehicle holding.

He blasted through the cordon, dragging the stanchions with them as he screeched to a halt, deftly avoiding slamming into any of the other vehicles. He looked in his rearview mirror.

"They're not crossing the barrier. Let's go! Everyone on the plane!"

All four doors flew open and Acton jumped out, pulling Laura with him. They sprinted toward the stairs as the news van came to a halt behind them. He glanced back and saw Stewart and Murphy running toward them, Stewart carrying the camera since Murphy had been driving. Acton frowned as he saw Murphy gripping his shoulder. That's when he noticed the bullet holes in their windshield.

But there was no time to worry about that now.

"Let's go! Let's go! Let's go!" cried a voice from up the stairs. He looked to see Dawson urging them forward. Niner reached the stairs first, turning to push Mai then Phong up. Laura was next, Acton on her heels as Niner went back to grab Murphy and help him along. He pointed at the camera.

"Keep that rolling!"

Stewart nodded and took up the rear, turning the camera on the Vietnamese troops still outside the cordon, uncertain as to what to do.

Acton crossed the threshold, entering the cabin, his heart racing a mile a minute as all thoughts of tactical breathing had been forgotten. He found everyone seated except for DSS agents who quickly showed them to seats. He and Laura were sat together with Sarkov, Mai and Phong across the aisle. Stewart went to the rear with Murphy, Niner, a trained medic, going with them.

Acton turned to Sarkov. "What made you change your mind?"

Sarkov said nothing, simply staring out the window. He finally spoke after a deep sigh.

"My wife and son."

Sarkov's phone rang. He pulled it out of his pocket, curious. "How's this working?" he asked. "I thought the cellular network was down."

A DSS agent standing nearby overheard. "The plane is equipped with its own cellular network with satellite relay. All your phones should now work."

The revelation caused almost every phone on the plane to appear. Sarkov took the call. "Hello?"

"What the hell are you doing?" It was Yashkin's voice, his rage crystal clear even if the signal wasn't.

"Saving Russia from itself."

"What?"

"These people are innocent and we are being made to look the fools on the international stage. The entire world knows what is going on yet our country under your orders pretends to continue believing Agent Green is the assassin. It's time to end the charade and show we aren't the fools the world would think us."

"You are a traitor!"

"No, I am a patriot, but to what the New Russia was to become, not this bastardized version the leadership of the Kremlin would have us believe is anything different from the former Soviet Union. The past should stay in the past. To try and recreate those perceived glory days of old is foolish and dangerous, and I won't let this continue."

"You will be hanged."

"If our glorious leader succeeds in bringing back the death penalty, then yes, I fully expect to be hanged. But since we don't have capital punishment anymore, I fully expect to die by some mysterious accident, a mere line item in some state controlled local newspaper."

"You'll never leave the ground."

Acton elbowed him and he looked to where he was pointing. The overhead television screens were showing CNN, a shot of their plane surrounded by troops with replays of the earlier action from Murphy's camera replayed in an inset.

Sarkov smiled.

"I think you should watch the news, *Comrade*. The entire world is watching what happens next."

"I could care less about what the world thinks. You. Aren't. Leaving."

"Very well."

Sarkov rose, looking for the head of security, Agent White, a name he knew to be an alias. He spotted him talking to Secretary Atwater in the first class section. "Agent White!" The man turned. "Mr. Yashkin says he will never let this plane leave. We have little time. I think he means to board us."

"Get this plane in the air!" ordered Atwater, the pilot standing behind Agent White. "I don't care what you have to do!"

"I can't leave until we get those stairs out of the way," he said. "Somebody is going to have to go out there and move them."

Phong had been listening, only a few rows back from where the conversation had been happening. He had been relieved when the Russian had agreed to take everyone to Moscow. He had resigned himself to his fate and was prepared to spend the rest of his life in prison, possibly being tortured. He had committed a horrible crime. Not in killing Petrov, but in not immediately turning himself in so the hundreds if not thousands of lives lost today might have been saved.

His shame knew no bounds.

And now he might be heading to America, where he wondered if justice would still be served. Balance in the universe was necessary, it was an inevitable imperative proven by the fact he had been able to deliver karmic justice forty years later. But his selfishness after this restoration had once again thrown things out of balance and there was only one way he could ensure things didn't go further astray.

Deliver himself to guaranteed justice.

He rose, striding quickly forward and past the conversation. The man who appeared in charge looked at him. "Where are you going?"

"I'll move the stairs," said Phong as he walked past.

"I can't let you do that." He felt a hand grab his arm and he yanked himself free, jumping toward the door. He pushed the guard at the door aside, hurtling himself toward the stairs and down the steps as shouts erupted behind him. He rounded the platform at the bottom, positioning himself behind the stairs and under the fuselage.

He pushed.

Nothing. The stairs swayed slightly, but didn't budge.

He looked and saw two manual brakes. He kicked them off with his feet and tried again.

This time it started to roll forward. He pushed, blind as to where he was going, instead looking at the wing. He continued forward when he heard the female professor's voice.

"Phong, come back!"

He turned to look up at the door. The two professors were there, waving for him to return, but he shook his head. "Leave! Now! Before it's too late!" he shouted. Car tires screeched nearby and he looked. A white man stepped out, pointing at him.

"Arrest that man!"

He pushed harder, picking up speed as he tried to clear the wing. Boots pounding on asphalt neared as he continued to shove the stairs. He collapsed to his knees, the end of the wing finally visible, and was quickly surrounded.

Somebody hit him across the shoulders, hard.

He fell forward, his hands breaking his fall as blows rained down on him, boots, clubs and rifle butts delivering agonizing punishment like he could never have imagined. He heard the female professor cry out, but also the sound of the plane's engines getting louder. Out of the corner of his eye he saw it begin to roll forward, the pilot turning sharply to avoid the vehicle blocking them.

He looked up at the doorway and saw the agent who had been accused of the assassination standing there. The man saluted him then closed the door, troops running after the plane, but none shooting.

And as the blows continued to fall, he prepared himself for the next life, a smile battling the grimaces on his face as he knew he had done the right thing in the end, and restored the balance that had been lost for so long.

Sarkov watched through the window in dismay as Phong was beaten to death, Yashkin watching on, nobody stopping the street justice being delivered. The door was now closed, Professor Acton helping his crying wife to her seat, most people, their faces pressed against windows watching the brutal horror unfold outside, unable to control their own tears.

But it wasn't over yet. The cockpit door was open, Agent White splitting his attention between the cabin and the view ahead.

"They're not getting out of the way!" shouted the pilot as they rolled forward. Sarkov looked up at the television screen and could see dozens of vehicles on the runway, blocking their path as they taxied toward it. He raised the phone to his ear.

"Are you still there?"

"You're a dead man."

"You fool! Look behind you! Look at the terminal! There's thousands of people recording this on their cellphones and who knows how many camera crews beaming it out to the entire world! Do you really think Moscow will be happy if you cause this plane to crash or worse, explode? These people are determined to leave, they will not stop!"

There was silence on the other end.

"Take action, you fool! Order them to let these people leave!"

There was an angry growl. "I will not rest until you are dead."

"So be it."

The call ended and Sarkov watched on the television screen the live shot from what apparently was a BBC film crew at the airport.

"They're moving!"

Somebody from behind him was first to notice one of the vehicles pulling away, followed by another, then suddenly they were all moving, bailing off the runway, leaving them a clear path as the plane turned off the taxiway and onto the runway.

The Captain's voice came over the PA system. "Everybody strap yourselves in, this is going to be an emergency takeoff and ascent. We're going to hit thirty thousand feet as fast as we can."

A flurry of activity filled the cabin as people who had been staring out the window at poor Phong's heroic death returned to their seats, the sounds of belt buckles clicking up and down the cabin. The DSS agents took their seats, including the man in charge as Laura Palmer continued to sob beside him, her husband's own cheeks stained with tears.

As they were pushed back into their seats, he made eye contact with Professor Acton who mouthed the words "Thank you."

Sarkov nodded, turning his head toward the window and watched as the plane left the ground, the cabin erupting in cheers, quickly stifled by the terrifying ascent the pilot began.

Sarkov closed his eyes and thought of his wife who had died instantly, then of his son who had suffered for days before finally being delivered from his pain.

And he silently prayed that poor Phong would be delivered quickly from his.

*The Pentagon, Washington, DC*

*The next day*

Acton looked up as Sarkov entered the room. It was some sort of fancy informal meeting room filled with comfortable leather chairs and couches. He was sitting on one of the couches with Dawson, Laura across from them with Mai. Niner was perched on a windowsill chatting with Jimmy and Spock who had taken up residence in two of the finer chairs.

Sarkov dropped into a chair beside him.

"How'd it go?" asked Acton.

"It looks like I will be given a new identity and a pension for my assistance."

"That's good," said Laura, who then sensed Sarkov wasn't too happy. "Isn't it?"

Sarkov shrugged. "It is generous of your country, yes, but it wasn't how I expected to live out my retirement years."

"You expected to retire in Russia," said Acton, nodding.

Sarkov surprisingly shook his head. "No, not for a long time. Today's Russia is not my Russia, and I don't mean the Soviet Union was either." He sighed. "It's hard to explain."

Acton smiled. "I think I understand."

Niner walked toward them, sitting on the arm of one of the couches. "For a while there I thought I'd be retiring to Russia."

Sarkov chuckled. "Yes, you were lucky. We were all lucky."

"Thanks to Phong."

Laura's voice cracked and Mai reached out, squeezing her hand. Word had arrived while they were in the air that the BBC crew had filmed

Phong's body being loaded into the back of an ambulance in a body bag, he thankfully dying from his beating quickly.

It was a small comfort.

Earlier today the embassy had reported that their attempts to contact Duy had failed, he apparently having taken Sarkov's advice and called in to the hotel announcing he was visiting a sick relative, hanging up before they could ask where or who.

Apparently the Vietnamese had privately promised he wouldn't be touched, nor would Mai's brother and associates.

*Believe that when I see it.*

Mai herself had been offered permission to stay in America and she had accepted. Acton was going to try and get her a position at the university so she could continue her studies.

Bombers had landed, navy's had parted, and things were settling down everywhere.

Except the Ukraine.

Eastern Ukraine was lost, and the Russians refused to answer questions on whether or not they would pull out. General consensus was they wouldn't until the separatist rebels were properly equipped and trained, then it would be merged with the Crimea.

A new state in Soviet Union 2.0.

At least the Russians and Vietnamese had acknowledged that the assassin was Phong and he acted alone. They refused however to acknowledge the validity of the motive.

It no longer mattered.

Phong was dead, his family avenged, his pain and suffering, both physical and mental, over.

Murphy was in a Japanese hospital being treated and word was he would be fine. He had lost a lot of blood before they reached Tokyo to offload him for treatment. Stewart had stayed behind with his partner, Acton insisting the two of them visit them once they were safely back in America.

They all had a tremendous debt to repay those two men.

It had been a terrifying twelve hours and he was sure his pulse rate hadn't returned to normal until they actually stepped onto US soil. Niner had actually dropped to the tarmac and given it a kiss, Pope style.

How that man was able to keep his sense of humor through everything he'd never know.

He looked at Laura as they all sat in silence, waiting for their official debriefings to finish. Sarkov had been last. He looked up as the door opened, one of the aides stepping into the room.

"You're all free to go under the parameters that were explained to you in your individual debriefs. Any questions?"

There were none.

"Good. Then you are free to leave with Secretary Atwater's thanks."

Acton rose and waited for Sarkov to struggle out of his seat. "What do you plan on doing now?" he asked.

"Apparently I will be meeting with some of your government officials to plan my retirement."

"I guess we won't be seeing you again," said Laura as they walked out of the room.

"No, I won't be allowed to see any of you. It is safer that way for all of us." He sighed, patting his jacket pocket. "But I must tie up one loose end before I leave."

"What's that?" asked Acton.

Sarkov smiled. "I'll never tell."

*The Kremlin, Moscow, Russia*

Yashkin sat comfortably in a high backed leather chair, sipping from a bottle of Evian. With the crisis in Vietnam over he had boarded an early morning flight, and with the time zone difference had arrived in Moscow around lunch. A lunch provided to him by the Kremlin, though he had enjoyed it alone.

It didn't bother him. His return had been unscheduled and he was sure the right officials were being summoned to greet him as a hero of the Russian Federation. He had successfully created the chaos they had demanded and the resulting distraction had allowed his country to send overwhelming forces, Blitzkrieg style, into Eastern Ukraine. Though there was still some fighting, it was sporadic, the Ukrainians not sending any more troops east and NATO sitting on its hands, rattling their sabers still sheathed in their scabbards.

It had been a good day for Russia.

The door opened and he rose, surprised to see the President's number two man, Ivan Churilla, enter the room with several others. "Comrade Churilla! It is a pleasure to finally meet you in person!" It had been Churilla who had given him his marching orders over the phone with the implicit understanding that they came from the top man himself.

A man he hoped to soon meet in person.

Churilla frowned, sitting at the head of the table, the others standing behind him like an impassive wall.

"You did poorly, Dimitri."

Yashkin's chest tightened and he suddenly felt lightheaded. Of all the words to come out of Churilla's mouth, those were the furthest from what he had imagined.

"I'm sorry? I don't understand."

"You have embarrassed us on the international stage."

"But I followed your orders! You said you wanted to create confusion, to have the Americans blamed and to ensure anything or anyone who might interfere with that conclusion be eliminated."

"And you failed."

"Only because I was betrayed. *We* were betrayed by that bastard Sarkov!"

"A man under your command while you were there."

Yashkin didn't know what to say, the man's statement true. Sarkov had been under his command. He should have had him arrested instead of sending him home. It had just never occurred to him that the man would actually have the balls to disobey his orders, he seeming so soft.

"I sent him home as soon as I realized he might be a problem," he said, his voice devoid of the confidence he had had only moments ago.

"Yet he didn't go home. Instead he found the people you were supposed to find, on his own, with no resources to assist him. Clearly he is the superior man."

Yashkin bristled at the very idea, but bit his tongue. "What is to become of me?" he asked, his voice subdued, his eyes lowered.

Churilla rose, Yashkin jumping to his feet as the door was opened by one of the aides. Churilla stepped out of the room without answering.

"Sir, Comrade, what is to happen?"

But Churilla continued to walk away, followed by his aides. Yashkin rounded the table to follow him but was blocked by two soldiers, one carrying a pair of handcuffs.

"No! Oh please no!" he cried, backing away. "Please, sir, everything I did, I did for my country!"

Churilla stopped and turned.

"And now the best thing you can do for your country is accept blame for your *independent* and *unauthorized* actions."

The handcuffs were slapped on his wrists and he knew then that the tables had turned. He was the patsy now, the patsy who would be blamed for the crimes committed by his superiors, he merely their minion ordered to carry them out.

And the harshness of the punishment, the swiftness of the justice, the efficiency with which the entire affair was swept under the proverbial rug, reminded him of the glorious days of the Soviet Union.

And the irony was lost on him.

*Valley of the Red River, Vietnam*

*Three weeks later*

"You've got mail, Grandmother."

Ly looked up as her grandson, Duc, entered the humble family home. They still led a simple life in the valley, farming and fishing, the busy life of modern day Vietnam a distant curiosity. Her husband had died years ago but she was surrounded by half a dozen of her children and dozens of grandchildren.

Her life was full, her life was happy.

And in all her seventy years, she had never received a letter.

Her grandson handed her the envelope, sitting down beside her as her shaking fingers took it. "It's postmarked from the United States!" he said, his voice clearly excited, pointing at the corner of the envelope.

"The United States? But who do we know in America?"

Duc laughed. "Grandmother, we know lots of people there." He was bouncing with excitement. "Come on, Grandmother, open it!"

She smiled. "You young ones are so impatient." She carefully tore the end of the envelope open and looked inside. "Curious." Inside there was another envelope. She pulled it out to find it too was addressed to her, and when she read the return address in the corner she gasped, her hand darting to her mouth as tears filled her eyes.

"Phong!"

THE END

# ACKNOWLEDGEMENTS

For some time now I've had the idea of one or more of the Delta boys being falsely accused of something and the rest of the team powerless to help them. Enter Acton and Laura to save the day for a change. Of course things never turn out exactly as I plan (because I rarely plan) so finding out what happens is just as fun for me as it hopefully is for you.

The history surrounding the death of Buddha is actually based on historical accounts excluding of course the mob. There were some who thought he had been poisoned, and the simple man who provided him his final meal was blamed by some, including himself. The Buddha did send a message through his trusted man Ananda, thanking him for the meal and to assure him he had already been sick.

The clay bowl of course was my invention.

Or was it?

One thing about the Internet I love is reviews. No, this isn't a plug for book reviews, though yes, I do love those. This is a plug for other review sites. In this case the story about the KFC in Hanoi that Niner hides in is actually based upon a customer review on one of the hotel and restaurant review sites. A tourist actually experienced this odd first floor ordering, second floor pickup, with the staff on the second floor playing tag rather than making the food.

Yet another Acton story torn from the headlines!

As usual there are people to thank. Brent Richards for some weapons info, Ian Davidson for some motorcycle info (and for proving I know nothing about these things), Fred Newton for some car racing advice, my Dad for researching as usual, and my wife, daughter, mother and friends for their continued support.

The Dong Son Drum Design used on the cover is copyrighted by Truong Viet Quoc and is licensed under fair use of copyrighted material via Wikipedia.

And to those who have not already done so, please visit my website at www.jrobertkennedy.com then sign up for the Insiders Club. You'll get emails about new book releases, new collections, sales, etc. and your email address will never be shared or sold.

# ABOUT THE AUTHOR

USA Today bestselling author J. Robert Kennedy has written over one dozen international bestsellers including the smash hit James Acton Thrillers series, the first installment of which, The Protocol, has been on the bestsellers list since its release, including a three month run at number one. In addition to the other novels from this series including The Templar's Relic, a USA Today bestseller and #1 overall bestseller on Barnes & Noble and #6 overall on Amazon, he writes the bestselling Special Agent Dylan Kane Thrillers and Detective Shakespeare Mysteries. Robert spends his time in Ontario, Canada with his family.

Visit Robert's website at www.jrobertkennedy.com for the latest news and contact information.

## Available James Acton Thrillers

### The Protocol (Book #1)

For two thousand years the Triarii have protected us, influencing history from the crusades to the discovery of America. Descendent from the Roman Empire, they pervade every level of society, and are now in a race with our own government to retrieve an ancient artifact thought to have been lost forever.

### Brass Monkey (Book #2)

A nuclear missile, lost during the Cold War, is now in play--the most public spy swap in history, with a gorgeous agent the center of international attention, triggers the end-game of a corrupt Soviet Colonel's twenty five year plan. Pursued across the globe by the Russian authorities, including a brutal Spetsnaz unit, those involved will stop at nothing to deliver their weapon, and ensure their pay day, regardless of the terrifying consequences.

### Broken Dove (Book #3)

With the Triarii in control of the Roman Catholic Church, an organization founded by Saint Peter himself takes action, murdering one of the new Pope's operatives. Detective Chaney, called in by the Pope to investigate, disappears, and, to the horror of the Papal staff sent to inform His Holiness, they find him missing too, the only clue a secret chest, presented to each new pope on the eve of their election, since the beginning of the Church.

### The Templar's Relic (Book #4)

The Vault must be sealed, but a construction accident leads to a miraculous discovery--an ancient tomb containing four Templar Knights, long forgotten, on the grounds of the Vatican. Not knowing who they can trust, the Vatican requests Professors James Acton and Laura Palmer examine the find, but what they discover, a precious Islamic relic, lost during the Crusades, triggers a set of events that shake the entire world, pitting the two greatest religions against each other. At risk is nothing less than the Vatican itself, and the rock upon which it was built.

## Flags of Sin (Book #5)

Archaeology Professor James Acton simply wants to get away from everything, and relax. A trip to China seems just the answer, and he and his fiancée, Professor Laura Palmer, are soon on a flight to Beijing. But while boarding, they bump into an old friend, Delta Force Command Sergeant Major Burt Dawson, who surreptitiously delivers a message that they must meet the next day, for Dawson knows something they don't. China is about to erupt into chaos.

## The Arab Fall (Book #6)

An accidental find by a friend of Professor James Acton may lead to the greatest archaeological discovery since the tomb of King Tutankhamen, perhaps even greater. And when news of it spreads, it reaches the ears of a group hell-bent on the destruction of all idols and icons, their mere existence considered blasphemous to Islam.

## The Circle of Eight (Book #7)

The Bravo Team is targeted by a madman after one of their own intervenes in a rape. Little do they know this internationally well-respected banker is also a senior member of an organization long thought extinct, whose stated goals for a reshaped world are not only terrifying, but with today's globalization, totally achievable.

## The Venice Code (Book #8)

A former President's son is kidnapped in a brazen attack on the streets of Potomac by the very ancient organization that murdered his father, convinced he knows the location of an item stolen from them by the late president.

A close friend awakes from a coma with a message for archeology Professor James Acton from the same organization, sending him along with his fiancée Professor Laura Palmer on a quest to find an object only rumored to exist, while trying desperately to keep one step ahead of a foe hell-bent on possessing it.

## Pompeii's Ghosts (Book #9)

Two thousand years ago Roman Emperor Vespasian tries to preserve an empire by hiding a massive treasure in the quiet town of Pompeii should someone challenge his throne. Unbeknownst to him nature is about to unleash its wrath upon the Empire during which the best and worst of Rome's citizens will be revealed during a time when duty and honor were more than words, they were ideals worth dying for.

## Amazon Burning (Book #10)

Days from any form of modern civilization, archeology Professor James Acton awakes to gunshots. Finding his wife missing, taken by a member of one of the uncontacted tribes, he and his friend INTERPOL Special Agent Hugh Reading try desperately to find her in the dark of the jungle, but quickly realize there is no hope without help. And with help three days away, he knows the longer they wait, the farther away she'll be.

## The Riddle (Book #11)

Russia accuses the United States of assassinating their Prime Minister in Hanoi, naming Delta Force member Sergeant Carl "Niner" Sung as the assassin. Professors James Acton and Laura Palmer, witnesses to the murder, know the truth, and as the Russians and Vietnamese attempt to use the situation to their advantage on the international stage, the husband and wife duo attempt to find proof that their friend is innocent.

## Available Special Agent Dylan Kane Thrillers

### Rogue Operator (Book #1)

Three top secret research scientists are presumed dead in a boating accident, but the kidnapping of their families the same day raises questions the FBI and local police can't answer, leaving them waiting for a ransom demand that will never come. Central Intelligence Agency Analyst Chris Leroux stumbles upon the story, and finds a phone conversation that was never supposed to happen but is told to leave it to the FBI. But he can't let it go. For he knows something the FBI doesn't. One of the scientists is alive.

### Containment Failure (Book #2)

New Orleans has been quarantined, an unknown virus sweeping the city, killing one hundred percent of those infected. The Centers for Disease Control, desperate to find a cure, is approached by BioDyne Pharma who reveal a former employee has turned a cutting edge medical treatment capable of targeting specific genetic sequences into a weapon, and released it.

The stakes have never been higher as Kane battles to save not only his friends and the country he loves, but all of mankind.

### Cold Warriors (Book #3)

While in Chechnya CIA Special Agent Dylan Kane stumbles upon a meeting between a known Chechen drug lord and a retired General once responsible for the entire Soviet nuclear arsenal. Money is exchanged for a data stick and the resulting transmission begins a race across the globe to discover just what was sold, the only clue a reference to a top secret Soviet weapon called Crimson Rush.

### Death to America (Book #4)

America is in crisis. Dozens of terrorist attacks have killed or injured thousands, and worse, every single attack appears to have been committed by an American citizen in the name of Islam.

A stolen experimental F-35 Lightning II is discovered by CIA Special Agent Dylan Kane in China, delivered by an American soldier reported dead years ago in exchange for a chilling promise.

And Chris Leroux is forced to watch as his girlfriend, Sherrie White, is tortured on camera, under orders to not interfere, her continued suffering providing intel too valuable to sacrifice.

## Available Detective Shakespeare Mysteries

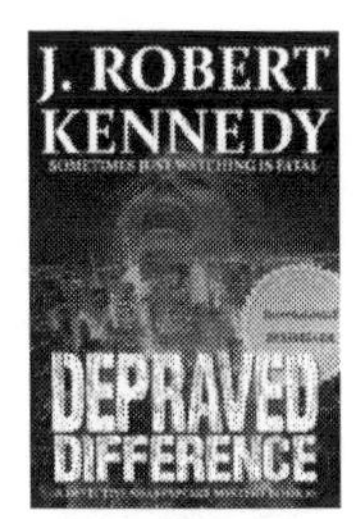


### Depraved Difference (Book #1)

**SOMETIMES JUST WATCHING IS FATAL**

When a young woman is brutally assaulted by two men on the subway, her cries for help fall on the deaf ears of onlookers too terrified to get involved, her misery ended with the crushing stomp of a steel-toed boot. A cellphone video of her vicious murder, callously released on the Internet, its popularity a testament to today's depraved society, serves as a trigger, pulled a year later, for a killer.

### Tick Tock (Book #2)

**SOMETIMES HELL IS OTHER PEOPLE**

Crime Scene tech Frank Brata digs deep and finds the courage to ask his colleague, Sarah, out for coffee after work. Their good time turns into a nightmare when Frank wakes up the next morning covered in blood, with no recollection of what happened, and Sarah's body floating in the tub.

### The Redeemer (Book #3)

**SOMETIMES LIFE GIVES MURDER A SECOND CHANCE**

It was the case that destroyed Detective Justin Shakespeare's career, beginning a downward spiral of self-loathing and self-destruction lasting half a decade. And today things are only going to get worse. The Widow Rapist is free on a technicality, and it is up to Detective Shakespeare and his partner Amber Trace to find the evidence, five years cold, to put him back in prison before he strikes again.

### The Turned: Zander Varga, Vampire Detective, Book #1

Zander has relived his wife's death at the hands of vampires every day for almost three hundred years, his perfect memory a curse of becoming one of The Turned—infecting him their final heinous act after her murder.

Nineteen year-old Sydney Winter knows Zander's secret, a secret preserved by the women in her family for four generations. But with her mother in a coma, she's thrust into the front lines, ahead of her time, to fight side-by-side with Zander.

Made in the USA
Middletown, DE
19 August 2019